WHO SAYS BEING A CAD IS EASY?

Flashy's off to Borneo to rescue his voluptuous but pea-brained wife from the ungentlemanly clutches of dastardly Don Haslam, the Eton-educated half-caste (who also happens to be a pirate). Swashbuckling his way through the South China Sea, Flashy picks up a bit of Oriental culture from some of the more fetching natives, and spends some time in the forced service of a lusty African queen who has only one use for philandering foreign men. . . .

Flashman's Lady

Also by
George MacDonald Fraser

1969   Flashman

1970   Royal Flash

1972   Flash for Freedom!

1972   The Steel Bonnets

1973   The General Danced at Dawn

1973   Flashman at the Charge

1974   McAuslan in the Rough

1975   Flashman in the Great Game

Flashman's Lady

George MacDonald Fraser

A PLUME BOOK

NEW AMERICAN LIBRARY

A DIVISION OF PENGUIN BOOKS USA INC., NEW YORK

Copyright © 1977 by George MacDonald Fraser

All rights reserved under International and Pan-American Copyright Conventions.
For information address Alfred A. Knopf, Inc., 201 East 50th Street, New York,
New York 10022.

This is an authorized reprint of a hardcover edition published by Alfred A. Knopf,
Inc., New York, and distributed by Random House, Inc., New York.

This book previously appeared in a Signet edition.

 PLUME TRADEMARK REG. U.S. PAT. OFF. AND FOREIGN COUNTRIES
REGISTERED TRADEMARK—MARCA REGISTRADA
HECHO EN BRATTLEBORO, VT., U.S.A.

SIGNET, SIGNET CLASSIC, MENTOR, ONYX, PLUME, MERIDIAN and
NAL BOOKS are published by New American Library, a division of
Penguin Books USA Inc., 1633 Broadway, New York, New York 10019

Library of Congress Cataloging-in-Publication Data

Fraser, George MacDonald, 1925–
    Flashman's Lady / George MacDonald Fraser.
        p.   cm.
    ISBN 0-452-26489-8
    I. Title.
    [PR6056.R287F8   1988]   87-30863
    823'.914—dc19   CIP

First Plume Printing, April, 1988

2 3 4 5 6 7 8 9 10

PRINTED IN THE UNITED STATES OF AMERICA

For
K, 6

Explanatory Note

Since the memoirs of Flashman, the notorious Rugby School bully and Victorian military hero, first came to light ten years ago, and have been laid before the public as each successive packet of manuscript was opened and edited, a question has arisen which many readers have found intriguing. The five volumes published so far have been in chronological order, spanning the period from 1839, when Flashman was expelled and entered the Army, to 1858, when he emerged from the Indian Mutiny. But not all the intervening years have been covered in the five volumes; one gap occurs between his first meeting with Bismarck and Lola Montez in 1842–3, and his involvement in the Schleswig-Holstein Question in 1848; yet another between 1849, when he was last seen on the New Orleans waterfront in the company of the well-known Oxford don and slave-trader, Captain Spring, M.A., and 1854, when duty called him to the Crimea. It has been asked, what of the "missing years"?

The sixth packet of the Flashman Papers supplies a partial answer, since it deals with its author's remarkable adventures from 1842 to 1845. It is clear from his manuscript that a chance paragraph in the sporting columns of a newspaper caused him to interrupt his normal chronological habit, to fill in this hiatus in his earlier years, and from the bulk of unopened manuscript remaining it appears that his memoirs of the Taiping Rebellion, the U.S. Civil War, and the Sioux and Zulu uprisings are still to come. (Indeed, since a serving officer of the United States Marines has informed me that his Corps' records contain positive pictorial evidence of Flashman's participation in the Boxer Rebellion of 1900, there is no saying where it may end.)

The historical significance of the present instalment may be thought to be threefold. As a first-hand account of the early Victorian sporting scene (on which Flashman now emerges as a distinguished if deplorable actor) it is certainly unique; on a

5

different plane it provides an eye-witness description of that incredible, forgotten private war in which a handful of gentlemen-adventurers pushed the British imperial frontier eastwards in the 1840s. Lastly, it sheds fresh light on the characters of two great figures of the time—one a legendary Empire-builder, the other an African queen who has been unfavourably compared to Caligula and Nero.

A small point which may be of interest to students of Flashman's earlier memoirs is that the present manuscript shows signs of having been lightly edited—as was one previous volume—by his sister-in-law, Grizel de Rothschild, probably soon after his death in 1915. She has modified his blasphemies, but has not otherwise tampered with the old soldier's narrative; indeed, she has embellished it here and there with extracts from the private diary of her sister Elspeth, Flashman's wife, and with her own pungent marginal comments. In the presence of such distinguished editing, I have confined myself to supplying foot-notes and appendices, and satisfying myself of the accuracy of Flashman's account of historical events so far as these can be checked.

G.M.F.

Flashman's Lady

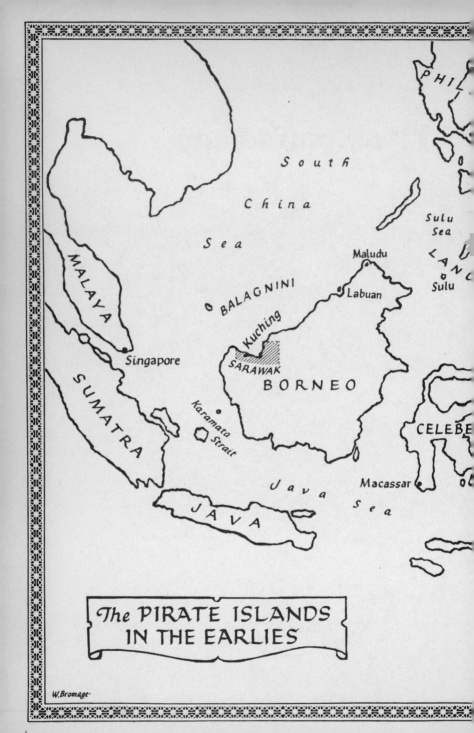

The PIRATE ISLANDS
IN THE EARLIES

W. Bromage

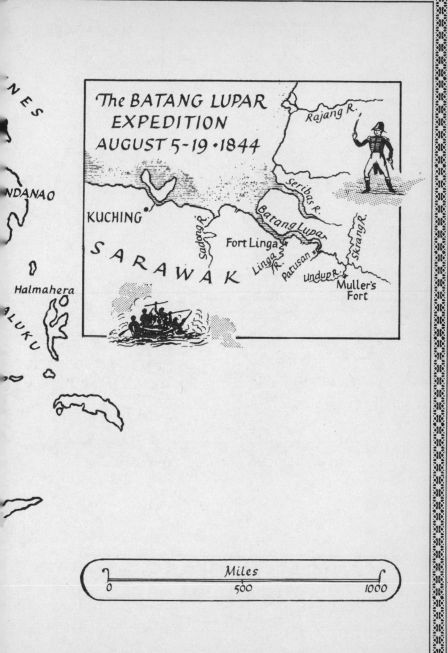

The BATANG LUPAR
EXPEDITION
AUGUST 5-19 • 1844

Rajang R.

KUCHING

SARAWAK

Sadong R.

Fort Linga

Linga R.

Seribas R.

Batang Lupar

Patusan

Undup R.

Skrang R.

Muller's Fort

NES

NDANAO

Halmahera

ALUKU

Miles

0   500   1000

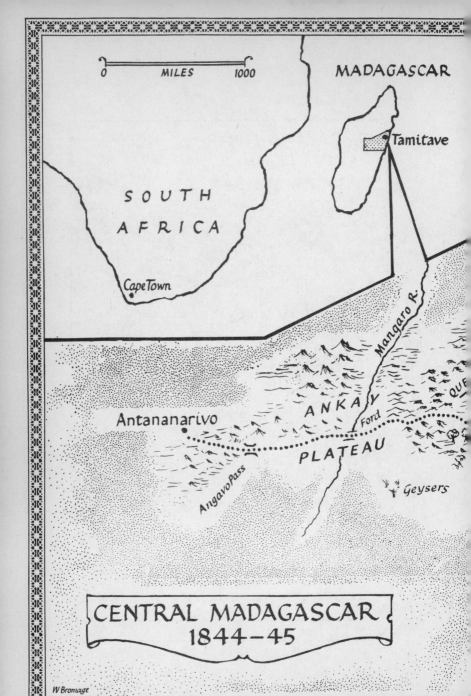

MILES 0 — 1000

MADAGASCAR

Tamitave

SOUTH AFRICA

Cape Town

Mangaro R.

ANKAY

Antananarivo

PLATEAU

Ford

QUE

Angavo Pass

Geysers

W Bromage

CENTRAL MADAGASCAR
1844–45

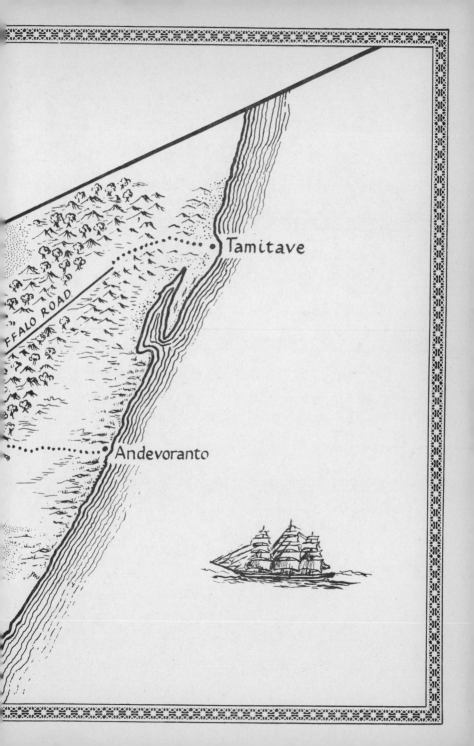

So they're talking about amending the leg-before-wicket rule again. I don't know why they bother, for they'll never get it right until they go back to the old law which said that if you put your leg in front of the ball a-purpose to stop it hitting the stumps, you were out, and d----d good riddance to you. That was plain enough, you'd have thought, but no; those mutton-brains in the Marylebone club have to scratch their heads over it every few years, and gas for days on end about the line of delivery and the point of pitch, and the L--d knows what other rubbish, and in the end they cross out a word and add another, and the whole thing's as incomprehensible as it was before. Set of doddering old women.

It all comes of these pads that batters wear nowadays. When I was playing cricket we had nothing to guard our precious shins except our trousers, and if you were fool enough to get your ankle in the way of one of Alfic Mynn's shooters, why, it didn't matter whether you were in front of the wicket or sitting on the pavilion privy—you were off to get your leg in plaster, no error. But now they shuffle about the crease like yokels in gaiters, and that great muffin Grace bleats like a ruptured choirboy if a fast ball comes near him. Wouldn't I just have liked to get him on the old Lord's wicket after a dry summer, with the pitch rock-hard, Mynn sending down his trimmers from one end and myself going all-out at t'other—they wouldn't have been calling him the "Champion" then, I may tell you; the old b-----'s beard would have been snow-white after two overs. And the same goes for that fat black nawab and the pup Fry, too.

From this you may gather that I was a bowler myself, not a batter, and if I say I was a d----d good one, well, the old scores are there to back me up. Seven for 32 against the Gentlemen of Kent, five for 12 against the England XI, and a fair number of runs as a tail-end slogger to boot. Not that I prided myself on my batting; as I've said, it could be a risky business against fast men in the old days, when wickets were rough, and I may tell you privately that I took care never to face up to a really scorching bowler without woollen scarves wrapped round my legs (under my flannels) and an old tin soup-bowl over my essentials; sport's all very well, but you mustn't let it incapacitate you for the manliest game of all. No, just let me go in about number eight or nine, when the slow lobbers and twisters were practising their wiles, and I could slash away in safety, and then, when t'other side had their innings—give me that ball and a thirty-pace run-up and just watch me make 'em dance.

It may strike you that old Flashy's approach to our great summer game wasn't *quite* that of your school-storybook hero, apple-cheeked and manly, playing up unselfishly for the honour of the side and love of his gallant captain, revelling in the jolly rivalry of bat and ball while his carefree laughter rings across the green sward. No, not exactly; personal glory and cheap wickets however you could get 'em, and d--n the honour of the side, that was my style, with a few quid picked up in side-bets, and plenty of skirt-chasing afterwards among the sporting ladies who used to ogle us big hairy fielders over their parasols at Canterbury Week. That's the spirit that wins matches, and you may take my word for it, and ponder our recent disastrous showing against the Australians while you're about it.[1]

Of course, I speak as one who learned his cricket in the golden age, when I was a miserable fag at Rugby, toadying my way up the school and trying to keep a whole skin in that infernal jungle —you took your choice of emerging a physical wreck or a moral one, and I'm glad to say I never hesitated, which is why I'm the man I am today, what's left of me. I snivelled and bought my way to safety when I was a small boy, and bullied and tyrannised when I was a big one; how the d---l I'm not in the House of Lords by now, I can't think. That's by the way; the point is that Rugby taught me only two things really well, survival and cricket, for I saw even at the tender age of eleven that while bribery, fawning, and deceit might ensure the former, they weren't enough to earn a popular reputation, which is a very necessary thing. For that, you had to shine at games, and cricket was the only one for me.

Not that I cared for it above half, at first, but the other great sport was football, and that was downright dangerous; I rubbed along at it only by limping up late to the scrimmages yelping: "Play up, you fellows, do! Oh, confound this game leg of mine!" and by developing a knack of missing my charges against bigger men by a fraction of an inch, plunging on the turf just too late with heroic gasps and roarings.[2] Cricket was peace and tranquillity by comparison, without any danger of being hacked in the members—and I turned out to be uncommon good at it.

I say this in all modesty; as you may know, I have three other prime talents, for horses, languages, and fornication, but they're all God-given, and no credit that I can claim. But I worked to make myself a cricketer, d----d hard I worked, which is probably why, when I look back nowadays on the rewards and trophies of an eventful life—the medals, the knighthood, the accumulated cash, the military glory, the drowsy, satisfied women—all in all, there's not much I'm prouder of than those five wickets for 12 runs against the flower of England's batters, or that one glorious over at Lord's in '42 when—but I'll come to that in a moment, for it's where my present story really begins.

I suppose, if Fuller Pilch had got his bat down just a split second sooner, it would all have turned out different. The Skrang pirates wouldn't have been burned out of their h--lish nest, the black queen of Madagascar would have had one lover fewer (not that she'd have missed a mere one, I dare say, the insatiable great b---h), the French and British wouldn't have bombarded Tamitave, and I'd have been spared kidnapping, slavery, blowpipes, and the risk of death and torture in unimaginable places—aye, old Fuller's got a lot to answer for, God rest him. However, that's anticipating—I was telling you how I became a fast bowler at Rugby, which is a necessary preliminary.

It was in the 'thirties, you see, that round-arm bowling came into its own, and fellows like Mynn got their hands up shoulder-high. It changed the game like nothing since, for we saw what fast bowling could be—and it *was* fast—you talk about Spofforth and Brown, but none of them kicked up the dust like those early trimmers. Why, I've seen Mynn bowl to five slips and three long-stops, and his deliveries going over 'em all, first bounce right down to Lord's gate. That's my ticket, thinks I, and I took up the new slinging style, at first because it was capital fun to buzz the ball round the ears of rabbits and funks who couldn't hit back, but I soon found this didn't answer against serious batters, who pulled and drove me all over the place. So I mended my ways until I could whip my fastest ball onto a crown piece, four times out of five, and as I grew tall I became faster still, and was in a fair way to being Cock of Big Side—until that memorable afternoon when the puritan prig Arnold took exception to my being carried home sodden drunk, and turfed me out of the school. Two weeks before the Marylebone match, if you please—well, they lost it without me, which shows that while piety and sobriety may ensure you eternal life, they ain't enough to beat the M.C.C.

However, that was an end to my cricket for a few summers, for I was packed off to the Army and Afghanistan, where I shuddered my way through the Kabul retreat, winning undeserved but undying fame in the siege of Jallalabad. All of which I've related elsewhere;* sufficient to say that I bilked, funked, ran for dear life and screamed for mercy as occasion demanded, all through that ghastly campaign, and came out with four medals, the Thanks of Parliament, an audience of our Queen, and a handshake from the Duke of Wellington. It's astonishing what you can make out of a bad business if you play your hand right and look noble at the proper time.

Anyway, I came home a popular hero in the late summer of '42, to a rapturous reception from the public and my beautiful idiot wife Elspeth. Being lionised and fêted, and making up for lost time by whoring and carousing to excess, I didn't have much time in the first few months for lighter diversions, but it chanced that I was promenading down Regent Street one afternoon, twirling my cane with my hat on three hairs and seeking what I might devour, when I found myself outside "The Green Man". I paused, idly—and that moment's hesitation launched me on what was perhaps the strangest adventure of my life.

It's long gone now, but in those days "The Green Man" was a famous haunt of cricketers, and it was the sight of bats and stumps and other paraphernalia of the game in the window that suddenly brought back memories, and awoke a strange hunger —not to play, you understand, but just to smell the atmosphere

* See *Flashman*.

12

again, and hear the talk of batters and bowlers, and the jargon and gossip. So I turned in, ordered a plate of tripe and a quart of home-brewed, exchanged a word or two with the jolly pipe-smokers in the tap, and was soon so carried away by the homely fare, the cheery talk and laughter, and the clean hearty air of the place, that I found myself wishing I'd gone on to the Haymarket and got myself a dish of hot spiced trollop instead. Still, there was time before supper, and I was just calling the waiter to settle up when I noticed a fellow staring at me across the room. He met my eye, shoved his chair back, and came over.

"I say," says he, "aren't you Flashman?" He said it almost warily, as though he didn't wish quite to believe it. I was used to this sort of thing by now, and having fellows fawn and admire the hero of Jallalabad, but this chap didn't look like a toad-eater. He was as tall as I was, brown-faced and square-chinned, with a keen look about him, as though he couldn't wait to have a cold tub and a ten-mile walk. A Christian, I shouldn't wonder, and no smoking the day before a match.

So I said, fairly cool, that I was Flashman, and what was it to him.

"You haven't changed," says he, grinning. "You won't remember me, though, do you?"

"Any good reason why I should try?" says I. "Here, waiter!"

"No, thank'ee," says this fellow. "I've had my pint for the day. Never take more during the season." And he sat himself down, cool as be-d----d, at my table.

"Well, I'm relieved to hear it," says, I, rising. "You'll forgive me, but—"

"Hold on," says he, laughing. "I'm Brown. Tom Brown—of Rugby. Don't say you've forgotten!"

Well, in fact, I had. Nowadays his name is emblazoned on my memory, and has been ever since Hughes published his infernal book in the 'fifties, but that was still in the future, and for the life of me I couldn't place him. Didn't want to, either; he had that manly, open-air reek about him that I can't stomach, what with his tweed jacket (I'll bet he'd rubbed down his horse with it) and sporting cap; not my style at all.

"You roasted me over the common-room fire once," says he, amiably, and then I knew him fast enough, and measured the distance to the door. That's the trouble with these snivelling little sneaks one knocks about at school; they grow up into hulking louts who box, and are always in prime trim. Fortunately this one appeared to be Christian as well as muscular, having swallowed Arnold's lunatic doctrine of love-thine-enemy, for as I hastily muttered that I hoped it hadn't done him any lasting injury, he laughed heartily and clapped me on the shoulder.

"Why, that's ancient history," cries he. "Boys will be boys, what? Besides, d'ye know—I feel almost that *I* owe *you* an apology. Yes," and he scratched his head and looked sheepish. "Tell the truth," went on this amazing oaf, "when we were youngsters I didn't care for you above half, Flashman. Well, you treated us fags pretty raw, you know—of course, I guess it was just thoughtlessness, but, well, we thought you no end of a cad, and—and . . . a coward, too." He stirred uncomfortably, and I wondered was he going to fart. "Well, you caught us out there, didn't you?" says he, meeting my eye again. "I mean, all this business in Afghanistan . . . the way you defended the old flag . . . that sort of thing. By George," and he absolutely had tears in his eyes, "it was the most splendid thing . . . and to think that you . . . well, *I* never heard of anything so heroic in my life, and I just wanted to apologise, old fellow, for thinking ill of you—'cos I'll own that I did, once—and ask to shake your hand, if you'll let me."

He sat there, with his great paw stuck out, looking misty and noble, virtue just oozing out of him, while I marvelled. The strange thing is, his precious pal Scud East, whom I'd hammered just as generously at school, said almost the same thing to me years later, when we met as prisoners in Russia—confessed how he'd loathed me, but how my heroic conduct had wiped away all old scores, and so forth. I wonder still if they believed that it did, or if they were being hypocrites for form's sake, or if they truly felt guilty for once having harboured evil thoughts of me? D----d if I know; the Victorian conscience is beyond me, thank G-d. I know that if anyone who'd done *me* a bad turn later turned out to be the Archangel Gabriel, I'd *still* hate the b-----d; but then, I'm a scoundrel, you see, with no proper feelings. However, I was so relieved to find that this stalwart lout was prepared to let bygones be bygones that I turned on all my Flashy charms, pumped his fin heartily, and insisted that he break his rule for once, and have a glass with me.

"Well, I will, thank'ee," says he, and when the beer had come and we'd drunk to dear old Rugby (sincerely, no doubt, on his part) he puts down his mug and says:

"There's another thing—matter of fact it was the first thought that popped into my head when I saw you just now—I don't know how you'd feel about it, though—I mean, perhaps your wounds ain't better yet?"

He hesitated. "Fire away," says I, thinking perhaps he wanted to introduce me to his sister.

"Well, you won't have heard, but my last half at school, when I was captain, we had no end of a match against the Marylebone men—lost on first innings, but only nine runs in it, and we'd have beat 'em, given one more over. Anyway, old Aislabie— you remember him?—was so taken with our play that he has asked me if I'd like to get up a side, Rugby past and present, for a match against Kent. Well, I've got some useful hands—you know young Brooke, and Raggles—and I remembered you were a famous bowler, so . . . What d'ye say to turning out for us— if you're fit, of course?"

It took me clean aback, and my tongue being what it is, I found myself saying: "Why, d'you think you'll draw a bigger gate with the hero of Afghanistan playing?"

"Eh? Good lord, no!" He coloured and then laughed. "What a cynic you are, Flashy! D'ye know," says he, looking knowing, "I'm beginning to understand you, I think. Even at school, you always said the smart, cutting things that got under people's skins—almost as though you were going out of your way to have 'em think ill of you. It's a contrary thing—all at odds with the truth, isn't it? Oh, aye," says he, smiling owlishly, "Afghanistan proved that, all right. The German doctors are doing a lot of work on it—the perversity of human nature, excellence bent on destroying itself, the heroic soul fearing its own fall from grace, and trying to anticipate it. Interesting." He shook his fat head solemnly. "I'm thinking of reading philosophy at Oxford this term, you know. However, I mustn't prose. What about it, old fellow?" And d--n his impudence, he slapped me on the knee. "Will you bowl your expresses for us—at Lord's?"

I'd been about to tell him to take his offer along with his rotten foreign sermonising and drop 'em both in the Serpentine, but that last word stopped me. Lord's—I'd never played there, but what cricketer who ever breathed wouldn't jump at the chance? You may think it small enough beer compared with the games I'd been playing lately, but I'll confess it made my heart leap. I was still young and impressionable then and I almost knocked his hand off, accepting. He gave me another of his thunderous shoulder-claps (they pawed each other something d--nable, those hearty young champions of my youth) and said, capital, it was settled then.

"You'll want to get in some practice, no doubt," says he, and promptly delivered a lecture about how he kept himself in condition, with runs and exercises and foregoing tuck, just as he had at school. From that he harked back to the dear old days, and how he'd gone for a weep and a pray at Arnold's tomb the previous month (our revered mentor having kicked the bucket earlier in the year, and not before time, in my opinion). Excited as I was at the prospect of the Lord's game, I'd had about my bellyful of Master Pious Brown by the time he was done, and as we took our leave of each other in Regent Street, I couldn't resist the temptation to puncture his confounded smugness.

"Can't say how glad I am to have seen you again, old lad," says he, as we shook hands. "Delighted to know you'll turn out for us, of course, but, you know, the best thing of all has been —meeting the new Flashman, if you know what I mean. It's odd," and he fixed his thumbs in his belt and squinted wisely at me, like an owl in labour, "but it reminds me of what the Doctor used to say at confirmation class—about man being born again— only it's happened to *you*—*for* me, if you understand me. At all events, I'm a better man now, I feel, than I was an hour ago. God bless you, old chap," says he, as I disengaged my hand before he could drag me to my knees for a quick prayer and a chorus of "Let us with a gladsome mind". He asked which way I was bound.

"Oh, down towards Haymarket," says I. "Get some exercise, I think."

"Capital," says he. "Nothing like a good walk."

"Well . . . I was thinking more of riding, don't you know."

"In Haymarket?" He frowned. "No stables thereaway, surely?"

"Best in town," says I. "A few English mounts, but mostly French fillies. Riding silks black and scarlet, splendid exercise, but d----d exhausting. Care to try it?"

For a moment he was all at a loss, and then as understanding dawned he went scarlet and white by turns, until I thought he would faint. "My G-d," he whispered hoarsely. I tapped him on the weskit with my cane, all confidential.

"You remember Stumps Harrowell, the shoemaker, at Rugby, and what enormous calves he had?" I winked while he gaped at me. "Well, there's a German wench down there whose poonts are even bigger. Just about your weight; do you a power of good."

He made gargling noises while I watched him with huge enjoyment.

"So much for the new Flashman, eh?" says I. "Wish you hadn't invited me to play with your pure-minded little friends? Well, it's too late, young Tom; you've shaken hands on it, haven't you?"

He pulled himself together and took a breath. "You may play if you wish," says he. "More fool I for asking you—but if you were the man I had hoped you were, you would—"

"Cry off gracefully—and save you from the pollution of my company? No, no, my boy—I'll be there, and just as fit as you are. But I'll wager I enjoy my training more."

"Flashman," cries he, as I turned away, "don't go to—to that place, I beseech you. It ain't worthy—"

"How would you know?" says I. "See you at Lord's." And I left him full of Christian anguish at the sight of the hardened sinner going down to the Pit. The best of it was, he was probably as full of holy torment at the thought of my foul fornications as he would have been if he'd galloped that German tart himself; that's unselfishness for you. But she'd have been wasted on him, anyway.

* * *

However, just because I'd punctured holy Tom's daydreams, don't imagine that I took my training lightly. Even while the German wench was recovering her breath afterwards and ringing

17

for refreshments, I was limbering up on the rug, trying out my old round-arm swing; I even got some of her sisters in to throw oranges to me for catching practice, and you never saw anything jollier than those painted dollymops scampering about in their corsets, shying fruit. We made such a row that the other customers put their heads out, and it turned into an impromptu innings on the landing, whores versus patrons (I must set down the rules for brothel cricket some day, if I can recall them; cover point took on a meaning that you won't find in "Wisden", I know). The whole thing got out of hand, of course, with furniture smashed and the sluts shrieking and weeping, and the madame's bullies put me out for upsetting her disorderly house, which seemed a trifle hard.

Next day, though, I got down to it in earnest, with a ball in the garden. To my delight none of my old skill seemed to have deserted me, the thigh which I'd broken in Afghanistan never even twinged, and I crowned my practice by smashing the morning-room window while my father-in-law was finishing his breakfast; he'd been reading about the Rebecca Riots[3] over his porridge, it seemed, and since he'd spent his miserable life squeezing and sweating his millworkers, and had a fearful guilty conscience according, his first reaction to the shattering glass was that the starving mob had risen at last and were coming to give him his just deserts.

"Ye d----d Goth!" he spluttered, fishing the fragments out of his whiskers. "Ye don't care who ye maim or murder; I micht ha'e been killed! Have ye nae work tae go tae?" And he whined on about ill-conditioned loafers who squandered their time and his money in selfish pleasure, while I nuzzled Elspeth good morning over her coffee service, marvelling as I regarded her golden-haired radiance and peach-soft skin that I had wasted strength on that suety frau the evening before, when this had been waiting between the covers at home.

"A fine family ye married intae," says her charming sire. "The son stramashin' aboot destroyin' property while the feyther's lyin' abovestairs stupefied wi' drink. Is there nae mair toast?"

"Well, it's our property and our drink," says I, helping myself to kidneys. "Our toast, too, if it comes to that."

"Aye, is't, though, my buckie?" says he, looking more like a spiteful goblin than ever. "And who peys for't? No' you an' yer wastrel parent. Aye, an' ye can keep yer sullen sniffs to yersel', my lassie," he went on to Elspeth. "We'll hae things aboveboard, plump an' plain. It's John Morrison foots the bills, wi' good Scots siller, hard-earned, for this fine husband o' yours an' the upkeep o' his hoose an' family; jist mind that." He crumpled up his paper, which was sodden with spilled coffee. "Tach! There my breakfast sp'iled for me. 'Our property' an' 'our drink', ye say? Grand airs and patched breeks!" And out he strode, to return in a moment, snarling. "And since you're meant tae be managin' this establishment, my girl, ye'll see tae it that we hae marmalade after this, and no' this d----d French jam! Con-fee—toor! Huh! Sticky rubbish!" And he slammed the door behind him.

"Oh, dear," sighs Elspeth. "Papa is in his black mood. What a shame you broke the window, dearest."

"Papa is a confounded blot," says I, wolfing kidneys. "But now that we're rid of him, give us a kiss."

You'll understand that we were an unusual menage. I had married Elspeth perforce, two years before when I had the ill-fortune to be stationed in Scotland, and had been detected tupping her in the bushes—it had been the altar or pistols for two with her fire-eating uncle. Then, when my drunken guv'nor had gone smash over railway shares, old Morrison had found himself saddled with the upkeep of the Flashman establishment, which he'd had to assume for his daughter's sake.

A pretty state, you'll allow, for the little miser wouldn't give me or the guv'nor a penny direct, but doled it out to Elspeth, on whom I had to rely for spending money. Not that she wasn't generous, for in addition to being a stunning beauty she was also as brainless as a feather mop, and doted on me—or at least, she seemed to, but I was beginning to have my doubts. She had a hearty appetite for the two-backed game, and the suspicion was growing on me that in my absence she'd been rolling the linen with any chap who'd come handy, and was still spreading her favours now that I was home. As I say, I couldn't be sure—for that matter, I'm still not, sixty years later. The trouble was and is, I dearly loved her in my way, and not only lustfully—although she was all you could wish as a nightcap—and however much I might stallion about the town and elsewhere, there was never another woman that I cared for besides her. Not even Lola Montez, or Lakshmibai, or Lily Langtry, or Ko Dali's daughter, or Duchess Irma, or Takes-Away-Clouds-Woman, or Valentina, or . . . or, oh, take your choice, there wasn't one to come up to Elspeth.

For one thing, she was the happiest creature in the world, and pitifully easy to please; she revelled in the London life, which was a rare change from the cemetery she'd been brought up in—Paisley, they call it—and with her looks, my new-won laurels, and (best of all) her father's shekels, we were well received everywhere, her "trade" origins being conveniently forgotten. (There's no such thing as an unfashionable hero or an unsuitable heiress.) This was just nuts to Elspeth, for she was an unconscionable little snob, and when I told her I was to play at Lord's, before the smartest of the sporting set, she went into raptures—here was a fresh excuse for new hats and dresses, and preening herself before the society rabble, she thought. Being Scotch, and knowing nothing, she supposed cricket was a gentleman's game, you see; sure enough, a certain level of the polite world followed it, but they weren't precisely the high cream, in those days —country barons, racing knights, well-to-do gentry, maybe a mad bishop or two, but pretty rustic. It wasn't quite as respectable as it is now.

One reason for this was that it was still a betting game, and the stakes could run pretty high—I've known £50,000 riding on a single innings, with wild side-bets of anything from a guinea to a thou on how many wickets Marsden would take, or how many catches would fall to the slips, or whether Pilch would reach fifty (which he probably would). With so much cash about, you may believe that some of the underhand work that went on would have made a Hays City stud school look like old maid's loo—matches were sold and thrown, players were bribed and threatened, wickets were doctored (I've known the whole eleven of a respected county side to sneak out en masse and p--s on the wicket in the dark, so that their twisters could get a grip next morning; I caught a nasty cold myself). Of course, corruption wasn't general, or even common, but it happened in those good old sporting days—and whatever the purists may say, there was a life and stingo about cricket then that you don't get now.

It *looked* so different, even; if I close my eyes I can see Lord's as it was then, and I know that when the memories of bed and battle have lost their colours and faded to misty grey, that at least will be as bright as ever. The coaches and carriages packed in the road outside the gate, the fashionable crowd streaming in by Jimmy Dark's house under the trees, the girls like so many gaudy butterflies in their summer dresses and hats, shaded by parasols, and the men guiding 'em to chairs, some in tall hats and coats, others in striped weskits and caps, the gentry uncomfortably buttoned up and the roughs and townies in shirt-sleeves and billycocks with their watch-chains and cutties; the bookies with their stands outside the pavilion, calling the odds, the flash chaps in their mighty whiskers and ornamented vests, the touts and runners and swell mobsmen slipping through the press like ferrets, the pot-boys from the Lord's pub thrusting along with trays loaded with beer and lemonade, crying "Way, order, gents! Way, order!"; old John Gully, the retired pug, standing like a great oak tree, feet planted wide, smiling his gentle smile as he talked to Alfred Mynn, whose scarlet waist-scarf and straw boater were a magnet for the eyes of the hero-worshipping youngsters, jostling at a respectful distance from these giants of the sporting world; the grooms pushing a way for some doddering old Duke, passing through nodding and tipping his tile, with his poule-of-the-moment arm-in-arm, she painted and bold-eyed and defiant as the ladies turned the other way with a rustle of skirts; the bowling green and archery range going full swing, with the thunk of the shafts mingling with the distant pomping of the artillery band, the chatter and yelling of the vendors, the grind of coach-wheels and the warm hum of summer ebbing across the great green field where Stevie Slatter's boys were herding away the sheep and warning off the bob-a-game players; the crowds ten-deep at the nets to see Pilch at batting practice, or Felix, agile as his animal namesake, bowling those slow lobs that seemed to hang forever in the air.

Or I see it in the late evening sun, the players in their white top hats trooping in from the field, with the ripple of applause running round the ropes, and the urchins streaming across to worship, while the old buffers outside the pavilion clap and cry "Played, well played!" and raise their tankards, and the Captain tosses the ball to some round-eyed small boy who'll guard it as a relic for life, and the scorer climbs stiffly down from his eyrie and the shadows lengthen across the idyllic scene, the very picture of merry, sporting old England, with the umpires bundling up the stumps, the birds calling in the tall trees, the gentle evenfall stealing over the ground and the pavilion, and the empty benches, and the willow wood-pile behind the sheep pen where Flashy is plunging away on top of the landlord's daughter in the long grass. Aye, cricket was cricket then.

Barring the last bit, which took place on another joyous occasion, that's absolutely what it was like on the afternoon when the Gentlemen of Rugby, including your humble servant, went out to play the cracks of Kent (twenty to one on, and no takers). At first I thought it was going to be a frost, for while most of my team-mates were pretty civil—as you'd expect, to the Hector of Afghanistan—the egregious Brown was decidedly cool, and so was Brooke, who'd been head of the school in my time and was the apple of Arnold's eye—that tells you all you need to know about him; he was clean-limbed and handsome and went to church and had no impure thoughts and was kind to animals and old ladies and was a midshipman in the Navy; what happened to him I've no idea, but I hope he absconded with the ship's funds and the admiral's wife and set up a knocking-shop in Valparaiso. He and Brown talked in low voices in the pavilion, and glanced towards me; rejoicing, no doubt, over the sinner who hadn't repented.

Then it was time to play, and Brown won the toss and elected to bat, which meant that I spent the next hour beside Elspeth's chair, trying to hush her imbecile observations on the game, and waiting for my turn to go in. It was a while coming, because either Kent were going easy to make a game of it, or Brooke and Brown were better than you'd think, for they survived the opening whirlwind of Mynn's attack, and when the twisters came on, began to push the score along quite handsomely. I'll say that for Brown, he could play a deuced straight bat, and Brooke was a hitter. They put on thirty for the first wicket, and our other batters were game, so that we had seventy up before the tail was reached, and I took my leave of my fair one, who embarrassed me d--nably by assuring her neighbours that I was sure to make a score, because I was so strong and clever. I hastened to the pavilion, collared a pint of ale from the pot-boy, and hadn't had time to do more than blow off the froth when there were two more wickets down, and Brown says: "In you go, Flashman."

So I picked up a bat from beside the flagstaff, threaded my way through the crowd who turned to look curiously at the next man in, and stepped out on to the turf—you must have done it yourselves often enough, and remember the silence as you walk out to the wicket, so far away, and perhaps there's a stray handclap, or a cry of "Go it, old fellow!", and no more than a few spectators loafing round the ropes, and the fielding side sit or lounge about, stretching in the sun, barely glancing at you as you come in. I knew it well enough, but as I stepped over the ropes I happened to glance up—and Lord's truly smote me for the first time. Round the great emerald field, smooth as a pool table, there was this mighty mass of people, ten-deep at the boundary, and behind them the coaches were banked solid, wheel to wheel, crowded with ladies and gentlemen, the whole huge multitude hushed and expectant while the sun caught the glittering eyes of thousands of opera-glasses and binocles glaring at me—it was d----d unnerving, with that vast space to be walked across, and my bladder suddenly holding a bushel, and I wished I could scurry back into the friendly warm throng behind me.

You may think it odd that nervous funk should grip me just then; after all, my native cowardice has been whetted on some real worth-while horrors—Zulu impis and Cossack cavalry and Sioux riders, all intent on rearranging my circulatory and nervous systems in their various ways; but there were others to share the limelight with me then, and it's a different kind of fear, anyway. The minor ordeals can be d----d scaring simply because you know you're going to survive them.

It didn't last above a second, while I gulped and hesitated and strode on, and then the most astounding thing happened. A murmur passed along the banks of people, and then it grew to a roar, and suddenly it exploded in the most deafening cheering you ever heard; you could feel the shock of it rolling across the ground, and ladies were standing up and fluttering their handkerchieves and parasols, and the men were roaring hurrah and waving their hats, and jumping up on the carriages, and in the middle of it all the brass band began to thump out "Rule, Britannia", and I realised they weren't cheering the next man in, but saluting the hero of Jallalabad, and I was fairly knocked sideways by the surprise of it all. However, I fancy I played it pretty well, raising my white topper right and left while the music and cheering pounded on, and hurrying to get to the wicket as a modest hero should. And here was slim little Felix, in his classroom whiskers and charity boy's cap, smiling shyly and holding out his hand—Felix, the greatest gentleman bat in the world, mark you, leading me to the wicket and calling for three cheers from the Kent team. And then the silence fell, and my bat thumped uncommon loud as I hit it into the block-hole, and the fielders crouched, and I thought, oh G-d, this is the serious business, and I'm bound to lay an egg on the scorer, I know I am, and after such a welcome, too, and with my bowels quailing I looked up the wicket at Alfred Mynn.

He was a huge man at the best of times, six feet odd and close on twenty stone, with a face like fried ham garnished with a double helping of black whisker, but now he looked like Goliath, and if you think a man can't tower above you from twenty-five yards off, you ain't seen young Alfie. He was smiling, idly tossing up the ball which looked no bigger than a cherry in his massive fist, working one foot on the turf—pawing it, bigod. Old Aislabie gave me guard, quavered "Play!" I gripped my bat, and Mynn took six quick steps and swung his arm.

I saw the ball in his hand, at shoulder height, and then something fizzed beside my right knee, I prepared to lift my bat—and the wicket-keeper was tossing the ball to Felix at point. I swallowed in horror, for I swear I never saw the d----d thing go, and someone in the crowd cries, "Well let alone, sir!" There was a little puff of dust settling about four feet in front of me; that's where he pitches, thinks I, oh J---s, don't let him hit me! Felix, crouching facing me, barely ten feet away, edged just a little closer, his eyes fixed on my feet; Mynn had the ball again, and again came the six little steps, and I was lunging forward, eyes tight shut, to get my bat down where the dust had jumped last time. I grounded it, my bat leaped as something hit it a hammer blow, numbing my wrists, and I opened my eyes to see the ball scuttling off to leg behind the wicket. Brooke yells "Come on!", and the lord knows I wanted to, but my legs didn't answer, and Brooke had to turn back, shaking his head.

This has got to stop, thinks I, for I'll be maimed for life if I stay here. And panic, mingled with hate and rage, gripped me as Mynn turned again; he strode up to the wicket, arm swinging back, and I came out of my ground in a huge despairing leap, swinging my bat for dear life—there was a sickening crack and in an instant of elation I knew I'd caught it low down on the outside edge, full swipe, the b----y thing must be in Wiltshire by now, five runs for certain, and I was about to tear up the pitch when I saw Brooke was standing his ground, and Felix, who'd been fielding almost in my pocket, was idly tossing the ball up in his left hand, shaking his head and smiling at me.

How he'd caught it only he and Satan know; it must have been like snatching a bullet from the muzzle. But he hadn't turned a hair, and I could only trudge back to the pavilion, while the mob groaned in sympathy, and I waved my bat to them and tipped my tile—after all I was a bowler, and at least I'd taken a swing at it. And I'd faced three balls from Alfred Mynn.

We closed our hand at 91, Flashy caught Felix, nought, and it was held to be a very fair score, although Kent were sure to pass it easily, and since it was a single-hand match that would be that. In spite of my blank score—how I wished I had gone for that single off the second ball!—I was well received round the pavilion, for it was known who I was by now, and several gentlemen came to shake my hand, while the ladies eyed my stalwart frame and simpered to each other behind their parasols; Elspeth was glowing at the splendid figure I had cut in her eyes, but indignant that I had been out when my wicket hadn't been knocked down, because wasn't that the object of the game? I explained that I had been caught out, and she said it was a most unfair advantage, and that little man in the cap must be a great sneak, at which the gentlemen around roared with laughter and ogled her, calling for soda punch for the lady and swearing she must be taken on to the committee to amend the rules.

I contented myself with a glass of beer before we went out to field, for I wanted to be fit to bowl, but d---e if Brown didn't leave me loafing in the outfield, no doubt to remind me that I was a whoremonger and therefore not fit to take an over. I didn't mind, but lounged about pretty nonchalant, chatting with the townies near the ropes, and shrugging my shoulders eloquently when Felix or his partner made a good hit, which they did every other ball. They fairly knocked our fellows all over the wicket, and had fifty up well within the hour; I observed to the townies that what we wanted was a bit of ginger, and limbered my arm, and they cheered and began to cry: "Bring on the Flash chap! Huzza for Afghanistan!" and so forth, which was very gratifying.

I'd been getting my share of attention from the ladies in the carriages near my look-out, and indeed had been so intent on winking and swaggering that I'd missed a long hit, at which Brown called pretty sharply to me to mind out; now one or two of the more spirited ladybirds began to echo the townies, who egged them on, so that "Bring on the Flash chap!" began to echo round the ground, in gruff bass and piping soprano. Finally Brown could stand it no longer, and waved me in, and the mob cheered like anything, and Felix smiled his quiet smile and took fresh guard.

On the whole he treated my first over with respect, for he took only eleven off it, which was better than I deserved. For of course I flung my deliveries down with terrific energy, the first one full pitch at his head, and the next three horribly short, in sheer nervous excitement. The crowd loved it, and so did Felix, curse him; he didn't reach the first one, but he drew the second beautifully for four, cut the third on tip-toe, and swept the last right off his upper lip and into the coaches near the pavilion.

How the crowd laughed and cheered, while Brown bit his lip with vexation, and Brooke frowned his disgust. But they couldn't take me off after only one turn; I saw Felix say something to his partner, and the other laughed—and as I walked back to my look-out a thought crept into my head, and I scowled horribly and clapped my hands in disgust, at which the spectators yelled louder than ever. "Give 'em the Afghan pepper, Flashy!" cries one, and "Run out the guns!" hollers another; I waved my fist and stuck my hat on the back of my head, and they cheered and laughed again.

They gave a huge shout when Brown called me up for my

second turn, and settled themselves to enjoy more fun and fury. You'll get it, my boys, thinks I, as I thundered up to the wicket, with the mob counting each step, and my first ball smote about half-way down the pitch, flew high over the batsman's head, and they ran three byes. That brought Felix to face me again, and I walked back, closing my ears to the shouting and to Brown's muttered rebuke. I turned, and just from the lift of Felix's shoulders I could see he was getting set to knock me into the trees; I fixed my eye on the spot dead in line with his off stump —he was a left-hander, which left the wicket wide as a barn door to my round delivery—and ran up determined to bowl the finest, fastest ball of my life.

And so I did. Very well, I told you I was a good bowler, and that was the best ball I ever delivered, which is to say it was unplayable. I had dropped the first one short on purpose, just to confirm what everyone supposed from the first over—that I was a wild chucker, with no more head than flat beer. But the second had every fibre directed at that spot, with just a trifle less strength than I could muster, to keep it steady, and from the moment it left my hand Felix was gone. Granted I was lucky, for the spot must have been bald; it was a shooter, skidding in past his toes when he expected it round his ears, and before he could smother it his stump was cart-wheeling away.

The yell that went up split the heaven, and he walked past me shaking his head and shooting me a quizzy look while the fellows slapped my back, and even Brooke condescended to cry "Well bowled!" I took it very offhand, but inside I was thinking: "Felix! Felix, by G-d!"—I'd not have swapped that wicket for a peerage. Then I was brought back to earth, for the crowd were cheering the new man in, and I picked up the ball and turned to face the tall, angular figure with the long-reaching arms and the short-handled bat.

I'd seen Fuller Pilch play at Norwich when I was a young shaver, when he beat Marsden of Yorkshire for the single-wicket championship of England; so far as I ever had a boyhood hero, it was Pilch, the best professional of his day—some say of any day, although it's my belief this new boy Rhodes may be as good. Well, Flash, thinks I, you've nothing to lose, so here goes at him.

Now, what I'd done to Felix was head bowling, but what came next was luck, and nothing else. I can't account for it yet, but it happened, and this is how it was. I did my d----dest to repeat my great effort, but even faster this time, and in consequence I was just short of a length; whether Pilch was surprised by the speed, or the fact that the ball kicked higher than it had any right to do, I don't know, but he was an instant slow in reaching forward, which was his great shot. He didn't ground his bat in time, the ball came high off the blade, and I fairly hurled myself down the pitch, all arms and legs, grabbing at a catch I could have held in my mouth. I nearly muffed it, too, but it stuck between finger and thumb, and the next I knew they were pounding me on the back, and the townies were in full voice, while Pilch turned away slapping his bat in vexation. "B----y gravel!" cries he. "Hasn't Dark got any brooms, then?" He may have been right, for all I know.

By now, as you may imagine, I was past caring. Felix—and Pilch. There was nothing more left in the world just then, or so I thought; what could excel those twin glorious strokes? My grandchildren will never believe this, thinks I, supposing I have any—by George, I'll buy every copy of the sporting press for the next month, and paper old Morrison's bedroom with 'em. And yet the best was still to come.

Mynn was striding to the crease; I can see him now, and it brings back to me a line that Macaulay wrote in that very year: "And now the cry is 'Aster'! and lo, the ranks divide, as the great Lord of Luna comes on with stately stride." That was Alfred the Great to a "t", stately and magnificent, with his broad crimson sash and the bat like a kid's paddle in his hand; he gave me a great grin as he walked by, took guard, glanced leisurely round the field, tipped his straw hat back on his head, and nodded to the umpire, old Aislabie, who was shaking with excitement as he called "Play!"

Well, I had no hope at all of improving on what I'd done, you may be sure, but I was determined to bowl my best, and it was only as I turned that it crossed my mind—old Aislabie's a Rugby man, and it was out of pride in the old school that he arranged this fixture; honest as God, to be sure, but like all enthusiasts he'll see what he wants to see, won't he?—and

Mynn's so tarnation big you can't help hitting him somewhere if you put your mind to it, and bowl your fastest. It was all taking shape even as I ran up to the wicket: I'd got Felix by skill, Pilch by luck, and I'd get Mynn by knavery or perish in the attempt. I fairly flung myself up to the crease, and let go a perfect snorter, dead on a length but a good foot wide of the leg stump. It bucked, Mynn stepped quickly across to let it go by, it flicked his calf, and by that time I was bounding across Aislabie's line of sight, three feet off the ground, turning as I sprang and yelling at the top of my voice: "How was he there, sir?"

Now, a bowler who's also a Gentleman of Rugby don't appeal unless he believes it; that gooseberry-eyed old fool Aislabie hadn't seen a d----d thing with me capering between him and the scene of the crime, but he concluded there must be something in it, as I knew he would, and by the time he had fixed his watery gaze, Mynn, who had stepped across, was plumb before the stumps. And Aislabie would have been more than human if he had resisted the temptation to give the word that everyone in that ground except Alfie wanted to hear. "Out!" cries he. "Yes, out, absolutely! Out! Out!"

It was bedlam after that; the spectators went wild, and my team-mates simply seized me and rolled me on the ground; the cheering was deafening, and even Brown pumped me by the hand and slapped me on the shoulder, yelling "Bowled, oh, well bowled, Flashy!" (You see the moral: cover every strumpet in London if you've a mind to, it don't signify so long as you can take wickets.) Mynn went walking by, shaking his head and cocking an eyebrow in Aislabie's direction—he knew it was a crab decision, but he beamed all over his big red face like the sporting ass he was, and then did something which has passed into the language: he took off his boater, presented it to me with a bow, and says:

"That trick's worth a new hat any day, youngster."

(I'm d----d if I know *which* trick he meant,[4] and I don't much care; I just know the leg-before-wicket rule is a perfectly splendid one, if they'll only let it alone.)

After that, of course, there was only one thing left to do. I told Brown that I'd sprained my arm with my exertions—

brought back the rheumatism contracted from exposure in Afghanistan, very likely . . . horrid shame . . . just when I was finding a length . . . too bad . . . worst of luck . . . field all right, though . . . (I wasn't going to run the risk of having the other Kent men paste me all over the ground, not for anything). So I went back to the deep field, to a tumultuous ovation from the gallery, which I acknowledged modestly with a tip of Mynn's hat, and basked in my glory for the rest of the match, which we lost by four wickets. (If only that splendid chap Flashman had been able to go on bowling, eh? Kent would have been knocked all to smash in no time. They do say he has a jezzail bullet in his right arm still—no it ain't, it was a spear thrust—I tell you I read it in the papers, etc., etc.)

It was beer all round in the pavilion afterwards, with all manner of congratulations—Felix shook my hand again, ducking his head in that shy way of his, and Mynn asked was I to be home next year, for if the Army didn't find a use for me, he could, in the casual side which he would get together for the Grand Cricket Week at Canterbury. This was flattery on the grand scale, but I'm not sure that the sincerest tribute I got wasn't Fuller Pilch's knitted brows and steady glare as he sat on a bench with his tankard, looking me up and down for a full two minutes and never saying a word.

Even the doddering Duke came up to compliment me and say that my style reminded him absolutely of his own—"Did I not remark it to you, my dear?" says he to his languid tart, who was fidgeting with her parasol and stifling a yawn while showing me her handsome profile and weighing me out of the corner of her eye. "Did I not observe that Mr Flashman's shooter was just like the one I bowled out Beauclerk with at Maidstone in '06?—directed to his off stump, sir, caught him goin' back, you understand, pitched just short, broke and shot, middle stump, bowled all over his wicket—ha! ha! what?"

I had to steady the old fool before he tumbled over demonstrating his action, and his houri, assisting, took the opportunity to rub a plump arm against me. "No doubt we shall have the pleasure of seeing you at Canterbury next summer, Mr Flashman," she murmurs, and the old pantaloon cries aye, aye, capital notion, as she helped him away; I made a note to look her up then, since she'd probably have killed him in the course of the winter.

It wasn't till I was towelling myself in the bathhouse, and getting outside a brandy punch, that I realised I hadn't seen Elspeth since the match ended, which was odd, since she'd hardly miss a chance to bask in my reflected glory. I dressed and looked about; no sign of her among the thinning crowd, or outside the pavilion, or at the ladies' tea tables, or at our carriage; coachee hadn't seen her either. There was a fairish throng outside the pub, but she'd hardly be there, and then someone plucked my sleeve, and I turned to find a large, beery-faced individual with black button eyes at my elbow.

"Mr Flashman, sir, best respex," says he, and tapped his low-crown hat with his cudgel. "You'll forgive the liberty, I'm sure —Tighe's the monicker, Daedalus Tighe, ev'yone knows me, agent an' accountant to the gentry—" and he pushed a card in my direction between sweaty fingers. "Takin' the hoppor-toonity, my dear sir an' sportsman, of presentin' my compliments an' best vishes, an'—"

"Thank'ee," says I, "but I've no bets to place."

"My dear sir!" says he, beaming. "The werry last idea!" And he invited his cronies, a seedy-flash bunch, to bear him witness. "My makin' so bold, dear sir, was to inwite you to share my good fortun', seein' as 'ow you've con-tribooted so 'andsome to same—namely, an' first, by partakin' o' some o' this 'ere French jam-pain—poodle's p--s to some, but as drunk in the bes' hestablishments by the werriest swells such as—your good self, sir. Wincent," says he, "pour a glass for the gallant—"

"Another time," says I, giving him my shoulder, but the brute had the effrontery to catch my arm.

" 'Old on, sir!" cries he. " 'Arf a mo', that's on'y the sociable pree-liminary. I'm vishful to present to your noble self the—"

"Go to the d---l!" snaps I. He stank of brandy.

"—sum of fifty jemmy o' goblins, as an earnest o' my profound gratitood an' respeck. Wincent!"

And d----d if the weasel at his elbow wasn't thrusting a glass of champagne at me with one hand and a fistful of bills in the other. I stopped short, staring.

"What the deuce . . .?"

"A triflin' token of my hes-teem," says Tighe. He swayed a little, leering at me, and for all the reek of booze, the flash cut of his coat, the watch-chain over his flowery silk vest, and the gaudy bloom in his lapel—the marks of the vulgar sport, in fact —the little eyes in his fat cheeks were as hard as coals. "You vun it for me, my dear sir—an' plenty to spare, d---e. Didn't 'e, though?" His confederates, crowding round, chortled and raised their glasses. "By the sweat—yore pardon, sir—by the peerspyration o' yore brow—an' that good right arm, vot sent back Felix, Pilch, 'an Alfred Mynn in three deliveries, sir. Look 'ere," and he snapped a finger to Vincent, who dropped the glass to whip open a leather satchel at his waist—it was stuffed with notes and coin.

"You, sir, earned that. You did, though. Ven you put avay Fuller Pilch—an' veren't that a 'andsome catch, now?—I sez to Fat Bob Napper, vot reckons e's king o' the odds an' evens— 'Napper,' sez I, 'that's a 'ead bowler, that is. Vot d'ye give me 'e don't put out Mynn, first ball?' 'Gammon,' sez 'e. 'Three in a row—never! Thahsand to one, an' you can pay me now.' Generous odds, sir, you'll allow." And the rascal winked and tapped his nose. "So—hon goes my quid—an' 'ere's Napper's thahsand, cash dahn, give 'im that—an' fifty on it's yore's, my gallant sir, vith the grateful compliments of Daedalus Tighe, Hesk-wire, agent an' accountant to the gentry, 'oo 'ereby salutes"—and he raised his glass and belched unsteadily —"yore 'onner's pardon, b----r them pickles—'oo salutes the most wicious right harm in the noble game o' cricket today! Hip-hip-hip—hooray!"

I couldn't help being amused at the brute, and his pack of rascals—drunken bookies and touts on the spree, and too far gone to appreciate their own impudence.

"My thanks for the thought, Mr Tighe," says I, for it don't harm to be civil to a bookie, and I was feeling easy, "you may drink my health with it." And I pushed firmly past him, at which he staggered and sat down heavily in a froth of cheap champagne, while his pals hooted and weaved in to help him. Not that I couldn't have used the fifty quid, but you can't be seen associating with cads of that kidney, much less accepting their gelt. I strode on, with cries of "Good luck, sir!" and

"Here's to the Flash cove!" following me. I was still grinning as I resumed my search for Elspeth, but as I turned into the archery range for a look there, the smile was wiped off my lips—for there were only two people in the long alley between the hedges: the tall figure of a man, and Elspeth in his arms.

I came to a dead halt, silent—for three reasons. First, I was astonished. Secondly, he was a big, vigorous brute, by what I could see of him—which was a massive pair of shoulders in a handsomely-cut broadcloth (no expense spared there), and thirdly, it passed quickly through my mind that Elspeth, apart from being my wife, was also my source of supply. Food for thought, you see, but before I had even an instant to taste it, they both turned their heads and I saw that Elspeth was in the act of stringing a shaft to a ladies' bow—giggling and making a most appealing hash of it—while her escort, standing close in behind her, was guiding her hands, which of course necessitated putting his arms about her, with her head against his shoulder.

All very innocent—as who knows better than I, who've taken advantage of many such situations for an ardent squeeze and fondle?

"Why, Harry," cries she, "where have you been all this while? See, Don Solomon is teaching me archery—and I have been making the sorriest show!" Which she demonstrated by fumbling the shaft, swinging her bow arm wildly, and letting fly into the hedge, squeaking with delighted alarm. "Oh, I am quite hopeless, Don Solomon, unless you hold my hands!"

"The fault is mine, dear Mrs Flashman," says he, easily. He managed to keep an arm round her, while bowing in my direction. "But here is Mars, who I'm sure is a much better instructor for Diana than I could ever be." He smiled and raised his hat. "Servant, Mr Flashman."

I nodded, pretty cool, and looked down my nose at him, which wasn't easy, since he was all of my height, and twice as big around—portly, you might say, if not fat, with a fleshy, smiling face, and fine teeth which flashed white against his swarthy skin. Dago, for certain, perhaps even Oriental, for his hair and whiskers were blue-black and curly, and as he came towards me he was moving with that mincing Latin grace, for all his flesh. A swell, too, by the elegant cut of his togs; diamond pin in his neckercher, a couple of rings on his big brown hands—and, by Jove, even a tiny gold ring in one ear. Part-nigger, not a doubt of it, and with all a rich nigger's side, too.

"Oh, Harry, we have had such fun!" cries Elspeth, and my heart gave a little jump as I looked at her. The gold ringlets under her ridiculous bonnet, the perfect pink and white complexion, the sheer innocent beauty of her as she sparkled with laughter and reached out a hand to me. "Don Solomon has shown me bowling, and how to shoot—ever so badly!—and entertained me—for the cricket came so dull when you were not playing, with those tedious Kentish people popping away, and—"

"Hey?" says I, astonished. "You mean you didn't see me bowl?"

"Why, no, Harry, but we had the jolliest time among the sideshows, with ices and hoop-la . . ." She prattled on, while the greaser raised his brows, smiling from one to the other of us.

"Dear me," says he, "I fear I have lured you from your duty, dear Mrs Flashman. Forgive me," he went on to me, "for I have the advantage of you still. Don Solomon Haslam, to command," and he nodded and flicked his handkerchief. "Mr Speedicut, who I believe is your friend, presented me to your so charming lady, and I took the liberty of suggesting that we . . . take a stroll. If I had known you were to be put on . . . but tell me . . . any luck, eh?"

"Oh, not too bad," says I, inwardly furious that while I'd been performing prodigies Elspeth had been fluttering at this oily flammer. "Felix, Pilch and Mynn, in three balls—if you call it luck. Now, my dear, if Mr Solomon will excuse—"

To my amazement he burst into laughter. "I would call it luck!" cries he. "That would be a daydream, to be sure! I'd settle for just one of 'em!"

"Well, I didn't," says I, glaring at him. "I bowled Felix, caught out Pilch, and had Mynn leg before—which probably don't mean much to a foreigner—"

"Good G-d!" cries he. "You don't mean it! You're bamming us, surely?"

"Now, look'ee, whoever you are—"

"But—but—oh, my G-d!" He was fairly spluttering, and

suddenly he seized my hand, and began pumping it, his face alight. "My dear chap—I can't believe it! All three? And to think I missed it!" He shook his head, and burst out laughing again. "Oh, what a dilemma! How can I regret an hour spent with the loveliest girl in London—but, oh, Mrs Flashman, what you've cost me! Why, there's never been anything like it! And to think that we were missing it all! Well, well, I've paid for my susceptibility to beauty, to be sure! Well done, my dear chap, well done! But this calls for celebration!"

I was fairly taken aback at this, while Elspeth looked charmingly bewildered, but nothing must do but he bore us off to where the liquor was, and demanded of me, action by action, a description of how I'd bowled out the mighty three. I've never seen a man so excited, and I'll own I found myself warming to him; he clapped me on the shoulder, and slapped his knee with delight when I'd done.

"Well, I'm blessed! Why, Mrs Flashman, your husband ain't just a hero—he's a prodigy!" At which Elspeth glowed and squeezed my hand, which banished the last of my temper. "Felix, Pilch, *and* Mynn! Extraordinary. Well—I thought I was something of a cricketer, in my humble way—I played at Eton, you know—we never had a match with Rugby, alas! but I fancy I'd be a year or two before your time, anyway, old fellow. But this quite beats everything!"

It was fairly amusing, not least for the effect it was having on Elspeth. Here was this gaudy foreign buck, who'd come spooning round her, d----d little flirt that she was, and now all his attention was for my cricket. She was between exulting on my behalf and pouting at being overlooked, but when we parted from the fellow, with fulsome compliments and assurances that we must meet again soon, on his side, and fair affability on mine, he won her heart by kissing her hand as though he'd like to eat it. I didn't mind, by now; he seemed not a bad sort, for a 'breed, and if he'd been to Eton he was presumably half-respectable, and obviously rolling in rhino. All men slobbered over Elspeth, anyway.

So the great day ended, which I'll never forget for its own splendid sake: Felix, Pilch, and Mynn, and those three ear-splitting yells from the mob as each one fell. It was a day that held the seed of great events, too, as you'll see, and the first tiny fruit was waiting for us when we got back to Mayfair. It was a packet handed in at the door, and addressed to me, enclosing bills for fifty pounds, and a badly-printed note saying "With the compliments of D. Tighe, Esq." Of all the infernal impudence; that b----y bookie, or whatever he was, having the starch to send cash to me, as though I were some pro. to be tipped.

I'd have kicked his backside to Whitechapel and back, or taken a cane to him for his presumption, if he'd been on hand. Since he wasn't, I pocketed the bills and burned his letter; it's the only way to put these upstarts in their place.

* * *

[Extract from the diary of Mrs H. Flashman, undated, 1842]
    . . . to be sure, it was very natural of H. to pay *some* attention to the other ladies at Lord's, for they were so *forward* in their admiration of him—and am I to blame you, less fortunate sisters? He looked *so* tall and proud and handsome, like the splendid English Lion that he is, that I felt quite *faint* with love and pride . . . to think that this striking man, the envy and admiration of all, is—*my husband* ! ! He is perfection, and I love him more than I can tell.

    Still, I could wish that he had been a *little* less attentive to those ladies near us, who smiled and waved to him when he was in the field, and some even so far forgot the obligations of modesty upon our tender sex, as to *call out* to him ! Of course, it is difficult for him to appear indifferent, so Admired as he is—and he has such an unaffected, gallant nature, and feels, I know, that he must acknowledge their flatteries, for fear that he should be thought lacking in that easy courtesy which becomes a gentleman. He is so Generous and Considerate, even to such *déclassé* persons as that *odious* Mrs Leo Lade, the Duke's *companion*, whose admiration of H. was so open and shameless that it caused some remark, and made me blush for her reputation—which to be sure, she hasn't any ! ! ! But H.'s simple, boyish goodness can see no fault in anyone—not even such an abandoned female as I'm sure she is, for they say . . . but I will not sully your fair page, dear diary, with such a Paltry Thing as Mrs Leo.

Yet mention of her reminds me yet again of my Duty to Protect my dear one—for he is still *such a boy*, with all a boy's *naiveté* and high spirit. Why, today, he looked quite *piqued and furious* at the attention shown to me by Don S.H., who is quite *sans reproche* and the most distinguished of persons. He has over fifty thousand a year, it is said, from estates and revenues in the Far East Indies, and is on terms with the Best in Society, and has been received by H.M. He is entirely English, although his mother was a Spanish Donna, I believe, and is of the most engaging manners and address, and the *jolliest* person besides. I confess I was not a little amused to find how I captivated him, which is quite *harmless* and *natural*, for I have noticed that Gentlemen of his Complexion are even more ardent in their addresses to the fair than those of Pure European Blood. Poor H. was not well pleased, I fear, but I could not help thinking it would do him no harm to be made aware that *both sexes* are wont to indulge in harmless gallantries, and if *he* is to be admired by such as Mrs L.L., he cannot object to the Don's natural regard for *me*. And to be sure, they are not to be compared, for Don S.H.'s addresses are of the *utmost* discretion and niceness; he is *amusing*, with propriety, engaging without familiarity. No doubt we shall see much of him in Society this winter, but not so much, I promise, as will make my Dear Hero *too* jealous—he has such sensibility . . .

[End of extract—G. de R.]

It was eight months before I so much as gave a thought to cricket again, but I'm bound to say that even if it had been blazing summer from October to March I'd still have been too busy. You can't conduct a passionate affair with Lola Montez, in which you fall foul of Otto Bismarck—which is what I was doing that autumn—and still have much time for recreation. Besides, this was the season when my fame was at its zenith, what with my visit to the Palace for the Kabul medal; in consequence I was in demand everywhere, and Elspeth, in her eagerness for the limelight, saw to it that I never had a moment's peace—balls and parties and receptions, and d---l a minute for serious raking. It was splendid, of course, to be the lion of the hour, but confounded exhausting.

But little enough happened to the point of my story, except that the stout Don Solomon Haslam played an increasingly lively part in our doings that winter. That was an odd fish, decidedly. Nobody, not even his old Eton chums, seemed to know much about him except that he was some kind of nabob, with connections in Leadenhall Street, but he was well received in Society, where his money and manners paid for all. And he seemed to be right in the know wherever he went—at the embassies, the smart houses, the sporting set, even at the political dinners; he was friendly with Haddington and Stanley at one end of the scale, and with such rascals as Deaf Jim Burke and Brougham at t'other. One night he would be dining with Aberdeen,[5] and the next at Rosherville Gardens or the Cider Cellars, and he had a quiet gift of being first with the word from all quarters: if you wanted to know what was behind the toll riots, or the tale of Peel's velveteens, ask Solomon; he had the latest joke about Alice Lowe, or Nelson's Column, could tell you beforehand about the new race cup for Ascot, and had songs from the "Bohemian Girl" played in his drawing-room months before the opera was seen in London.[6] It wasn't that he was a gossip or couch-whisperer, either; whatever way the talk turned, he just knew the answers.

He ought to have been detestable, but strangely enough he wasn't, for he didn't push or show off. His entertainment was lavish, in his house on Brook Street, where he gave a Chinese Party that was said to have cost twenty thou., and was the talk for weeks, and his appearance was what the ladies called Romantic—I've told you about the earring, enough said—but with it all he managed to appear modest and unaffected. He could charm, I'll say that for him, for he had the true gift of flattery, which is to show the keenest possible interest—and, of course, he had money to burn.

I didn't mind him much, myself; he went out of his way to be pleasant to me, and once I had satisfied myself that his enthusiasm for Elspeth wasn't likely to go the length, I tolerated him. She was ready to flirt with anything in breeches—and more than flirt, I suspected, but there were horny captains I was far leerier of than the Don. That b-----d Watney, for one, and the lecherous snob Ranelagh, and I fancy young Conyngham was itching after her, too. But Solomon had no name as a rake; didn't even keep a mistress, apparently, and did no damage round Windmill Street or any of *my* haunts, leastways. Another odd thing: he didn't touch liquor, in any form.

Oddest of all, though, was the way that my father-in-law took to him. From time to time during that winter old Morrison came south from his lair in Paisley to inflict himself on us and carp about expense, and it was during one of these visits that we had Solomon to dine. Morrison took one look at the fashionable cut of his coat and Newgate knockers,* sniffed, and muttered about "anither scented gommeril wi' mair money than sense", but before that dinner was through Solomon had him eating out of his palm.

Old Morrison had started off on one of his usual happy harangues about the state of the nation, so that for the first course we had cockaleekie soup, halibut with oyster sauce, and the income tax, removed with minced chicken patties, lamb cutlets, and the Mines Act, followed by a second course of venison in burgundy, fricassee of beef, and the Chartists, with

* Side-whiskers.

grape ices, bilberry tart, and Ireland for dessert. Then the ladies (Elspeth and my father's mistress, Judy, whom Elspeth had a great fancy for, G-d knows why) withdrew, and over the port we had the miners' strike and the General Ruin of the Country.

Fine stuff, all of it, and my guv'nor went to sleep in his chair while Morrison held forth on the iniquity of those scoundrelly colliers who objected to having their infants dragging tubs naked through the seams for a mere fifteen hours a day.

"It's the infernal Royal Commission," cries he. "Makin' mischief—aye, an' it'll spread, mark me. If bairns below the age o' ten year is no' tae work underground, how long will it be afore they're prohibitin' their employment in factories, will ye tell me? D--n that whippersnapper Ashley! 'Eddicate them', says he, the eejit! I'd eddicate them, would I no'! An' then there's the Factory Act—that'll be the next thing."

"The amendment can't pass for another two years," says Solomon quietly, and Morrison glowered at him.

"How d'ye ken that?"

"It's obvious, surely. We have the Mines Act, which is all the country can digest for the moment. But the shorter hours will come—probably within two years, certainly within three. Mr Horne's report will see to that."

His easy certainty impressed Morrison, who wasn't used to being lectured on business; however, the mention of Horne's name set him off again—I gathered this worthy was to publish a paper on child employment, which would inevitably lead to bankruptcies all round for deserving employers like my father-in-law, with free beer and holidays for the paupers, a workers' rebellion, and invasion by the French.

"Not quite so much, perhaps," smiles Solomon. "But his report will raise a storm, that's certain. I've seen some of it."

"Ye've seen it?" cries Morrison. "But it's no' oot till the New Year!" He glowered a moment. "Ye're gey far ben,* sir." He took an anxious gulp of port. "Does it . . . was there . . . that is, did ye chance tae see any mention o' Paisley, maybe?"

Solomon couldn't be certain, but said there was some shocking stuff in the report—infants tied up and lashed unmercifully by

---

* In the know, well-informed.

overseers, flogged naked through the streets when they were late; in one factory they'd even had their ears nailed down for bad work.

"It's a lie!" bawls Morrison, knocking over his glass. "A d----d lie! Never a bairn in oor shop had hand laid on it! Ma Goad—prayers at seeven, an' a cup o' milk an' a piece tae their dinner—oot o' ma ain pocket! Even a yard o' yarn, whiles, as a gift, an' me near demented wi' pilferin'—"

Solomon soothed him by saying he was sure Morrison's factories were paradise on earth, but added gravely that between the Horne report[7] and slack trade generally, he couldn't see many good pickings for manufacturers for some years to come. Overseas investment, that was the thing; why, there were millions a year to be made out of the Orient, by men who knew their business (as he did), and while Morrison sniffed a bit, and called it prospectus talk, you could see he was interested despite himself. He began to ask questions, and argue, and Solomon had every answer pat; I found it a dead bore, and left them prosing away, with my guv'nor snoring and belching at the table head—the most sensible noises I'd heard all night. But later, old Morrison was heard to remark that yon young Solomon had a heid on his shoothers, richt enough, a kenspeckle lad—no' like some that sauntered and drank awa' their time, an' sponged off their betters, etc.

One result of all this was that Don Solomon Haslam was a more frequent visitor than ever, dividing his time between Elspeth and her sire, which was perverse variety, if you like. He was forever talking Far East trade with Morrison, urging him to get into it—he even suggested that the old b-----d should take a trip to see for himself, which I'd have seconded, nem. con. I wondered if perhaps Solomon was some swell magsman trying to diddle the old rascal of a few thou.; some hopes, if he was. Anyway, they got along like a matched pair, and since Morrison was at this time expanding his enterprises, and Haslam was well-connected in the City, I dare say my dear relative found the acquaintance useful.

So winter and spring went by, and then in June I had two letters. One was from my Uncle Bindley at the Horse Guards, to say that negotiations were under way to procure me a lieutenancy in the Household Cavalry; this great honour, he was careful to point out, was due to my Afghan heroics, not to my social desirability, which in his opinion was negligible—he was from the Paget side of our family, you see, and affected to despise us common Flashmans, which showed he had more sense than manners. I was quite flown by this news, and almost equally elated by the other letter, which was from Alfred Mynn, reminding me of his invitation to play in his casual side at Canterbury. I'd been having a few games for the Montpeliers at the old Beehive field, and was in form, so I accepted straight off. It wasn't just for the cricket, though: I had three good reasons for wanting to be out of Town just then. First, I had just encompassed Lola Montez's ruin on the London stage,[8] and had reason to believe that the mad b---h was looking for me with a pistol—she was game for anything, you know, including murder; secondly, a female acrobat whom I'd been tupping was pretending that she was in foal, and demanding compensation with tears and menaces; and thirdly, I recalled that Mrs Lade, the Duke's little piece, was to be in Canterbury for the Cricket Week.

So you can see a change of scene was just what old Flashy needed; if I'd known the change I was going to get I'd have paid off the acrobat, let Mrs Lade go hang, and allowed Montez one clear shot at me running—and thought myself lucky. But we can't see into the future, thank God.

I'd intended to go down to Canterbury on my own, but a week or so beforehand I happened to mention my visit to Haslam, in Elspeth's presence, and right away he said famous, just the thing; he was keen as mustard on cricket himself, and he'd take a house there for the week: we must be his guests, he would get together a party, and we'd make a capital holiday of it. He was like that, expense was no object with him, and in a moment he had Elspeth clapping her hands with promises of picnic and dances and all sorts of junketings.

"Oh, Don, how delightful!" cries she. "Why, it will be the jolliest thing, and Canterbury is the most *select* place, I believe—yes, there is a regiment there—but, oh, what shall I have to wear? One needs a very different style out of London, you see, especially if many of our lunches are to be *al fresco*, and some of the evening parties are sure to be out of doors—oh, but what about poor, dear Papa?"

I should have added that another reason for my leaving London was to get away from old Morrison, who was still infesting our premises. In fact, he'd been taken ill in May—not fatally, unfortunately. He claimed it was overwork, but I knew it was the report of the child employment commission which, as Don Solomon had predicted, had caused a shocking uproar when it came out, for it proved that our factories were rather worse than the Siberian salt mines. Names hadn't been named, but questions were being asked in the Commons, and Morrison was terrified that at any moment he'd be exposed for the slave-driving swine he was. So the little villain had taken to his bed, more or less, with an attack of the nervous guilts, and spent his time d---ing the commissioners, snarling at the servants, and snuffing candles to save money.

Of course Haslam said he must come with us; the change of air would do him good; myself, I thought a change *from* air was what the old pest required, but there was nothing I could do about it, and since my first game for Mynn's crew was on a Monday afternoon, it was arranged that the party should travel down the day before. I managed to steer clear of that ordeal, pleading business—in fact, young Conyngham had bespoken a room at the Magpie for a hanging on the Monday morning, but I didn't let on to Elspeth about that. Don Solomon convoyed the party to the station for the special he'd engaged, Elspeth with enough trunks and bandboxes to start a new colony, old Morrison wrapped in rugs and bleating about the iniquity of travelling by railroad on the sabbath, and Judy, my father's bit, watching the performance with her crooked little smile.

She and I never exchanged a word, nowadays. I'd rattled her (once) in the old days, when the guv'nor's back was turned, but then she'd called a halt, and we'd had a fine, shouting turn-up in which I'd blacked her eye. Since then we'd been on civil-sneer terms, for the guv'nor's sake, but since he'd recently been carted away again to the blue-devil factory to have the booze bogies chased out of his brain, Judy was devoting her time to being Elspeth's companion—oh, we were a conventional little menage, sure enough. She was a handsome, knowing piece, and I squeezed her thigh for spite as I handed her into the carriage, got a blood-freezing glare for my pains, and waved them farewell, promising to meet them in Canterbury by noon next day.

I forget who they hung on the Monday, and it don't matter anyway, but it was the only Newgate scragging I ever saw, and I had an encounter afterwards which is part of my tale. When I got to the Magpie on Sunday evening, Conyngham and his pals weren't there, having gone across to the prison chapel to see the condemned man attend his last service; I didn't miss a great deal apparently, for when they came back they were crying that it had been a dead bore—just the chaplain droning away and praying, and the murderer sitting in the black pen talking to the turnkey.

"They didn't even have him sitting on his coffin," cries Conyngham. "I thought they always had his coffin in the pew with him—d--n you, Beresford, you told me they did!"

"Still, t'aint every day you see a chap attend his own burial service," says another. "Don't you just wish you may look as lively at your own, Conners?"

After that they all settled down to cards and boozing, with a buffet supper that went on all evening, and of course the girls were brought in—Snow Hill sluts that I wouldn't have touched with a long pole. I was amused to see that Conyngham and the other younger fellows were in a rare sweat of excitement—quite feverish they got in their wining and wenching, and all because they were going to see a chap turned off. It was nothing to me, who'd seen hangings, beheadings, crucifixions and the L--d knows what in my wanderings; *my* interest was to see an English felon crapped in front of an English crowd, so in the meantime I settled down to écarté with Speedicut, and by getting him well foxed I cleaned him out before midnight.

By then most of the company were three-parts drunk or snoring, but they didn't sleep long, for in the small hours the gallows-builders arrived, and the racket they made as they hammered up the scaffold in the street outside woke everyone. Conyngham remembered then that he had a sheriff's order, so we all trooped across to Newgate to get a squint at the chap in the condemned cell, and I remember how that boozy, rowdy party fell silent once we were in Newgate Yard, with the dank black walls crowding in on either side, our steps sounding hollow in the stone passages, breathing short and whispering while the turnkey grinned horribly and rolled his eyes to give Conyngham his money's worth.

I reckon the young sparks didn't get it, though, for all they saw in the end was a man lying fast asleep on his stone bench, with his jailer resting on a mattress alongside; one or two of our party, having recovered their spunk by that time, wanted to wake him up, in the hope that he'd rave and pray, I suppose; Conyngham, who was wilder than most, broke a bottle on the bars and roared at the fellow to stir himself, but he just turned over on his side, and a little beadle-like chap in a black coat and tall hat came on the scene in a tearing rage to have us turned out.

"Vermin!" cries he, stamping and red in the face. "Have you no decency? Dear G-d, and these are meant to be the leaders of the nation! D--n you, d--n you, d--n you all to h--l!" He was incoherent with fury, and vowed the turnkey would lose his place; he absolutely threw Conyngham out bodily, but our bold boy wasn't abashed; when he'd done giving back curse for curse he made a drunken dash for the scaffold, which was erected by now, black beams, barriers, and all, and managed to dance on the trap before the scandalised workmen threw him into the road.

His pals picked him up, laughing and cheering, and got him back to the Magpie; the crowd that was already gathering in the warm summer dawn grinned and guffawed as we went through, though there were some black looks and cries of "Shame!" The first eel-piemen were crying their wares in the street, and the vendors of tiny model gibbets and Courvoisier's confession and pieces of rope from the last hanging (cut off some chandler's stock that very morning, you may be sure) were having their breakfast in Lamb's and the Magpie common room, waiting for the real mob to arrive; the lower kind of priggers and whores were congregating, and some family parties were already established at the windows, making a picnic of it; carters were putting their vehicles against the walls and offering places of vantage at sixpence a time; the warehousemen and porters who had their business to do were d--ning the eyes of those who obstructed their work, and the constables were sauntering up and down in pairs, moving on the beggars and drunks, and keeping a cold eye on the more obvious thieves and flash-tails. A bluff-looking chap in clerical duds was watching with lively interest as Conyngham was helped into the Magpie and up the stairs; he nodded civilly to me.

"Quiet enough so far," says he, and I noticed that he carried his right arm at an odd angle, and his hand was crooked and waxy. "I wonder, sir, if I might accompany your party?" He gave me his name, but I'm shot if I recall it now.

I didn't mind, so he came abovestairs, into the wreck of our front room, with the remains of the night's eating and drinking being cleared away and breakfast set, and the sluts being chivvied out by the waiters, complaining shrilly; most of our party were looking pretty seedy, and didn't make much of the chops and kidneys at all.

"First time for most of them," says my new acquaintance. "Interesting, sir, most interesting." At my invitation he helped himself to cold beef, and we talked and ate in one of the windows while the crowd below began to increase, until the whole street was packed tight as far as you could see both sides of the scaffold; a great, seething mob, with the peelers guarding the barriers, and hardly room enough for the dippers and mobsmen to ply their trade—there must have been every class of mortal in London there; all the dross of the underworld rubbing shoulders with tradesmen and City folk; clerks and counter-jumpers; family men with children perched on their shoulders; beggar brats scampering and tugging at sleeves; a lord's carriage against a wall, and the mob cheering as its stout occupant was heaved on to the roof by his coachmen; every window was jammed with onlookers at two quid a time; there were galleries on the roofs with seats to let, and even the gutters and lamp-brackets had people clinging to them. A ragged little urchin came swinging along the Magpie's wall like a monkey; he clung to our window-ledge with naked, grimy toes and fingers, his great eyes staring at our plates; my companion held out a chop to him, and it vanished in a twinkling into the ugly, chewing face.

Someone hailed from beneath our window, and I saw a burly, pug-nosed fellow looking up; my crooked-arm chap shouted down to him, but the noise and hooting and laughter of the crowd was too much for conversation, and presently my companion gave up, and says to me:

"Thought he might be here. Capital writer, just you watch; put us all in the shade presently. Did you follow Miss Tickletoby last summer?" From which I've since deduced that the cove beneath our window that day was Mr William Makepeace Thackeray. That was my closest acquaintance with him, though.

"It's a solemn thought," went on my companion, "that if executions were held in churches, we'd never lack for congregations—probably get much the same people as we do now, don't you think? Ah—there we are!"

As he spoke the bell boomed, and the mob below began to roar off the strokes in unison: "One, two, three . . ." until the eighth peal, when there was a tremendous hurrah, which echoed between the buildings, and then died away in a sudden fall, broken only by the shrill wail of an infant. My companion whispered:

> "St Sepulchre's bell begins to toll,
> The Lord have mercy on his soul."

As the chatter of the crowd grew again, we looked across that craning sea of humanity to the scaffold, and there were the constables hurrying out of the Debtors' Door from the jail, with the prisoner bound between them, up the steps, and on to the platform. The prisoner seemed to be half-asleep ("drugged," says my companion; "they won't care for that"). They didn't, either, but began to stamp and yell and jeer, drowning out the clergyman's prayer, while the executioner made fast the noose, slipped a hood over the condemned man's head, and stood by to slip the bolt. There wasn't a sound now, until a drunk chap sings out, "Good health, Jimmy!" and there were cries and laughter, and everyone stared at the white-hooded figure under the beam, waiting.

"Don't watch him," whispers my friend. "Look at your companions."

I did, glancing along at the next window: every face staring, every mouth open, motionless, some grinning, some pale with fear, some in an almost vacant ecstasy. "Keep watching 'em," says he, and pat on his words came the rattle and slam of the drop, an almighty yell from the crowd, and every face at the next window was eagerly alight with pleasure—Speedicut grinning and crowing, Beresford sighing and moistening his lips, Spottswood's heavy face set in grim satisfaction, while his fancy woman clung giggling to his arm, and pretended to hide her face.

"Interesting, what?" says the man with the crooked arm.[9] He put on his hat, tapped it down, and nodded amiably. "Well, I'm obliged to you, sir," and off he went. Across the street the white-capped body was spinning slowly beneath the trap, a constable on the platform was holding the rope, and directly beneath me the outskirts of the crowd was dissolving into the taverns. Over in a corner of the room Conyngham was being sick.

I went downstairs and stood waiting for the crowd to thin, but most of 'em were still waiting in the hopes of catching a glimpse of the hanging corpse, which they couldn't see for the throng in front. I was wondering how far I'd have to walk for a hack, when a man loomed up in front of me, and after a moment I recognised the red face, button eyes, and flash weskit of Mr Daedalus Tighe.

"Vell, vell, sir," cries he, "here ve are again! I hears as you're off to Canterbury—vell, you'll give 'em better sport than *that*, I'll be bound!" And he nodded towards the scaffold. "Did you ever see poorer stuff, Mr Flashman? Not vorth the vatchin', sir, not vorth the vatchin'. Not a word out o' him—no speech, no repentance, not even a struggle, blow me! That's not vot ve'd 'ave called a 'angin', in my young day. You'd think," says he, sticking his thumbs in his vest, "that a young cribsman like that there, vot 'adn't no upbringin' to speak of, nor never amounted to nothin'—till today—you'd think, sir, that on *the* great hocassion of 'is life, 'e'd show appreciation, 'stead o' lettin' them drug 'im vith daffy. Vere vas his ambition, sir, allowin' 'imself to be crapped like that there, ven 'e might 'ave reckernised the interest, sir, of all these people 'ere, an' responded to same?" He beamed at me, head on one side. "No bottom, Mr Flashman; no game. Now, *you*, sir—*you'd* do your werry best if *you* vas misfortinit enough to be in his shoes—vhich Gawd forbid—an' so should I, eh? Ve'd give the people vot they came for, like good game Henglishmen.

"Speakin' of game," he went on, "I trust you're in prime condition for Canterbury. I'm countin' on you, sir, countin' on you, I am."

Something in his tone raised a tiny prickle on my neck. I'd been giving him a cool stare, but now I made it a hard one.

"I don't know what you mean, my man," says I, "and I don't care. You may take yourself——"

"No, no, no, my dear young sir," says he, beaming redder than ever. "You've mistook me quite. Vot I'm indicatin', sir, is that I'm interested—werry much interested, in the success of Mr Mynn's Casual XI, vot I hexpec' to carry all before 'em, for your satisfaction an' my profit." He closed an eye roguishly. "You'll remember, sir, as 'ow I expressed my appreciation o' your notable feat at Lord's last year, by forwardin' a token, a small gift of admiration, reelly——"

"I never had a d----d thing from you," says I, perhaps just a shade too quickly.

"You don't say, sir? Vell, blow me, but you astonish me, sir—you reelly do. An' me takin' werry partikler care to send it to yore direction—an' you never received same! Vell, vell," and the little black eyes were hard as pebbles. "I vonder now, if that villain o' mine, Wincent, slipped it in 'is cly, 'stead o' deliverin' same to you? Hooman vickedness, Mr Flashman, sir, there ain't no end to it. Still, sir, ve needn't repine," and he laughed heartily, "there's more vere that come from, sir. An' I can tell you, sir, that if you carries yore bat against the Irreg'lars this arternoon—vell, you can count to three hundred, I'll be bound, eh?"

I stared at him, speechless, opened my mouth—and shut it. He regarded me benignly, winked again, and glanced about him.

"Terrible press, sir; shockin'. Vhy the peelers don't chivvy these d----d magsmen an' cly-fakers—vhy, a gent like you ain't safe; they'll 'ave the teeth out yore 'ead, 'less you looks sharp. Scandalous, sir; vot you need's a cab; that's vot you need."

He gave a nod, a burly brute close by gave a piercing whistle, and before you could wink there was a hack pushing through the crowd, its driver belabouring all who didn't clear out fast enough. The burly henchman leaped to the horse's head, another held the door, and Mr Tighe, hat in hand, was ushering me in, beaming wider than ever.

"An' the werry best o' luck this arternoon, sir," cries he. "You'll bowl them Irreg'lars aht in no time, I'll wager, an' "—he winked again—"I do 'ope as you carries your bat, Mr Flashman. Charin' Cross, cabby!" And away went the cab, carrying a very thoughtful gentleman, you may be sure.

I considered the remarkable Mr Tighe all the way to Canterbury, too, and concluded that if he was fool enough to throw money away, that was his business—what kind of odds could he hope to get on my losing my wicket, for after all, I batted well down the list, and might easily carry my bat through the hand?[10] Who'd wager above three hundred on that? Well, that was his concern, not mine—but I'd have to keep a close eye on him, and not become entangled with his sort; at least he wasn't expecting me to throw the game, but quite the reverse; he was trying to bribe me to do well, in fact. H'm.

The upshot of it was, I bowled pretty well for Mynn's eleven, and when I went to the wicket to bat, I stuck to my block-hole like glue, to the disappointment of the spectators, who expected me to slog. I was third last man in, so I didn't have to endure long, and as Mynn himself was at t'other end, knocking off the runs, my behaviour was perfectly proper. We won by two wickets, Flashy not out, nil—and next morning, after breakfast, there was a plain packet addressed to me, with three hundred in bills inside.

I near as a toucher sealed it up again and told the footman to give it back to whoever had brought it—but I didn't. Warm work—but three hundred is three hundred—and it was a gift, wasn't it? I could always deny I'd ever seen it—G-d, I was an innocent then, for all my campaign experience.

This, of course, took place at the house which Haslam had taken just outside Canterbury, very splendid, gravel walks, fine lawns, shrubbery and trees, gaslight throughout, beautifully-appointed rooms, best of food and drink, flunkeys everywhere, and go-as-you-please. There were about a dozen house guests, for it was a great rambling place, and Haslam had seen to every comfort. He gave a sumptuous party on that first Monday night, at which Mynn and Felix were present, and the talk was all cricket, of course, but there were any number of ladies, too, including Mrs Leo Lade, smouldering at me across the table from under a heap of sausage curls, and in a dress so *décolleté* that her udders were almost in her soup. That's one over we'll bowl this week that won't be a maiden, thinks I, and flashed my most loving smile to Elspeth, who was sparkling radiantly beside Don Solomon at the top of the table.

Presently, however, her sparkle was wiped clean away, for Don Solomon was understood to say that this week would be his last fling in England; he was leaving at the end of the month to visit his estates in the East, and had no notion when he would return; it might be years, he said, at which there were genuine expressions of sorrow round the table, for those assembled knew a dripping roast when they saw one. Without the lavish Don Solomon, there would be one luxurious establishment less for the Society hyenas to guzzle at. Elspeth was quite put out.

"But dear Don Solomon, what shall we do? Oh, you're teasing —why, your tiresome estates will do admirably without you, for I'm sure you employ only the cleverest people to look after them." She pouted prettily. "You would not be so cruel to your friends, surely—Mrs Lade, we shan't let him, shall we?"

Solomon laughed and patted her hand. "My dear Diana," says he—Diana had been his nickname for her ever since he'd tried to teach her archery—"you may be sure nothing but harsh necessity would take me from such delightful company as your own—and Harry's yonder, and all of you. But—a man must work, and my work is overseas. So—" and he shook his head, his smooth, handsome face smiling ruefully. "It will be a sore wrench—sorest of all in that I shall miss both of you"—and he looked from Elspeth to me and back again—"above all the rest, for you have been to me like a brother and sister." And, d---e, the fellow's great dark eyes were positively glistening; the rest of the table murmured sympathetically, all but old Morrison, who was champing away at his blancmange and finding bones in it, by the sound of him.

At this Elspeth was so overcome that she began piping her eye, and her tits shook so violently that the old Duke, on Solomon's other side, coughed his false teeth into his wine-glass and had to be put to rights by the butler. Solomon, for once, was looking a little embarrassed; he shrugged and gave me a look that was almost appealing. "I'm sorry, old boy," says he, "but I mean it." I couldn't fathom this—he might be sorry to miss Elspeth; what man wouldn't? But had I been so friendly? —well, I'd been civil enough, and I was her husband; perhaps that charming manner of mine which Tom Hughes mentioned had had its effect on this emotional dago. Anyway, something seemed called for.

"Well, Don," says I, "we'll all be sorry to lose you, and that's a fact. You're a d----d stout chap—that is, I mean, you're one of the best, and couldn't be better if . . . if you were English." I wasn't going to gush all over him, you understand, but the company murmured "Hear, hear," and after a moment Mynn tapped the table to second me. "Well," says I, "let's drink his health, then." And everyone did, while Solomon gave me his bland smile, inclining his head.

"I know," says he, "just how great a compliment that is. I thank you—all of you, and especially you, my dear Harry. I only wish—" and then he stopped, shaking his head. "But no, that would be too much to ask."

"Oh, ask anything, Don!" cries Elspeth, all idiot-imploring. "You know we could not refuse you!"

He said no, no, it had been a foolish thought, and at that of course she was all over him to know what it was. So after a moment, toying with his wine-glass, he says: "Well, you'll think it a very silly notion, I dare say—but what I was about to propose, my dear Diana, for Harry and yourself, and for your father, whom I count among my wisest friends—" and he inclined his head to old Morrison, who was assuring Mrs Lade that he didn't want any blancmange, but he'd like anither helpin' o' yon cornflour puddin' "—I was about to say, since I must go—why do the three of you not come with me?" And he smiled shyly at us in turn.

I stared at the fellow to see if he was joking; Elspeth, all blonde bewilderment, looked at me and then at Solomon, open-mouthed.

"Come with you?"

"It's only to the other side of the world, after all," says he, whimsically. "No, no—I am quite serious; it is not as bad as that. You know me well enough to understand that I wouldn't propose anything that you would not find delightful. We should cruise, in my steam-brig—it's as well-appointed as any royal yacht, you know, and we'd have the most splendid holiday. We would touch wherever we liked—Lisbon, Cadiz, the Cape, Bombay, Madras—exactly as the fancy took us. Oh, it would be quite capital!" He leaned towards Elspeth, smiling. "Think of the places we'd see! The delight it would give me, Diana, to show you the wonder of Africa, as one sees it at dawn from the quarterdeck—such colours as you cannot imagine! The shores of the Indian Ocean—yes, the coral strand! Ah, believe me, until you have anchored off Singapore, or cruised the tropical coasts of Sumatra and Java and Borneo, and seen that glorious China Sea, where it is always morning—oh, my dear, you have seen nothing!"

Nonsense, of course; the Orient stinks. Always did. But Elspeth was gazing at him in rapture, and then she turned eagerly to me. "Oh, Harry—could we?"

"Out o' the question," says I. "It's the back of beyond."

"In these days?" cries Solomon. "Why, with steam you may be in Singapore in—oh, three months at most. Say, three months as my guests while we visit my estates—and you would learn, Diana, what it means to be a queen in the Orient, I assure you—and three months to return. You'd be home again by next Easter."

"Oh, Harry!" Elspeth was positively squeaking with joy. "Oh, Harry—may we? Oh, please, Harry!" The chaps at the table were nodding admiringly, and the ladies murmuring enviously; the old Duke was heard to say that it was an adventure, d----d if it wasn't, and if he was a younger man, by George, wouldn't he jump at the chance?

Well, they weren't getting me East again; once had been enough. Besides, I wasn't going anywhere on the charity of some rich dago show-off who'd taken a shine to my wife. And there was another reason, which enabled me to put a good face on my refusal.

"Can't be done, m'dear," says I. "Sorry, but I'm a soldier with a living to make. Duty and the Life Guards call, what? I'm desolate to deny you what I'm sure would be the jolliest trip"—I felt a pang, I'll admit, at seeing that lovely child face fall—"but

I can't go, you see. I'm afraid, Don, we'll have to decline your kind offer."

He shrugged good-humouredly. "That's settled, then. A pity, but—" he smiled consolingly at Elspeth, who was looking down-in-the-mouth "—perhaps another year. Unless, in Harry's enforced absence, your father could be persuaded to accompany us?"

It was said so natural it took my breath away, but as it sank home I had to bite back an angry refusal. You b-----d, thinks I, that's the game, is it? Wait till old Flashy's put himself out of the running, and then innocently propose a scheme to get my wife far away where you can cock a leg over her at leisure. It was plain as a pikestaff; all my dormant suspicions of this smooth tub of nigger suet came back with a rush, but I kept mum while Elspeth looked down the table towards me—and, bless her, it was a doubtful look.

"But . . . but it would be no fun without Harry," says she, and if ever I loved the girl it was then. "I . . . I don't know—what does Papa say?"

Papa, who appeared to be still tunnelling away at his pudding, had missed nothing, you may be sure, but he kept quiet while Solomon explained the proposal. "You remember, sir, we spoke of the possibility that you might accompany me to the East, to see for yourself the opportunities of business expansion," he was adding, but Morrison cut him short in his charming way.

"You spoke of it, no' me," says he, busily engulfing blanc-mange. "I've mair than enough o' affairs here, withoot galli-vantin' tae China at my time o' life." He waved his spoon. "Forbye, husband an' wife should be thegither—it was bad enough when Harry yonder had tae be away in India, an' my wee lassie near heartbroken." He made a noise which the company took for a sentimental sniff; myself I think it was another spoonful being pried loose. "Na, na—I'll need a guid reason afore I'll stir forth o' England."

And he got it—to this day I can't be certain that it was contrived by Solomon, but I'll wager it was. For next morning the old hound was taken ill again—I don't know if surfeit of blancmange can cause nervous collapse, but by afternoon he was groaning in bed, shuddering as with a fever, and Solomon insisted on summoning his own medico from Town, a dundreary-looking cove with a handle to his name and a line in unctuous gravity that must have been worth five thousand a year in Mayfair. He looked down solemnly at the sufferer, who was huddled under the clothes like a rat in its burrow, two beady eyes in a wrinkled face, and his nose quivering in apprehension.

"Overstrained," says the sawbones, when he had completed his examination and caught the tune of Morrison's whimpering. "The system is simply tired; that is all. Of organic deterioration there is no sign whatever; internally, my dear sir, you are sound as I am—as I hope I am, ha-ha!" He beamed like a bishop. "But the machine, while not in need of repair, requires a rest— a long rest."

"Is it serious, doacter?" quavers Morrison. Internally, as the quack said, he might be in A1 trim, but his exterior suggested James I dying.

"Certainly not—unless you make it so," says the poultice-walloper. He shook his head in censorious admiration. "You captains of commerce—you sacrifice yourselves without thought for personal health, as you labour for family and country and mankind. But, my dear sir, it won't do, you know. You forget that there is a limit—and you have reached it."

"Could ye no' gi' me a line for a boatle?" croaks the captain of commerce, and when this had been translated the medico shook his head.

"I can prescribe," says he, "but no medicine could be as efficacious as—oh, a few months in the Italian lakes, or on the French coast. Warmth, sunshine, rest—complete rest in congenial company—that is my 'line' for you, sir. I won't be answerable for the consequences if you don't take it."

Well, there it was. In two seconds I had foreseen what was to follow—Solomon's recollection that he had only yesterday proposed just such a holiday, the quack's booming agreement that a sea voyage in comfort was the ideal thing, Morrison's reluctance being eventually overborne by Elspeth's entreaties and the pill-slinger's stern admonition—you could have set it all to music and sung the d----d thing. Then they all looked at me, and I said no.

There followed painful private scenes between Elspeth and

me. I said if old Morrison wanted to sail away with Don Solomon, he was more than welcome. She replied that it was *unthinkable* for dear Papa to go without her to look after him; it was absolutely her *duty* to accept Don Solomon's generous offer and accompany the old goat. If I insisted on staying at home in the Army, of course she would be desolate without me —but why, oh why, could I not come anyway?—what did the Army matter, we had money enough, and so forth. I said no again, and added that it was a piece of impudence of Solomon's even to suggest that she should go without me, at which she burst into tears and said I was *odiously* jealous, not only of her, but of Don Solomon's breeding and address and money, just because I hadn't any myself, and I was *spitefully* denying her a little pleasure, and there could be no *possible* impropriety with dear Papa to chaperon her, and I was trying to shovel the old sod into an early grave, or words to that effect.

I left her wailing, and when Solomon tried to persuade me later himself, took the line that military duty made the trip impossible for me, and I couldn't bear to be parted from Elspeth. He sighed, but said he understood only too well—in my shoes, he said with disarming frankness, he'd do the same. I wondered for a moment if I had wronged him—for I know I tend to judge everyone by myself, and while I'm usually not far wrong to do so, there *are* decent and disinterested folk about, here and there. I've seen some.

Old Morrison, by the way, didn't say a word; he could have forced my hand, of course, but being as true a Presbyterian hypocrite as ever robbed an orphan, he held that a wife should abide by her husband's rule, and wouldn't interfere between Elspeth and me. So I continued to say "no", and Elspeth sulked until the time came to put on her next new bonnet.

So a couple of days passed, in which I played cricket for Mynn's side, tumbling a few wickets with my shiverers, and slogging a few runs (not many, but 18 in one innings, which pleased me, and catching out Pilch again, one hand, very low down, when he tried to cut Mynn past point and I had to go full length to it. Pilch swore it was a bump, but it wasn't—you may be sure I'd tell you if it had been). Meanwhile Elspeth basked in admiration and the gay life, Solomon was the perfect host and escort, old Morrison sat on the terrace grumbling and reading sermons and share prices, and Judy promenaded with Elspeth, looking cattish and saying nothing.

Then on Friday things began to happen, and as so often is the case with catastrophe, all went splendidly at first. All week I'd been trying to arrange an assignation with the tantalising Mrs Leo Lade, but what with my own busy affairs and the fact that the old Duke kept a jealous eye on her, I'd been out of luck. It was just a question of time and place, for she was as ready as I; indeed, we'd near got to grips on the Monday after dinner, when we strolled in the garden, but I'd no sooner got her panting among the privet with her teeth half-way through my ear than that bl----d minx Judy came to summon us to hear Elspeth sing "The Ash Grove" in the drawing-room; it *would* be Judy, smiling her knowing smile, telling us to be sure not to miss the treat.

However, on Friday morning Elspeth went off with Solomon to visit some picture gallery, Judy was shopping with some of the guests, the house was empty except for old Morrison on the terrace, and Mrs Lade bowled up presently to say that the Duke was abed with an attack of gout. For show's sake we made small talk with Morrison, which infuriated him, and then went our separate ways in leisurely fashion, meeting again in the drawing-room in a fine frenzy of fumbling and escaping steam. We weren't new to the business, either of us, so I had her breasts out with one hand and my breeches down with the other while I was still kicking the door to, and she completed her undressing while we were positively humping the mutton all the way to the couch, which argued sound training on her part. By George, she was a heavy woman, but nimble as an eel for all her elegant poundage; I can't think offhand of a partner who could put you through as many different mounting-drills in the course of one romp, except perhaps Elspeth herself when she had a drink in her.

It was exhilarating work, and I was just settling myself for the finish, and thinking, we'll have to have more of this another time, when I heard a sound that galvanised me so suddenly that it's a wonder the couch didn't give way—rapid footsteps were approaching the drawing-room door. I took stock—breeches down, one shoe off, miles from the window or any convenient cover, Mrs Lade kneeling on the couch, me peering from behind through her feathered headdress (which she had forgotten to remove; quite a compliment, I remember thinking), the doorknob turning. Caught, hopeless, not a chance of escape—nothing for it but to hide my face in the nape of her neck and trust that the visible side of me wouldn't be recognised by whoever came in. For they wouldn't linger—not in 1843—unless it was the Duke, and those footsteps didn't belong to a gout patient.

The door opened, the footsteps stopped—and then there was what a lady novelist would call a pregnant pause, lasting about three hours, it seemed to me, and broken only by Mrs Lade's ecstatic moanings; I gathered she was unaware that we were observed. I stole a peep through her feathers at the mirror above the fireplace—and almost had convulsions, for it was Solomon reflected in the doorway, his hand on the latch, taking in the scene.

He never even blinked an eye; then, as other footsteps sounded somewhere behind him he stepped back, and as the door closed I heard him saying: "No, there is no one here; let us try the conservatory." Dago or not, he was a d----d considerate host, that one.

The door hadn't closed before I was trying to disengage, but without success, for Mrs Lade's hands reached back in an instant, clamping her claws into my rear, her head tilting back beside mine. "No, no, no, not yet!" gasps she, chewing away at me. "Don't go!"

"The door," I explained. "Must lock the door. Someone might see."

"Don't leave me!" she cried, and I doubt if she knew where she was, even, for her eyes were rolling in her head, and d----d if I could get loose. Mind you, I was reluctant; torn two ways, as it were.

"The key," I mumbled, thrusting away. "Only take a moment —back directly."

"Take me with you!" she moans, and I did, heaven knows how, hobbling along with all that flesh to carry. Fortunately it all ended happily just as my legs gave way, and we collapsed at the threshold in joyous exhaustion; I even managed to get the key turned.

Whether she could dress as quickly as she stripped, I can't say, for she was still swooning and gasping against the panels, with her feathers awry, when I flung on my last garment and shinned down the ivy. Feverish work it had been, and the sooner I was elsewhere, establishing an alibi, the better. A brisk walk was what I needed just then—anyway, I had a match in the afternoon, and wanted to be in trim.

* * *

[Extract from the diary of Mrs Flashman, June —, 1843]
    . . . never have I felt so guilty—and yet, what could I *do*? My heart *warned* me, when Don S. cut short our visit to the gallery—and there were some Exquisite Water-colours which I would have liked to view at leisure—that he had some Purpose in returning early to the house. What my Foreboding was I cannot explain, but alas! it was justified, and I am the most Wretched Creature in the world!! The house was quite *deserted*, except for Papa asleep on the terrace, and Something in Don S.'s manner—it may have been the Ardent Expression in his eyes—led me to insist that we should seek out my Dear H. at once. Oh, would that we had found him! We looked every-where, but there was no one to be seen, and when we came to the conservatory, Don S. filled me with Alarm and Shame by *declaring* himself in the most forward manner—for the atmosphere of the plants, being extremely Oppressive, and my own *agitation*, made me feel so faint that I was forced to support myself by leaning on his arm, and find relief by resting my head on his shoulder. (A likely story!!!—G. de R.) In that moment of faintness, picture my *utter distress* when he took advantage of the situation to press his lips to mine!! I was so affronted that it was ~~some moments~~ a moment before I could find the strength to make him desist, and it was only with difficulty that I at last Escaped his Embrace. He used the most Passionate Expressions to me, calling me his Dear Diana and his Golden Nymph (which struck me, even in that Moment of Perturbation, as a *most poetic* conceit), and the Effect was so *weakening* that I was unable to resist

when he clasped me to his bosom yet again, and Kissed me with even greater Force than before. Fortunately, one of the gardeners was heard approaching, and I was able to make good my retreat, with my wits *quite disordered*.

My Shame and Remorse may be imagined, and if aught could have increased them it was the sudden sight of *my darling* H. in the garden, taking his exercise, he explained, before his match in the afternoon. The sight of his flushed, manly countenance, and the knowledge that he had been engaged in such a healthy, innocent pursuit while I had been helpless in the Heated Embrace of another, however much *against my will*, were as a knife in my heart. To make it worse, he called me his Jolly Old Girl, and asked eagerly after the picture gallery; I was moved almost to tears, and when we went together to the terrace, and found Mrs L.L., I could not but remark that H. paid her no more than the barest civility (and, indeed, there was very little about her to Entice any man, for she appeared *quite bedraggled*), but was all kindness and attentiveness to me, like the dear *best of husbands* that he is.

But what am I to think of Don S.'s conduct? I must try not to judge him *too harshly*, for he is of such a *warm temperament*, and given to passionate disclosure of it in every way, that it is not to be wondered at if he is Susceptible to that which he finds attractive. But surely I am not to blame if—through no fault of mine—I have been cast by Kind Nature in a form and feature which the Stronger Sex find pleasing? I console myself with the thought that it is Woman's Portion, if she is fortunate in her endowments, to be *adored*, and she has little to reproach herself with so long as she does not Encourage Familiarity, but comports herself with Proper Modesty . . .
[Conceit and humbug! End of extract—G. de R.]

There's no doubt that a good gallop before work is the best training you can have, for that afternoon I bowled the best long spell of my life for Mynn's Casuals against the All-England XI: five wickets for 12 in eleven overs, with Lillywhite. leg before and Marsden clean bowled amongst them. I'd never have done *that* on cold baths and dumbbells, so you can see that what our present Test match fellows need is some sporting female like Mrs Leo Lade to look after 'em, then we'd have the Australians begging for mercy.

The only small cloud on my horizon, as we took tea afterwards in the marquee among the fashionable throng, with Elspeth clinging to my arm and Mynn passing round bubbly in the challenge cup we'd won, was whether Solomon had recognised me in the drawing-room that morning, and if so, would he keep his mouth shut? I wasn't over-concerned, for all he'd had in view was my stalwart back and buttocks heaving away and Mrs Lade's stupefied face reflected in the mirror—it didn't matter a three-ha'penny what he said about *her*, and even if he'd recognised me as t'other coupler, it wasn't likely that he'd bruit it about; chaps didn't, in those days. And there wasn't even a hint of a knowing twinkle in his eye as he came over to congratulate me, all cheery smiles, refilling my glass and exclaiming to Elspeth that her husband was the most tearaway bowler in the country, and ought to be in the All-England side himself, blessed if he shouldn't. A few of those present cried, "Hear, hear," and Solomon wagged his head admiringly—the artful, conniving scoundrel.

"D'ye know," says he, addressing those nearest, who included many of his house party, as well as Mynn and Felix and Ponsonby-Fane, "I shouldn't wonder if Harry wasn't the fastest man in England just now—I don't say the best, in deference to distinguished company"—and he bowed gracefully towards Mynn —"but certainly the quickest; what d'you think, Mr Felix?"

Felix blinked and blushed, as he always did at being singled out, and said he wasn't sure; when he was at the crease, he added gravely, he didn't consider miles per hour, but any batter who faced Mynn at one end and me at t'other would have something to tell his grandchildren about. Everyone laughed, and Solomon cries, lucky men indeed; wouldn't tyro cricketers like himself just jump at the chance of facing a few overs from us. Not that they'd last long, to be sure, but the honour would be worth it.

"I don't suppose," he added, fingering his earring and looking impish at me, "you'd consider playing me a single-wicket match, would you?"

Being cheerful with bubbly and my five for 12, I laughed and said I'd be glad to oblige, but he'd better get himself cover from Lloyd's, or a suit of armour. "Why," says I, "d'you fancy your chance?" and he shrugged and said no, not exactly; he knew he mightn't make much of a show, but he was game to try. "After all," says he, tongue in cheek, "you ain't Fuller Pilch as a batter, you know."

There are moments, and they have a habit of sticking in memory, when light-hearted, easy fun suddenly becomes dead serious. I can picture that moment now; the marquee with its throng of men in their whites, the ladies in their bright summer confections, the stuffy smell of grass and canvas, the sound of the tent-flap stirring in the warm breeze, the tinkle of plates and glasses, the chatter and the polite laughter, Elspeth smiling eagerly over her strawberries and cream, Mynn's big red face glistening, and Solomon opposite me—huge and smiling in his bottle-green coat, the emerald pin in his scarf, the brown varnished face with its smiling dark eyes, the carefully-dressed black curls and whiskers, the big, delicately-manicured hand spinning his glass by the stem.

"Just for fun," says he. "Give me something to boast about, anyway—play on my lawn at the house. Come on"—and he poked me in the ribs—"I dare you, Harry," at which they chortled and said he was a game bird, all right.

I didn't know, then, that it mattered, although something warned me that there was a hint of humbug about it, but with the champagne working and Elspeth miaowing eagerly I couldn't see any harm.

"Very good," says I, "they're your ribs, you know. How many a side?"

"Oh, just the two of us," says he. "No fieldsmen; bounds, of course, but no byes or overthrows. I'm not built for chasing," and he patted his guts, smiling. "Couple of hands, what? Double my chance of winning a run or two."

"What about stakes?" laughs Mynn. "Can't have a match like this for just a tizzy*," winking at me.

"What you will," says Solomon easily. "All one to me—fiver, pony, monkey, thou.—don't matter, since I shan't be winning it anyway."

Now that's the kind of talk that sends any sensible man diving for his hat and the nearest doorway, usually; otherwise you find yourself an hour later scribbling I.O.U.s and trying to think of a false name. But this was different—after all, I was first-class, and he wasn't even thought about; no one had seen him play, even. He couldn't hope for anything against my expresses—and one thing was sure, he didn't need my money.

"Hold on, though," says I. "We ain't all nabob millionaires, you know. Lieutenant's half-pay don't stretch—"

Elspeth absolutely reached for her reticule, d--n her, whispering that I *must* afford whatever Don Solomon put up, and while I was trying to hush her, Solomon says:

"Not a bit of it—*I'll* wager the thou., on my side; it's my proposal, after all, so I must be ready to stand the racket. Harry can put up what he pleases—what d'ye say, old boy?"

Well, everyone knew he was filthy rich and careless with it, so if he wanted to lose a thousand for the privilege of having me trim him up, I didn't mind. I couldn't think what to offer as a wager against his money, though, and said so.

"Well, make it a pint of ale," says he, and then snapped his fingers. "Tell you what—I'll name what your stake's to be, and I promise you, if you lose and have to stump up, it's something that won't cost you a penny."

"What's that?" says I, all leery in a moment.

"Are you game?" cries he.

"Tell us my stake first," says I.

"Well, you can't cry off now, anyway," says he, beaming

* Sixpence.

triumphantly. "It's this: a thou. on my side, if you win, and if *I* win—which you'll admit ain't likely"—he paused, to keep everyone in suspense—"if I win, you'll allow Elspeth and her father to come on my voyage." He beamed round at the company. "What's fairer than that, I should like to know?"

The bare-faced sauce of it took my breath away. Here was this fat upstart, with his nigger airs, who had proclaimed his interest in my wife and proposed publicly to take her jaunting while I was left cuckolded at home, had been properly and politely warned off, and was now back on the same tack, but trying to pass it off as a jolly, light-hearted game. My skin burned with fury—had he cooked this up with Elspeth?—but one glance told me she was as astonished as I was. Others were smiling, though, and I saw two ladies whispering behind their parasols; Mrs Lade was watching with amusement.

"Well, well, Don," says I, deliberately easy. "You don't give up in a hurry, do you?"

"Oh, come, Harry," cries he. "What hope have I? It's just nonsense, for you're sure to win. Doesn't he always win, Mrs Lade?" And he looked at her, smiling, and then at me, and at Elspeth, without a flicker of expression—by G-d, had he recognised my heaving stern in the drawing-room, after all, and was he daring to say: "Accept my wager, give me this chance, or I'll blow the gaff"? I didn't know—but it made no odds, for I realised I had to take him on, for my credit's sake. What—Flashy, the heroic sport, back down against a mere tyro, and thereby proclaim that he was jealous of his wife where this fat swaggerer was concerned? No—I had to play, and look pleasant. He had, as the Duke would say, humbugged me, by G-d.

But what was he hoping for? A fluke in a million? Single-wicket's a chancy game, but even so, he couldn't hope to beat me. And yet, he was so set on having his way, like the spoiled, arrogant pup he was (for all his modest air), that any chance, however slim, he'd snatch at. He'd nothing to lose except a thousand quid, and that was ha'pence to him. Very well, then—I'd not only beat the brute; I'd milk him for the privilege.

"Done, then," says I, cheerfully. "But since you've set my stake, I'll set yours. If you lose, it'll cost you two thousand—not one. Suit you?"

Of course he had to agree, laughing and saying I drove such a hard bargain I must give him the tie as well—which meant that if the scores finished even, I would forfeit my stake. I had to *win* to collect—but it was a trivial thing, since I was bound to drub him handsomely. Just to be sure, though, I asked Felix then and there if he'd stand umpire; I wasn't having some creature of Solomon's handing him the game in a box.

So the match was made, and Elspeth had the grace not to say she hoped I would lose; indeed, she confided later that she thought Don Solomon had been just a *little sharp*, and not *quite refined* in taking her for granted.

"For you know, Harry, I would never accompany him with Papa against your wishes. But if you *choose* to accept his wager, that is different—and, oh! it would be such fun to see India and . . . all those splendid places! But of course, you must play your best, and not lose on *my* account—"

"Don't worry, old girl," says I, climbing aboard her, "I shan't."

That was before dinner. By bed-time I wasn't so sure.

I was taking a turn about the grounds while the others were at their port, and had just strolled abreast the gates, when someone goes "Psst!" from the shadows, and to my astonishment I saw two or three dark figures lurking in the roadway. One of them advanced, and I choked on my cheroot when I recognised the portly frame of Daedalus Tighe, Heskwire.

"What the d---l are you doing here?" I demanded. I'd seen the brute at one or two of the games, but naturally had avoided him. He touched his hat, glanced about in the dusk, and asked for a word with me, if he might make so bold. I told him to go to blazes.

"Oh, never that, sir!" says he. "You couldn't vish that, now —not you. Don't go, Mr Flashman; I promise not to detain you —vhy, the ladies an' gents will be waitin' in the drorin'-room, I dare say, and you'll want to get back. But I hear as 'ow you're playin' a single-wicket match tomorrow, 'gainst that fine sportsman Mr Solomon Haslam—werry esteemed cove 'e is, quite the slap-up—"

"What d'ye know about his cricket?" says I, and Mr Tighe chuckled beerily.

"Well, sir, they do say 'e plays a bit—but, lor' bless yer, 'e'll be a babby against the likes o' you. Vhy, in the town I could get fifty to one against 'im, an' no takers; mebbe even a hundred—"

"I'm obliged to you," says I, and was turning away when he said:

"Mind you, sir, there might be some as would put money on 'im, just on the chance that 'e'd win—vhich is himpossible, o' course, 'gainst a crack player like you. Then again, even cracks lose *sometimes*—an' *if* you lost, vhy, anyone who'd put a thousand on Haslam—vell spread about, o' course—vhy, he'd pick up fifty thousand, wouldn't 'e? I think," he added, "me calkerlation is about right."

I nearly swallowed my cheroot. The blind, blazing impudence of it was staggering—for there wasn't the slightest doubt what the scoundrel was proposing. (And without even a word of what cut he was prepared to offer, rot his insolence.) I hadn't been so insulted all day, and I d----d his eyes in my indignation.

"I shouldn't raise your voice, sir," says he. "You wouldn't want to be over'eard talkin' to the likes o' me, I'm sure. Or to 'ave folks know that you've 'ad some o' my rhino, in the past, for services rendered—"

"You infernal liar!" cries I. "I've never seen a penny of your d----d money!"

"Vell, think o' that, now," says he. "D'you suppose that Wincent 'as been pocketin' it again? I don't see 'ow 'e could ha' done, neither—seein' as my letters to you vas writ an' sealed, vith cash henclosed, in the presence of two reliable legal friends o' mine, who'd swear that same vas delivered to your direction. An' you never got 'em, you say? Vell, that Wincent must be sharper than I thought; I'll just 'ave to break 'is b----y legs to learn 'im better. Still, that's by the by; the point is"— and he poked me in the ribs—"if my legal friends vas to svear to vot they know—there's some as might believe you'd been takin' cash from a bookie—oh, to win, granted, but it'd make a nasty scandal. Werry nasty it would be."

"D--n you!" I was nearly choking with rage. "If you think you can scare me—"

He raised his hands in mock horror. "I'd never think any such thing, Mr Flashman! I know you're brave as a lion, sir—vhy, you ain't even afraid to walk the streets o' London alone at nights—some rare strange places you gets to, I b'lieve. Places vhere young chaps 'as come adrift afore now—set on by footpads an' beat almost to death. Vhy, a young friend o' mine—vell, 'e vasn't much of a friend, 'cos 'e velched on me, 'e did. Crippled for life, sir, I regret to say. Never did catch the willains that done it, neither. Course, the peelers is shockin' lax these days—"

"You villain! Why, I've a mind to—"

"No, you 'aven't, Mr Flashman. Werry inadwisable it vould be for you to do anythin' rash, sir. An' vhere's the necessity, arter all?" I could imagine the greasy smile, but all I could see was shadow. "Mr Haslam just 'as to vin termorror—an' I'll see you're five thahsand richer straight avay, my dear sir. My legal friends'll forget . . . vot they know . . . an' I dare say no footpads nor garroters von't never come your vay, neither." He paused, and then touched his hat again. "Now, sir, I shan't detain you no more—your ladies vill be gettin' impatient. A werry good night to you—an' I'm mortal sorry you ain't goin' to vin in the mornin'. But think of 'ow cock-a-hoop Mr Haslam'll be, eh? It'll be such a hunexpected surprise for 'im."

And with that he faded into the darkness; I heard his beery chuckle as he and his bullies went down the road.

When I'd got over my indignation, my first thought was that Haslam was behind this, but saner judgement told me he wouldn't be such a fool—only young idiots like me got hooked by the likes of Daedalus Tighe. G-d, what a purblind ass I'd been, ever to touch his dirty money. He could make a scandal, not a doubt of that—and I didn't question either that he was capable of setting his roughs on to waylay me some dark night. What the d---l was I to do? If I didn't let Haslam win—no, by G-d, I was shot if I would! Let him go fornicating round the world with Elspeth while I rotted in my tin belly at St James's? Not likely. But if I beat him, Tighe would split, for certain, and his thugs would pulp me in some alley one fine night . . .

You can understand that I didn't go to bed in any good temper, and I didn't sleep much, either.

It never rains but it pours, though. I was still wrestling with my dilemma next morning when I received another blow, this time through the smirking agency of Miss Judy, the guvnor's trull. I had been out on the gravel watching Solomon's gardeners roll the wicket on the main lawn for our match, smoking furiously and drumming my fingers, and then took a restless turn round the house; Judy was sitting in one of the arbours, reading a journal. She didn't so much as glance up as I walked by, ignoring her, and then her voice sounded coolly behind me:

"Looking for Mrs Leo Lade?"

That was a nasty start, to begin with. I stopped, and turned to look at her. She leafed over a page and went on: "I shouldn't, if I were you. She isn't receiving this morning, I fancy."

"What the d---l have I to do with her?" says I.

"That's what the Duke is asking, I dare say," says Miss Judy, giving the journal her sly smile. "He has not directed his inquiries to you as yet? Well, well, all in good time, no doubt." And she went on reading cool as be-d----d, while my heart went like a hammer.

"What the h--l are you driving at?" says I, and when she didn't answer I lost my temper and knocked the paper from her hand.

"Ah, that's my little man!" says she, and now she was looking at me, sneering in scornful pleasure. "Are you going to strike me, as well? You'd best not—there are people within call, and it would never do for them to see the hero of Kabul assaulting a lady, would it?"

"Not 'lady'!" says I. "Slut's the word."

"It's what the Duke called Mrs Lade, they tell me," says she, and rose gracefully to her feet, picking up her parasol and spreading it. "You mean you haven't heard? You will, though, soon enough."

"I'll hear it now!" says I, and gripped her arm. "By G-d, if you or anyone else is spreading slanders about me, you'll answer for it! I've nothing to do with Mrs Lade or the Duke, d'you hear?"

"No?" She looked me up and down with her crooked smile and suddenly jerked her arm free. "Then Mrs Lade must be a liar—which I dare say she is."

"What d'you mean? You'll tell me, this instant, or—"

"Oh, I wouldn't deny myself the pleasure," says she. "I like to see you wriggle and mouth first, though. Well, then—a little bird from the Duke's hotel tells me that he and Mrs Lade quarrelled violently last night, as I believe they frequently do—his gout, you know. There were raised voices—his, at first, and then hers, and all manner of names called—you know how these things develop, I'm sure. Just a little domestic scene, but I'm afraid Mrs Lade is a stupid woman, because when the talk touched on his grace's . . . capabilities—how it did, I can't imagine—she was ill-advised enough to mention your name, and make unflattering comparisons." Miss Judy smiled sweetly, and patted her auburn curls affectedly. "She must be singularly easy to please, I think. Not to say foolish, to taunt her admirer so. In any event, his grace was so tender as to be jealous—"

"It's a d----d lie! I've never been near the b---h!"

"Ah, well, no doubt she is confusing you with someone else. It is probably difficult for her to keep tally. However, I dare say his grace believed her; jealous lovers usually think the worst. Of course, we must hope he will forgive her, but his forgiveness won't include you, I'll be bound, and—"

"Shut your lying mouth!" cries I. "It's all false—if that slattern has been lying about me, or if you are making up this malicious gossip to discredit me, by G-d I'll make you both wish you'd never been born—"

"Again, you're quoting the Duke. A hot-tempered old gentleman, it seems. He spoke—at the top of his voice, according to a guest at the hotel—of setting a prize-fighter on to you. It seems he is the backer of some persons called Caunt and the Great Gun—but I don't know about such things . . ."

"Has Elspeth heard this foul slander?" I shouted.

"If I thought she would believe it, I would tell her myself," says the malicious tart. "The sooner she knows what a hound she has married, the better. But she's stupid enough to worship you—most of the time. Whether she'll still find you so attractive when the Duke's pugilists have done with you is another matter." She sighed contentedly and turned away up the path. "Dear me, you're shaking, Harry—and you will need a steady hand, you know, for your match with Don Solomon. Everyone is so looking forward to it . . ,"

She left me in a fine state of rage and apprehension, as you can imagine. It almost passed belief that the idiot heifer Lade had boasted to her protector of her bout with me, but some women are stupid enough for anything, especially when tempers are flying—and now that doddering, vindictive old pander of a Duke would sick his bullies onto me[11]—on top of Tighe's threats of the previous evening it was the wrong side of enough. Couldn't the selfish old lecher realise that his flash-tail needed a young mount from time to time, to keep her in running condition? But here I was, under clouds from all directions, still undecided what I should do in my match with Solomon—and at that moment Mynn hove up to bear me away to the pitch for the great encounter. I wasn't feeling like cricket one little bit.

Our party, and a fair number of local quality riff-raff, were already arranging themselves on chairs and couches set on the gravel before the house—the Duke and Mrs Lade weren't there, thank G-d: probably still flinging furniture at each other in the hotel—but Elspeth was the centre of attraction, with Judy at her side looking as though she'd just swallowed the last of the cream. Tattling trollop—I gritted my teeth and vowed I'd be even with her yet.

On the other sides of the lawn was the popular mob, for Solomon had thrown open his grounds for the occasion, and had set up a marquee where free beer and refreshments were being doled out to the thirsty; well, if the d----d show-off wanted to let 'em see him being thoroughly beat, that was his business. Oh, Ch---t, though—*was* I going to beat him? And to compound my confusion, what should I see among a group of flash coves under the trees but the scarlet weskit and face of Daedalus Tighe, Heskwire, come to oversee his great coup, no doubt; he had some likely-looking hard cases with him, too, all punishing the ale and chortling.

"Breakfast disagree with you, Flashy?" says Mynn. "You look a mite peaky—hollo, though, there's your opponent all ready. Come along."

Solomon was already on the lawn, very business-like in corduroys and pumps, with a straw hat on his black head, smiling at me and shaking hands while the swells clapped politely and the popular crowd shouted and rattled their pots. I stripped off my coat and donned my pumps, and then little Felix spun the bat; I called "blade", and so it was. "Very good," says I to Solomon, "you'll bat first."

"Capital!" cries he, with a flash of teeth. "Then may the better man win!"

"He will," says I, and called for the ball, while Solomon, rot his impudence, went across to Elspeth and made great play of having her wish him luck; he even had the gall to ask her for her handkerchief to tie in his belt—"for I must carry the lady's colours, you know," cries he, making a great joke of it.

Of course she obliged him, and then, catching my glare, fluttered that of course I must carry her colours, too, to show no favouritism. But she hadn't another wipe, so the minx Judy said she must borrow hers to give me—and I finished up with that sly slut's snot-rag in my belt, and she sitting with her acid tongue in her cheek.

We went out to the wicket together, and Felix gave Solomon guard; he took his time over it, too, patting his block-hole and feeling the pitch before him, very business-like, while I fretted and swung my arm. It was spongy turf, I realised, so I wasn't going to get much play out of it—no doubt Solomon had taken *that* into account, too. Much good might it do him.

"Play!" calls Felix, and a hush fell round the lawn, everyone expectant for the first ball. I tightened my belt, while Solomon waited in his turn, and then let him have one of my hardest—I'll swear he went pale as it shot past his shins and went first bounce into the bushes. The mob cheered, and I turned and bowled again.

He wasn't a bad batter. He blocked my next ball with his hanging guard, played the third straight back to me, and then got a great cheer when he ran two off the fourth. Hollo, thinks I, what have we here? I gave him a slower ball, and he pulled it into the trees, so that I had to plough through the chattering mob to reach it, while he ran five; I was panting and furious when I got back to the crease, but I held myself in and gave him a snorter, dead straight; he went back, and pushed it to his off-side for a single. The crowd yelled with delight, and I ground my teeth.

I was beginning to realise what a desperate business single-wicket can be when you haven't got fieldsmen, and have to chase every run yourself. You're tuckered in no time, and for a fast bowler that won't do. Worse still, no fieldsmen meant no catches behind the stumps, which is how fast men like me get half their wickets. I had to bowl or catch him out myself, and what with the plump turf and his solid poking away, it looked like being the deuce of a job. I took a slow turn, recovering my breath, and then bowled him four of my fastest; the first shaved his stumps, but he met the other three like a game-cock, full on the blade, and they brought him another five runs. The crowd applauded like anything, and he smiled and tipped his hat. Very good, thinks I, we'll have to see to this in short order.

I bowled him another score or so of balls—and he took another eight runs, carefully—before I got what I wanted, which was a push shot up the wicket, slightly to my left. I slipped deliberately as I went to gather it, and let it run by, at which Solomon, who had been poised and waiting, came galloping out to steal a run. Got you, you b-----d, thinks I, and as I scrambled up, out of his path, pursuing the ball, I got him the deuce of a crack on the knee with my heel, accidental-like. I heard him yelp, but by then I was lunging after the ball, scooping it up and throwing down the wicket, and then looking round all eager, as though to see where he was. Well, I *knew* where he was—lying two yards out of his ground on his big backside, holding his knee and cursing.

"Oh, bad luck, old fellow!" cries I. "What happened? Did you slip?"

"Aaarr-h!" says he, and for once he wasn't smiling. "You hacked me on the leg, confound it!"

"What?" cries I. "Oh, never! Good l--d, did I? Look here, I'm most fearfully sorry. I slipped myself, you know. Oh, my G-d!" says I, clapping my brow. "And I threw down your wicket! If I'd realised—I say, Felix, he don't have to be out, does he? I mean, it wouldn't be fair?"

Feiix said he was run out, no question; it hadn't been my fault I'd slipped and had Solomon run into me. I said, no, no, I wouldn't have it, I couldn't take advantage, and he must carry on with his innings. Solomon was up by now, rubbing his knee, and saying, no, he was out, it couldn't be helped; his grin was back now, if a bit lop-sided. So we stood there, arguing like little

Christians, myself stricken with remorse, pressing him to bat on, until Felix settled it by saying he was out, and that was that. (About time, too; for a moment I'd thought I was going to convince him.)

So it was my turn to bat, shaking my head and saying what a d----d shame it had been; Solomon said it was his clumsiness, and I mustn't fret, and the crowd buzzed with admiration at all this sporting spirit. "Kick 'im in the crotch next time!" bawls a voice from the trees, and the quality pretended not to hear. I took guard; twenty-one he'd scored; now we'd see how he bowled.

It was pathetic. As a batter he'd looked sound, if dull, with some good wrist-work, but from the moment I saw him put the ball to his eye and waddle up with that pregnant-duck look of earnestness on his face, I knew he was a duffer with the ball. Quite astonishing, for he was normally a graceful, sure-moving man, and fast for all his bulk, but when he tried to bowl he was like a Shire horse on its way to the knackers. He lobbed with the solemn concentration of a dowager at a coconut shy, and I gloated inwardly, watched it drop, drove with confidence—and mishit the first ball straight down his throat for the simplest of catches.

The spectators yelled in amazement, and by George, they weren't alone. I flung down my bat, cursing; Solomon stared in disbelief, half-delighted, half-frowning. "I believe you did that on purpose," cries he.

"Did I ——!" says I, furious. I'd meant to hit him into the next county—but ain't it the way, if a task is too easy, we botch it often as not? I could have kicked myself for my carelessness —thinking like a cricketer, you understand. For with 21 runs in it, I might easily lose the match now—the question was: did I want to? There was Tighe's red waistcoat under the trees—on the other hand, there was Elspeth, looking radiant, clapping her gloved hands and crying "Well played!" while Solomon tipped his hat gracefully and I tried to put on a good face. By Jove, though, it was him she was looking at—no doubt picturing herself under a tropic moon already, with inconvenient old Flashy safely left behind—no, by G-d, to the d---l with Tighe, and his threats and blackmail—I was going to win this match, and be d----d to everyone.

We had a sandwich and a glass, while the swells chattered round us, and the Canterbury professional rubbed embrocation on Solomon's knee. "Splendid game, old fellow!" cries the Don, raising his lemonade in my direction. "I'll have some more of my lobs for you directly!" I laughed and said I hoped they weren't such twisters as his first one, for it had had me all at sea, and he absolutely looked pleased, the b----y farmer.

"It is *so* exciting!" cries Elspeth. "Oh, *who* is going to win? I don't think I could bear it for either of them to lose—could you, Judy?"

"Indeed not," says Judy. "Capital fun. Just think, my dear— you cannot lose, either way, for you will gain a jolly voyage if the Don wins, or if Harry succeeds, why, he will have two thousand pounds to spend on you."

"Oh I can't think of it that way!" cries my darling spouse. "It is the game that counts, I'm sure." D----d idiot.

"Now then, gentlemen," cries Felix, clapping his hands. "We've had more eating and drinking than cricket so far. Your hand, Don," and he led us out for the second innings.

I had learned my lesson from my first bowling spell, and had a good notion now of where Solomon's strength and weakness lay. He was quick, and sure-footed, and his back game was excellent, but I'd noticed that he wasn't too steady with his forward strokes, so I pitched well up to him, on the leg stump; the wicket was getting the green off it, with being played on, and I'd hopes of perhaps putting a rising ball into his groin, or at least making him hop about. He met my attack pretty well, though, and played a hanging guard, taking the occasional single on the on side. But I pegged away, settling him into place, with the ball going into his legs, and then sent one t'other way; he didn't come within a foot of it, and his off-stump went down flat.

He'd made ten runs that hand, so I had 32 to get to win—and while it ain't many against a muffin of a bowler, well, you can't afford a single mistake. And I wasn't a batter to trade; however, with care I should be good enough to see Master Solomon away —if I wanted to. For as I took guard, I could see Tighe's red weskit out of the corner of my eye, and felt a tremor of fear up my spine. By George, if I won and sent his stake money down the drain, he'd do his best to ruin me, socially and physically, no error—and what was left the Duke's bruisers would no doubt share between 'em. Was anyone ever in such a cursed fix—but here was Felix calling "Play!" and the Don shuffling up to deliver his donkey-drop.

It's a strange thing about bad bowling—it can be deuced difficult to play, especially when you know you have only one life to lose, and have to abandon your usual swiping style. In an ordinary game, I'd have hammered Solomon's rubbish all over the pasture, but now I had to stay cautiously back, while he dropped his simple lobs on a length—no twist at all but dead straight—and I was so nervous that I edged some of them, and would have been a goner if there'd been even an old woman fielding at slip. It made him look a deal better than he was, and the crowd cheered every ball, seeing the slogger Flashy pinned to his crease.

However, I got over my first shakes, tried a drive or two, and had the satisfaction of seeing him tearing about and sweating while I ran a few singles. That was a thing about single wicket; even a good drive might not win you much, for to score one run you had to race to the bowler's end *and back*, whereas in an ordinary match the same work would have brought you two. And all his careering about the outfield didn't seem to trouble his bowling, which was as bad—but still as straight—as ever. But I hung on, and got to a dozen, and when he sent me a full pitch, I let fly and hit him clean over the house, running eight while he vanished frantically round the building, with the small boys whooping in his wake, and the ladies standing up and squeaking with excitement. I was haring away between the wickets, with the mob chanting each run, and was beginning to think I'd run past his total when he hove in sight again, trailing dung and nettles, and threw the ball across the crease, so that I had to leave off.

So there I was, with 20 runs, 12 still needed to win, and both of us blowing like whales. And now my great decision could be postponed no longer—was I going to beat him, and take the consequences from Tighe, or let him win and have a year in which to seduce Elspeth on his confounded boat? The thought of him murmuring greasily beside her at the taffrail while she got drunk on moonlight and flattery fairly maddened me, and I banged his next delivery against the front door for another three runs—and as I waited panting for his next ball, there under the trees was the beast Tighe, hat down on his brows and thumbs hooked in his weskit, staring at me, with his cudgel-coves behind him. I swallowed, missed the next ball, and saw it shave my bails by a whisker.

What the blazes should I do? Tighe was saying a word over his shoulder to one of his thugs—and I swung wildly at the next ball and sent it high over Solomon's head. I was bound to run, and that was another two—seven to get to win. He bowled again, and for once produced a shooter; I poked frantically at it, got the edge, and it went scuttling away in front of the bounds for a single. Six to get, and the spectators were clapping and laughing and egging us on. I leaned on my bat, watching Tighe out of the corner of my eye and conjuring up nameless fears—no, they weren't nameless. I couldn't face the certainty of it being published that I'd taken money from a tout, and having his assassins walk on my face in a Haymarket alley into the bargain. I *must* lose—and if Solomon rogered Elspeth all over the Orient, well, I'd not be there to see it. I turned to look in her direction, and she stood up and waved to me, ever so pretty, calling encouragement; I looked at Solomon, his black hair wet with perspiration and his eyes glittering as he ran up to bowl—and I roared "No, by G-d!" and cut him square and hard, clean through a ground-floor window.

How they cheered, as Solomon thundered through the quality seats, the ladies fluttering to let him by, and the men laughing fit to burst; he hurtled through the front door, and as I completed my second run I turned to see that ominous figure in the red weskit; he and his cronies were the only still, silent members of that whole excited assembly. D--n Solomon—was he going to take all day finding the b----y ball? I *had* to run, with my nerve failing again; I lumbered up the pitch, and there was a great howl from the house; Solomon was emerging dishevelled and triumphant as I made the third run—only another three and the match was mine.

But I couldn't face it; I knew I daren't win—after all, I wasn't any too confident of Elspeth's virtue as it was; one Solomon more or less wasn't going to make all that much difference—better be a cuckold than a disgraced cripple. I had wobbled in intent all through the past half-hour, but now I did my level best to hand Solomon the game. I swiped and missed, but my wicket remained intact; I prodded a catch at him, and it fell short; I played a ball to the off, went for a single that I hadn't a hope of getting—and the great oaf, with nothing to do but throw down my wicket for victory, shied wildly wide in his excitement. I stumbled home, with the mob yelling delightedly; Solomon 31, Flashy 30, and even little Felix was hopping from one leg to the other as he signalled Solomon to bowl on.

There wasn't a whisper round the field now. I waited at the crease, bowels dissolving, as Solomon stood doubled over, regaining his breath, and then picked up the ball. I was settled in my mind now: I'd wait for a straight one and miss it, and let myself be bowled out.

Would you believe it, his next three balls were as squint as a Jew's conscience? He was dead beat with running, labouring like a cow in milk, and couldn't keep direction at all. I let 'em go by, while the crowd groaned in disappointment, and when his next one looked like going wide altogether I *had* to play at it, like it or not; I scrambled across, trying desperately to pull it in his direction, muttering to myself: "If you can't bowl me, for Ch---t's sake catch me out, you ham-fisted buttock," and in my panic I stumbled, took a frantic swipe—and drove the confounded ball miles over his head, high into the air. He turned and raced to get under it, and there was nothing I could do but leg it for the other end, praying to G-d he'd catch it. It was still in the air when I reached the bowler's crease and turned, running backwards to watch; he was weaving about beneath it with his mouth open, arms outstretched, while the whole field waited breathless—down it came, down to his waiting hands, he clutched at it, held it, stumbled, fumbled—and to my horror and a great shriek from the mob, it bounced free—he made a despairing grab, measured his length on the turf, and there was the b----y ball rolling across the grass away from him.

"You—oh, you butter-fingered b-----d!" I roared, but it was lost in the tumult. I had regained my crease having scored one—

but I was bound to try for the second, winning run with Solomon prostrate and the ball ten yards from him. "Run!" they were yelling, "run, Flashy!" and poor despairing Flashy couldn't do anything else but obey—the match was in my grasp, and with hundreds watching I couldn't be seen deliberately ignoring the chance to win it.

So I bounded forward again, full of sham eagerness, tripping artistically to give him a chance to reach the ball and run me out; I went down, rolling, and d---e, the brute was still grovelling after his dropped catch. I couldn't lie there forever, so I went plunging on, as slowly as possible, like a man exhausted; even so, I had reached the bowler's crease before he'd recovered the ball, and now his only chance was to shy the thing a full thirty yards and hit my wicket as I careered back to the batter's end. I knew he hadn't a hope in h--l, at that distance; all I could do was forge ahead to victory—and ruin at the hands of Tighe. The crowd were literally dancing as I bore down on the crease —three more strides would see me home and doomed—and then the ground rose up very gently in front of me, crowd and wicket vanished from view, the noise died away into a soothing murmur, and I was nestling comfortably against the turf, chewing placidly at the grass, thinking, this is just the thing, a nice, peaceful rest, how extremely pleasant . . .

I was staring up at the sky, with Felix in between, peering down anxiously, and behind him Mynn's beefy face saying: "Get his head up—give him air. Here, a drink"—and a glass rattling against my teeth and the burning taste of brandy in my mouth. There was the deuce of a pain in the back of my head, and more anxious faces, and I heard Elspeth's voice in distant, shrill inquiry, amidst a babble of chatter.

"What—what happened?" says I, as they raised me; my legs were like jelly, and Mynn had to hold me up.

"It's all right!" cries Felix. "He tried to shy down your wicket —and the ball hit you crack on the back of the skull. Why, you went down like a shot rabbit!"

"He threw down your wicket, too—afterwards," says Mynn. "D--n him."

I blinked and touched my head; there was a lump growing like a football. Then here was Solomon, panting like a bellows, clasping my hand and crying: "My dear Harry—are you all right? My poor chap—let me see!" He was volleying out apologies, and Mynn was looking at him pretty cool, I noticed, while Felix fidgeted and the assembling mob were gaping at the sensation.

"You mean—I was out?" says I, trying to collect my wits.

"I'm afraid so!" cries Solomon. "You see, I was so confused, when I shied the ball, I didn't realise it had hit you . . . saw you lying there, and the ball loose . . . well, in my excitement I just ran in and snatched it . . . and broke your wicket. I'm sorry," he repeated, "for of course I'd never have taken advantage . . . if I'd had time to think. It all happened so quickly, you see." He looked round at the others, smiling whimsically. "Why—it was just like our accident in the first innings—when Flashy put *me* out."

At that the chatter broke out, and then Elspeth was all over me, exclaiming about my poor head, and calling for salts and hartshorn. I quieted her while I regained my wits and listened to the debate: Mynn was maintaining stoutly that it wasn't fair, running a chap out when he was half-stunned, and Felix said, well, according to the rules, I was fairly out, and anyway, the same sort of thing had happened in Solomon's first hand, which was extraordinary, when he came to think of it—Mynn said that was different, because I hadn't *realised* Solomon was crocked, and Felix said, ah well, that was the point, but Solomon hadn't realised I was crocked, either, and Mynn muttered, didn't he, by George, and if that was the way they played at Eton, he didn't think much of it . . .

"But . . . who has *won*?" demanded Elspeth.

"No one," says Felix. "It's a tie. Flashy ran one run, which made the scores level at 31, and was run out before he could finish the second. So the game's drawn."

"And if you remember," says Solomon—and although his smile was as bland as ever, he couldn't keep the triumphant gleam out of his eye—"you gave me the tie, which means"— and he bowed to Elspeth—"that I shall have the joy of welcoming you, my dear Diana, and your father, aboard my vessel for our cruise. I'm truly sorry our game ended as it did, old chap— but I feel entitled to claim my wager."

Oh, he was indeed, and I knew it. He'd paid me back in my own coin, for felling him in the first innings—it was no consolation that I'd done my dirty work a sight more subtly than he had—not with Elspeth hopping with excitement, clapping her hands, exulting and trying to commiserate with me all at once.

"Tain't cricket," Mynn mutters to me, "but there's nothing for it. Pay up, look pleasant—that's the d---able thing about being English and playing against foreigners; they ain't gentlemen." I doubt if Solomon heard him; he was too busy beaming, with his arm round my shoulders, calling out that there was champagne and oysters in the house, and more beer for the groundlings. So he'd won his bet, without winning the match—well, at least I was clear where Tighe was concerned, for . . . and then the horrid realisation struck me, at the very moment when I looked up and saw that red weskit on the outskirts of the crowd, with the boozy, scowling face above it—he was glaring at me, tight-lipped, shredding what I guessed was a betting-slip between his fingers. He nodded at me twice, ominously, turned on his heel, and stalked away.

For Tighe had lost his bet, too. He'd backed me to *lose*, and Solomon to *win*—and we had tied. With all my floundering indecision and bad luck, I'd achieved the worst possible result all round. I'd lost Elspeth to Solomon and his d----d cruise (for I couldn't oil out of paying now) and I'd cost Tighe a thousand to boot. He'd expose me for taking his money, and set his ruffians after me—oh, J---s, and there was the Duke, too, vowing vengeance on me for deflowering his tiger lily. What a b----y pickle—

"Why, are you all right, old fellow?" cries Solomon. "You've gone pale again—here, help me get him into the shade—fetch some ice for his head—"

"Brandy," I croaked. "No, no, I mean . . . I'm first-rate; just a passing weakness—the bump, and my old wound, you know. I just need a moment . . . to recover . . . collect my thoughts . . ."

Horrid thoughts they were, too—how the deuce was I going to get out of this mess? And they say cricket's an innocent pastime!

* * *

The most famous thing has happened—darling Harry has consented to come with us on our voyage ! ! ! and I am happy beyond all telling ! He has even put aside the Prospect of his Appointment in the Life Guards—and all for Me ! It was so *unexpected* (but that is so like my Dear Hero), for almost as soon as the match was over, and Don S. had claimed his Prize, H. said very seriously, that he had thought the matter over, and while he was reluctant to decline the Military Advancement that had been offered him, *he could not bear to be parted from me* ! ! Such Proof of his Devotion moved me to tears, and I could not forbear to embrace him—which display I suppose caused *some* remark, but I don't care !

Don S., of course, was very warm in agreeing that H. should come, once he had satisfied himself that my dear one was quite determined. Don S. is *so* good; he reminded H. of what a signal honour he was declining, in not going to the Life Guards, and asked was he *perfectly certain* he wished to come with us, explaining that he would not have H. make any sacrifice on our account. But My Darling said "No, thank'ee, I'll come, if you don't mind," in that straightforward way of his, rubbing his poor head, and looking *so pale* but *determined*. I was overjoyed, and longed to be private with him, so that I might better express my Deep Gratification at his decision, as well as my *undying love*. But—alas !—that is denied me for the moment, for almost at once H. announced that his decision necessitated his immediate departure for Town, where he has many Affairs to attend to before we sail. I offered to accompany him, of course, but he wouldn't hear of it, so reluctant is he to interrupt my holiday here—he is the Dearest of Husbands ! *So* considerate. He explained that his Business would take him about a good deal, and he could not say *where* he would be for a day or so, but would join us at Dover, whence we sail for the Mysterious Orient.

So he has gone, not even staying to answer an invitation from our *dear friend* the Duke, to call upon him. I am instructed to say to *all inquiries* that he is gone away, on Private Business—for of course there are always People anxious to see and solicit my darling, so celebrated as he has become—not only Dukes and the like, but quite Ordinary Mortals as well, who hope to shake his hand, I dare say, and then tell their Acquaintances of it afterwards. In the meantime, dear diary, I am left alone—except for the company of Don S., of course, and dear Papa—to anticipate the Great Adventure which lies before us, and await that Joyous Reunion with my Beloved at Dover, which will be but the Prelude, I trust, to our Fairytale Journey into the Romantic Unknown . . .

[End of extract—G. de R.]

It was one thing to decide to go on Solomon's cruise, but quite another to get safe aboard; I had to spend ten days lurking in and about London like a gunpowder plotter, starting at my own shadow and keeping an eye skinned for the Duke's pluggers—and Daedalus Tighe's. You may think I was over-timid, and the danger none so great, but you don't know what people like the Duke were capable of in my young days; they thought they were still in the eighteenth century, and if you offended 'em they could have their bullies thrash you, and then trust to their title to keep them clear of the consequences. I was never a Reform Bill man myself, but there's no doubt the aristocracy needed its comb cutting.

In any event, it required no great arithmetic to decide to flee the country for a spell. It was sickening to have to give up the Life Guards, but if Tighe spread a scandal about me it might well force me to resign anyway—you could be an imbecile viscount with a cleft palate and still fit to command in the Household Brigade, but if they found you were taking a bookie's tin for favours, heaven help you, however famous a soldier you were. So there was nothing for it but to lie doggo until the boat sailed, and make one furtive visit to Horse Guards to tip Uncle Bindley the bad news. He quivered with disbelief down the length of his aristocratic spine when I told him.

"Do I apprehend," says he, "that you are refusing an appointment—free of purchase, may I remind you—in the Household Brigade, which has been specially procured for you at Lord Wellington's instance, in order to go junketing abroad with your wife, her extraordinary father, and this . . . this person from Threadneedle Street?" He shuddered. "It is nothing short of commercial travelling."

"Can't be helped," says I. "There's no staying in England just now."

"You realise this is tantamount to refusing an honour from

the Throne itself? That you can never again hope for any similar mark of favour? I know that you are dead to most dictates of decent behaviour and common discretion, but surely even you can see—"

"D----t, uncle!" cries I. "I've got to go!"

He squinted down his long nose. "You sound almost desperate. Am I right in supposing there will be some scandal if you do not?"

"Yes," says I, reluctantly.

"Well, then that is entirely different," cries he. "Why could you not say so at once? I suppose it is some woman or other."

I admitted it, and dropped a hint that the Duke of —— was involved, but that it was all a misunderstanding, and Bindley sniffed again and said he had never known a time when the quality of the House of Peers was quite so low. He would speak to Wellington, he said, and since it was advisable for the family's credit that I should not be seen to be cutting the painter, he would see if some official colour couldn't be given to my Far Eastern visit. The result was that a day or two later, at the room over the pawn-shop where I was hiding out, I got a note instructing me to proceed forthwith to Singapore, there to examine and approve the first consignment of Australian horses which would be arriving next spring[12] for the Company's Indian Army. Well done, old Bindley; he had his uses.

So then it was just a question of skulking down to Dover for the last of the month, which I accomplished, arriving after dark and legging it along the crowded quay with my valise, hoping to G-d that neither Tighe nor the Duke had camped out their ruffians to intercept me (they hadn't, of course, but if I've lived this long it's because I've always feared the worst and been ready for it). A boat took me out to Solomon's steam-brig, and there was a great reunion with my loved ones—Elspeth all over me clamouring to know where I had *been*, she was quite *distracted*, and Old Morrison grunting: "Huh, ye've come, at the coo's tail as usual," and muttering about a thief in the night. Solomon seemed delighted to see me, but I wasn't fooled—he was just masking his displeasure that he wouldn't have a clear run at Elspeth. That quite consoled me to making the voyage; it might be d---lish inconvenient, in some ways, and I couldn't be quite easy in my mind at venturing East again, but at least I'd have my flighty piece under my eye. Indeed, when I reflected, that was my prime reason for going, and rated even above escaping Tighe and the Duke; looking back from mid-Channel, they didn't seem nearly so terrible, and I resigned myself to enjoying the cruise; why, it might turn out to be quite fun.

I'll give it to Solomon, he hadn't lied about the luxury of his brig, the *Sulu Queen*. She was quite the latest thing in screw vessels, driven by a wheel through her keel, twin-masted for sail, and with her funnel well back, so that the whole forward deck, which was reserved for us, was quite free of the belching smoke which covered the stern with smuts and left a great black cloud in our wake. Our cabins were under-deck aft, though, out of the reek, and they were tip-top; oak furniture screwed down, Persian carpets, panelled bulkheads with watercolour paintings, a mirrored dressing-table that had Elspeth clapping her hands, Chinese curtains, excellent crystal and a well-stocked cellarette, clockwork fans, and a double bed with silk sheets that would have done credit to a New Orleans sporting-house. Well, thinks I, this is better than riding the gridiron*; we'll be right at home here.

The rest of the appointment was to match; the saloon, where we dined, couldn't have been bettered for grub, liquor and service—even old Morrison, who'd been groaning reluctantly, I gathered, ever since he'd agreed to come, had his final doubts settled when they set his first sea meal before him; he was even seen to smile, which I'll bet he hadn't done since he last cut the mill-hands' wages. Solomon was a splendid host, with every thought for our comfort; he even spent the first week pottering about the coast while we got our sea-legs, and was full of consideration for Elspeth—when she discovered that she had left her toilet water behind he had her maid landed at Portsmouth to go up to Town for some, with instructions to meet us at Plymouth; it was royal treatment, no error, and d--n all expense.

Only two things raised a prickle with me in all this idyllic luxury. One was the crew: there wasn't a white face among 'em. When I was helped aboard that first night, it was by two grinning

* Travelling on an East Indiaman.

yellow-faced rascals in reefer jackets and bare feet; I tried 'em in Hindi, but they just grinned with brown fangs and shook their heads. Solomon explained that they were Malays; he had a few half-caste Arabs aboard as well, who were his engineers and black gang, but no Europeans except the skipper, a surly enough Frog with a touch of nigger in his hair, who messed in his cabin, so that we never saw him, hardly. I didn't quite care for the all-yellow crew, though—I like to hear a British or Yankee voice in the foc'sle; it's reassuring-like. Still, Solomon was a Far East trader, and part-breed himself, so it was perhaps natural enough. He had 'em under his heel, too, and they kept well clear of us, except for the Chink stewards, who were sleek and silent and first-rate.

The other thing was that the *Sulu Queen*, while she was fitted like a floating palace, carried ten guns, which is about as many as a brig will bear. I said it seemed a lot for a pleasure-yacht, and Solomon smiled and says:

"She is too valuable a vessel to risk, in Far Eastern waters, where even the British and Dutch navies can afford little protection. And"—bowing to us—"she carries a precious cargo. Piracy is not unknown in the islands, you know, and while its victims are usually defenceless native craft—well, I believe in being over-cautious."

"Ye mean—there's danger?" goggled Morrison.

"Not," says Solomon, "with ten guns aboard."

And to settle old Morrison's qualms, and show off to Elspeth, he had all forty of his crew perform a gun practice for our benefit. They were handy, all right, scampering about the white-scrubbed deck in their tunics and short breeches, running out the pieces and ramming home cold shot to the squeal of the Arab bosun's pipe, precise as guardsmen, and afterwards standing stock-still by their guns, like so many yellow idols. Then they performed cutlass-drill and arms drill, moving like clockwork, and I had to admit that trained troops couldn't have shaped better; what with her speed and handiness, the *Sulu Queen* was fit to tackle anything short of a man-of-war.

"It is merely precaution piled on precaution," says Solomon. "My estates lie on peaceful lanes, on the Malay mainland for the most part, and I take care never to venture where I might be blown into less friendly waters. But I believe in being prepared," and he went on to talk about his iron water-tanks, and stores of sealed food—I'd still have been happier to see a few white faces and brown whiskers around us. We were three white folk—and Solomon himself, of course—and we were outward bound, after all.

However, these thoughts were soon dispelled in the interest of the voyage. I shan't bore you with descriptions, but I'm bound to say it was the pleasantest cruise of my life, and we never noticed how the weeks slipped by. Solomon had spoken of three months to Singapore; in fact, it took us more than twice as long, and we never grudged a minute of it. Through the summer we cruised gently along the French and Spanish coasts, looking in at Brest and Vigo and Lisbon, being entertained lavishly by local gentry—for Solomon seemed to have a genius for easy acquaintance—and then dipping on down the African coast, into the warm latitudes. I can look back now and say I've made that run more times than I can count, in everything from an Indiaman to a Middle Passage slaver, but this was not like any common voyage—why, we picnicked on Moroccan beaches, made excursions to desert ruins beyond Casablanca, were carried on camels with veiled drivers, strolled in Berber market-places, watched fire-dancers under the massive walls of old corsair castles, saw wild tribesmen run their horse races, took coffee with turbanned, white-bearded governors, and even bathed in warm blue water lapping on miles and miles of empty silver sand with palms nodding in the breeze—and every evening there was the luxury of the *Sulu Queen* to return to, with its snowy cloths and sparkling silver and crystal, and the delicate Chink stewards attending to every want in the cool dimness of the saloon. Well, I've *been* a Crown Prince, once, in my wanderings, but I've never seen the like of that voyage.

"It is a fairy-tale!" Elspeth kept exclaiming, and even old Morrison admitted it wasn't half bad—the old b-----d became positively mellow, as why shouldn't he, waited on hand and foot, with two slant-eyed and muscular yellow devils to carry him ashore and bear him in a palki on our excursions? "It's daein' me guid," says he. "I can feel the benefit." And Elspeth would sigh dreamily while they fanned her in the shade, and Solomon would smile and beckon the steward to put more ice in the glasses—oh, aye, he even had a patent ice-house stowed away somewhere, down by the keel.

Farther south, along the jungly and desert coasts, there was no lack of entertainment—a cruise up a forest river in the ship's launch, with Elspeth wide-eyed at the sight of crocodiles, which made her shudder deliciously, or laughing at the antics of monkeys and marvelling at the brilliance of foliage and bird-life. "Did I not tell you, Diana, how splendid it would be?" Solomon would say, and Elspeth would exclaim rapturously, "Oh, you did, you did—but this is *quite* beyond imagination!" Or there would be flying-fish, and porpoises, and once we were round the Cape—where we spent a week, dining out ashore and attending a ball at the Governor's, which pleased Elspeth no end—there was the real deep blue sea of the Indian Ocean, and more marvels for my insatiable relatives. We began the long haul across to India in perfect weather, and at night Solomon would fetch his guitar and sing dago dirges in the dusk, with Elspeth drowsing on a daybed by the rail, while Morrison cheated me at écarté, or we would play whist, or just laze the time contentedly away. It was tame stuff, if you like, but I put up with it—and kept my eye on Solomon.

For there was no doubt about it, he changed as the voyage progressed. He took the sun pretty strong, and was soon the brownest thing aboard, but in other ways, too, I was reminded that he was at least half-dago or native; instead of the customary shirt sleeves and trousers he took to wearing a tunic and sarong, saying jokingly that it was the proper tropical style; next it was bare feet, and once when the crew were shark-fishing Solomon took a hand at hauling in the huge threshing monster—if you had seen him, stripped to the waist, his great bronze body dripping with sweat, yelling as he heaved on the line and jabbering orders to his men in coast lingo . . . well, you'd have wondered if it was the same chap who'd been bowling slow lobs at Canterbury, or talking City prices over the port.

Afterwards, when he came to sit on the deck for an iced soda, I noticed Elspeth glancing at his splendid shoulders in a lazy sort of way, and the glitter in his dark eyes as he swept back his moist black hair and smiled at her—he'd been the perfect family friend for months, mind you, never so much as a fondling paw out of place—and I thought, hollo, he's looking d----d dashing and romantic these days. To make it worse, he'd started growing a chin-beard, a sort of nigger imperial; Elspeth said it gave him *quite* the corsair touch, so I made a note to roger her twice that night, just to quell these girlish fancies. All this reading Byron ain't good for young women.

It was the very next day that we came on deck to see a huge green coastline some miles to port; jungle-clad slopes beyond the beach, and mountains behind, and Elspeth cried out to know where it might be. Solomon laughed in an odd way as he came to the rail beside us.

"That's the strangest country, perhaps, in the whole wide world," says he. "The strangest—and the most savage and cruel. Few Europeans go there, but I have visited it—it's very rich, you see," he went on, turning to old Morrison, "gums and balsam, sugar and silk, indigo and spices—I believe there is coal and iron also. I have hopes of improving on the little trade I have started there. But they are a wild, terrible people; one has to tread warily—and keep an eye on your beached boat."

"Why, Don Solomon!" cries Elspeth. "We shall not land there, surely?"

"I shall," says he, "but not you; the *Sulu Queen* will lie well off—out of any possible danger."

"What danger?" says I. "Cannibals in war canoes?" He laughed.

"Not quite. Would you believe it if I told you that the capital of that country contains fifty thousand people, half of 'em slaves? That it is ruled by a monstrous black queen, who dresses in the height of eighteenth-century fashion, eats with her fingers from a table laden with gold and silver European cutlery, with place-cards at each chair and wall-paper showing Napoleon's victories on the wall—and having dined she will go out to watch robbers being burned alive and Christians crucified? That her bodyguard go almost naked—but with pipe-clayed cartridge belts, behind a band playing 'The British Grenadiers'? That her chief pleasures are torture and slaughter—why, I have seen a ritual execution at which hundreds were buried alive, sawn in half, hurled from—"

"No, Don Solomon, no!" squeals Elspeth, covering her ears, and old Morrison muttered about respecting the presence of ladies—now, the Don Solomon of London would never have mentioned such horrors to a lady, and if he had, he'd have been profuse in his apologies. But here he just smiled and shrugged, and passed on to talk of birds and beasts such as were known nowhere else, great coloured spiders in the jungle, fantastic chameleons, and the curious customs of the native courts, which decided guilt or innocence by giving the accused a special drink and seeing whether he spewed or not; the whole place was ruled by such superstitions and crazy laws, he said, and woe betide the outsider who tried to teach 'em different.

"Odd spot it must be," says I. "What did you say it was called?"

"Madagascar," says he, and looked at me. "You have been in some terrible places, Harry—well, if ever you chance to be wrecked *there*"—and he nodded at the green shore—"pray that you have a bullet left for yourself." He glanced to see that Elspeth was out of earshot. "The fate of any stranger cast on those shores is too shocking to contemplate; they say the queen has only two uses for foreign men—first, to subdue them to her will, if you follow me, and afterwards, to destroy them by the most fearful tortures she can devise."

"Playful little lady, is she?"

"You think I'm joking? My dear chap, she kills between twenty and thirty thousand human beings each year—she means to exterminate all tribes except her own, you see. When she came to the throne, some years ago, she had twenty-five thousand enemies rounded up, forced to kneel all together in one great enclosure, and at a given signal, swish! They were all executed at once. She kept a few thousand over, of course, to hang up sewed in ox skins until they rotted—or to be boiled or roasted to death, by way of a change. That's Madagascar."

"Ah, well," says I, "Brighton for me next year, I think. And you're going ashore?"

"For a few hours. The governor of Tamitave, up the coast, is a fairly civilised savage—all the ruling class are, including the queen: Bond Street dresses, as I said, and a piano in the palace. That's a remarkable place, by the way—big as a cathedral, and covered entirely by tiny silver bells. G-d knows what goes on in there."

"You've visited it?"

"I've seen it—but not been to tea, as you might say. But I've talked to those who have been inside it, and who've even seen Queen Ranavalona and lived to tell the tale. Europeans, some of 'em."

"What are they doing there, for G-d's sake?"

"The Europeans? Oh, they're slaves."

At the time, of course, I suspected he was drawing the long bow to impress the visitors—but he wasn't. No, every word he'd said about Madagascar was gospel true—and not one-tenth of the truth. I know; I found out for myself.

But from the sea it looked placid enough. Tamitave was apparently a very large village of yellow wooden buildings set out in orderly rows back from the shore; there was a fairish-sized fort with a great stockade some distance from the town, and a few soldiers drilling outside it. While Haslam was ashore, I examined them through the glass—big buck niggers in white kilts, with lances and swords, very smart, and moving in time, which is unusual among black troops. They weren't true niggers, though, it seemed to me; when Haslam was rowed out to the ship again there was an escorting boat, with a chap in the stern in what was a fair imitation of our naval rig: blue frock coat, epaulettes, cocked hat and braid, saluting away like anything—*he* looked like a Mexican, if anything, with his round, oily black face, but the rowers were dark brown and woolly haired, with straight noses and quite fine features.

That was the closest I got to the Malagassies, just then, and you may come to agree that it was near enough. Solomon seemed well satisfied with whatever business he had done ashore, and by next morning we were far out to sea with Madagascar forgotten behind us.

Now, I said I wouldn't weary you with our voyage, so I shall do no more than mention Ceylon and Madras—which is all they deserve, anyway, and take you straight away across the Bengal Bay, past the infernal Andamans, south by the heel of Great Nicobar, and into the steaming straits where the great jelly-fishes swim between the mainland of Malaya and the strange jungle island of Sumatra with its man-monkeys, down to the sea where the sun comes from, and the Islands lie ahead of you in a great brilliant chain that runs thousands of miles from the South China Sea to Australia and the far Pacific on the other side of the world. That's the East—the Islands; and you may take it from one who has India in his bones, there's no sea so blue, no lands so green, and no sun so bright, as you'll find beyond Singapore. What was it Solomon had said—"where it's always morning." So it was, and in that part of my imagination where I keep the best memories, it always will be.

That's one side of it. I wasn't to know, then, that Singapore was the last jumping-off place from civilisation into a world as terrible as it was beautiful, rich and savage and cruel beyond belief, of land and seas still unexplored where even the mighty Royal Navy sent only a few questing warships, and the handful of white adventurers who voyaged in survived by the speed of their keels and slept on their guns. It's quiet now, and the law, British and Dutch, runs from Sunda Strait to the Solomons; the coasts are tamed, the last trophy heads in the long-houses are ancient and shrivelled,[13] and there's hardly a man alive who can say he's heard the war gongs booming as the great robber fleets swept down from the Sulu Sea. Well, I heard 'em, only too clearly, and for all the good I've got to say of the Islands, I can tell you that if I'd known on that first voyage what I learned later, I'd have jumped ship at Madras.

But I was happily ignorant, and when we slipped in past the green sugar-loaf islands one fine April morning of '44, and dropped anchor in Singapore roads, it looked safe enough to me. The bay was alive with shipping, a hundred square-riggers if there was one: huge Indiamen under the gridiron flag, tall clippers of the Southern Run wearing the Stars and Stripes, British merchantmen by the bucketful, ships of every nationality —Solomon pointed out the blue crossed anchors of Russia, the red and gold bars of Spain, the blue and yellow of Sweden, even a gold lion which he said was Venice. Closer in, the tubby junks and long trading praus were packed so close it seemed you could have walked on them right across the bay, fairly seething with half-naked crews of Malays, Chinese, and every colour from pale yellow to jet black, deafening us with their high-pitched chatter as Solomon's rowers threaded the launch through to the river quay. There it was bedlam; all Asia seemed to have congregated on the landing, bringing their pungent smells and deafening sounds with them.

There were coolies everywhere, in straw hats or dirty turbans, staggering half-naked under bales and boxes—they swarmed on the quays, on the sampans that choked the river, round the warehouses and go-downs, and through them pushed Yankee captains in their short jackets and tall hats, removing their cheroots from their rat-trap jaws only to spit and cuss; Armenian Jews in black coats and long beards, all babbling; British blue-jackets in canvas shirts and ducks; long-moustached Chinese merchants in their round caps, borne in palkis; British traders from the Sundas with their pistols on their hips; leathery clipper men in pilot caps, shouting oaths of Liverpool and New York; planters in wideawakes making play among the niggers with their stout canes; a file of prisoners tramping by in leg-irons, with scarlet-coated soldiers herding them and bawling the step—I heard English, Dutch, German, Spanish, and Hindi all in the first minute, and most of the accents of England, Scotland, Wales, Ireland and the American seaboards to boot. God knows what the native tongues were, but they were all being used at full pitch, and after the comparative quiet we'd been used to it was enough to make you dizzy. The stink was fearful, too.

Of course, waterfronts are much the same everywhere; once you were away from the river, out on the "Mayfair" side of the town, which lay east along Beach Road, it was pleasant, and that was where Solomon had his house, a fine two-storey mansion set in an extensive garden, facing the sea. We were installed in cool, airy rooms, all complete with fans and screens, legions of Chinese servants to look after us, cold drinks by the gallon, and nothing to do but rest in luxury and recover from the rigours of our voyage, which we did for the next three weeks.

Old Morrison was all for it; he had gluttonised to such a tune that he'd put on flesh alarmingly, and all he wanted to do was lie down, belching and refreshing his ill nature in a hot climate. Elspeth, on the other hand, must be up and doing at once; she was off almost before she'd changed her shift, carried in a palki by menials, to pay calls on what she called The Society People, find out who was who, and squander money in the shops and bazaars. Solomon pointed her in the right directions, made introductions, and then explained apologetically that he had weeks of work to do in his 'changing-house at the quays; after that, he assured us, we would set off on our tour of his possessions, which I gathered lay somewhere on the east coast of the peninsula.

So there was I, at a loose end—and not before time. I didn't know when I had been so d---ably bored; a cruise of wonders was all very well, but I'd had my bellyful of Solomon and his floating mansion with its immaculate appointments and unvarying luxury and everything so exactly, confoundedly right, and the finest foods and wines coming out of my ears—I was surfeited with perfection, and sick of the sight of old Morrison's ugly mug, and the sound of Elspeth's unwearying imbecile chatter, and having not a d----d thing to do but stuff myself and sleep. I'd not had a scrap of vicious amusement for six months —and, for me, that's a lifetime of going hungry. Well, thinks I, if Singapore, the fleshpot of the Orient, can't supply my urgent needs, and give me enough assorted depravity in three weeks to last the long voyage home, there's something amiss; just let me shave and change my shirt, and we'll stand this town on its head.

I took a long slant, to get my bearings, and then plunged in, slavering. There were eight cross-streets in the Mayfair section, where all the fine houses were, and a large upland park below Governor's Hill where Society congregated in the evening—and, by Jove, wasn't it wild work, though? Why, you might raise your hat to as many as a hundred couples in two hours, and when you were fagged out with this, there was the frantic debauch of a gig drive along Beach Road, to look at the ships, or a dance at the assembly rooms, where a married woman might even polka with you, provided your wife and her husband were on hand—unmarried ladies didn't waltz, except with each other, the daring little hussies.

Then there were dinners at Dutranquoy's Hotel, with discussions afterwards about whether the Raffles Club oughtn't to be revived, and how the building of the new Chinese Pauper Hospital was progressing, and the price of sugar, and the latest leaderette in the "Free Press", and for the wilder spirits, a game of pyramids on the hotel billiard table—I played twice, and felt soiled at my beastly indulgence. Elspeth was indefatigable, of course, in her pursuit of pleasure, and dragged me to every soirée, ball, and junket that she could find, including church twice each Sunday, and the subscription meetings for the new theatre, and several times we even met Colonel Butterworth, the Governor—well, thinks I, this *is* Singapore, to be sure, but I'm shot if I can stand this pace for long.[14]

Once, I asked a likely-looking chap—you could tell he was a rake; he was using pomade—where the less respectable entertainments were to be found, supposing there were any, and he coloured a bit and shuffled and said :

"Well, there are the Chinese processions—but not many people would care to be seen looking at them, I dare say. They begin in the—ahem—native quarter, you know."

"By George," says I, "that's bad. Perhaps we could look at 'em for just a moment, though—we needn't stay long."

He didn't care for it, but I prevailed on him, and we hurried down to the promenade, with him muttering that it wasn't at all the thing, and what Penelope would say if she got to hear of it, he couldn't imagine. He had me in a fever of excitement, and I was palpitating by the time the procession hove in view—twenty Chinks beating gongs and letting off smoke and whistles, and half a dozen urchins dressed in Tartar costumes with umbrellas, all making a h--l of a din.

"Is that it?" says I.

"That's it," says he. "Come along, do—or someone will see us. It's—it's not done, you know, to be seen at these native displays, my dear Flashman."

"I'm surprised the authorities allow it," says I, and he said the "Free Press" was very hot against it, but the Indian processions were even worse, with chaps swinging on poles and carrying torches, and he'd even heard rumours that there were fakirs walking on hot coals, on the other side of the river.

That was what put me on the right track. I'd seen the waterfront, of course, with its great array of commercial buildings and warehouses, but the native town that lay beyond it, on the west bank, had looked pretty seedy and hardly worth exploring. Being desperate by this time, I ventured across one evening when Elspeth was at some female gathering, and it was like stepping into a brave new world.

Beyond the shanties was China Town—streets brilliantly-lit with lanterns, gaming houses and casinos roaring away on every corner, side-shows and acrobats—Hindoo fire-walkers, too, my pomaded chum had been right—pimps accosting you every other step, with promises of their sister who was, of course, every bit as voluptuous as Queen Victoria (how our sovereign lady became the carnal yardstick for the entire Orient through most of the last century, I've never been able to figure; possibly they imagined all true Britons lusted after her), and on all sides, enough popsy to satisfy an army—Chinese girls with faces like pale dolls at the windows; tall, graceful Kling tarts from the Coromandel, swaying past and smiling down their long noses; saucy Malay wenches giggling and beckoning from doorways, popping out their boobies for inspection; it was Vanity Fair come true—but it wouldn't do, of course. Poxed to a turn, most of 'em; they were all right for the drunken sailors lounging on the verandahs, who didn't care about being fleeced—and possibly knifed—but I'd have to find better quality than that. I didn't doubt that I would, and quickly, now that I knew where to begin, but for the present I was content to stroll and look about, brushing off the pimps and the more forward whores, and presently walking back to the river bridge.

And who should I run slap into but Solomon, coming late from his office. He stopped short at sight of me.

"Good G-d," says he, "you ain't been in bazaar-town, surely? My dear chap, if I'd known you wanted to see the sights, I'd have arranged an escort—it ain't the safest place on earth, you know. Not quite your style, either, I'd have thought."

Well, he knew better than that, but if he wanted to play innocent, I didn't mind. I said it had been most interesting, like all native towns, and here I was, safe and sound, wasn't I?

"Sure enough," says he, laughing and taking my arm. "I was forgetting—you've seen quite a bit of local colour in your time. But Singapore's—well, quite a surprising place, even for an old hand. You've heard about our Black-faced gangs, I suppose? Chinese, you know—nothing to do with the *tongs* or *hues*, who are the secret societies who rule down yonder—but murderous villains, just the same. They've even been coming east of the river lately, I'm told—burglary, kidnapping, that sort of thing, with their faces blacked in soot. Well, an unarmed white civilian on his own—he's just their meat. If you want to go again"—he gave me a quick look and away—"let me know; there are some really fine eating-houses on the north edge of the native town—the rich Chinese go there, and it's much more genteel. The Temple of Heaven's about the best—no sharking or rooking, or anything of that kind, and first-class service. Good cabarets, native dancing . . . that order of thing, you know."

Now why, I wondered, was Solomon offering to pimp for me —for that's what it struck me he was doing. To keep me sinfully amused while he paid court to Elspeth, perhaps—or just in the way of kindness, to steer me to the best brothels in town? I was pondering this when he went on:

"Speaking of rich Chinese—you and Elspeth haven't met any yet, I suppose? Now *they* are the most interesting folk in this settlement, altogether—people like Whampoa and Tan Tock Seng. I must arrange that—I'm afraid I've been neglecting you all shockingly, but when one's been away for three years—well, there's a great deal to do, as you can guess." He grinned whimsically. "Confess it—you've found our Singapore gaiety just a trifle tedious. Old Butterworth prosing—and Logan and Dyce ain't quite Hyde Park style, are they? Ne'er mind—I'll see to it that you visit one of old Whampoa's parties—*that* won't bore, I promise you!"

And it didn't. Solomon was as good as his word, and two nights later Elspeth and I and old Morrison were driven out to Whampoa's estate in a four-wheel palki; it was a superb place, more like a palace than a house, with the garden brilliant with lanterns, and the man himself bowing us in ceremonially at the door. He was a huge, fat Chinese, with a shaven head and a pigtail down to his heels, clad in a black silk robe embroidered with shimmering green and scarlet flowers—straight from Aladdin, except that he had a schooner of sherry in one paw; it never left him, and it was never empty either.

"Welcome to my miserable and lowly dwelling," says he, doubling over as far as his belly would let him. "That is what the Chinese always say, is it not? In fact, I think my home is perfectly splendid, and quite the best in Singapore—but I can truthfully say it has never entertained a more beautiful visitor." This was to Elspeth, who was gaping round at the magnificence of lacquered panelling, gold-leafed slender columns, jade ornaments, and silk hangings, with which Whampoa's establishment appeared to be stuffed. "You shall sit beside me at dinner, lovely golden-haired lady, and while you exclaim at the luxury of my house, I shall flatter your exquisite beauty. So we shall both be assured of a blissful evening, listening to what delights us most."

Which he did, keeping her entranced beside him, sipping continually at his sherry, while we ate a Chinese banquet in a dining-room that made Versailles look like a garret. The food was atrocious, as Chinese grub always is—some of the soups, and the creamed walnuts, weren't bad, though—but the servants were the most delightful little Chinese girls, in tight silk dresses each of a different colour; even ancient eggs with sea-weed dressing and carrion sauce don't seem so bad when they're offered by a slant-eyed little goer who breathes perfume on you and wriggles in a most entrancing way as she takes your hand in velvet fingers to show you how to manage your chop-sticks. D----d if I could get the hang of it at first; it took two of 'em to show me, one either side, and Elspeth told Whampoa she was sure I'd be much happier with a knife and fork.

There were quite a few in the party, apart from us three and Solomon—Balestier, the American consul, I remember, a jolly Yankee planter with a fund of good stories, and Catchick Moses,[15] a big noise in the Armenian community, who was the decentest Jew I ever met, and struck up an immediate rapport with old Morrison—they got to arguing about interest rates, and when Whampoa joined in, Balestier said he wouldn't rest until he'd made up a story which began "There was a Chinaman, a Scotchman, and a Jew", which caused great merriment. It was the cheeriest party I'd struck yet, and no lack of excellent drink, but after a while Whampoa called a halt, and there was a little cabaret, of Chinese songs, and plays, which were the worst kind of pantomime drivel, but very pretty costumes and masks, and then two Chinese dancing girls—exquisite little trollops, but clad from head to foot, alas.

Afterwards Whampoa took Elspeth and me on a tour of his amazing house—all the walls were carved screens, in ivory and ebony, which must have been h---ish draughty, but splendid to look at, and the doors were all oval in shape, with jade handles and gold frames—I reckon half a million might have bought the place. When we were finished, he presented me with a knife, inlaid with mother-of-pearl, in the shape of a miniature scimitar —to prove its edge, he dropped a filmy scrap of muslin on the blade, and it fell in half, sheared through by its own insignificant weight. (I've never sharpened it since, and it's as keen as ever, after sixty years.) To Elspeth he gave a model jade horse, whose bridle and stirrups were tiny jade chains, all cut out of one solid block—G-d knows what it was worth.

She scampered off to show it to the others, calling on Solomon to admire it, and Whampoa says quietly to me:

"You have known Mr Solomon Haslam for a long time?"

I said a year or so, in London, and he nodded his great bald head and turned his Buddha-like face to me.

"He is taking you on a cruise round his plantations, I believe. That will be interesting—I must ask him where they are. I should much like to visit them myself some day."

I said I thought they were on the peninsula, and he nodded gravely and sipped his sherry.

"No doubt they are. He is a man of sufficient shrewdness and enterprise, I think—he does business well." The sound of Elspeth's laughter sounded from the dining-room, and Whampoa's fat yellow face creased in a sudden smile. "How fortunate you are, Mr Flashman. I have, in my humble way—which is not at all humble, you understand—a taste for beautiful things, and especially in women. You have seen"—he fluttered his hand, with its beastly long nails—"that I surround myself with them. But when I see your lady, Elspet', I understand why the old story-tellers always made their gods and goddesses fair-skinned and golden-haired. If I were forty years younger, I should try to take her from you"—he sluiced down some more Amontillado—"without success, of course. But so much beauty—it is dangerous."

He looked at me, and I can't think why, but I felt a chill of sudden fear—not of him, but of what he was saying. Before I could speak, though, Elspeth was back, to exclaim again over her present, and prattle her thanks, and he stood smiling down at her, like some benign, sherry-soaked heathen god.

"Thank me, beautiful child, by coming again to my humble palace, for hereafter it will truly be humble without your presence," says he. Then we joined the others, and the thanks and compliments flew as we took our leave in that glittering place, and everything was cheery and happy—but I found myself shivering as we went out, which was odd, for it was a warm and balmy night.

I couldn't account for it, after such a jolly affair, but I went to bed thoroughly out of sorts. At first I put it down to foul Chinese grub, and certainly something gave me the most vivid nightmares, in which I was playing a single-wicket match up and downstairs in Whampoa's house, and his silky little Chinese tarts were showing me how to hold my bat—that part of it was all right, as they snuggled up, whispering fragrantly and guiding my hands, but all the time I was conscious of dark shapes moving behind the screens, and when Daedalus Tighe bowled to me it was a Chinese lantern that I had to hit, and it went ballooning up into the dark, bursting into a thousand rockets, and Old Morrison and the Duke came jumping out at me in sarongs, crying that I must run all through the house to score a single, at compound interest, and I set off, blundering past the screens, where nameless horrors lurked, and I was trying to catch Solomon, who was flitting like a shadow before me, calling out of the dark that there was no danger, because he carried ten guns, and I could feel someone or something drawing closer behind me, and Elspeth's voice was calling, fainter and fainter, and I knew if I looked back I should see something terrible—and there I was, gasping into the pillow, my face wet with sweat, and Elspeth snoring peacefully beside me.

It rattled me, I can tell you, because the last time I'd had a nightmare was in Gul Shah's dungeon, two years before, and that was no happy recollection. (It's a strange thing, by the way, that I usually have my worst nightmares in jail; I can remember some beauties, in Fort Raim prison, up on the Aral Sea, where I imagined old Morrison and Rudi Starnberg were painting my backside with boot polish, and in Gwalior Fort, where I waltzed in chains with Captain Charity Spring conducting the band, and the beastliest of all was in a Mexican clink during the Juarez business, when I dreamed I was charging the Balaclava guns at the head of a squadron of skeletons in mortar-boards, all chanting "Ab and absque, coram de", while just ahead of me Lord Cardigan was sailing in his yacht, leering at me and tearing Elspeth's clothes off. Mind you, I'd been living on chili and beans for a week.)

In any event, I didn't sleep well after Whampoa's party, and was in a fine fit of the dismals next day, as a result of which Elspeth and I quarrelled, and she wept and sulked until Solomon came to propose a picnic on the other side of the island. We would sail round in the *Sulu Queen*, he said, and make a capital day of it. Elspeth cheered up at once, and old Morrison was game, too, but I cried off, pleading indisposition. I knew what I needed to lift my gloom, and it wasn't an al fresco lunch in the mangrove swamps with those three; let them remove themselves, and it would leave me free to explore China Town at closer quarters, and perhaps sample the menu at one of those exclusive establishments that Solomon had mentioned; the Temple of Heaven was the name that stuck in my mind. Why, they might even have dainty little waitresses like Whampoa's, to teach you how to use your chopsticks.

So when the three of them had left, Elspeth with her nose in the air because I wasn't disposed to make up, I loafed about until evening and then whistled up a palki. My bearers jogged away through the crowded streets, and presently, just as dusk was falling, we reached our destination in what seemed to be a pleasant residential district inland from China Town, with big houses half-hidden in groves of trees from which paper lanterns hung; all very quiet and discreet.

The Temple of Heaven was a large frame house on a little hill, entirely surrounded by trees and shrubs, with a winding drive up to the front verandah, which was all dim lights and gentle music and Chinese servants scurrying to make the guests at home. There was a large cool dining-room, where I had an excellent European meal with a bottle and a half of champagne, and I was in capital fettle and ready for mischief when the Hindoo head waiter sidled up to ask if all was in order, and was there anything else that the gentleman required? Would I care to see a cabaret, or an exhibition of Chinese works of art, or a concert, if my tastes were musical, or . . .

"The whole d----d lot," says I, "for I ain't going home till morning, if you know what I mean. I've been six months at sea, so drum 'em up, Sambo, and sharp about it."

He smiled and bowed in his discreet Indian way, clapped his hands, and into the alcove where I was sitting there stepped the most gorgeous creature imaginable. She was Chinese, with blue-black hair coiled above a face that was pearl-like in its perfection and colour, with great slanting eyes, and her gown of crimson silk clung to a shape which English travellers are wont to describe as "a thought too generous for the European taste" but which, if I'd been a classical sculptor, would have had me dropping my hammer and chisel and reaching for the meat. Her arms were bare, and she spread them in the prettiest curtsey, smiling with perfect teeth between lips the colour of good port.

"This is Madame Sabba," says the waiter. "She will conduct you, if your excellency will permit . . .?"

"I may, just about," says I. "Which way's upstairs?"

I imagined it was the usual style, you see, but Madame Sabba, indicating that I should follow, led the way through an arch and down a long corridor, glancing behind to see that I was following. Which I was, breathing heavy, with my eyes on that trim waist and wobbling bottom; I caught her up at the end door, and was just clutching a handful when I realised that we were on a porch, and she was slipping out of my fond embrace and indicating a palki which was waiting at the foot of the steps.

"What's this?" says I.

"The entertainment," says she, "is a little way off. They will take us there."

"The entertainment," says I, "is on this very spot." And I took hold of her, growling, and hauled her against me. By George, she was a randy armful, wriggling against me and pretending she wanted to break loose, while I nuzzled into her, inhaling her perfume and munching away at her lips and face.

"But I am only your guide," she giggled, turning her face aside. "I shall take you—"

"Just to the nearest bed, ducky. I'll do the guiding after that."

"You like—me?" says she, playing coy, while I overhauled her lustfully. "Why, then—this is not suitable, here. We must go a little way—but I believe that when you see what else is offered, you will not care for Sabba." And she stuck her tongue into my mouth and then pulled me towards the palki. "Come—they will take us quickly."

"If it's more than ten yards, it'll be a wasted trip," says I, pawing away as we clambered aboard and pulled the curtains. I was properly on the boil, and intent on giving her the business then and there, but to my frustration the palki was one of those double sedans, where you sit opposite each other, and all I could do was paw at her frontage in the dark, swearing as I tried to unbutton her dress, and squeezing at the delights beneath it, while she kissed and fondled, laughing, telling me not to be impatient, and the palki men jogged along, bouncing us in a way that made it impossible to get down to serious work. Where they were taking us I didn't care; what with champagne and passion I was lost to everything but the scented beauty teasing me in the dark; at last I managed to get one tit clear and was nibbling away when the palki stopped, and Madame Sabba gently disengaged herself.

"A moment," says she, and I could imagine her adjusting her gown in the darkness. "Wait here;" her fingers gently stroked my lips, there was a glimpse of dusk as she slipped through the palki curtain—and then silence.

I waited, fretting and anticipating, for perhaps half a minute, and then stuck my head out. For a moment I couldn't make out anything in the gloom, and then I saw that the palki was stopped in a mean-looking street, between dark and shuttered buildings —but of the palki men and Madame Sabba there wasn't a sign. Just deserted shadow, not a light anywhere, and not a sound except the faint murmur of the town a long way off.

My blank astonishment lasted perhaps two seconds, to be replaced by rage as I tore back the palki curtain and stumbled out, cursing. I hadn't had time to feel the first chill of fear before I saw the black shapes moving out of the shadows at the end of the street, gliding silently towards me.

I'm not proud of what happened in the next moment. Of course, I was very young and thoughtless, and my great days of instant flight and evasion were still ahead of me, but even so, with my Afghan experience and my native cowardice to boot, my reaction was inexcusable. In my riper years I'd have lost no precious seconds in bemused swearing; long before those stealthy figures even appeared, I'd have realised that Madame Sabba's disappearance portended deadly danger, and been over the nearest wall and heading for the high country. But now, in my youthful folly and ignorance, I absolutely stood there gaping, and calling out:

"Who the d---l are you, and what d'ye want? Where's my whore, confound it?"

And then they were running towards me, on silent feet, and I saw in a flash that I'd been lured to my death. Then, at last, was seen Flashy at his best, when it was all but too late. One scream, three strides, and I was leaping for the rickety fence between two houses; for an instant I was astride of it, and had a glimpse of four lean black shapes converging on me at frightening speed; something sang past my head and then I was down and pelting along the alley beyond, hearing the soft thuds behind as they vaulted over after me. I tore ahead full tilt, bawling "Help!" at the top of my lungs, shot round the corner, and ran for dear life down the street beyond.

It was my yellow belly that saved me, nothing else. A hero wouldn't have stood and fought—not against those odds, in such a place—but he'd at least have glanced back, to see how close the pursuit was, or maybe even have drawn rein to consider which way to run next. Which would have been fatal, for the speed at which they moved was fearful. One glimpse I caught of the leader as I turned the corner—a fell black shape moving like a panther, with something glittering in his hand—and in pure panic I went hurtling on, from one street to another, leaping every obstruction, screaming steadily for aid, but going at my uttermost every stride. That's what you young chaps have got to remember—when you run, *run*, full speed, with never a thought for anything else; don't look or listen or dither even for an instant; let terror have his way, for he's the best friend you've got.

He kept me ahead of the field for a good quarter of a mile, I reckon, through deserted streets and lanes, over fences and yards and ditches, and never a glimpse of a human soul, until I turned a corner and found myself looking down a narrow alley which obviously led to a frequented street, for at the far end there were lanterns and figures moving, and beyond that, against the night sky, the spars and masts of ships under riding lights.

"Help!" I bawled. "Murder! Assassins! H--l and d---ation! Help!"

I was pelting down the alley as I shouted, and now, like a fool, I stole a glance back—there he was, like a black avenging angel gliding round the corner a bare twenty yards behind. I raced on, but in turning my head I'd lost my direction; suddenly there was an empty handcart in my path—left by some infernally careless coolie in the middle of the lane—and in trying to clear it I caught my foot and went sprawling. I was afoot in an instant, ahead of me someone was shouting, but my pursuer had halved the distance behind me, and as I shot another panic-stricken glance over my shoulder I saw his hand go back behind his head, something glittered and whirled at me, a fearful pain drove through by left shoulder, and I went sprawling into a pile of boxes, the flung hatchet clattering to the ground beside me.

He had me now; he came over the handcart like a hurdle racer, landed on the balls of his feet, and as I tried vainly to scramble to cover among the wrecked boxes, he plucked a second hatchet from his belt, poised it in his hand, and took deliberate aim. Behind me, along the alley, I could hear boots pounding, and a voice shouting, but they were too late for me—I can still see that horrible figure in the lantern light, the glistening black paint like a mask across the skull-like Chinese head, the arm swinging back to hurl the hatchet—

"Jingo!" a voice called, and pat on the word something whispered in the air above my head, the hatchet-man shrieked, his body twisted on tip-toe, and to my amazement I saw clearly in silhouette that an object like a short knitting-needle was protruding from beneath his upturned chin. His fingers fluttered at it, and then his whole body seemed to dissolve beneath him, and he sprawled motionless in the alley. Without being conscious of imitation, I followed suit.

If I fainted, though, with pain and shock, it can only have been for a moment, for I became conscious of strong hands raising me, and an English voice saying: "I say, he's taken a bit of a cut. Here, sit him against the wall." And there were other voices, in an astonishing jumble: "How's the Chink?" "Dead as mutton—Jingo hit him full in the crop." "By Jove, that was neat—I say, look here, though, he's starting to twitch!" "Well, I'm blessed, the poison's working, even though he's dead. If that don't beat everything!" "Trust our little Jingo—cut his throat and poison him afterwards, just for luck, what?"

I was too dazed to make anything of this, but one word in their crazy discussion struck home in my disordered senses.

"Poison!" I gasped. "The axe—poisoned! My G-d, I'm dying, get a doctor—my arm's gone dead already—"

And then I opened my eyes, and saw an amazing sight. In front of me was crouching a squat, hideously-featured native, naked save for a loin-cloth, gripping a long bamboo spear. Alongside him stood a huge Arab-looking chap, in white ducks and crimson sash, with a green scarf round his hawk head and a great red-dyed beard rippling down to his waist. There were a couple of other near-naked natives, two or three obvious seamen in ducks and caps, and kneeling at my right side a young, fair-haired fellow in a striped jersey. As motley a crowd as ever I opened eyes on, but when I turned my head to see who was poking painfully at my wounded shoulder, I forgot all about the others—this was the chap to look at.

It was a boy's face; that was the first impression, in spite of the bronzed, strong lines of it, the touches of grey in the dark curly hair and long side-whiskers, the tough-set mouth and jaw, and the half-healed sword cut that ran from his right brow onto his cheek. He was about forty, and they hadn't been quiet years, but the dark blue eyes were as innocent as a ten-year-old's and when he grinned, as he was doing now, you thought at once of stolen apples and tacks on the master's chair.

"Poison?" says he, ripping away my blood-sodden sleeve. "Not a bit of it. Chink hatchet-men don't go in for it, you know. That's for ignorant savages like Jingo here—say 'How-de-do' to the gentleman, Jingo." And while the savage with the spear bobbed his head at me with a frightful grin, this chap left off mauling my shoulder, and reaching over towards the body of my fallen pursuer, pulled the knitting-needle thing from his neck.

"See there," says he, holding it gingerly, and I saw it was a thin dart about a foot long. "That's Jingo's delight—saved your life, I dare say, didn't it, Jingo? Of course, any Iban worth his salt can hit a farthing at twenty yards, but Jingo can do it at fifty. *Radjun* poison on the tip—not fatal to humans, as a rule, but it don't need to be if the dart goes through your jugular, does it?" He tossed the beastly thing aside and poked at my wound again, humming softly:

> "Oh, say was you ever in Mobile bay,
> A-screwin' cotton at a dollar a day,
> Sing 'Johnny come down to Hilo'."

I yelped with pain and he clicked his tongue reprovingly.

"Don't swear," says he. "Just excite yourself, and you won't go to heaven when you die. Anyway, squeaking won't mend it—it's just a scrape, two stitches and you'll be as right as rain."

"It's agony!" I groaned. "I'm bleeding buckets!"

"No, you ain't, either. Anyway, a great big hearty chap like you won't miss a bit of blood. Mustn't be a milksop. Why, when I got this"—he touched his scar—"I didn't even cheep. Did I, Stuart?"

"Yes, you did," says the fair chap. "Bellowed like a bull and wanted your mother."

"Not a word of truth in it. Is there, Paitingi?"

The red-bearded Arab spat. "You enjoy bein' hurt," says he, in a strong Scotch accent. "Ye gaunae leave the man lyin' here a' nicht?"

"We ought to let Mackenzie look at him, J.B.," says the fair chap. "He's looking pretty groggy."

"Shock," says my ministering angel, who was knotting his handkerchief round my shoulder, to my accompanying moans. "There, now—that'll do. Yes, let Mac sew him together, and he'll be ready to tackle twenty hatchet-men tomorrow. Won't you, old son?" And the grinning madman winked and patted my head. "Why was this one chasing you, by the way? I see he's a Black-face; they usually hunt in packs."

Between groans, I told him how my palki had been set on by four of them—I didn't say anything about Madame Sabba—and he stopped grinning and looked murderous.

"The cowardly, sneaking vagabonds!" cries he. "I don't know what the police are thinking about—leave it to me and I'd clear the rascals out in a fortnight, wouldn't I just!" He looked the very man to do it, too. "It's too bad altogether. You were lucky we happened along, though. Think you can walk? Here, Stuart, help him up. There now," cries the callous brute, as they hauled me to my feet, "you're feeling better already, I'll be bound!"

At any other time I'd have given him a piece of my mind, for if there's one thing I detest more than another it's these hearty, selfish, muscular Christians who are forever making light of your troubles when all you want to do is lie whimpering. But I was too dizzy with the agony of my shoulder, and besides, he and his amazing gang of sailors and savages had certainly saved my bacon, so I felt obliged to mutter my thanks as well as I could. J.B. laughed at this and said it was all in a good cause, and duty-free, and they would see me home in a palki. So while some of them set off hallooing to find one, he and the others propped me against the wall, and then they stood about and discussed what they should do with the dead Chinaman.

It was a remarkable conversation, in its way. Someone suggested, sensibly enough, that they should cart him along and give him to the police, but the fair chap, Stuart, said no, they ought to leave him lying and write a letter to the "Free Press" complaining about litter in the streets. The Arab, whose name was Paitingi Ali, and whose Scotch accent I found unbelievable, was for giving him a Christian burial, of all things, and the hideous little native, Jingo, jabbering excitedly and stamping his feet, apparently wanted to cut his head off and take it home.

"Can't do that," says Stuart. "You can't cure it till we get to Kuching, and it'll stink long before that."

"I won't have it," says the man J.B., who was evidently the leader. "Taking heads is a beastly practice, and one I am resolved to suppress. Mind you," he added, "Jingo's suggestion, by his own lights, has a stronger claim to consideration than yours—it is his head, since he killed the fellow. Hollo, though, here's Crimble with the palki. In you go, old chap."

I wondered, listening to them, if my wound had made me delirious; either that, or I had fallen in with a party of lunatics. But I was too used up to care; I let them stow me in the palki, and lay half-conscious while they debated where they might find Mackenzie—who I gathered was a doctor—at this time of night. No one seemed to know where he might be, and then someone recalled that he had been going to play chess with Whampoa. I had just enough of my wits left to recall the name, and croak out that Whampoa's establishment would suit me splendidly—the thought that his delectable little Chinese girls might be employed to nurse me was particularly soothing just then.

"You know Whampoa, do you?" says J.B. "Well, that settles it. Lead on, Stuart. By the way," says he to me, as they picked up the palki, "my name's Brooke—James Brooke[16]—known as J.B. You're Mr . . .?"

I told him, and even in my reduced condition it was a satisfaction to see the blue eyes open wider in surprise.

"Not the Afghan chap? Well, I'm blessed! Why, I've wanted to meet you this two years past! And to think that if we hadn't happened along, you'd have been . . ."

My head was swimming with pain and fatigue, and I didn't hear any more. I have a faint recollection of the palki jogging, and of the voices of my escort singing:

"Oh, say have you seen the plantation boss,
With his black-haired woman and his high-tail hoss,
Sing 'Johnny come down to Hilo',
Poor . . . old . . . man!"

But I must have gone under, for the next thing I remember is the choking stench of ammonia beneath my nose, and when I opened my eyes there was a glare of light, and I was sitting in a chair in Whampoa's hall. My coat and shirt had been stripped away, and a burly, black-bearded chap was making me wince and cry out with a scalding hot cloth applied to my wound— sure enough, though, at his elbow was one of those almond-eyed little beauties, holding a bowl of steaming water. She was the only cheery sight in the room, for as I blinked against the light reflected from the magnificence of silver and jade and ivory I saw that the ring of faces watching me was solemn and silent and still as statues.

There was Whampoa himself, in the centre, impassive as ever in his splendid gown of black silk; next to him Catchick Moses, his bald head gleaming and his kindly Jewish face pale with grief; Brooke, not smiling now—his jaw and mouth were set like stone, and beside him the fair boy Stuart was a picture of pity and horror—what the h--l are they staring at, I wondered, for I ain't as ill as all that, surely? Then Whampoa was talking, and I understood, for what he said made the terror of that night, and the pain of my wound, seem insignificant. He had to repeat it twice before it sank in, and then I could only sit staring at him in horror and disbelief.

"Your beautiful wife, the lady Elspet', has gone. The man Solomon Haslam has stolen her. The *Sulu Queen* sailed from Singapore this night, no one knows where."

*   *   *

[Extract from the diary of Mrs Flashman, July —, 1844]

Lost! lost! lost! I have never been so Surprised in my life. One moment *secure* in Tranquillity and Affection, among Loving Friends and Relations, shielded by the Devotion of a Constant Husband and Generous Parent—the next, horribly ~~ravished~~ stolen away by one ~~whom~~ ~~who~~ that I had *esteemed* and *trusted* almost beyond any gentleman of my acquaintance (excepting of course H. and dear Papa). Shall I ever see them again? What terrible fate lies ahead— ah, I can guess *all too well*, for I have seen the Loathsome Passion in his eyes, and it is not to be thought that he has so *ruthlessly* abducted me to any end but one! I am so distracted by Shame and Terror that I believe my Reason will be unseated—lest it should, I must record my Miserable Lot while *clarity of thought* remains, and I can still hold my trembling pen!

Oh, alas, that I parted from my darling H. in *discord* and *sulks*—and over the Merest Trifle, because he threw the coffee pot against the wall and kicked the servant—

110

which was no more than that minion deserved, for his bearing had been Careless and Familiar, and he would not clean his nails before waiting upon us. And I, sullen Wretch that I was, reproved my Dearest One, and took that Bad Servant's part, so that we were at odds over breakfast, and exchanged only the most Brief Remarks for the better part of the day, with Pouting and Missishness on my *unworthy* part, and Dark Looks and Exclamations from my Darling—but I see now how *forbearing* he was with such a Perverse and Contrary creature as ~~are~~ I. Oh, Unhappy, *unworthy* woman that I am, for it was in Cruel Huff that I accompanied Don S., that Viper, on his proposed excursion, thinking to Punish my dear, patient, sweet Protector—oh, it is I who am punished for my *selfish* and *spiteful* conduct!

All went well until our picnic ashore, although I believe the champagne was flat, and made me feel strangely drowsy, so that I must go aboard the vessel to lie down. With no thought of Peril, I slept, and awoke to find we were under way, with Don S. upon deck instructing his people to make all speed. "Where is Papa?" I cried, "and why are we sailing away from Land? See, Don Solomon, the sun is sinking; we must return!" His face was Pale, despite his warm complection, and his look was Wild. With brutal frankness, yet in a Moderate Tone, he told me I should Resign myself, for I should never see my dear Papa again.

"What do you mean, Don Solomon?" I cried. "We are bidden to Mrs Alec Middleton's for dinner!" It was then, in a voice which shook with Feeling, so unlike his usual Controll'd form of address, although I could see he was striving to master his Emotion, that he told me there could be no going back; that he was subject to an Overmastering Passion for me, and had been from our Moment of First Meeting. "The die is cast," he declared. "I cannot live without you, so I must make you *my own*, in the face of the world and your husband, tho' it means I must cut all my ties with civilised life, and take you beyond pursuit, to my own distant kingdom, where, I assure you, you will rule as Queen not only over my Possessions, but over my Heart."

"This is madness, Don Solomon," I cried. "I have no clothes with me. Besides, I am a *married woman*, with a Position in Society." He said it was no matter for that, and Seizing me suddenly in his Powerful Embrace, which took my breath away, he vowed that I loved him too—that he had known it from Encouraging Signs he had detected in me—which, of course, was the Odious Construction which his Fever'd Brain had placed on the common civilities and little pleasantries which a Lady is accustomed to bestow on a Gentleman.

I was *quite overcome* at the fearful position in which I found myself, so unexpectedly, but not so much that I lost my capacity for Careful Consideration. For having pleaded with him to repent this *madness*, which could lead only to *shame* for myself, and Ruin for him, and even having demeaned myself to the extent of struggling vainly in his crushing embrace, so Brutally Strong and *inflexible*, as well as calling loudly for assistance and kicking his shins, I became calmer, and feigned to Swoon. I recollected that there is no Emergency beyond the Power of a Resolute Englishwoman, especially if she is Scotch, and took heart from the lesson enjoined by our dominie, Mr Buchanan, at the Renfrew Academy for Young Ladies and Gentlewomen—ah, dear home, am I parted forever from the Scenes of Childhood?—that in Moments of Danger, it is of the *first importance* to take Accurate Measurements and then *act* with boldness and dispatch.

Accordingly, I fell *limp* in my Captor's cruel—altho' no doubt he meant it to be Affectionate—clasp, and he relaxing his vigilance, I *broke free* and sped to the rail, intending to cast myself upon the mercy of the waves, and swim ashore—for I was a Strong Swimmer, and hold the West of Scotland Physical Improvement Society's certificate for Saving Life from Drowning, having been among the First to receive it when that Institution was founded in 1835, or it may have been 1836, when I was still a child. It was not very far to the shore, either, but before I could *fling* myself into the sea, in the Trust of Almighty God, I was seized by one of Don S.'s Hideous and Smelling natives, and despite my struggles, I was carried below, at Don S.'s orders, and am confined in the saloon, where I write this melancholy account.

What shall I do? Oh, Harry, Harry, darling Harry, come and save me! Forgive my Thoughtless and Wayward behaviour, and Rescue me from the Clutches of this Improper Person. I think he must be *mad*—and yet, such Passionate Obsessions are not uncommon, I believe, and I am not insensible of the Regard that I have been shown by others of his sex, who have praised my attractions, so I must not pretend that I do not understand the reason for his Horrid and Ungallant Conduct. My dread is that before Aid can reach me, his Beast may overpower his Finer Feelings—and even now I cannot suppose that he is altogether Dead to Propriety, though how long such Restraint will continue I cannot say.

So come *quickly*, *quickly*, my own love, for how can I, *weak* and *defenceless* as I am, resist him unaided? I am in terror and distraction at 9 p.m. The weather continues fine.

[End of extract—this is what comes of forward and immodest behaviour—G. de R.]

"I blame myself," says Whampoa, sipping his sherry. "For years one does business with a man, and if his credit is good and his merchandise sound, one clicks the abacus and sets aside the doubts one feels on looking into his eyes." He was enthroned behind his great desk, impassive as Buddha, with one of his little tarts beside him holding the Amontillado bottle. "I knew he was not safe, but I let it go, even when I saw how he watched your golden lady two evenings since. It disturbed me, but I am a lazy, stupid and selfish fool, so I did nothing. You shall tell me so, Mr Flashman, and I shall bow my unworthy head beneath your deserved censure."

He nodded towards me while his glass was refilled, and Catchick Moses burst out:

"Not as stupid as I, for G-d's sake, and I'm a man of business, they say! Yeh! Haven't I for the past week been watching him liquidate his assets, closing his warehouses, selling his stock to my committee, auctioning his lighters?" He spread his hands. "Who cared? He was a cash-on-the-table man, so did I mind where he came from, or that nobody knew him before ten years back? He was in spice, they said, and silk, and antimony, and G-d-knows-what, with plantations up the coast and something-or-other in the Islands—and now you tell us, Whampoa, that no one has ever seen these estates of his?"

"That is my information in the past few hours," says Whampoa gravely. "It amounts to this: he has great riches, but no one knows where they come from. He is a Singapore middleman, but he is not alone in that. His name was good, because he did good business—"

"And now he has done us!" cries Catchick. "This, in Singapore! Under our very noses, in the most respectable community in Asia, he steals a great English lady—what will they say in the world, hey? Where's our reputation, *our* good name, I should like to know. It's gone out yonder, heaven knows where, aboard his accursed brig! Pirates, they'll call us—thieves and kidnappers! I tell you, Whampoa, this could ruin trade for five years—"

"In G-d's name, man!" cries Brooke. "It could ruin Mrs Flashman forever!"

"Oi-hoi!" cries Catchick, clutching his head with his hands, and then he came trotting across to me and dropped his hand on my shoulder, kneading away at me. "Oh, my poor friend, forgive me!" he groans. "My poor friend!"

It was just on dawn, and we had been engaged in such useful conversation for two hours past. At least, they had; I had been sitting in silence, sick with shock and pain, while Catchick Moses apostrophised and tore his whiskers, Whampoa reviled himself in precise, grammatical terms and sank half a gallon of Manzanilla, Balestier, the American consul, who had been summoned, d----d Solomon to Hades and beyond, and two or three other leading citizens shook their heads and exclaimed from time to time. Brooke just listened, mostly, having sent his people out to pick up news; there was a steady trickle of Whampoa's Chinese, too, coming in to report, but adding little to what we already knew. And that was knowledge enough, stark and unbelievable.

Most of it came from old Morrison, who had been abandoned on the bay island where the party had picnicked. He had gone to sleep, he said—full of drugged drink, no doubt, and had come to in the late evening to find the *Sulu Queen* hull down on the horizon, steaming away east—this was confirmed by the captain of an American clipper, one Waterman, who had passed her as he came into port. Morrison had been picked up by some native fishermen and had arrived at the quay after nightfall to pour out his tale, and now the whole community was in uproar. Whampoa had taken it upon himself to get to the bottom of the thing—he had feelers everywhere, of course—and had put Morrison to bed upstairs, where the old goat was in a state of prostration. The Governor had been informed, with the result that brows were being clutched, oaths sworn, fists shaken, and sal volatile sold out in the shops, no doubt. There hadn't been a sensation like it since the last Presbyterian Church jumble sale. But of course nothing was done.

At first, everyone had said it was a mistake; the *Sulu Queen* was off on some pleasure jaunt. But when Catchick and Whampoa pieced it all together, that wouldn't do: it was discovered that Solomon had been quietly selling up in Singapore, that when all was said, no one knew a d----d thing about him, and that all the signs were that he was intending to clear out, leaving not a wrack behind. Hence the loud recriminations, and the dropped voices when they remembered that I was present, and the repeated demands as to what should be done now.

Only Brooke seemed to have any notions, and they weren't much help. "Pursuit," cries he, with his eyes blazing. "She's going to be rescued, don't doubt that for a moment." He dropped a hand on my uninjured shoulder. "I'm with you in this; we all are, and as I've a soul to save I won't rest until you have her safe back, and this evil rascal has received condign punishment. So there—we'll find her, if we have to rake the sea to Australia and back! My word on it."

The others growled agreement, and looked resolute and sympathetic and scratched themselves, and then Whampoa signs to his girl for more liquor and says gravely:

"Indeed, everyone supports your majesty in this"—it says much about my condition that I never thought twice about that remarkable form of address to an English sailor in a pea-jacket and pilot cap—"but it is difficult to see how pursuit can be made until we have precise information about where they have gone."

"My G-d, that is the truth," groans Catchick Moses. "They may be anywhere. How many millions of miles of sea, how many islands, half of them uncharted—two thousand, five, ten? Does anyone know, even? And such islands—swarming with pirates, cannibals, head-takers—in G-d's name, my friend, this rascal may have taken her anywhere. And there is no vessel in port fit to pursue a steam-brig."

"It's a job for the Royal Navy," says Balestier. "Our navy boys, too—they'll have to track this villain, run him to earth, and—"

"Jeesh!" cries Catchick, heaving himself up. "What are you saying? What Royal Navy? What navy boys? Where is Belcher with his squadron—two t'ousand miles away, chasing the Lanun brigands round Mindanao! Where is your one American navy boat? Do you know, Balestier? Somewhere between Japan and

New Zealand—maybe! Where is Seymour's *Wanderer*, or Hastings with the *Harlequin*—?"

"*Dido*'s due from Calcutta in two or three days," says Balestier. "Keppel knows these seas as well as anyone—"

"And how well is that?" croaks Catchick, flapping his hands and stalking about. "Be practical! Be calm! It is terra incognita out yonder—as we all know, as everyone knows! And it is vast! If we had the whole Royal Navy, American and Dutch as well, from all the oceans of the world, they could search to the end of the century and never cover half the places where this rascal may be hiding—why, he may have gone anywhere. Don't we know his brig can sail round the world if need be?"

"I think not," says Whampoa quietly. "I have reason—I fear I may have reason—to believe that he will not sail beyond our Indies."

"Even then—haven't I told you that there are ten million lurking places between Cochin and Java?"

"And ten million eyes that won't miss a steam-brig, and will pass word to us wherever she anchors," snaps Brooke. "See here—" and he slapped the map they had unrolled on Whampoa's desk. "The *Sulu Queen* was last seen heading east, according to Bully Waterman. Very well—he won't double back, that's certain; Sumatra's no use to him, anyway. And I don't see him turning north—that's either open sea or the Malay coast, where we'd soon have word of him. South—perhaps, but if he runs through Karamata we'll hear of it. So I'll stake my head he'll stay on the course he's taken—and that means Borneo."

"Oi-hoi!" cries Catchick, between derision and despair. "And is that nothing, then? Borneo—where every river is a pirate nest, where every bay is an armed camp—where even you don't venture far, J.B., without an armed expedition at your back. And when you do, you know where you are going—not like now, when you might hunt forever!"

"I'll know where I'm going," says Brooke. "And if I have to hunt forever . . . well, I'll find him, sooner or later."

Catchick shot an uneasy glance across at me where I sat in the corner, nursing my wound, and I saw him pluck at Brooke's sleeve and mutter something of which I caught only the words ". . . too late by then." At that they fell silent, while Brooke pored over his map and Whampoa sat silent, sipping his d----d sherry. Balestier and the others talked in low voices, and Catchick slumped in a chair, hands in pockets, the picture of gloom.

You may wonder what I was thinking while all this hot air was being expelled, and why I wasn't taking part as a bereaved and distracted husband should—wild cries of impotent rage and grief, prayers to heaven, vows of revenge, and all the usual preliminaries to inaction. The fact was, I had troubles enough—my shoulder was giving me gyp, and having not recovered from the terror I'd faced myself that night, I didn't have much emotion left to spare, even for Elspeth, once the first shock of the news had worn off. She was gone—kidnapped by that half-caste scum, and what feelings I had were mostly about him. The slimy, twisting, insinuating hound had planned all this, over months—it was incredible, but he must have been so infatuated with her that he was prepared to steal her, make himself an outcast and outlaw, put himself beyond the bounds of civilisation for good, just on her account. There was no sense in it—no woman's worth that. Why, as I sat there, trying to take it in, I knew I wouldn't have done it, not for Elspeth and a pound of tea—not for Aphrodite herself and ten thousand a year. But I'm not a rich, spoiled dago, of course. Even so, it was past belief.

Don't misunderstand me—I loved Elspeth, pretty well, no error; still do, if being used to having her about the place is anything to go by, and missing her if she's too long gone. But there are limits, and I was suddenly aware of them now. On the one hand, she was a rare beauty, the finest mount I'd ever struck, and an heiress to boot, but on t'other, I hadn't wed her willingly, we'd spent most of our married life apart, and no harm done, and I couldn't for the life of me work up a frenzy of anxiety on her account now. After all, the worst that could happen, *to her*, was that this scoundrel would roger her, if he hadn't done it already while my back was turned—well, that was nothing new to her; she'd had me, and enjoyed it, and I hadn't been her only partner, I was certain. So being rattled stupid by Solomon would be no fate worse than death to her; if I knew the little trollop, she'd revel in it.

Beyond that, well, if he didn't tire of her (and considering the sacrifices he'd made to get her, he presumably intended to keep her) he'd probably look after her well enough; he wasn't short of blunt, and could no doubt support her in luxury in some exotic corner of the world. She'd miss England, of course, but taking the long view, her prospects weren't unendurable. It would make a change for her.

But that was only one side of it, of course—her side, which shows, since I've put it first, that I ain't so selfish after all. What did twist my innards with fury was shame and injured pride. Here was *my* wife—the beloved of the heroic Flashy—stolen from him by a swarthy, treacherous, lecherous, Etonian nigger, who'd be bulling her all over the shop, and what the deuce was I to do about it? He was cuckolding *me*, by G-d, as he might well have done twenty times already—by George, there was a fine thought—who was to say she hadn't gone with him willingly? But no, idiot and flirt that she was, she knew better than that. Either way, though, I looked d----d ridiculous, and there wasn't a thing to be done. Oh, there would have to be racing and chasing after her and Solomon, to no avail—in those first hours, you see, I was certain that she was gone for good: Catchick was right, we hadn't a hope of getting her back. What then? There would still have to be months, perhaps years, of fruitless searching, for form's sake, expensive, confounded risky, and there I'd be, at the end of it, going home, and when people asked after her, saying: "Oh, she was kidnapped, don't you know, out East. No, never did discover what happened to her." J---s, I'd be the laughing-stock of the country—Flashy, the man whose wife was pinched by a half-breed millionaire . . . "Close friend of the family, too . . . well, they *say* she was pinched, but who knows? . . . probably tired of old Flash, what?—felt like some Oriental mutton for a change, ha-ha."

I ground my teeth and cursed the day I'd ever set eyes on her, but above all, I felt such hatred of Solomon as I've never felt for any other human being. That he'd done this to *me*— there was no fate too horrible for the greasy rat, but precious little chance of inflicting it, so far as I could see at the moment. I was helpless, while that b----y wop steamed off with my wife— I could just picture him galloping away at her while she pretended maiden modesty, and the world roared with laughter at me, and in my rage and misery I must have let out a muffled yowl, for Brooke turned away from his map, strode across, dropped on one knee beside my chair, gripped my arm, and cries:

"You poor chap! What must you be feeling! It must be unbearable—the thought of your loved one in the hands of that dastard. I can share your anguish," he went on, "for I know how I should feel if it were my mother. We must trust in God and our own endeavours—and don't you fret, we shall win her back."

He absolutely had tears in his eyes, and had to turn his head aside to hide his emotion; I heard him muttter about "a captive damosel" and "blue eyes and golden hair of hyacinthine flow" or some fustian of that sort.[17] Then, having clasped my hand, he went back to his map and said that if the b----r had taken her to Borneo he'd turn the place inside out.

"An unexplored island the size of Europe," says Catchick mournfully. "And even then you are only guessing. If he has gone east, it may as well be to the Celebes or the Philippines."

"He burns wood, doesn't he?" says Brooke. "Then he'll touch Borneo—and that's my bailiwick. Let him show his nose there, and I'll hear of it."

"But you are not *in* Borneo, my friend—"

"I will be, though, within a week of Keppel's getting here in *Dido*. You know her—eighteen guns, two hundred blue-jackets, and Keppel would sail her to the Pole and back on a venture like this!" He was fairly glittering with eagerness. "He and I have run more chases than you can count, Catchick. Once we get this fox's scent, he can double and turn till he's dizzy, but we'll get him! Aye, he can sail to China—"

"Needle in a haystack," says Balestier, and Catchick and the others joined in, some supporting Brooke and others shaking their heads; while they were at it, one of Whampoa's Chinese slipped in and whispered in his master's ear for a full minute, and our host put down his sherry glass and opened his slit eyes a fraction wider, which for him was the equivalent of leaping to his feet and shouting "Great Scott!" Then he tapped the table, and they shut up.

"If you will forgive my interruption," says Whampoa, "I have information which I believe may be vital to us, and to the safety of the beautiful Mrs Flashman." He ducked his head at me. "A little time ago I ventured the humble opinion that her abductor would not sail beyond the Indies waters; I had developed a theory, from the scant information in my possession; my agents have been testing it in the few hours that have elapsed since this deplorable crime took place. It concerned the identity of this mysterious Don Solomon Haslam, whom Singapore has known as a merchant and trader—for how long?"

"Ten years or thereabouts," says Catchick. "He came here as a young man, in about '35."

Whampoa bowed acknowledgement. "Precisely; that accords with my own recollection. Since then, when he established a warehouse here, he has visited our port only occasionally, spending most of his time—where? No one knows. It was assumed that he was on trading ventures, or on these estates about which he talked vaguely. Then, three years ago, he returned to England, where he had been at school. He returns now, with Mr and Mrs Flashman, and Mr Morrison."

"Well, well," cries Catchick. "We know all this. What of it?"

"We know nothing of his parentage, his birth, or his early life," says Whampoa. "We know he is fabulously rich, that he never touches strong drink, and I gather—from conversation I have had with Mr Morrison—that on his brig he commonly wore the sarong and went barefoot." He shrugged. "These are small things; what do they indicate? That he is half-caste, we know; I suggest the evidence points to his being a Muslim, although there is no proof that he ever observes the rituals of that faith. Now then, a rich Muslim, who speaks fluent Malay—"

"The Islands are full of 'em," cries Brooke. "What are you driving at?"

"—who has been known in these waters for ten years, except for the last three, when he was in England. And his name is Solomon Haslam, to which he attaches the Spanish honorific 'Don'."

They were still as mice, listening. Whampoa turned his expressionless yellow face, surveying them, and tapped his glass, which the wench refilled.

"This suggests nothing to you? Not to you, Catchick? Mr Balestier? Your majesty?" This to Brooke, who shook his head.

"It did not to me, either," Whampoa continued, "until I considered his name, and something stirred in my poor memory. Another name. Your majesty knows, I am sure, the names of the principal pirates of the Borneo coast for several years back —could you recall some of them to us now?"

"Pirates?" cries Brooke. "You're not suggesting—"

"If you please," says Whampoa.

"Why—well then, let's see," Brooke frowned. "There's Jaffir, at Fort Linga; Sharif Muller of the Skrang—nearly cornered him on the Rajang last year—then there's Pangeran Suva, out of Brunei; Suleiman Usman of Maludu, but no one's heard of him for long enough; Sharif Sahib of Patusan; Ranu—"

He broke off, for Catchick Moses had let fly one of his amazing Hebrew exclamations, and was staring at Whampoa, who nodded placidly.

"You noticed, Catchick. As I did—I ask myself why I did not notice five years ago. That name," and he looked at Brooke, and sipped his sherry. " 'Suleiman Usman of Maludu, but no one has heard of him for long enough'," he repeated. "I think —indeed, I know, that no one has heard of him for precisely three years. Suleiman Usman—Solomon Haslam." He put down his sherry glass.

For a moment there was stupefied silence, and then Balestier burst out:

"But that can't be! What—a coast pirate, and you suggest he set up shop here, amongst us, as a trader, and carried on business, and went a-pirating on the side? That's not just too rich— it's downright crazy—"

"What better cover for piracy?" wonders Whampoa. "What better means of collecting information?"

"But d--n it, this fellow Haslam's a public school man!" cries Brooke. "Isn't he?"

"He attended Eton College," says Whampoa gravely, "but that is not, in itself, necessarily inconsistent with a later life of crime."

"But consider!" cries Catchick. "If it were as you say, would any sane man adopt an alias so close to his own name? Wouldn't he call himself Smith, or Brown, or—or anything?"

"Not necessarily," says Whampoa. "I do not doubt that when

his parent—or whoever it was—arranged for his English education, he entered school under his true name, which might well be rendered into English as Solomon Haslam. The first name is an exact translation; the second, an English name reasonably close to Usman. And there is nothing impossible about some wealthy Borneo raja or sharif sending his child to an English school—unusual, yes, but it has certainly happened in this case. And the son, following in his father's footsteps, has practised piracy, which we know is the profession of half the population of the Islands. At the same time, he has developed business interests in England and Singapore—which he has now decided to cut."

"And stolen another man's wife, to carry her off to his pirate lair?" scoffs Balestier. "Oh, but this is beyond reason—"

"Hardly more unreasonable than to suppose that Don Solomon Haslam, if he were *not* a pirate, would kidnap an English lady," says Whampoa.

"Oh, but you're only guessing!" cries Catchick. "A coincidence in names—"

"And in times. Solomon Haslam went to England three years ago—and Suleiman Usman vanished at the same time."

That silenced them, and then Brooke says slowly:

"It might be true, but if it was, what difference does it make, after all—"

"Some, I think. For if it is true you need look no farther than Borneo for the *Sulu Queen*'s destination. Maludu lies north, beyond the Papar river, in unexplored country. He may go there, or take cover among his allies on the Seribas river or the Batang Lupar—"

"If he does, he's done for!" cries Brooke excitedly. "I can bottle him there, or anywhere between Kuching and Serikei Point!"

Whampoa sluiced down some more sherry. "It may not be so easy. Suleiman Usman was a man of power; his fort at Maludu was accounted impregnable, and he could draw at need on the great pirate fleets of the Lanun and Balagnini and Maluku of Gillalao. You have fought pirates, your majesty, I know—but hardly as many as these."

"I'd fight every sea-robber from Luzon to Sumatra in this

quarrel," says Brooke. "And beat 'em. And swing Suleiman Usman from the *Dido's* foretop at the end of it."

"If he is the man you are looking for," says Catchick. "Whampoa may be wrong."

"Undoubtedly, I make frequent mistakes, in my poor ignorance," says Whampoa. "But not, I think, in this. I have further proof. No one among us, I believe, has ever seen Suleiman Usman of Maludu—or met anyone who has? No. However, my agents have been diligent tonight, and I can now supply a brief description. About thirty years old, over two yards in height, of stout build, unmarked features. Is it enough?"

It was enough for one listener, at any rate. Why not—it was no more incredible than all the rest of the events of that fearful night; indeed, it seemed to confirm them, as Whampoa pointed out.

"I would suggest also," says he, "that we need look no further for an explanation of the attack by Black-faces on Mr Flashman," and they all turned to stare at me. "Tell me, sir—you dined at a restaurant, before the attack? The Temple of Heaven, as I understand—"

"By G-d!" I croaked. "It was Haslam who recommended it!"

Whampoa shrugged. "Remove the husband, and the most ardent pursuer is disposed of. Such an assassination might be difficult to arrange, for an ordinary Singapore merchant, but to a pirate, with his connections with the criminal community, it would be simple."

"The cowardly swine!" cries Brooke. "Well, his ruffians were out of luck, weren't they? The pursuer's ready for the chase, ain't you, Flashman? And between us we'll make this scoundrel Usman or Haslam rue the day he dared to cast eyes on an Englishwoman. We'll smoke him out, and his foul crew with him. Oh, let me alone for that!"

I wasn't thinking that far ahead, I confess, and I didn't know James Brooke at this moment for anything but a smiling madman in a pilot-cap, with an odd taste in friends and followers. If I'd known him for what he truly was, I'd have been in an even more agitated condition when our discussion finally ended, and I was helped up Whampoa's staircase to a magnificent bed-chamber, and tucked in between silk sheets, bandaged shoulder and all, by his stewards and Dr Mackenzie. I hardly knew where I was; my mind was in a perfect spin, but when they'd left me, and I was lying staring up at the thin rays of sunlight that were breaking through the screens—for it was now full day outside—there broke at last the sudden dreadful realisation of what had happened. Elspeth was gone; she was in the clutches of a nigger pirate, who could take her beyond the maps of Europeans, to some horrible stronghold where she'd be his slave, where we could never hope to find her—my beautiful, idiot Elspeth, with her creamy skin and golden hair and imbecile smile and wonderful body, lost to me, forever.

I ain't sentimental, but suddenly I could feel the tears running down my face, and I was muttering her name in the darkness, over and over, alone in my empty bed, where she ought to have been, all soft and warm and passionate—and just then there was a scratching at my door, and when it opened, there was Whampoa, bowing from his great height on the threshold. He came forward beside the bed, his hands tucked into his sleeves, and looked down at me. Was my shoulder, he asked, giving me great pain? I said it was agony.

"But no greater," says he, "than your torment of mind. That, too, nothing can alleviate. The loss you have suffered, of the loveliest of companions, is a deprivation which cannot but excite compassion in any man of feeling. I know that nothing can take the place of the beautiful golden lady, and that every thought of her must be a pang of the most exquisite agony. But as some small, poor consolation to your grief of mind and body, I humbly offer the best that my poor establishment provides." He said something in Chinese, and through the door, to my amazement, glided two of his little Chink girls, one in red silk, t'other in green. They came forward and stood either side of the bed, like voluptuous little dolls, and began to unbutton their dresses.

"These are White Tigress and Honey-and-Milk," says Whampoa. "To offer you the services of only one would have seemed an insulting comparison with the magic of your exquisite lady, therefore I send two, in the hope that quantity may be some trivial amend for a quality which they cannot hope to approach. Triflingly inadequate as they are, their presence may soothe your pains in some infinitesimal degree. They are skilful by our mean standards, but if their clumsiness and undoubted ugliness are offensive, you should beat them for their correction and your pleasure. Forgive my presumption in presenting them."

He bowed, retreating, and the door closed behind him just as the two dresses dropped to the floor with a gentle swish, and two girlish giggles sounded in the dimness.

You must never refuse an Oriental's hospitality, you know. It doesn't do, or they get offended; you just have to buckle to and pretend it's exactly what you wanted, whether you like it or not.

*   *   *

For four days I was confined in Whampoa's house with my gashed shoulder, recuperating, and I've never had a more bliss-fully ruinous convalescence in my life. It would have been interesting, had there been time, to see whether my wound healed before Whampoa's solicitous young ladies killed me with their attentions; my own belief is that I would have expired just about the time the stitches were ready to come out. As it was, my confinement was cut short by the arrival and swift departure of H.M.S. *Dido*, commanded by one Keppel, R.N.; willy-nilly, I had to sail with her, staggering aboard still weak with loss of blood, et cetera, clutching the gangway not so much for support as to prevent my being wafted away by the first puff of breeze.

You see, it was taken for granted that as a devoted husband and military hero, I was in a sweat to be off in quest of my abducted spouse and her pirate ravisher—that was one of the disadvantages of life on the frontiers of Empire in the earlies, that you were expected to do your own avenging and recovering, with such assistance as the authorities might lend. Not my style at all; left to old Flash it would have been a case of tooling round to the local constabulary, reporting a kidnapped wife, leaving my name and address, and letting 'em get on with it. After all, it's what they're paid for, and why else was I stump-ing up sevenpence in the pound income tax?

I said as much to old Morrison, thinking it was the kind of view that would appeal to him, but all I got for my pains was tears and curses.

"You're tae blame!" whimpers he, for he was far too reduced to bawl; he looked fit to pass away, his eyes sunk and his cheeks blenched, but still full of spite against me. "If you had been daein' your duty as a husband, this would never have happened. Oh, Goad, ma puir wee lamb! My wee bit lassie—and you, where were ye? Whoorin' away in some hoose o' ill fame, like enough, while—"

"Nothing of the sort!" cries I indignantly. "I was at a Chinese restaurant," at which he set up a great wail, burying his head in the bed-clothes and bawling about his wee bairn.

"Ye'll bring her back!" he croaks presently. "Ye'll save her —you're a military man, wi' decorations, an' she's the wife o' your boozum, so she is! Say ye'll bring her back tae her puir auld faither? Aye, ye'll dae that—ye're a guid lad, Harry—ye'll no' fail her." And more in the same nauseating vein, interspersed with curses that he had ever set foot outside Glasgow. No doubt it was very pitiable, and if I'd been less disturbed myself and hadn't despised the little swine so heartily, I might have felt sorry for him. I doubt it, though.

I left him lamenting, and went off to nurse my shoulder and reflect gloomily that there was no help for it—I would have to be first in the field when the pursuit got under way. The fellow Brooke, who—for reasons that I couldn't fathom just then— seemed to have taken on himself the planning of the expedition, obviously took it for granted that I would go, and when Keppel arrived and agreed at once to put *Dido* and her crew into the business, there was no hanging back any longer.

Brooke was in a great lather of impatience to be away, and stamped and ground his teeth when Keppel said it would be at least three days before he could sail; he had treasure from Calcutta to unload, and must lay in stores and equipment for the expedition. "It'll be river fighting, I dare say," says he, yawning; he was a dry, likely-looking chap with blazing red hair and sleepy, humorous eyes.[18] "Cutting out, jungle work, ambushes, that sort of thing? Ye-es, well, we know what happens if you rush into it at half-cock—remember how Belcher ripped the bottom out of *Samarang* on a shoal last year? I'll have to restow *Dido*'s ballast, for one thing, and take on a couple of extra launches."

"I can't wait for that!" cries Brooke. "I must get to Kuching, for news of this villain Suleiman and to get my people and boats together. I hear *Harlequin*'s been sighted; I'll go ahead in her—Hastings will take me when I tell him how fearfully urgent it is. We must run down this scoundrel and free Mrs Flashman without a moment's delay!"

"You're sure it'll be Borneo, then?" says Keppel.

"It has to be!" cried Brooke. "No ship from the south in the last two days has sighted him. Depend upon it, he'll either run for Maludu or the rivers."

It was all Greek to me, and sounded horribly active and risky, but everyone deferred to Brooke's judgement, and next day off he sailed in *Harlequin*. Because of my wound I was to rest in Singapore until *Dido* sailed two days later, but perforce I must be down at the quay when Brooke was rowed out with his motley gang by *Harlequin*'s boat crew. He seized my hand at parting.

"By the time you reach Kuching, we'll be ready to run up the flag and run out the guns!" cried he. "You'll see! And don't fret yourself, old fellow—we shall have your dear lady back safe and sound before you know it. Just you limber up that sword-arm, and between us we'll give these dogs a bit of your Afghan sauce. Why, in Sarawak we do this sort of thing before breakfast! Don't we, Paitingi? Eh, Mackenzie?"

I watched them go—Brooke in the stern with his pilot-cap tipped at a rakish angle, laughing and slapping his knee in eagerness; the enormous Paitingi at his elbow, the black-bearded Mackenzie with his medical bag, and the other hard-cases disposed about the boat, with the hideous little Jingo in his loin-cloth nursing his blow-pipe spear. That was the fancy-dress crowd that I was to accompany on what sounded like a most hair-raising piece of madness—it was a dreadful prospect, and on the heels of my apprehension came fierce resentment at the frightful luck that was about to pitch me headlong into the stew again. D--n Elspeth, for a hare-brained, careless, wanton, ogling little slut, and d--n Solomon for a horny thief who hadn't the decency to be content with women of his own beastly colour, and d--n this officious, bloodthirsty lunatic Brooke—who the d---l was he to go busybodying about uninvited, dragging me into his idiot enterprises? What right had he, and why did everyone defer to him as though he was some mixture of God and the Duke of Wellington?

I found out, the evening *Dido* sailed, after I had taken my fond farewells—whining and shouting with Morrison, stately and generous with the hospitable Whampoa, and ecstatically frenzied in the last minute of packing with my dear little nurses. I went aboard almost on my hands and knees, as I've said, with Stuart helping me, for he had stayed behind to bear me company and execute some business for Brooke. It was while we were at the stern rail of the corvette, watching the Singapore islands sinking black into the fiery sunset sea, that I dropped some chance remark about his crazy commander—as you know, I still had precious little idea who he was, and I must have said so, for Stuart started round, staring at me.

"Who's J.B.?" he cried. "You can't mean it! Who's J.B.? You don't know? Why, he's the greatest man in the East, that's all! You're not serious—bless me, how long have you been in Singapore?"

"Not long enough, evidently. All I know is that he and you and your . . . ah, friends . . . rescued me mighty handy the other night, and that since then he's very kindly taken charge of operations to do the same for my wife."

He blessed himself again, heartily, and enlightened me with frightening enthusiasm.

"J.B.—His Royal Highness James Brooke—is the King of Sarawak, that's who he is. I thought the whole world had heard of the White Raja! Why, he's the biggest thing in these parts since Raffles—bigger, even. He's the law, the prophet, the Grand Panjandrum, the *tuan besar**—the whole kitboodle! He's the scourge of every pirate and brigand on the Borneo coast—the best fighting seaman since Nelson, for my money—he tamed Sarawak, which was the toughest nest of rebels and head-hunters this side of Papua, he's its protector, its ruler, and to the natives, its saint! Why, they worship him down yonder—and more power to 'em, for he's the truest friend, the fairest judge, and the noblest, whitest man in the whole wide world! *That's* who J.B. is."

* Great lord.

"My word, I'm glad he happened along," says I. "I didn't know we had a colony in—Sarawak, d'you call it?"

"We haven't. It's not British soil. J.B. is nominal governor for the Sultan of Brunei—but it's his kingdom, not Queen Victoria's. How did he get it? Why, he sailed in there four years ago, after the d-mfool Company Army pensioned him off for overstaying his furlough. He'd bought this brig, the *Royalist*, you see, with some cash his guv'nor left him, and just set off on his own account." He laughed, shaking his head. "G-d, we were mad! There were nineteen of us, with one little ship, and six six-pounder guns, and we got a kingdom with it! J.B. delivered the native people from slavery, drove out their oppressors, gave 'em a proper government—and now, with a few little boats, his loyal natives, and those of us who've survived, he's fighting single-handed to drive piracy out of the Islands and make them safe for honest folk."[19]

"Very commendable," says I. "But isn't that the East India Company's job—or the navy's?"

"Bless you, they couldn't even begin it!" cries he. "There's barely a British squadron in all these enormous waters—and the pirates are numbered in tens upon tens of thousands. I've seen fleets of five hundred praus and bankongs—those are their warboats—cruising together, crammed with fighting men and cannon, and behind them hundreds of miles of coastline in burning ruin—towns wiped out, thousands slaughtered, women carried off as slaves, every peaceful vessel plundered and sunk—I tell you, the Spanish Main was nothing to it! They leave a trail of destruction and torture and abomination wherever they go. They set our navy and the Dutch at defiance, and hold the Islands in terror—they have a slave-market at Sulu where hundreds of human beings are bought and sold daily; even the kings and rajas pay them tribute—when they aren't pirates themselves. Well, J.B. don't like it, and he means to put a stop to it."

"Hold on, though—what can he do, if even the navy's powerless?"

"He's J.B.," says Stuart, simply, with that drunk, smug look you see on a child's face when his father mends a toy. "Of course, he gets the navy to help—why, we had three navy vessels at Murdu in February, when he wiped out the Sumatra

robbers—but his strength is with the honest native peoples—
some of 'em were once pirates themselves, and head-hunters,
like the Sea Dyaks, until J.B. showed 'em better. He puts spirit
into them, bullies and wheedles the rajas, gathers news of the
pirates, and when they least expect it, takes his expeditions
against their forts and harbours, fights 'em to a standstill, burns
their ships, and either makes 'em swear to keep the peace, or
else! That's why everyone in Singapore jumps when he whistles
—why, how long d'you think it would have taken them to do
anything about your missus—months, years even? But J.B. says
"Go!" and don't they just! And if I'd gone along Beach Road
this morning looking for people to bet that J.B. couldn't rescue
her, good as new, and destroy this swine Suleiman Usman—well,
I'd not have got a single taker, at a hundred to one. He'll do it,
all right. You'll see."

"But why?" says I, without thinking, and he frowned. "I
mean," I added, "he hardly knows me—and he's never even met
my wife—but the way he's gone about this, you'd think we were
—well, his dearest relatives."

"Well, that's his way, you know. Anything for a friend—and
with a lady involved, of course, that makes it all the more
urgent—to him. He's a bit of a knight-errant, is J.B. Besides, he
likes you."

"What? He don't even know me."

"Don't he, though! Why, I remember when we got the news
of the great deeds you'd done at Kabul, J.B. talked of nothing
else for days, read all the papers, kept exclaiming over your
defence of Piper's Fort. 'That's the man for me!' he kept saying. 'By Jingo, what wouldn't I give to have him out here! We'd
see the last pirate out of the China Sea between us!' Well, now
he's got you—I shouldn't wonder if he doesn't move heaven
and earth to keep you."

You can guess how this impressed me. I could see, of course,
that J.B. was just the man for the task in hand—if anyone could
bring Elspeth off, more or less undamaged, it was probably he,
for he seemed to be the same kind of desperate, stick-at-nothing
adventurer I'd known in Afghanistan—wild men like Georgie
Broadfoot and Sekundar Burnes. The trouble with fellows like
those is that they're d----d dangerous to be alongside; it would

be capital if I could arrange it that Brooke went off a-rescuing while I stayed safe in the rear, hallooing encouragement, but my wound was healing nicely, b---t it, and the outlook was disquieting.

It was a question which was still vexing me four days later when the *Dido*, under sweeps, came gliding over a sea like blue glass to the mouth of the Kuching river, and I saw for the first time those brilliant golden beaches washed with foam, the low green flats of mangrove creeping to the water's edge among the little islands, the palm-fringed creeks, and in the distant southern haze the mountains of Borneo.

"Paradise!" exclaims Stuart, breathing in the warm air, "and I don't give a d--n if I never see Dover cliffs again. Look at it— half a million square miles of the loveliest land in the world, unexplored, except for this little corner. Sarawak's where civilisation begins and ends, you know—go a day's march in yonder"— he pointed towards the mountains—"and if you're still alive you'll be among head-hunters who've never seen a white man. Ain't it capital, though?"

I couldn't say it was. The river, as we went slowly up it, was broad enough, and the land green and fertile, but it had that steamy look that spells fever, and the air was hot and heavy. We passed by several villages, some of them partly built over the water on stilts, with long, primitive thatched houses; the water itself was aswarm with canoes and small boats, manned by squat, ugly, grinning little men like Jingo; I don't suppose one of them stood more than five feet, but they looked tough as teak. They wore simple loin-cloths, with rings round their knees, and head-cloths; some had black and white feathers in their hair. The women were fairer than the men, although no taller, and decidedly good-looking, in an impudent, pug-nosed way; they wore their hair long, down their backs, and went naked except for kilts, swinging their bums and udders in a way that did your heart good to see. (They couple like stoats, by the way, but only with men of proved bravery. In a country where the usual engagement ring is a human head, it follows that you have to be bloodthirsty in order to get your muttons.)

"Sea Dyaks," says Stuart. "The bravest, cheeriest folk you'll ever see—fight like tigers, cruel as the grave, but loyal as Swiss.

Listen to 'em jabber—that's the coast *lingua franca*, part Malay, but with Portuguese, French, Dutch, and English thrown in. *Amiga sua!*" cries he, waving to one of the boatmen—that, I learned, means "my friend", which gives you some notion.

Sarawak, as Stuart said, might be the civilised corner of Borneo, but as we drew closer to Kuching you could see that it was precious like an armed camp. There was a huge log boom across the river, which had to be swung open so that *Dido* could warp through, and on the low bluffs either side there were gun emplacements, with cannon peeping through the earthworks; there were cannon, too, on the three strange craft at anchor inside the boom—they were like galleys, with high stern and forecastles, sixty or seventy feet long, with their great oars resting in the water like the legs of some monstrous insect.

"War praus," cries Stuart. "By Jove, there's something up—those are Lundu boats. J.B.'s mustering his forces with a vengeance!"

We rounded a bend, and came in sight of Kuching proper; it wasn't much of a place, just a sprawling native town, with a few Swiss cottages on the higher ground, but the river was jammed with ships and boats of every description—at least a score of praus and barges, light sailing cutters, launches, canoes, and even a natty little paddle-steamer. The bustle and noise were tremendous, and as *Dido* dropped anchor in mid-stream she was surrounded by swarms of little boats, from one of which the enormous figure of Paitingi Ali came swinging up to the deck, to present himself to Keppel, and then come over to us.

"Aye, weel," says he, in that astonishing accent which sounded so oddly with his occasional pious Muslim exclamations. "He was right again. The Praise tae the One."

"What d'ye mean?" cries Stuart.

"A spy-boat came in frae Budraddin yesterday. A steam-brig —which cannae be any other than the *Sulu Queen*—put into Batang Lupar four days ago, and went upriver. Budraddin's watching the estuary, but there's nae fear she'll come out again, for the word along the coast is that the great Suleiman Usman is back, and has gone up tae Fort Linga tae join Sharif Jaffir. He's in there, a' richt; a' we have tae do is gang in an' tak' him."

"Huzza!" roars Stuart, capering and seizing his hand. "Good

133

old J.B.! Borneo he said it would be, and Borneo it is!" He swung to me. "You hear that, Flashman—it means we know where your lady is, and that kidnapping rascal, too! J.B. guessed exactly right—now do you believe that he's the greatest man in the East?"

"Will ye tell me how he does it?" growled Paitingi. "If I didnae ken he was a guid Protestant I'd say he was in league wi' Shaitan. Come awa'—he's up at the hoose, gey pleased wi' himsel'. Bismillah! Perhaps when he's told you in person he'll be less insufferable."

But when we went ashore to Brooke's house, "The Grove", as it was called, the great man hardly referred to Paitingi's momentous news—I discovered later that this was delicacy on his part; he didn't want to distress me by even talking about Elspeth's plight. Instead, when we had been conducted to that great shady bungalow on its eminence, commanding a view of the teeming river and landing-places, he sat us down with glasses of arrack punch, and began to talk, of all things, about— roses.

"I'm goin' to make 'em grow here if it kills me," says he. "Imagine that slope down to the river below us, covered with English blooms; think of warm evenings in the dusk, and the perfume filling the verandah. By George, if I could raise Norfolk apples as well, that would be perfect—great, red beauties like the ones that grow on the roadside by North Walsham, what? You can keep your mangoes and paw-paws, Stuart—what wouldn't I give for an honest old apple, this minute! But I might manage the roses, one day." He jumped up. "Come and see my garden, Flashman—I promise you won't see another like it in Borneo, at any rate!"

So he took me round his place, pointing out his jasmine and sundals and the rest, exclaiming about their night scents, and suddenly snatching up a trowel and falling on some weeds. "These confounded Chinese gardeners!" cries he. "I'd be better served by Red Indians, I believe. But I suppose it's asking too much to expect," he cries, trowelling away, "that a people as filthy, ugly, and ungraceful as the Chinks should have any feeling for flowers. Mind you, they're industrious and cheery, but that ain't the same."

He chattered on, pointing out how his house was built carefully on palm piles to defy the bugs and damp, and telling me how he had come to design it. "We'd had the deuce of a scrap with Lundu head-hunters just across the river yonder, and were licking our wounds in a dirty little kampong, waiting for 'em to attack again—it was evening, and we were out of water altogether, and pretty used up, down to our last ounces of powder, too—and I thought to myself, what you need, J.B. my boy, is an easy chair and an English newspaper and a vase of roses on the table. It seemed such a splendid notion—and I resolved that I'd make myself a house, with just those things, so that wherever I went in Borneo, it would always be here to return to." He waved at the house. "And there she is—all complete, except for the roses. I'll get those in time."

It was true enough; his big central room, with the bedrooms arranged round it, and an opening on to his front verandah, was for all the world like a mixture of drawing-room and gun-room at home, except that the furniture was mostly bamboo. There were easy chairs, and old copies of *The Times* and *Post* neatly stacked, couches, polished tables, an Axminster, flowers in vases, and all manner of weapons and pictures on the walls.

"If ever I want to forget wars and pirates and fevers and ong-ong-ongs—that's my own word for anything Malay, you know—I just sit down and read about how it rained in Bath last year, or how some rascal was jailed for poaching at Exeter Assizes," says he. "Even potato prices in Lancashire will do—oh, I say . . . I'd meant to put that away . . ."

I'd stopped to look at a miniature on the table, of a most peachy blonde girl, and Brooke jumped up and reached out towards it. I seemed to know the face. "Why," says I, "that's Angie Coutts, surely?"

"You know her?" cries he, and he was pink to the gills, and right out of countenance for once. "I have never had the honour of meeting her," he went on, in a hushed, stuffed way, "but I have long admired her, for her enlightened opinions, and unsparing championship of worthy causes." He looked at the miniature like a contemplative frog. "Tell me— is she as . . . as . . . well—ah—as her portrait suggests?"

"She's a stunner, if that's what you mean," says I, for like every other grown male in London I, too, had admired little Angie, though not entirely for her enlightened opinions—more for the fact that she had a superb complexion, tits like footballs, and two million in the bank, really. I'd taken a loving fumble at her myself, during blind-man's-buff at a party in Stratton Street, but she'd simply stared straight ahead of her and dislocated my thumb. Wasteful little prude.[20]

"Perhaps, one of these days, when I return to England, you will present me," says he, gulping, and shovelled her picture into a drawer. Well, well, thinks I, who'd have thought it: the mad pirate-killer and rose-fancier, spoony on Angie Coutts's picture —I'll bet that every time he contemplates it the local Dyak lasses have to scamper for cover.

I must have said something to this effect, in my tasteful way, that same evening to Stuart, no doubt with my lewd Flashy nudge and leer, but he was such an innocent that he just shook his head and sighed deeply.

"Miss Burdett-Coutts?" says he. "Poor old J.B. He has told me of his deep regard for her, although he's a very secret man about such things. I dare say they'd make a splendid match, but it can't be, of course—even if he realised his ambition to meet her."

"Why not?" says I. "He's a likely chap, and just the kind to fire a romantic piece like young Angie. Why, they'd go like duck and green peas." Kindly old match-maker Flash, you see.

"Impossible," says Stuart, and then he went red in the face and hesitated. "You see—it's a shocking thing—but J.B. can never marry—it wouldn't do, at all."

Hollo, thinks I, he ain't one of the Dick's hatband brigade, surely?—I'd not have thought it.

"It is never mentioned, of course," says Stuart, uncomfortably, "but it is as well you should know—in case, in conversation, you unwittingly made any reference that might . . . well, be wounding. It was in Burma, you see, when he was in the army. He received an . . . incapacitating injury in battle. It was put about that it was a bullet in the lung . . . but in fact . . . well, it wasn't."

"Good G-d, you don't mean to say," cries I, genuinely appalled, "that he got his knocker shot off?"

"Let's not think about it," says he, but I can tell you I went about wincing for the rest of the evening. Poor old White Raja —I mean, I'm a callous chap enough, but there are some tragedies that truly wring the heart. Mad about that delectable little bouncer Angie Coutts, despot of a country abounding with the juiciest of dusky flashtails just itching for him to exercise the droit de seigneur, and there he was with a broken firing-pin. I don't know when I've been more deeply moved. Still, if J.B. was the first man in to rescue Elspeth, she'd be safe enough.[21]

It was an appropriate thought, for that same evening, after dinner at The Grove, we held the council at which Brooke announced his plan of operations. It followed a dinner as formal in its way as any I've ever attended—but that was Brooke all over: when we had our pegs on the verandah beforehand he was laughing and sky-larking, playing leap-frog with Stuart and Crimble and even the dour Paitingi, the bet being that he could jump over them one after another with a glass in one hand, and not spill a drop—but when the bell sounded, everyone quieted down, and filed silently into his great room.

I can still see it, Brooke at the head of the table in his big armchair, stiff in his white collar and carefully-tied black neckercher, with black coat and ruffled cuffs, the eager brown face grave for once, and the only thing out of place his untidy black curls—he could never get 'em to lie straight. On one side of him was Keppel, in full fig of uniform dress coat and epaulette, with his best black cravat, looking sleepy and solemn; Stuart and I in the cleanest ducks we could find; Charlie Wade, Keppel's lieutenant; Paitingi Ali, very brave in a tunic of dark plaid trimmed with gold and with a great crimson sash, and Crimble, another of Brooke's lieutenants, who absolutely had a frock coat and fancy weskit. There was a Malay steward behind each chair, and over in the corner, silent but missing nothing, the squint-faced Jingo; even he had exchanged his loin-cloth for a silver sarong, with hornbill feathers in his hair and decorating the shaft of his *sumpitan** standing handy against the wall. I never saw him without it, or the little bamboo quiver of his beastly darts.

I don't remember much of the meal, except that the food was

* Blowpipe.

good and the wine execrable, and that conversation consisted of Brooke lecturing interminably; like most active men, he had all the makings of a thoroughgoing bore.

"There shan't be a missionary in Borneo if I can help it," I remember him saying, "for there are only two kinds, bad ones and Americans. The bad ones ram Christianity down the natives' throats and tell them their own gods are false—"

"Which they are," says Keppel quietly.

"Of course, but a gentleman doesn't tell 'em so," says Brooke. "The Yankees have the right notion; they devote themselves to medicine and education, and don't talk religion or politics. And they don't treat natives as inferiors—that's where we've gone wrong in India," says he, wagging his finger at me, as though I had framed British policy. "We've made them conscious of their inferiority, which is a great folly. After all, if you've a weaker younger brother, you *encourage* him to think he can run as fast as you can, or jump as far without a race, don't you? He *knows* he can't, but that don't matter. In the same way, natives *know* they're inferior, but they'll love you all the better if they think you are unconscious of it."

"Well, you may be right," says Charlie Wade, who was Irish, "but I don't for the life of me see how you can ever expect 'em to grow up, at that rate, or achieve any self-respect at all."

"You can't," says Brooke briskly. "No Asiatic is fit to govern, anyway."

"And Europeans are?" says Paitingi, snorting.

"Only to govern Asiatics," says Brooke. "A glass of wine with you, Flashman. But I'll give you this, Paitingi—you can rule Asiatics only by living among them. You cannot govern them from London, or Paris, or Lisbon—"

"Aye, but Dundee, now?" says Paitingi, stroking his red beard, and when the roar of laughter had died down Brooke cries:

"Why, you old heathen, you have never been nearer to Dundee than Port Said! Observe," says he to me, "that in old Paitingi you have the ultimate flowering of a mixture of east and west— an Arab-Malay father and a Caledonian mother. Ah, the cruel fate of the half-caste—he has spent fifty years trying to reconcile the Kirk with the Koran."

"They're no' that different," says Paitingi, "an' at least they're baith highly superior tae the Book o' Common Prayer."

I was interested to see the way they railed at each other, as only very close friends do. Brooke obviously had an immense respect for Paitingi Ali; however, now that the talk had touched on religion, he began to hold forth again on an interminable prose about how he had recently written a treatise against Article 90 of the "Oxford Tracts", whatever they were, which lasted to the end of the meal. Then, with due solemnity, he proposed the Queen, which was drunk sitting down, Navy fashion, and while the rest of us talked and smoked, Brooke went through a peculiar little ceremony which, I suppose, explained better than anything else the hold he had on his native subjects.

All through the meal, a most curious thing had been happening. While the courses and wine had come with all due ceremony, and we had been buffing in, I'd noticed that every few minutes a Malay, or Dyak, or half-breed would come into the room, touch Brooke's hand as they passed his chair, and then go to squat near the wall by Jingo. No one paid them any notice; they seemed to be all sorts, from a near-naked beggarly rascal to a well-dressed Malay in gold sarong and cap, but they were all armed—I learned later that it was a great insult to come into the White Raja's presence without your *krees*, which is the strange, wavy-bladed knife of the people.

In any event, while the rest of us gassed, Brooke turned his chair, beckoned each suppliant in turn, and talked with him quietly in Malay. One after another they came to hunker down beside him, putting their cases or telling their tales, while he listened, leaning forward with elbows on knees, nodding attentively. Then he would pronounce, quietly, and they would touch hands again and go; the rest of us might as well not have been there. When I asked Stuart about it later, he said: "Oh, that's J.B. ruling Sarawak. Simple, ain't it?"[22]

When the last native had gone Brooke sat in a reverie for a moment or two, and then swung abruptly to the table.

"No singing tonight," says he. "Business. Let's have that map, Crimble." We crowded round, the lamps were turned up, shining on the ring of sunburned faces under the wreath of cigar smoke, and Brooke tapped the table. I felt my belly muscles tightening.

"We know what's to do, gentlemen," cries he, "and I'll answer that the task is one that strikes a spark in the heart of every one of us. A fair and gentle lady, the beloved wife of one here, is in the hands of a bloody pirate; she is to be saved, and he destroyed. By God's grace, we know where the quarry lies, not sixty miles from where we sit, on the Batang Lupar, the greatest lair of robbers in these Islands, save Mindanao itself. Look at it" —his finger stabbed the map—"first, Sharif Jaffir and his slaver fleet, at Fort Linga; beyond him, the great stronghold of Sharif Sahib at Patusan; farther on, at Undup, the toughest nut of all— the fortress of the Skrang pirates under Sharif Muller. Was ever a choicer collection of villains on one river? Add to 'em now the arch-d---l, Suleiman Usman, who has stolen away Mrs Flashman in dastardly fashion. She is the key to his vile plan, gentlemen, for he knows we cannot leave her in his clutches an hour longer than we must." He gave my shoulder a manly squeeze; everyone else was carefully avoiding my eye. "He realises that chivalry will not permit us to wait. You know him, Flashman; is this not how his scheming mind will reason?"

I didn't doubt it, and said so. "He's made a fortune in the City, too, and plays a d----d dirty game of single-wicket," I added, and Brooke nodded sympathetically.

"He knows I dare not delay, even if it means going after him with only the piecemeal force I have here—fifty praus and two thousand men, a third of which I must leave to garrison Kuching. Even so, Usman knows I must take at least a week to prepare—a week in which he can muster his praus and savages, outnumbering us ten to one, and make ready his ambushes along the Lupar, confident that we'll stumble into them half-armed and ill-prepared—"

"Stop it, before I start wishin' I was on their side," mutters Wade, and Brooke laughed in his conceited fashion and threw back his black curls.

"Why, he'll wipe us out to the last man!" cries he. "That's his beastly scheme. That," he smiled complacently round at us, "is what Suleiman Usman thinks."

Paitingi sighed. "But, of course, he's wrong, the puir heathen," says he with heavy sarcasm. "Ye'll tell us how."

"You may wager the Bank to a tinker's dam he's wrong!" cries Brooke, his face alive with swank and excitement. "He expects us in a week—he shall have us in two days! He expects us with two-thirds of our strength—well, we'll show him all of it! I'll strip Kuching of every man and gun and leave it defence-less—I'll stake everything on this throw!" He beamed at us, bursting with confidence. "Surprise, gentlemen—that's the thing! I'll catch the rascal napping before he's laid his infernal toils! What d'you say?"

I know what I'd have said, if I'd been talking just then. I'd never heard such lunacy in my life, and neither had the others by the look of them. Paitingi snorted.

"Ye're mad! It'll no' do."

"I know, old fellow," grins Brooke. "What then?"

"Ye've said it yersel'! There's a hundred mile o' river between Skrang creek and the sea, every yard o' it hotchin' wi' pirates, slavers, *nata-hutan*,* an' heid-hunters by the thousand, every side-stream crawlin' wi' war-praus an' bankongs, tae say nothin' o' the forts! Surprise, says you? By Eblis, I ken who'll be surprised! We've done oor share o' river-fightin', but this—" he waved a great red hand. "Withoot a well-fitted expedition in strength—man, it's fatal folly."

"He's right, J.B.," says Keppel. "Anyway, even the poor force we've got couldn't be ready in two days—"

"Yes, it can, though. In one, if necessary."

"Well, even then—you might catch Fort Linga unprepared, but after that they'll be ready for you upriver."

"Not at the speed I'll move!" cries Brooke. "The messenger of disaster from Linga to Patusan will have us on his heels! We'll carry all before us, all the way to Skrang if need be!"

"But Kuching?" Stuart protested. "Why, the Balagnini or those beastly Lanun could sweep it up while our back was turned."

"Never!" Brooke was exultant. "They won't know it's naked! And suppose they did—why, we'd just have to begin all over again, wouldn't we? You talk about the odds against us on the

* "Wood devils", i.e. users of the *sumpitan*.

141

Lupar—were they a whit better at Seribas, or Murdu? Were they any better when you and I, George, took all Sarawak with six guns and a leaky pleasure-yacht? I tell you, gentlemen, I can have this thing over and done in a fortnight! D'you doubt me? Have I ever failed, and will I fail now, when there is a poor, weak creature crying out for rescue, and I, a Briton, hear that cry? When I have the stout hearts and good keels that will do the thing, and crush this swarm of hornets, too, before they can scatter on their accursed errands? What? I tell you, all the Queen's ships and all the Queen's men could not bring such a chance together again,[23] and I mean to take it!"

I'd never seen it before, although I've seen it more times than I care to count since—one man, mad as a hatter and drunk with pride, sweeping sane heads away against their better judgement. Chinese Gordon could do it, and Yakub Beg the Kirghiz; so could J. E. B. Stuart, and that almighty maniac George Custer. They and Brooke could have formed a club. I can see him still: erect, head thrown back, eyes blazing, like the worst kind of actor mouthing the Agincourt speech to a crowd of yokels in a tent theatre in the backwoods. I don't believe he convinced them—Stuart and Crimble, perhaps, but not Keppel and the others; certainly not Paitingi. But they couldn't resist him, or the force that beat out of him. He was going to have his way, and they knew it. They stood silent; Keppel, I think, was embarrassed. And then Paitingi says:

"Aye. Ye'll want me to have charge o' the spy-boats, I suppose?"

That settled it, and at once Brooke quieted down, and they set to earnestly to discuss ways and means, while I sat back contemplating the horror of the whole thing, and wondering how I could weasel out of it. Plainly they were going to catastrophe, lugging me along with them, and not a thing to be done about it. I turned over a dozen schemes in my mind, from feigning insanity to running away; finally, when all but Brooke had hurried off to begin the preparations which were to take them all night and the following day, I had a feeble shot at turning him from his hare-brained purpose. Perhaps, I suggested diffidently, it might be possible to ransom Elspeth; I'd heard of such things being done among the Oriental pirates, and old Morrison was stiff with blunt which he'd be glad . . .

"What?" cries Brooke, his brow darkening. "Treat with these scoundrels? Never! I should not contemplate such—ah, but I see what it is!" He came over all compassionate, and laid a hand on my arm. "You are fearful for your dear one's safety, when battle is joined. You need have no such fear, old fellow; no harm will come to her."

Well, it was beyond me how he could guarantee that, but then he explained, and I give you my word that this is what he said. He sat me down in my chair and poured me a glass of arrack first.

"It is natural enough, Flashman, that you should believe this pirate's motives to be of the darkest kind . . . where your wife is concerned. Indeed, from what I have heard of her grace and charm of person, they are such as might well excite . . . ah, that is, they might awaken—well, unworthy passion—in an unworthy person, that is." He floundered a bit, and took a pull at his glass, wondering how to discuss the likelihood of her being rogered without causing me undue distress. At last he burst out:

"He won't do it!—I mean, that is—I cannot believe she will be . . . ill-used, in any way, if you follow me. I am confident that she is but a pawn in a game which he has planned with Machiavellian cunning, using her as a bait to destroy me. That," says this swollen-headed lunatic smugly, "is his true purpose, for he and his kind can know no safety while I live. His design is not principally against her, of that I am certain. For one thing, he is married already, you know. Oh, yes, I have gleaned much information in the past few days, and it's true—five years ago he took to wife the daughter of the Sultan of Sulu, and while Muslims are not, of course, monogamous," he went on earnestly, "there is no reason to suppose that their union was not a . . . a happy one." He took a turn round the room, while I gaped, stricken speechless. "So I'm sure your dear lady is perfectly safe from any . . . any . . . anything like that. Anything . . ." he waved his glass, sloshing arrack broadcast ". . . anything awful, you know."

Well, that is what he said, as I hope to die. I couldn't credit

143

my ears. For a moment I wondered if having his love-muscle shot off had affected his brain; then I realised that, in his utterly daft way, he was simply talking all this rubbish to reassure me. Possibly he thought I was so distraught that I'd be ready to believe anything, even that a chap with one wife would never think of bulling another. Maybe he even believed it himself.

"She will be restored to you . . ." he searched for a suitable word, and found one, "unblemished, you may be sure. Indeed, I am certain that her preservation must be his first concern, for he must know what a terrific retribution will follow if any harm should come to her, either in the violence of battle or . . . in any other way. And after all," says he, apparently quite struck with the thought, "he may be a pirate, but he has been educated as an English gentleman. I cannot believe that he is dead to all feelings of honour. Whatever he has become—here, let me fill your glass, old chap—we must remember that there was a time when he was, well . . . one of us. I think you can take comfort in that thought, what?"

*　　*　　*

[Extract from the diary of Mrs Flashman, August —, 1844]
I am now Beyond Hope, and *Utterly Desolate* in my Captivity, like the Prisoner of Chillon, except that he was in a dungeon and I am in a steamship, which I am sure is a *thousand times* worse, for at least in a dungeon one stays still, and is not conscious of being carried away far beyond the reach of Loving Friends! A week have I been in *durance*—nay, it seems like a Year!! I can only pine my *lost love*, and await in Terror whatever Fate is in store for me at the hands of my *heartless abductor*. My knees tremble at the thought and my heart fails me—how enviable does the lot of the Prisoner of Chillon seem (see Above), for no such Dread hung over *his* captivity, and at least he had mice to play with, laying their wrinkly wee noses in his hand in *sympathy*. Although to be sure I don't like mice, but no more than I don't like the Odious Native who brings my food, which I cannot endure to eat anyway, although there have been some Pleasant Fruits added to my diet the last day or two, when we came in

sight of land as I saw from my porthole. Is this *strange* and *hostile* tropic shore to be the Scene of my Captivity? Shall I be sold on Indian Soil? Oh, dear Father—and *kind, noble,* generous H., thou art lost to me forever!!

Yet even such loss is no worse than the Suspense which *wracks* my brain. Since the first *dreadful* day of my abduction I have not seen Don S., which at first I supposed was because he was so a prey to Shame and Remorse, that he could not look me *in the eye.* I pictured him, Restless on his Prow, torn by *pangs of conscience,* gnawing at his nails and Oblivious of his sailors' requests for directions, as the vessel plow'ed on heedless over the waves. Oh, how *well deserved* his Torment!—and yet it is *extremely strange,* after his Passionate Protestations, that he should Restrain himself for *seven whole days* from seeing me, the Object of his Madness. I don't understand it, for I don't believe he feels Remorse at all, and the affairs of his boat cannot take all his time, surely! Why, then, does the Cruel Wretch not come to *gloat* over his Helpless Prey, and Jeer at her *sorry condition,* for my white taffeta is now quite soiled, and so *oppressively hot* in the confines of my cabin, that I have perforce discarded it in favour of some of the native dresses called *sarongas,* which have been provided by the *creeping* little Chinese woman who waits upon me, a sallow creature, and not a word of English, tho' not as handless as some I've known. I have a *saronga* of red silk which is, I think, the most becoming, and another in blue and gold embroidery, quite pretty, but of course they are very *simple* and *slight,* and would not be the thing at all for European Wear, except in *déshabillé.* But to these am I *reduced,* and the left heel of my shoe broken, so I must put them both off, and no proper articles for *toilette,* and my hair a *positive* fright. Don. S. is a Brute and Beast, first to *wrench* me away, and then so heartlessly to *neglect* me in this sorry condition!

~~Post merid~~ P.M.

He came at last, and I am *distraught!* While I was repairing as best I might the ~~ravages~~ slight disorders in my appearance which my *cruel confinement* has wrought, and

trying how my *saronga* (the red one) might fold most elegantly—for it is an *excellent rule* that in all Circumstances a
Gentlewoman should make the best of things, and strive
to present a *collected appearance*—I was of a sudden Aware
of his Presence. To my Startled Protest, he replied with an
insinuating compliment on how well my *saronga* became
me, and such a Look of *ardent yearning* that I at once
regretted my poor discarded taffeta, fearing the *base ardour*
that the sight of me in Native Garb might kindle in him.
To my instant and repeated demands that I be taken Home
at once, and my Upbraidings for his *scandalous usage*
and *neglect* of me, he replied with the *utmost composure*
and odiously solicitous inquiries for my Comfort! I replied
with *icy disdain*. "Restore me instantly to my family, and
keep your tiresome comforts!" He received this rebuff
quite unabashed, and said I must put such hopes from my
mind forever.

"What!" I cried, "you will deny me even some suitable
clothing, and proper toilet articles, and a change of bed
linen every day, and a proper variety in diet, instead of
roast pork, of which I am *utterly tired*, and a thorough
airing and cleaning of my accommodation?" "No, no," he
protested, "these things you shall have, and whatever else
your heart desires, but as for returning to your family, it
is out of the question, for the *die is cast!*" "We shall see
about that, my lad!" I cried, masking the Terror which his
Grim and Unrelenting manner inspired in my Quaking
Bosom, and presenting a Bold Front, at which to my
astonishment he dropped to his knees, and taking my hand
—but with every sign of respect—he spoke in so *moving*
and *pleading* a manner, protesting his *worship*, and vowing
that when I returned his Love, he would make me a Queen
Indeed, and my lightest whim instantly obeyed, that I
could not but be *touched*. Seeing me weaken, he spoke
earnestly of the Kindness and Companionship which we
had shared, at which, despising my own Frailty, I was
moved to tears.

"Why, oh, why, Don S., did you have to spoil it all by
this *thoughtless* and *ungenteel* behaviour, and after such a

jolly cruise?" I cried. "It is most disobliging of you!" "I could not bear the torture of seeing you possessed by another!" cried he. I asked, "Why, ~~whom~~ who do you mean, Don S.?" "Your husband!" cries he, "but, by h——n, he shall be your husband no longer!" and springing up, he cried that my Spirit was as matchless as my Beauty, which he praised in terms that I cannot bring myself to *repeat*, although I dare say the compliment was kindly intended, and adding fiercely that he should *win me*, at whatever cost. Despite my struggles and reproaches, and *feeble cries* for an Aid which I knew could not be forthcoming, he repeatedly subjected me to the *assault* of his *salutes* upon my lips, so fervently that I *fainted* into a Merciful Oblivion for between five and ten minutes, after which, by the Intervention of Heaven, he was called on deck by one of his sailors, leaving me, with repeated oaths of his Fidelity, in a state of *perturbed delicacy*.

There is *still* no sign of pursuit by H., which I had so wildly hoped for. Am I, then, forgotten by those dearest to me, and is there *no hope* indeed? Am I doomed to be carried off forever, or will Don S. yet repent the intemperate regard for me—nay, for my mere Outward Show— which drove him to this *inconsiderate folly*? I pray it may be so, and hourly I lament—nay, I curse— that Fairness of Form and Feature of which I was once so vain. Ah, why could I not have been born *safe* and *plain* like my dearest sister Agnes, or our Mary, who is even less favoured, altho' to be sure her complection is none too bad, or............* Oh, sweet sisters three, gone beyond hope of recall! Could you but know, and pity me in my affliction! Where *is* H.? Don S. has sent down a great posy of flowers to my cabin, jungle blossoms, pretty but quite *gaudy*.
[End of extract, which passes belief for shamelessness, hypocrisy, and *unwarranted* conceit!—G. de R.]

* At this point a heavy deletion of two lines occurs in the manuscript, doubtless to excise some unflattering reference to Lady Flashman's third sister, Grizel de Rothschild, who edited the journal.

We dropped down Kuching river on the evening tide of the day following, a great convoy of ill-assorted boats gliding silently through the opened booms, and down between banks dark and feathery in the dusk to the open sea. How Brooke had done it I don't know—I dare say you can read in his journal, and Keppel's, how they armed and victualled and assembled their ramshackle war fleet of close on eighty vessels, loaded with the most unlikely crew of pirates, savages, and lunatics, and launched them on to the China Sea like a d----d regatta; I don't remember it too clearly myself, for all through a night and a day it had been bedlam along the Kuching wharves, in which, being new to the business, I'd borne no very useful part.

I have my usual disjointed memories of it, though. I remember the long war-praus with their steep sheers and forests of oars, being warped one after another into the jetty by sweating, squealing Malay steersmen, and the Raja's native allies pouring aboard—a chattering, half-naked horde of Dyaks, some in kilts and sarongs, others in loin-cloths and leggings, some in turbans, some with feathers in their hair, but all grinning and ugly as sin, loaded with their vile *sumpitan*-pipes and arrows, their *kreeses* and spears, all fit to frighten the French.

Then there were the Malay swordsmen who filled the sampans —big, flat-faced villains with muskets and the terrible, straight-bladed *kampilan* cleavers in their belts; the British tars in their canvas smocks and trousers and straw hats, their red faces grinning and sweating while they loaded *Dido*'s pinnace, singing "Whisky, Johnny" as they stamped and hauled; the silent Chinese cannoneers whose task it was to lash down the small guns in the bows of the sampans and long-boats, and stow the powder kegs and matches; the slim, olive-skinned Linga pirates who manned Paitingi's spy-boats—astonishing craft these, for all the world like Varsity racing-shells, slim frail needles with thirty paddles that could skim across the water as fast as a man can run. They darted among the other vessels—the long, stately praus, the *Dido*'s pinnace, the cutters and launches and canoes, the long sloop *Jolly Bachelor*, which was Brooke's own flagship; and the flower of our fleet, the East India paddle-steamer *Phlegethon*, with her massive wheel and platform, and her funnel belching smoke. They all packed the river, in a great tangle of oars and cordage and rubbish, and over it rang the constant chorus of curses and commands in half a dozen languages; it looked like a waterman's picnic gone mad.

The variety of weapons was an armourer's nightmare; aside from those I've mentioned there were bows and arrows, every conceivable kind of sword, axe, and spear, modern rifled muskets, pepper-pot revolvers, horse-pistols, needle-guns, fantastically-carved Chinese flintlocks, six-pounder naval guns, and stands of Congreve rockets with their firing-frames mounted on the forecastles of three of the praus. God help whoever gets in the way of this collection, thinks I—noting especially a fine comparison on the shore: a British naval officer in tail-coat and waterproof hat testing the hair-triggers of a pair of Mantons, his blue-jackets sharpening their brass-hilted cutlasses on a grindstone, and within a yard of them a jabbering band of Dyaks dipping their *langa* darts in a bubbling cauldron of the beastly white *radjun* poison.

"Let's see you puff your pop-gun, Johnny," cries one of the tars, and they swung a champagne cork on a string as a target, twenty yards off; one of the grinning little brutes slipped a dart into his *sumpitan*, clapped it to his mouth—and in a twinkling there was the cork, jerking on its string, transfixed by the foot-long needle. "Ch---t!" says the blue-jacket reverently, "don't point that b----y thing at my backside, will you?" and the others cheered the Dyak, and offered to swap their gunner for him.

So you can see the kind of army that James Brooke took to sea from Kuching on the morning of August 5, 1844, and if, like me, you had shaken your head in despair at the motley, rag-bag confusion of it as it assembled by the wharves, you would have held your breath in disbelief as you watched it sweeping in silent, disciplined order out on to the China Sea in the breaking dawn. I'll never forget it: the dark purple water, ruffled by the morning wind; the tangled green mangrove shore a cable's length to our right; the first blinding rays of silver turning the sea into a molten lake ahead of our bows as the fleet ploughed east.

First went the spy-boats, ten of them in line abreast a mile long, seeming to fly just above the surface of the sea, driven by the thin antennae of their oars; then the praus, in double column, their sails spread and the great sweeps thrashing the water, with the smaller sampans and canoes in tow; the *Dido*'s pinnace and the *Jolly Bachelor* under sail, and last, shepherding the flock, the steamer *Phlegethon*, her big wheel thumping up the spray, with Brooke strutting under her awning, monarch of all he surveyed, discoursing to the admiring Flashy. (It wasn't that I sought his company, but since I had to go along, I'd figured it would be safest to stick close by him, on the biggest boat available; something told me that whoever came home feet first, it wasn't going to be him, and the rations would probably be better. So I toadied him in my best style, and he bored me breathless in return.)

"There's something better than inspecting stirrup straps on Horse Guards!" cries he gaily, flourishing a hand at our fleet driving over the sunlit sea. "What more could a man ask, eh?— a solid deck beneath, the old flag above, stout fellows alongside, and a bitter foe ahead. That's the life, my boy!" It seemed to me it was more likely to be the death, but of course I just grinned and agreed that it was capital. "And a good cause to fight in," he went on. "Wrongs to punish, Sarawak to defend—and your lady to rescue, of course. Aye, it'll be a sweeter, cleaner coast by the time we've done with it."

I asked him if he meant to devote his life to chasing pirates, and he came all over solemn, gazing out over the sea with the wind ruffling his hair.

"It may well be a life's work," says he. "You see, what our people at home will not understand is that a pirate here is not a criminal, in our sense; piracy is the profession of the Islands, their way of life—just as trading or keeping shop is with Englishmen. So it is not a question of rooting out a few scoundrels, but of changing the minds of whole nations, and turning them to honest, peaceful pursuits." He laughed and shook his head. "It will not be easy—d'you know what one of them said to me once?—and this was a well-travelled, intelligent head-man—he said: 'I know your British system is good, *tuan besar*; I have seen Singapura and your soldiers and traders and great ships. But I was brought up to plunder, and I laugh when I think that I have fleeced a peaceful tribe right down to their cooking-pots.' Now, what d'you do with such a fellow?"

"Hang him," says Wade, who was sitting on the deck with little Charlie Johnson, one of Brooke's people,[24] playing *main chatter*.* "That was Makota, wasn't it?"

"Yes, Makota," says Brooke, "and he was the finest of 'em. One of the stoutest friends and allies I ever had—until he deserted to join the Sadong slavers. Now he supplies labourers and concubines to the coast princes who are meant to be our allies, but who deal secretly with the pirates for fear and profit. That's the kind of thing we have to fight, quite apart from the pirates themselves."

"Why d'you do it?" I asked, for in spite of what Stuart had told me, I wanted to hear it from the man himself; I always suspect these buccaneer-crusaders, you see. "I mean, you have Sarawak; don't that keep you busy enough?"

"It's a duty," says he, as one might say it was warm for the time of year. "I suppose it began with Sarawak, which at first seemed to me like a foundling, which I protected with hesitation and doubt, but it has repaid my trouble. I have freed its people and its trade, given it a code of laws, encouraged industry and Chinese immigration, imposed only the lightest of taxes, and protected it from the pirates. Oh, I could make a fortune from it, but I content myself with a little—I'm either a man of worth, you see, or a mere adventurer after gain, and God forbid I should ever be that. But I'm well rewarded," says he blandly, "for all the good that I do ministers to my satisfaction."

Pity you couldn't set it to music and sing it as an anthem, thinks I. Old Arnold would have loved it. But all I said was that it was undoubtedly God's work, and it was a crying shame that it went unrecognised; worth a knighthood at least, I'd have said.

"Titles?" cries he, smiling. "They're like fine clothes, penny

* Malay chess, an interesting variant of the game in which the king can make the knight's move when checked.

trumpets, and turtle soup—all of slight but equal value. No, no, I'm too quiet to be a hero. All my wish is for the good of Borneo and its people—I've shown what can be done here, but it is for our government at home to decide what means, if any, they put at my disposal to extend and develop my work." His eyes took on that glitter that you see in camp-meeting preachers and company accountants. "I've only touched the surface here— I want to open the interior of this amazing land, to exploit it for the benefit of its people, to correct the native character, to improve their lot. But you know our politicians and departments —they don't care for foreign ventures, and they're jolly wary of me, I can tell you."

He laughed again. "They suspect me of being up to some job or other, for my own good. And what can I tell 'em?—they don't know the country, and the only visits I ever get are brief and official. Well, what can an admiral learn in a week? If I'd any sense I'd vamp up a prospectus, get a board of directors, and hold public meetings. 'Borneo Limited', what? That'd interest 'em, all right! But it would be the wrong thing, you see—and it'd only convince the government that I'm a filibuster myself— Blackbeard Teach with a clean shirt on. No, no, it wouldn't do." He sighed. "Yet how proud I should be, some day, to see Sarawak, and all Borneo, under the British flag—for their good, not ours. It may never happen, more's the pity—but in the meantime, I have my duty to Sarawak and its people. I'm their only protector, and if I leave my life in the business, well, I shall have died nobly."

Well, I've seen pure-minded complacency in my time, and done a fair bit in that line myself, when occasion demanded, but J.B. certainly beat all. Mind you, unlike most Arnoldian hypocrites, I think he truly believed what he said; at least, he was fool enough to live up to it, so far as I could see, which is consistent with my conclusion that he was off his head. And when you remember that he excited the wrath of Gladstone[25]— well, that speaks volumes in a chap's favour, doesn't it? But at the time I was just noting him down as another smug, lying, psalm-smiter devoted to prayer and profit, when he went and spoiled it all by bursting into laughter and saying:

"Mind you, if it's in a good cause, it's still the greatest fun! I don't know that I'd enjoy the protection and improvement of Sarawak above half, if it didn't involve fighting these piratical, head-taking vagabonds! It's just my good luck that duty combines with pleasure—maybe I'm not so different from Makota and the rest of these villains after all. They go a-roving for lust and plunder, and I go for justice and duty. It's a nice point, don't you think? You'll think me crazy, I dare say"—he little knew how right he was—"but sometimes I think that rascals like Sharif Sahib and and Suleiman Usman and the Balagnini sea-wolves are the best friends I've got. Perhaps our radical M.P.s are right, and I'm just a pirate at heart."

"Well, you look enough like one, J.B.," says Wade, getting up from the board. "*Main chatter, sheikh matter*—it's my game, Charlie." He came to the rail and pointed, laughing, at the Dyaks and Malay savages who were swarming on the platform of the prau just ahead of us. "They don't look exactly like a Sunday School treat, do they, Flashman? Pirates, if you like!"

"Flashman hasn't seen real pirates yet," says Brooke. "He'll see the difference then."

I did, too, and before the day was out. We cruised swiftly along the coast all day, before the warm breeze, while the sun swung over and dropped like a blood-red rose behind us, and with the cooler air of evening we came at last to the broad estuary of the Batang Lupar. It was miles across, and among the little jungly islands of its western shore we disturbed an anchorage of squalid sailor-folk in weather-beaten sampans—*orang laut*, the Malays called them, "sea-gipsies", the vagrants of the coast, who were always running from one debt-collector to another, picking up what living they could.

Paitingi brought their headman, a dirty, bedraggled savage, to the *Phlegethon* in one of the spy-boats, and after Brooke had talked to him he beckoned me to follow him down into Paitingi's craft, saying I should get the "feel" of a spy-boat before we got into the river proper. I didn't much care for the sound of it, but took my seat behind him in the prow, where the gunwales were tight either side, and you put your feet delicately for fear of sending them clean through the light hull. Paitingi crouched behind me, and the Linga look-out straddled above me, a foot on either gunwale.

"Don't like it altogether," says Brooke. "Those *bajoos* say there are villages burning up towards the Rajang, and that ain't natural, when all that's sinful should be congregated up the Lupar, getting ready for us. We'll take a sniff about. Give way!"

The slender spy-boat shot away like a dart, trembling most alarmingly under my feet, with the thirty paddlers sweeping us silently forward. We threaded through the little islands, Brooke staring over towards the far shore, which was fading in the gathering dusk. There was a light mist coming down behind us, concealing our fleet, and a great bank of it was slowly rolling in from the sea, ghostly above the oily water. It was dead calm now, and the dank air made your flesh crawl; Brooke checked our pace, and we glided under the overhanging shelter of a mangrove bank, where the fronds dripped eerily. I saw Brooke's head turning this way and that, and then Paitingi stiffened behind me.

"Bismillah! J.B.!" he whispered. "Listen!"

Brooke nodded, and I strained my ears, staring fearfully across that limpid water at the fog blanket creeping towards us. Then I heard something—at first I thought it was my heart, but gradually it resolved itself into a faint, regular, throbbing boom, coming faintly out of the mist, growing gradually louder. It was melodious but horrible, a deep metallic drumming that raised the hairs on my neck; Paitingi whispered behind me:

"War-gong. Bide you; don't even breathe!"

Brooke gestured for silence, and we lay hidden beneath the mangrove fronds, waiting breathlessly, while that h---ish booming grew to a slow thunder, and it seemed to me that behind it I could hear a rushing, as of some great thing flying along; my mouth was dry as I stared at the fog, waiting for some horror to appear—and then suddenly it was upon us, like a train rushing from a tunnel, a huge, scarlet shape bursting out of the mist. I only had a glimpse as it swept by, but the image is stamped on my memory of that long, gleaming red hull with its towering forecastle and stern; the platform over its bulwark crowded with men—flat yellow faces with scarves round their brows, lank hair flowing down over their sleeveless tunics; the glitter of swords and spear-heads, the ghastly line of white bobbing globes hanging like a horrible fringe from stem to stern beneath the platform—skulls, hundreds of them; the great sweeps churning the water; the guttering torches on the poop; the long silken pennants on the upper works writhing in the foggy air like coloured snakes; the figure of a half-naked giant beating the oar-stroke on a huge bronze gong—and then it was gone as swiftly as it had come, the booming receding into the mist as it drove up the Batang Lupar.[26]

The sweat was starting out on me as we waited, while two more praus like the first emerged and vanished in its wake; then Brooke looked past me at Paitingi.

"That's inconvenient," says he. "I made 'em Lanun, the first two; the third one Maluku. What d'ye think?"

"Lagoon pirates from Mindanao," says Paitingi, "but what the h--l are they doin' here?" He spat into the water. "There's an end tae our expedition, J.B.—there's a thousand men on each o' those devil-craft, more than we muster all told, and—"

"—and they've gone to join Usman," says Brooke. He whistled softly to himself, scratching his head beneath the pilot cap. "Tell you what, Paitingi—he's taking us seriously, ain't he just?"

"Aye, so let's pay him the same compliment. If we beat back tae Kuching in the mornin', we can put oursel's in a state o' defence, at least, because, by G-d's beard, we're goin' tae have such a swarm roond oor ears—"

"Not us," says Brooke. "Them." His teeth showed white in the gathering dark; he was quivering with excitement. "D'ye know what, old 'un? I think this is just what we wanted—now I know what we can expect! I've got it all plain now—just you watch!"

"Aye, weel, if we get home wi' all speed—"

"Home nothing!" says Brooke. "We're going in tonight! Give way, there!"

For a moment I thought Paitingi was going to have the boat over; he exploded in a torrent of disbelief and dismay, and expostulations concerning Scottish Old Testament fiends and the hundred names of Allah flew over my head; Brooke just laughed, fidgeting with impatience, and Paitingi was still cursing and arguing when our spy-boat reached *Phlegethon* again. A hasty summons brought the commanders from the other vessels, and Brooke, who looked to me as though he was in the grip of some stimulating drug, held a conference on the platform by the light of a single storm lantern.

"Now's the time—I know it!" says he. "Those three lagoon praus will be making for Linga—they've been butchering and looting on the coast all day, and they'll never go farther tonight. We'll find 'em tied up at Linga tomorrow dawn. Keppel, you'll take the rocket-praus—burn those pirates at their anchorage, land the blue-jackets to storm the fort, and boom the Linga river to stop anything coming down. You'll find precious little fight in Jaffir's people, or I'm much mistaken.

"Meanwhile, the rest of us will sweep past upriver, making for Patusan. That's where we'll find the real thieves' kitchen; we'll strike it as soon as Keppel's boats have caught us up—"

"You'll leave no one at Linga?" says Keppel. "Suppose more praus arrive from Mindanao?"

"They won't," says Brooke confidently. "And if they do, we'll turn in our tracks and blow them all the way back to Sulu!" His laugh sent shivers down my spine. "Mind, Keppel, I want those three praus destroyed utterly, and every one of their crews killed or scattered! Drive 'em into the jungle; if they have slaves or captives, bring 'em along. Paitingi, you'll take the lead to Linga, with one spy-boat; we don't need more while the river's still wide. Now then, what time is it?"

It may have been my army training, or my experience in Afghanistan, where no one even relieved himself without a staff conference's approval, but this haphazard, neck-or-nothing style appalled me. We were to go careering upriver in the dark, after those three horrors that I'd seen streaking out of the mist—I shuddered at the memory of the evil yellow faces and that hideous skull fringe—and tackle them and whatever other cut-throat horde happened to be waiting at this Linga fort. He was crazy, whipped into a drunken enthusiasm by his own schoolboy notions of death or glory; why the devil didn't Keppel and the other sane men take him in hand, or drop him overboard, before he wrecked us all? But there they were, setting their watches, hardly asking a question even, suggesting improvisations in an offhand way that made your hair curl, no one so much as hinting at a written order—and Brooke laughing and slapping Keppel on the back as he went down into his long-boat.

"And mind now, Paitingi," he cries cheerily, "don't go skedaddling off on your own. As soon as those praus are well alight, I want to see your ugly old mug heading back to *Phlegethon*, d'you hear? Look after him, Stuart—he's a poor old soul, but I'm used to him!"

The spy-boat vanished into the dark, and we heard the creak of the long-boats' oars as they dispersed. Brooke rubbed his hands and winked at me. "Now's the day and now's the hour," says he. "Charlie Johnson, pass my compliments to the engineer, and tell him I want steam up. We'll have Fort Linga for our *chota hazri*!"*

It sounded like madman's babble at the time, but as I look back, it seems reasonable enough—for, being J.B., he got what he wanted. He spent all night in the *Phlegethon*'s wheel-house, poring over maps and sipping Batavia arrack, issuing orders to Johnson or Crimble from time to time, and as we thrashed on into the gloom the spy-boats would come lancing out of the misty darkness, hooking on, and then gliding away again with messages for the fleet strung out behind us; one of them kept scuttling to and fro between *Phlegethon* and the rocket-praus, which were somewhere up ahead. How the deuce they kept order I couldn't fathom, for each ship had only one dark lantern gleaming faintly at its stern, and the mist seemed thick all round. There was no sign, in that clammy murk, of the river-banks, a mile either side of us, and no sound except the steady thumping of *Phlegethon*'s engines; the night was both chill and sweating at once, and I sat huddled in wakeful apprehension in the lee of the wheel-house, drawing what consolation I could from the knowledge that *Phlegethon* would be clear of the morning's action.

She had a grandstand seat, though; when dawn came, pale and sudden, we were thrashing full tilt up the oily river, a bare half-mile from the jungle-covered bank to starboard, and nothing ahead of us but one spy-boat, loitering on the river bend. Even as we watched her, there was a distant crackle of musketry from up ahead, and from the spy-boat a blue light shot into the foggy

* Early morning tea.

air, barely visible against the pale grey sky; "Keppel's there!" yells Brooke. "Full ahead, Charlie!" and right on the heels of his words came a thunderous explosion that seemed to send a tremor across the swirling water.

Phlegethon tore down on the spy-boat, and then as we rounded the bend, I saw a sight I'll never forget. A mile away, on the right-hand shore, was a great clearing, with a big native village sprawling down to the shore, and behind it, on the fringe of the forest, a stockaded fort on a slight rise, with a green banner waving above its walls. There were twists of smoke, early cooking-fires, rising above the village, but down on the river-bank itself there was a great pall of sooty cloud rising from the glittering red war-prau which I recognised as one of those we had seen the previous evening; there was orange flame creeping up her steep side. Beyond her lay the two other praus, tied up to the bank and swinging gently in the current.

Keppel's praus were standing in towards them, in line ahead, like ghost ships floating on the morning mist which swirled above the river's surface. There was white smoke wreathing up from Keppel's own prau, and now the prau behind rocked and shuddered as fire blinked on her main-deck, and the white trails of the Congreves went streaking out from her side; you could see the rockets weaving in the air before they smashed into the sides of the anchored vessels at point-blank range; orange balls of fire exploded into torrents of smoke, with debris, broken sweeps, and spars flying high into the air, and then across the water came the thunder of the explosions, seconds later.

There were human figures swarming like ants on the stricken pirate vessels, dropping into the river or scattering up the shore; another salvo of rockets streaked across the smoking water, and as the reek of the explosions cleared we could see that all three targets were burning fiercely, the nearest one, a flaming wreck, already sinking in the shallows. From each of Keppel's craft a longboat was pulling off for the shore, and even without the glass I could make out the canvas shirts and straw hats of our salts. As the boats pulled past the blazing wrecks and touched shore, Keppel's rockets began firing at higher elevation, towards the stockaded fort, but at that range the rockets weaved and

trailed all over the place, most of them plunging down somewhere in the jungle beyond. Brooke handed me his glass.

"That's cost the Sultan of Sulu a penny or two," says he. "He'll
think twice before he sends his skull-fanciers this way again."

I was watching our seamen landing through the glass: there
was Wade's burly figure leading them at a fast trot through the
village towards the fort, the cutlasses glittering in the early light.
Behind, the boat crews were hauling their bow-chasers ashore,
manhandling them on to wheeled sledges to run them forward
so that they could be brought to play against the fort. Others
were trailing bamboo ladders, and from one of the boats there
were landing a group of Malay archers, with firepots—it was
beginning to dawn on me that for all his bull-at-a-gate style,
Brooke—or someone—knew his business; they had all the right
gear, and were moving like clockwork. Keppel's praus must
have rounded the bend and come in sight of the town at the
precise minute when there was light enough to shoot by; any
later and their approach might have been seen, and the pirates
been on the q.v.

"Wonder if Sharif Jaffir's awake yet, what?" Brooke was
striding about the platform, grinning like a schoolboy. "What
d'you bet, Charlie, he'll be scampering out of the fort this minute,
taking to the jungle? We can leave it to Keppel, now, I think—
full ahead!"

While we had been watching, the rest of our fleet had passed
by, and was surging upriver, the sweeps going like billy-oh, and
the square sails of the praus set to catch the light sea-breeze. A
spy-boat was scooting out towards us from Keppel's prau, the
burly figure of Paitingi in the bow; beyond him the village was
half-hidden by the smoke from the pirate praus, which were
burning down to the waterline, and the rockets were firing again,
this time against the smaller praus which were assembled farther
up, near the Linga river mouth. I watched until my eye ached,
and just before the *Phlegethon* rounded the next bend, a couple
of miles upstream, cheering broke out from the vessels around
us—I turned my glass, and saw that the green flag on the distant
fort was coming down, and the Union Jack was running up in
its place.

Well, I was thinking, if it's as easy as this, we don't need to break much sweat; with any luck you'll have a quiet passage, Flash, my boy—and at that very moment Brooke was at my elbow.

"Tame work for you?" says he. "Don't you fret, old fellow, you'll get a swipe at them presently, when we come to Patusan! There'll be some capital fun there, you'll see!" And just to give me the idea, he took me below and offered me the choice of some Jersey revolvers with barrels as long as my leg.[27] "And a cutlass, of course," says he, "you'll feel naked without that."

He little knew that I could feel naked in a suit of armour in the bowels of a dreadnought being attacked by an angry bumboat-woman. But one has to show willing, so I accepted his weapons with a dark scowl, and tried a cut or two with the cutlass for display, muttering professionally and praying to God I'd never have the chance to use it. He nodded approvingly, and then laid a hand on my shoulder.

"That's the spirit!" says he, "but, I say, Flashman—I know you feel you've got a lot to repay, and the thought of that dear, sweet creature of yours—well, I can see from your face the rage that is in you—and I don't blame you, mind. But, d'you know what?—whenever I go to battle, I try to remember that Our Saviour, when He had laid out those money-changing chaps in the temple, felt remorse, didn't He, for having got in such a bait? So I try to restrain my anger, and temper justice with mercy—not a bad mixture, what? God bless you, old chap." And off he went, no doubt for another gloat over the burning praus.

He baffled me, but then so many good Christians do, probably because I'm such a d----d bad one myself. And not having much of a conscience, I'm in no position to judge those that are apparently made of indiarubber—not that I gave a rap how many pirates he'd roasted before giving me his cautionary pi-jaw. As it turned out, not many—when Keppel caught us up he reported that the fort had fallen without a shot, Sharif Jaffir having legged it for the jungle with most of the Lanun pirates in tow; those remaining had thrown in their hand when they saw their vessels destroyed and the size of our fleet. So that was all good business, and what pleased Brooke most was that Keppel had brought along three hundred women whom the Lanuns had been carrying off as slaves; he visited them on Keppel's prau, patting their heads and promising them they'd soon be safe home again; I'd have consoled some of 'em more warmly than that, myself—good taste, those Lanun pirates had—but of course there was none of that, under our peckerless leader.

Thereafter he had a quick look at the pirates and slavers who'd been taken prisoner, and ordered the execution of two of them on the spot. One of them was the renegade Makota, I think; at any rate he and Brooke conversed earnestly for about five minutes, while the squat little villain grinned and shuffled his bare feet, looking bashful—according to Stuart, he was confessing to indescribable tortures which he and his pal had inflicted on some of the women prisoners the previous evening—Keppel's party had found the grisly evidence in the village. Finally, when Brooke told him his course was run, the horrid fellow nodded cheerfully, touched hands, and cries "Salaam, tuan besar", the hovering Jingo slipped a mosquito net and a rope over his head, and pfft!—one quick jerk and that was Makota off to the happy head-hunting grounds.[28]

The other condemned chap kicked up a frightful row at this, exclaiming "Krees, krees!" and eyeing the rope and mosquito net as though they were port being passed to the right. What his objection to strangulation was, I'm not certain, but they humoured him, taking him ashore so as not to make a mess. I watched from the rail; he stood up straight, his toad-like face impassive, while Jingo laid his krees point delicately inside the clavicle on the left side, and thrust down hard. The fellow never even twitched.

"A sorry business," says Brooke, "but before such atrocities I find it hard to remain composed."

After that it was all aboard the Skylark again, bound for Patusan, which lay about twenty miles farther upstream. "They'll stand and fight there, where the river narrows," says Keppel. "Two hundred praus, I dare say, and their jungle-men peppering us with blow-pipes from the trees."

"That don't matter," says Brooke. "It'll be a case of bursting the booms, and then run up and board, hand-to-hand. It's the forts that count—five of 'em, and you may be sure there'll be a thousand men in each—we must smoke 'em out with rockets and cannon and then charge home, in the old style. That'll be your innings, Charles, as usual," says he to Wade, and to my horror he added: "We'll take Flashman with us—make use of your special talents, what?" And he grinned at me as though it were my birthday.

"Couldn't be better!" cries Wade, slapping me on the back. "Sure an' we'll show you some pretty mixed scrappin', old son. Better than Afghanistan, and you may lay to that. I'll wager ye didn't see many praus rammed in the Khyber Pass, or have obligin' Paythans droppin' tree-trunks on you! What the d---l, though—as long as ye can run, swim, scale a bamboo wall, an' keep your sword-arm swingin', ye'll soon get the hang of it. Like Trafalgar an' Waterloo rolled into one, with a row in a Silver Street pub thrown in!"

They all crowed at this delightful prospect, and Stuart says:

"Remember Seribas last year, when they dropped the booms behind us. My stars, that was a go! Our Ibans had to shoot 'em out of the trees with *sumpitans*!"

"An' Buster Anderson got shot in the leg when he boarded that bankong—the one that was sinkin'," cries Wade, "an' Buster had to swim for it, wi' the pirates one side of him an' crocodiles on t'other—an' he comes rollin' ashore, plastered wi' mud an' gore, yellin': 'Anyone seen me baccy pouch?—it's got me initials on it!'"

They roared again, and said Buster was a rare card, and Wade recalled how he'd gone ploughing through the battle, performing prodigies in search of his pouch. "The best of it was," says he, spluttering, "Buster didn't smoke!"

This tickled them immensely, of course, and Keppel asked where old Buster was these days.

"Alas, we lost him at Murdu," says Brooke. "Same cutting-out party I got this"—he tapped his scar—"and a slug in the bicep. Balagnini jumped on him as he was scrambling up their stern-cable—Buster's pistol misfired—he was the most confounded careless chap imaginable with firearms, you know—and the Balagnini took the dear old chap's head almost clean off with his *parang*. Bad business."

They shook their heads and agreed it was a d----d shame, but cheered up presently when someone recalled that Jack Penty had settled the Balagnini with a lovely backhand cut soon after, and from this they passed to recalling similar happy memories of old pals and enemies, most of 'em deceased in the most grisly circumstances, apparently. Just the kind of thing I like to hear before breakfast—but, d'you know, I learned from Brooke afterwards, that they'd absolutely been trying to raise my spirits!

"Forgive their levity," says he, "it is kindly meant. Charlie Wade sees you are quite down in the dumps, fretting about your lady, and he tries to divert you with his chatter about battles past and brave actions ahead—well, when the warhorse hears the trumpets, he don't think about much else, does he? If you just give your mind to what's to do—and I know you're itching to be at it—you'll feel ever so much better." He muttered something else about my heart being tender enough to suffer, but tough enough not to break, and tooled off to see that we were still headed in the right direction.

By this time I was ready to bolt, but that's the trouble with being afloat—you can only run in circles. There was land not far off, of course, if one could have reached it through water that was no doubt well-stocked with crocodiles, and was prepared to wander in unexplored jungle full of head-hunters. And the prospect got worse through that steaming, fevered day; the river twisted and got narrower, until there was a bare few hundred yards of sluggish water either side of the vessels, with a solid jungle wall hemming us in. Whenever a bird screamed in the undergrowth I almost had a seizure, and we were tormented by mosquito clouds which added their unceasing buzzing to the monotonous throb of *Phlegethon*'s engines and the rhythmic swish of the praus' sweeps.

Worst of all was the stench—the farther we went on, the closer the jungle loomed in on us, the more unbearable became that rotten, musky, choking atmosphere, stifling in its steaming intensity. It conjured up nightmares of corpses decaying in loathsome swamps—I found the sweat which bathed me turning to ice as I watched that hostile green forest wall, conjuring up hideous faces in its shadows, imagining painted horrors lurking in its depths, waiting.

If day was bad, night was ten times worse. Dark found us still a few miles from Patusan, and the mist came with the dusk;

as we swung at anchor in midstream there was nothing to be seen but pale white wraiths coming and going in the festering gloom. With all engines stopped you could hear the water gurgling oozily by, even above the d---l's chorus of screams and yells from the darkness—I was new to jungle, and had no conception of the appalling din with which it is filled at night. I stayed on deck about ten minutes, in which time I saw at least half a dozen skull-laden praus crammed with savages starting to emerge from the shadows, at which point they dissolved into shadows themselves—after that I decided I might as well turn in, which I did by plumbing the depths of that sweltering iron tub, finding a hole in the corner of the engine-room, and crouching there with my Colt in my fist, listening to the evil whispers of head-hunters congregating on the other side of the half-inch plate.

And barely ten days before I'd been unbuttoning in that Singapore chop-house, bursting with best meat and drink, and running a lascivious eye over Madame Sabba! Now, thanks to Elspeth's wantoning, I was on the eve of death, or worse—if I get out of this, thinks I, I'll divorce the b---h, that's flat. I'd been a fool ever to marry her—and brooding on that I must have dozed, for I could see her in that sunny field by the river, golden hair tumbled in the grass, cheeks moist and pink from the ecstasy of our first acquaintance, smiling at me. That lovely white body— and then like a black shadow came the recollection of the hideous fate of those captive women at Linga—those same bestial savages had Elspeth at their mercy—even now she might be being ravished by some filthy dacoit, or suffering unmentionable agonies . . . I was awake, gasping, drenched on the cold iron.

"They shan't hurt you, old girl!" I was absolutely croaking in the dark. "They shan't! I'll—I'll—"

What would I do? Rush to her rescue, like Dick Dauntless, against the kind of human ghouls I'd seen on that pirate prau? I wouldn't dare—it wasn't a question I'd even have asked myself, normally, for the great advantage to real true-blue cowardice like mine, you see, was that I'd always been able to take it for granted and no regrets or qualms of conscience; it had served its turn, and I'd never lost a wink over Hudson or old Iqbal or any of the other honoured dead who'd served me as stepping-stones to safety. But Elspeth . . . and to haunt me in that stinking stokehold came the appalling question: suppose it was my skin or *hers*—would I turn tail then? I didn't know, but judging by the form-book I could guess, and for once the alternative to suffering and death was as horrible as death itself. I even found myself wondering if there was perhaps a limit to my funk, and that was such a fearful thought that between it and the terrors ahead I was driven to prayer, along the lines of Oh, kind God, forgive all the beastly sins I've committed, and a few that I'll certainly commit if I get out of this, or rather, pay no attention to 'em, Heavenly Father, but turn all Thy Grace on Elspeth and me, and save us both—but if it's got to be one or t'other of us, for Ch----'s sake don't leave the decision to me. And whatever Thy will, don't let me suffer mutilation or torment —if it'll save her, you can even blot me out suddenly so that I don't know about it—no, hold on, though, better still, take Brooke—the b-----'s been asking for it, and he'll adore a martyr's crown, and be a credit to Thy company of saints. But save Elspeth, and me, too, for I'll get no benefit from her salvation if I'm dead . . .

Which was all wasted piety, if you like, since Elspeth was presumably snug in Solomon's bed aboard the *Sulu Queen* and a d----d sight safer than I was, but there's nothing like the fear of violent death for playing havoc with reason and logic. I dare say if Socrates had been up the Batang Lupar that night he might have put my thoughts in order—not that he'd have had much chance; he'd have had a Colt thrust into his fist and been pushed over the side with instructions to lay on like fury, look out for a blonde female in distress, and give me a shout when the coast was clear. As it was, having no counsel but my own, I went to sleep.

* * *

[Extract from the diary of Mrs Flashman, August —, 1844]
    An *extremely* uncomfortable night—oppressive heat— and much plagued by Insects. The noise of the Natives is too much to be *borne*. Why should they beat their Gongs after dark? No doubt it has some Religious Purpose; if so, it is *trying* to a degree. I despair of sleep, even in Nature's

Garb, so intense is the *heat* and *drumliness* of the air; it is with difficulty that I pen even these few lines; the paper is *quite damp*, and blots most provokingly.

No sign of Don S. since this morning, when I was allowed briefly on deck for air and exercise. Almost forgot my *pitiful* condition in the interest of what I saw, of which I have Rough Notes, and a few modest sketches. The colours of the Forest Blooms are most exquisite, but Pale to Nothing before the Extravagance of the Natives themselves. So many Splendid and Barbaric galleys, adorned with streamers and flags, like Corsairs of yore, manned by Swarthy Crews, many of *repulsive appearance*, but others quite commanding. As I stood in the bows, one such galley swept by on the bosom of the stream, urged on by the oars plied by Dusky Argonauts, and at the back of the boat, plainly its Chief, a Tall and Most Elegantly Shaped Young Barbarian, clad in a *saronga* of Shimmering Gold, with many ornaments on his exposed arms and legs—really a most Noble Carriage and quite handsome for a Native, who inclined his head to me and smiled *pleasantly*, very respectfully, yet with a Natural Dignity. Not at all Yellow, but quite pale of skin, as I had imagined an Aztec God. His name, as I discovered by discreet inquiry of Don S., is Sheriff Saheeb, and I suppose from this title that he is at least a Justice of the Peace.

I believe he would have come aboard our vessel, but Don S. spoke to him from the Gangway, which I confess was a Disappointment, for he seemed a Personage of some *gentility*—if one may use the word of a Heathen—and I should have liked time to sketch him, and try if I could not capture some of that Savage Nobility of his bearing.

However, I have not passed my time in *idle staring*, but recollecting what Lord Fitzroy Somerset told me at the Guards Ball, have made *careful count* of all the armaments I have seen, and the disposition of the Enemy's Strength, which I have noted *separately*, both the number of large guns and ships, or galleys. There seem to be a *vast host* of these people, on land and water, which fills me with dread—how can I *hope* to be delivered?—but I shall not waste my pen on *that*, or other *vain repining*.

A diverting occurrence, which I should *not* record, I know—I am a sadly undutiful daughter. Among the animals and birds (of the most *beautiful* plumage) I have seen, was a most droll Ape on one of the native boats, where I guess he is a pet creature—a most astonishing Pug, for never was *anything* more like a Human—quite as tall as a small man, and covered with an overcoat of *red hair* of remarkable Luxuriance. He had such a Melancholy Expression, but with so *appealing* a "glint tae his e'en", and the aspect of a dour wee old man, that I was greatly amused, and his captors, seeing my interest, made him perform *most divertingly*, for he had the trick of Perfect Imitation, and even essay'd to kindle a fire as they did, putting together twigs to himself—but poor Pug, they did not take light by themselves, as he *expected they would*! He was quite *cast down*, and Annoy'd, and it was when he Mouthed his Discontent and *scattered* his twigs in Temper, that I saw he was the Speaking Likeness of dear Papa, even to the way he screwed up his eyes! Almost I expected him to express himself with a round "De'il tak' it!" What a preposterous fancy, to see a resemblance in that Brute to one's parent—but he did look *exactly* like Papa in one of his tantrums! But this awoke such Poignant Memories, that I could not look long.

So to my Prison again, and Forebodings, which I put *resolutely* from me. I am alive, so I hope—and *will not be cast down*!!! Don S. continues attentive, though I see little of him; he tells me the name of my Ape is Man of the Forest. I close this day with a Prayer to my Merciful Father in Heaven—oh, let him send my H. soon to me!

[End of extract—and a *most malicious* libel on a good and honest Parent who, whatever his faults, deserved kinder usage from an Ungrateful Child whom he indulged far too much!!— G. de R.]

I was back in Patusan just a few years ago, and it's changed beyond belief. Now, past the bend of the river, there is a sleepy, warm little village of bamboo huts and booths, hemmed in by towering jungle trees, drowsing in the sunlight; fowls scratching in the dirt, women cooking, and no greater activity than a child tumbling and crying. However much I walked round, and squinted at it from odd angles, I couldn't match it to my memory of bristling stockades along the banks, with five mighty wooden forts fringing the great clearing—the jungle must have been farther back then, and even the river has changed: it is broad and placid now, but I remember it narrow and choppy, and everything more cramped and enclosed; even the sky seems farther away nowadays, and there's a great peace where once there was pandemonium of smoke and gunfire and rending timber and bloody water.

They were waiting for us when we swept round the bend in line abreast, *Phlegethon* and the rocket-praus leading, with our spy-boats lurking under the counters waiting to strike. Although it was broad dawn you couldn't see the water at all; there was a blanket of mist a yard deep on its surface, cutting off not only sight but sound, so that even the *Phlegethon*'s wheel gave only a muffled thump as it hit the water, and the splash of the sweeps was a dull, continuous churning as we ploughed the fog.

There was a huge log-boom just visible above the mist fifty yards ahead, and beyond it a sight to freeze your blood—from bank to bank, a line of great war-praus, swarming with armed men, pennants hanging from their masts, skull-fringes bobbing, and as we came into view, a hideous yell going up from every deck, the war-gongs booming, and that d---l's horde shaking their fists and brandishing their weapons. It was taken up from the manned stockades on the right bank, and the wooden forts behind—and then the fort guns and the praus' bow-chasers belched smoke, and the air was thick with screaming shot, whining overhead, driving up jets of water from the misty surface or crashing home into the timbers of our craft. The rocket-praus fired back, and in a moment the still air was criss-crossed with the smoky vapour trails, and the pirate battle-line shuddered under the pounding of the Congreves; shattering explosions on their decks, bursts of flame and smoke, men diving from their upper works, and then their cannon roaring back again, turning the narrow river into an inferno of noise and destruction.

"Spy-boats away!" bawls Brooke from the *Phlegethon's* rail, and out from under the counters raced half a dozen of Paitingi's shells, darting in towards the boom, only the rowers visible above the mist, so that each crew was just a line of heads and shoulders cleaving through that woolly blanket. Just beyond the boom the foggy water was thick with enemy canoes, their musketeers firing raggedly at our spy-boats. I saw heads vanish here and there as the shots took effect, but the spy-boats forged on, and now the pirates were closing on the boom itself, scrambling on to the huge logs, swords and *parangs* in hand, to deny our men a foot-hold. And above both sides the great gun duel continued, between our praus and theirs, in one continuous h--lish din of explosion and crashing timber, punctuated by screams of wounded men and bellowed commands.

You couldn't hear yourself think, but at such times it's best not to, anyway. I was at Brooke's elbow, straining every nerve to keep his body between mine and the enemy's fire without being too obvious about it. Now he was directing our musketeers' fire from the *Phlegethon's* bow, to cover our spy-boatmen, who were fighting furiously to drive the pirates from the boom so that the great binding-ropes could be cut and the boom broken to give our vessels passage; I flung myself down, yelling nonsense, between two of our riflemen, seizing a piece myself and making great play at loading it. Brooke, on his feet, was walking from man to man, pointing out targets.

"That one in the yellow scarf—lively, now! Got him! The big fellow with the spear—the Malay beyond Paitingi—there, now, the fat one in the stern of yon canoe. Blaze away, boys! They're failing—go on, Stuart, get the axes going on those cables! Come on, Flashman, off we go!"

He slapped me on the shoulder—just when I'd got myself

nice and snug behind the sandbags, too—and perforce I had to tumble after him over the *Phlegethon's* side into the *Jolly Bachelor*, which was bobbing alongside, packed with *Dido's* men. I heard a shot clang on the *Phlegethon's* plates just above my head as I went sprawling into the sloop, and then hands were hauling me upright, and a bearded tar was grinning and yelling: " 'Ere we go, sir! Twice round the light'ouse for a penny!" I plunged after Brooke, stumbling over the cursing, cheering men who squatted on the deck, and fetched up beside him near the bow-chaser, where he was trying to make himself heard above the din, and pointing ahead.

We were driving in towards the boom, under a canopy of rocket-smoke, and now the gunfire was dispersing the mist, and you could see the oily water, already littered with broken timbers, and even a body here and there, rolling limp. On the boom it was a hand-to-hand mêlée between the pirate canoes and our spy-boatmen, a slippering, slashing dog-fight of glittering *parangs* and thrusting spears, with crashing musketry at point-blank range over the logs. I saw Paitingi, erect on the boom, laying about him with a broken oar; Stuart, holding off a naked pirate with his cutlass, shielding two Chinese who were swinging their axes at the great rattan cables securing the boom. Even as I watched, the cables parted, and the logs rolled, sending friend and foe headlong into the water; the *Jolly Bachelor* gave a great yell of triumph, and we were heading for the gap, into the smoke, while from our bow a blue light went up to signal the praus.

There was a frantic five minutes while we backed water in the space between the broken sides of the boom, Brooke and the bow-chaser crew spraying grape ahead of us, and the rest of us banging away at anything that looked like a hostile shape, either on the boom itself or in the canoes beyond. I used my Colt sparingly, crouched down by the bulwark, and keeping as well snuggled into the mob of tars as possible; once, when a canoe came surging out of the smoke, with a great yellow d---l in a quilted tunic and spiked helmet in the prow, brandishing a barbed lance, I took a steady sight and missed him twice, but my third shot got him clean amidships as he was preparing to leap for our rail, and he tumbled into the water.

"Bravo, Flashman!" cries Brooke. "Here, come up beside

me!" And there I was again, red in the face with panic, stumbling up beside him as he leaned over the side, helping to haul Stuart out of the water—he'd swum from the broken boom, and was gasping on the deck, sodden wet, with a trickle of blood running from his left sleeve.

"Steady all!" roars Brooke. "Ready, oarsmen! Every musket primed? Right, hold on, there! Wait for the praus!"

Beyond the tangle of wreckage and foundering canoes, beyond the struggling swimmers and floating bodies, the two ends of the boom were now a good fifty yards apart, drifting slowly behind us on the current. The spy-boats had done their work, and our praus were moving ahead under their sweeps, coming up into line, half a dozen on either side, while the rocket-praus, farther back, were still cannonading away at the pirate line, perhaps two cables' lengths ahead. Three or four of them were burning furiously, and a great reek of black smoke was surging down river towards us, but their line was still solid, and their bow guns fired steadily, sending up clouds of water round our praus and battering their upper works. Between them and us their canoes were in retreat, scurrying for the safety of the larger craft; Brooke nodded with satisfaction.

"So far, so good!" cries he, and standing up in the bows, he waved his hat. "Now then, you fellows, put your backs into it! Two blue lights, there—signal the advance! Cutlasses and small arms, everyone—tally-ho!"

The blue-jackets yelled and stamped, and as the blue lights went up the cheering spread along our line, and on either side the praus drove forward, bow-chasers blazing away, musketeers firing from the platforms, the crews crowding forward to the bows. As our line steadied the gunfire rose to a new crescendo; we were crouching down as the shot whined above us, and suddenly there was an appalling smash, a chorus of shrieks, and I found myself sodden with blood, staring in horror at two legs and half a body thrashing feebly on the deck in front of me, where an instant before a seaman had been ramming shot into the bow-chaser. I sat down heavily, pawing at the disgusting mess, and then Brooke had me on my feet again, yelling to know if I was all right, and I was yelling back that the corn on my big toe was giving me h--l—G-d knows why one says these things, but he gave a wild laugh and pushed me forward to the bow rail. I crouched down, shuddering and ready to vomit, helpless with fear—but who would have recognised it then?

Suddenly the cannonading died, and for a few seconds there was a silence in which you could hear the water chuckling under the *Jolly Bachelor*'s forefoot as she went gliding forward. Then the musketry crashed out again, as our sharpshooters on the praus poured their fire into the pirate line, and the pirates gave us back volley for volley. Thank G-d the *Jolly Bachelor* was too low and too close now for them to get at us with cannon, but as we drove in towards them the water either side was boiling with their small shot, and behind me there were cries and oaths of men hit; our whole line was charging across the water, praus on the flanks, *Jolly Bachelor* in the centre, towards the pirate vessels; they were barely fifty yards off, and I could only stare in horror at the nearest one, dead ahead, the platform which jutted out from her rails crowded with savage howling faces, brandished steel, and smoking barrels—"They'll shoot us to pieces! We'll founder—Jesus loves me!" someone was shouting, but nobody heard me in that fearful din. A seaman at my elbow screamed and stood up, tearing at a *sumpitan* dart in his arm; as I dived for the cover of the rail another stood quivering in a cable a foot from my face; Brooke leaned over, grinning, snapped it off, tossed it away, and then did an unbelievable thing. I didn't credit it then, and scarcely do now, but it's a fact.

He stood up, full height in the bows, one foot on the rail, threw away his straw hat, and folded his arms, staring straight ahead at that yelling, grimacing Death that was launching shot, steel, and poisoned arrows at us in clouds. He was smiling serenely, and seemed to be saying something. "Get down, you mad b----r!" I shouted, but he never even heard, and then I realised that he wasn't speaking—he was singing. Above the crash of musketry, the whistle and thump of those horrid darts, the screams and the yells, you could hear it:

> "Come, cheer up, my lads,
> 'Tis to glory we steer,
> To add something new
> To this wonderful year—"

He was turning now, one hand on a stay for balance, thumping the time with his other fist, his face alight with laughter, roaring to us to sing—and from the mob behind it came thundering out:

"Heart of oak are our ships,
Jolly tars are our men,
We always are ready,
Steady, boys, steady,
We'll fight and we'll conquer again and again!"

The *Jolly Bachelor* shuddered in the water as we scraped under the platform of the pirate prau, and then shrieking, slashing figures were dropping among us; I went sprawling on the deck, with someone treading on my head, and came up to find myself staring into a contorted, screaming yellow face; I had an instant's glimpse of a jade earring carved like a half-moon, and a scarlet turban, and then he had gone over the side with a cutlass jammed to the hilt in his stomach; I fired at him as he fell, slipped in the blood on the deck, and finished up in the scuppers, glaring about me in panic. The deck was in turmoil, resolving itself into knots of blue-jackets, each killing a struggling pirate in their midst and heaving the bodies overside; the prau we had scraped was behind us now, and Brooke was yelling:

"Steady, oarsmen! Pull with a will! There's our quarry, you chaps! Straight ahead!"

He was pointing to the right bank, where the stockade, hit by rocket fire, was collapsed in smouldering ruin; beyond it lay one of the forts, its stockade blazing fiercely, with figures scattering away, and a gallant few trying to douse the flames. Behind us was an unbelievable carnage; our praus and the pirates' locked together in a bloody hand-to-hand struggle, and through the gaps our longboats surging in the wake of the *Jolly Bachelor*, loaded with Malay swordsmen and Dyaks. The water was littered with smoking wreckage and struggling forms; men were falling from the platforms, and our boats were picking them up when they were friends, or butchering them in the bloody current if they were pirates. Smoke from the burning praus was swirling in a great pall above the infernal scene; I remembered that line about "a death-shade round the ships"—and then someone was shaking my arm, and Brooke was shouting at me, pointing ahead to the nearing shore and the smoking breach in the stockade.

"Take that fort!" he was yelling. "Lead the blue-jackets! Charge in, d'ye hear, no covering, no halting! Just tear in with the cutlass—watch out for women and kids, and prisoners! Chase 'em, Flashy! Good luck to you!"

I inquired tactfully if he was b----y mad, but he was ten yards away by then, plunging through the shallows as our boat scraped into the shelving bank; he scrambled up the shore, waving to the other longboats to close on him; they were turning at his signal —and there was I, revolver in shaking fist, staring horrified over the bows at the charred ruins of the stockade, and beyond it, a good hundred yards of hard-beaten earth, already littered with cannon casualties, and beyond that again, the blazing barrier of the fort's outer wall. Ch---t knew how many slashing fiends were waiting in there, ready to blast us with musketry and then rip us up at close quarters—if we ever got that far. I looked round at the *Jolly Bachelor*, crammed with yelling sailors, straw hats, bearded faces, white smocks, glaring eyes, cutlasses at the ready, waiting for the word. And the word, no doubt about it, was with old Flash.

Well, whatever you may say of me, I know my duty, and if there was one thing Afghanistan had taught me, it was the art of leadership. In a trice I had seized a cutlass, thrust it aloft, and turned to the maddened crew behind me. "Ha, ha, you fellows!" I bellowed. "Here we go, then! Who'll be first after me into yonder fort?" I sprang to the bank, waved my cutlass again, and bawled, "Follow me!"

They came tumbling out of the boat on my heels, yelling and cheering, brandishing their weapons, and as I stood shouting, "On! On! Rule, Britannia!" they went pouring up the shore, scattering the embers of the stockade. I advanced with them, of course, pausing only to encourage those in the rear with manly cries, until I reckoned there were about a score in front of me; then I lit out in pursuit of the vanguard, not leading from behind, exactly—more from the middle, really, which is the safest place to be unless you're up against civilised artillery.

We charged across the open space, howling like hounds; as we ran, I saw that on our right flank Brooke was directing the Malay swordsmen towards another fort; they were drawing those dreadful *kampilans* with the hair-tufts on their hilts, and behind them came a second wave from the boats, of half-naked Iban, carrying their *sumpitan* spears and screeching "Dyak! Dyak!" as they ran. But none of 'em matched the speed and fury of my tars, who were now almost up to the blazing fort stockade; just as they reached it the whole thing, by great good luck, fell inwards with a great whooshing of sparks and smoke, and as the foremost leaped through the burning rubbish I was able to see how wise I'd been in not leading the charge myself—there, in a ragged double line, was a troop of pirate musketeers presenting their pieces. Out crashed their volley, knocking over one or two of our first fellows, and then the rest were into them, cutlasses swinging, with old Flash arriving full of noble noise at the point where our chaps were thickest.

It seemed to me that I could employ my best efforts picking off the enemy with my Colt, and this gave me the opportunity to watch something which is worth going a long way to see, provided you can find a safe vantage—the terrible cut-and-thrust, shoulder to shoulder, of British blue-jackets in a body. I dare say the Navy has been teaching it since Blake's day, and Mr Gilbert, who never dreamed what it was like, makes great fun of it nowadays, but I've seen it—and I know now why we've been ruling the oceans for centuries. There must have been a hundred pirates to our first line of twenty, but the tars just charged them in a solid wedge, cutlasses raised for the backhand cut—stamp and slash, then thrust, stamp and slash, then thrust, stamp-slash-thrust, and that pirate line melted into a fallen tangle of gashed faces and shoulders, through which the sailors ploughed roaring. Those pirates who still stood, turned tail and fairly pelted for the fort gates, with our chaps chasing and d--ning 'em for cowardly swabs—made me quite proud to be British, I can tell you.

I was fairly close up with the front rank, by now, bellowing the odds and taking a juicy swipe at any wounded who happened to be looking t'other way. The defenders had obviously hoped their musketeers would hold us beyond the gate, but we were in before they knew it. There was a party of pirates trying to swing a great gun round to blast us at the entrance; one of 'em was snatching at a linstock, but before he could touch it off there were half a dozen thrown sheath-knives in his body, and he sprawled over the gun while the others turned and fled. We were in, and all that remained was to ferret out every pirate for the place to be ours.

This presented no difficulty, since there weren't any—for the simple reason that the cunning b-----ds had all sneaked out the back way, and were even now scurrying round to take us in the rear at the gate. I didn't know this, of course, at the time; I was too busy despatching armed parties under petty officers to overrun the interior, which was like no fort I'd ever seen. In fact, it was Sharif Sahib's personal bamboo palace and head-quarters, a great labyrinth of houses, some of 'em even three storeys high, with outside staircases, connecting walkways, verandahs, and screened passages everywhere. We had just begun to ransack and loot, and had discovered the Sharif's private wardrobe— an astonishing collection which included such varying garments as cloth-of-gold turbans, jewelled tiaras, toppers, and morning dress—when all h--l broke out from the direction of the main gate, and there was a general move in that direction. General, but not particular—while the loyal tars surged off in search of further blood, I was skipping nimbly out of Sharif Sahib's wardrobe in the opposite direction. I didn't know where it would lead, but it was at least away from the firing—I'd seen enough gore and horror for one day, and I sped quickly across a bamboo bridge into the adjoining house, which appeared to be deserted. There was a long passage, with doors on one side, and I was hesitating over which would be the safest bolt-hole, when one of them shot open and out rushed the biggest man I've ever seen in my life.

He was at least seven feet tall, and as hideous as he was big —a great yellow, globular face set on massive shoulders, with a tasselled cap on top, staring pop-eyes, and a great sword clutched in his pudgy hands. He screamed at the sight of me, backing down the passage in a strange, waddling run, and then he swung his sword back over his head, squealing like a steam-whistle, overbalanced, and vanished with a rending crash down a steep flight of stairs. By the sound of it he must have carried away two floors with him, but I wasn't waiting about for any more like him—I leaped through the nearest door, and stopped dead in my tracks, unable to believe my eyes. I was in a great room full of women.

I closed my eyes, and opened them, wondering if I was dreaming, or having hallucinations after my trying day. It was still there, like something out of Burton's "Arabian Nights"—the illustrated one that you can only get on the Continent. Silken hangings, couches, carpets, cushions, a stink of perfume coming at you in waves—and the ladies, a round score of them—beautifully round, I realised, and evidently proud of it, for there wasn't clothing enough among the lot of 'em to cover one body respectably. A few sarongs, wisps of silk, bangles, satin trousers, a turban or two, but not worth a d--n when it came to concealing those splendid limbs, shapely hips, plump buttocks, and pouting tits. I could only gape, disbelieving, and tear my eyes from the bodies to the faces—every shade from coffee and beige to honey and white, and all beautiful; red lips parted and trembling, dark, kohl-fringed eyes wide with terror.

I wondered for a moment if I'd been killed in the fight and transported to some delightful paradise; but celestial or earthly, I couldn't pass up a chance like this, and the thought must have shown in my expression, for with one accord the whole gorgeous assembly screamed in unison, and turned to flee—mind, I don't blame 'em, for Flashy leering in your doorway, covered in blood and grime, pistol in one hand and bloody cutlass in t'other, ain't quite the vicar dropping in to tea. They ran pell-mell, falling over cushions, blundering into each other, scrambling for the other doors in the room, and it seemed only common sense to grab for the nearest, a voluptuous little thing whose entire wardrobe was a necklace and gauzy trousers; it may have been my hand on her ankle, or her top-heavy bosom, that made her overbalance; either way, she fell through a curtained alcove and slithered headlong down a narrow stairway, scrambling and shrieking with Flashy in hot pursuit. She fetched up against a screen wall at the bottom, I seized her joyfully—and in that moment I was recalled to a sense of my true position by a sound that drove all carnal thoughts from my mind: a deafening volley of musketry crashed in the street just outside the flimsy house-wall, there was a clash of steel, a jabber of native voices —pirates, for certain—and in the distance an English voice bawling orders to take cover.

It seemed a capital notion; I pinned the wriggling wench to the floor, brandished my pistol, and mouthed at her to be silent. She lay shuddering in my grip, her face working with terror— lovely little face it was, part Chink-Indian-Malay, probably, great eyes filled with tears, short nose, plump little lips—and, by George, she was handsomely built, too; more by instinct than a-purpose, I found myself taking an appraising fondle, and she trembled under my hand, but had sense enough to keep her mouth shut.

I listened fearfully; the pirates were moving just beyond our screen wall, and then suddenly they were blazing away again, yelling and cursing or crying out in agony, feet running and shots whining horribly near—I clapped a hand over her mouth and gripped her close, terrified that she would scream and bring some bestial savage cleaving through the flimsy wall to fillet me; we lay there, in the stuffy dimness of the stair-foot, with the noise of battle pounding by not six feet away, and once, during a second's lull in the tumult, I heard the sounds of squealing and wailing somewhere overhead—the other young ladies of the Patusan finishing school waiting to be ravished and murdered, presumably. I found I was hissing hysterically in her ear: "Quiet, quiet, quiet, for G-d's sake!" and to my astonishment she was whimpering tearfully back, "Amiga sua, amiga sua!" stroking my sweating face with her hand, a look of terrified entreaty in her eyes—she was even trying to smile, too, a pathetic little grimace, straining to bring her slobbering lips up to mine, making little moaning noises.

Well, I've seen women in the grip of terror often enough, but I couldn't account for this passionate frenzy—until I realised that my shuddering was of a curiously rhythmic nature, that I had a quivering tit in one hand and a plump thigh in the other, that our nether garments seemed to have come adrift somehow, and that my innards were convulsing with another sensation besides fear. I was so startled I nearly broke stride—I'd never have believed that I could gallop a female without realising I was doing it, yet here we were, thundering away like King Hal on honeymoon, after all I'd been through that day, and with battle, murder, and sudden death raging around us. It just shows how your better instinct will prevail in a crisis—some fall to prayer, others cry upon Queen and Country, but here's one, I'm proud to say, who instinctively fornicated in the jaws of death, gibbering with fright and reckless lust, but giving of his best, for when you realise it may be your last ride you make the most of it. And, d'you know, it may well be true that perfect love casteth out fear, as Dr Arnold used to say; leastways, I doubt if I can ever have been in finer tupping trim, for in the last ecstatic moment my partner fainted clean away, and you can't do better by 'em than that.

They were still going at it hammer and tongs outside, but after a while the action seemed to move along, and when presently I heard in the distance the unmistakable sound of a British cheer, I judged it was safe to venture forth again. My wench had come to, and was lying limp and blubbering, too scared to stir; I had to lay the flat of my sword across her rump to drive her up the stairs, and then, after a cautious prowl, I sallied out.

It was all over by then. My blue-jackets, who didn't seem to have missed me, had driven off the pirate attack, and were busy emptying the fort of its valuables before it was burned, for Brooke was determined to destroy the pirate nests utterly. I told 'em that during the fighting I'd heard the cries of women in one of the buildings, and that the poor creatures must be sought out and treated with all consideration—I was very stern about that, but when they went to look it appeared that the whole gaggle had decamped into the jungle; there wasn't a living soul left in the place, so I went off to find Brooke and report.[29]

Outside the fort it was a nightmare. The open space down to the river was littered with enemy corpses—most of them headless, for the victorious Dyaks had been busy at their ghastly work of collecting trophies, and the river itself was just a mess of smoking wreckage. The pirate praus had either been burned in the battle or had fled upriver; fewer than a quarter of them had escaped, scores of their crews had been killed or driven into the jungle, and great numbers of wounded and prisoners had been herded into one of the captured forts. All five of them had been taken, and two of them were already alight; when night came down on Patusan it was still as bright as day from the orange glare of the burning buildings, the heat was so intense that for a time we had to retire to our boats, but all through the night the work had to go on—prisoners to be guarded and fed, our own wounded to be cared for, the loot of the forts assessed and shipped, our vessels repaired, stores replenished, fresh weapons and ammunition issued, dead counted, and the whole sickening confusion restored to some sort of order.

I've seen the aftermath of battle fifty times if I've seen it once, and it's h-ll, but through all the foulness and exhaustion there's always one cheery thought—I'm here. Sick and sore and weary, perhaps, but at least alive and sound with a place to lie down—and I'd had a good if somewhat alarming rattle into the bargain. The one snag was that there'd been no sign of the *Sulu Queen*, so the whole filthy business would have to be gone through again, which was not to be contemplated.

I said as much to Brooke, in the faint hope that I might get him to give up—of course, I played it full of manly anguish, torn between love of Elspeth and concern at what her rescue had already cost. "T'ain't right, raja," says I, looking piously constipated. "I can't ask this kind of . . . of sacrifice from you and your people. G-d knows how many lives will be lost—how many noble fellows . . . no, it won't do. She's my wife, and—well, it's up to me, don't you see . . ."

It was dreadful humbug, hinting I'd take on the job single-handed, in some unspecified fashion—given the chance I'd have legged it for Singapore that instant, sent out reward notices, and sat back out of harm's way. From which you may gather that a busy day among the Borneo pirates had quite dissipated the conscientious lunacy which had temporarily come over me in the stokehold the previous night. But I was wasting my time, of course; he just gripped my hand with tears in his eyes and cried:

"Do you truly think there's a man of us who would fail you now? We'll win her back at any cost! Besides," and he gritted his teeth, "there are these pirate rascals to stamp out still—we've won the decisive battle, thanks to valour such as yours, but we must give 'em the coup de grâce! So you see, I'd be bound to go on, even if your loved one were not in their foul hands." He gripped my shoulder. "You're a white man, Flashman—and I know you'd go on alone if you had to; well, you can count on J.B. to blazes and beyond, so there!" That was what I'd been afraid of.

We were another two days at Patusan, waiting for news from Brooke's spies and keeping to windward of the Dyaks' funeral pyres on the river-bank, before word came that the *Sulu Queen* had been sighted twenty miles farther upstream, with a force of enemy praus, but when we cruised up there on the 10th the birds had flown to Sharif Muller's fort on the Undup river, so for two more days we must toil after them, plagued by boiling heat and mosquitoes, the stream running stronger all the time and our pace reduced to a struggling crawl. The *Phlegethon* had to be left behind because of the current and snags, to which the pirates had added traps of tree-trunks and sunken rattan nets to trammel our sweeps; every few minutes there would have to be a halt while we cut our way loose, hacking at the creeper ropes, and then hauling on, drenched with sweat and oily water, panting for breath, eyes forever turning to that steaming olive wall that hemmed us in either side, waiting for the whistle of a *sumpitan* dart that every now and then would come winging out of the jungle to strike a paddler or quiver in the gunwales. Beith, Keppel's surgeon, was up and down the fleet constantly, digging the beastly things out of limbs and cauterising wounds; fortunately they were seldom fatal, but I reckoned we were suffering a casualty every half-hour.

It wouldn't have been too bad if I'd still had the *Phlegethon*'s iron sheets to skulk behind, but I had been assigned to Paitingi's spy-boat, which was as often as not in the lead; only at night did I go back aboard the *Jolly Bachelor* with Brooke, and that wasn't much comfort—huddled up for sleep at the foot of her ladder after the tintacks had been scattered on her deck against night attack, sweating in the cramped dark, filthy and unkempt, listening to the screaming noise of the jungle and the occasional distant thob of a war-gong—doom, doom, doom, out of the misty dark.

"Drum away, Muller," Brooke would say, "we'll be playing you a livelier tune presently, just you wait. We'll see some fun then—eh, Flashy?"

By his lights, I suppose that what happened on the third day along the Undup *was* fun—a dawn attack on Muller's fort, which was a great stockaded bamboo castle on a steep hill. The rocket-praus pounded it, and the remnants of the pirate fleet in their anchorage, and then *Dido*'s men and the Dyaks swarmed ashore, the latter war-dancing on the landing-ground before the assault, leaping, shaking their *sumpitans* and yelling "Dyak!" ("that's aye their way," says Paitingi to me as we watched from the spy-boat, "they'd sooner yelp than fight"—which I thought pretty hard). Poor Charlie Wade was killed storming the fort; I heard later he'd been shot while carrying a Malay child to shelter, which shows what Christian charity gets you.

The only part I took in the fight, though, was when a prau broke free from the pirate anchorage and made off upriver, sweeps going like blazes and war-gong thundering. Paitingi danced up and down, roaring in Scotch and Arabic that he could see Muller's personal banner on her, so our spy set off in pursuit. The prau foundered, burning from rocket-fire, but Muller, a persevering big villain in quilted armour and black turban, took to a sampan; we overhauled it, banging away, and I was having the horrors at the thought of boarding when the sensible chap dived overboard with his gang at his heels and swam for it. We lost him near the jungle-edge, and Paitingi tore his beard, cussing as only an Arab can.

"Come back and fight, ye son-of-a-Malay-b---h!" cries he, shaking his fist. "Istagfurallah! Is it thus that pirates prove their courage? Aye, run to the jungle, ye Port Said pimp, you! By the Seven Heroes, I shall give thy head to my Lingas yet, thou uncircumcised carrion! Ach! Burn his grandmither—he's awa' wi' it, so he is!"

By this time the fort was taken,[30] and we left it burning, and the dead unburied, for it had been discovered from a prisoner that our principal quarry, Suleiman Usman, with the *Sulu Queen* —and presumably my errant wife—had taken refuge up the Skrang river with a force of praus. So it was back down the Undup again, a good deal faster than we had come up, to the mainstream, where *Phlegethon* was guarding the junction.

"You can't run much farther now, Usman, my son," says Brooke. "Skrang's navigable for a few miles at most; if he takes

Sulu Queen any distance up he'll ground her. He's bound to stand and fight—why, he's still got more men and keels than we have, and while we've been chasing Muller he's had time to put 'em in order. He must know we're pretty used up and thinned out, too."

That was no lie, either. The faces round the table in *Phlegethon*'s tiny ward-room were puffy and hollow-eyed with fatigue; Keppel, the spruce naval officer of a week ago, looked like a scarecrow with his unshaven cheeks and matted hair, his uniform coat cut and torn and the epaulette burned away; Charlie Johnson, with his arm in a blood-stained sling, was dozing and waking like a clockwork doll; even Stuart, normally the liveliest of fellows, was sitting tuckered out, with his head in his hands, his half-cleaned revolver on the table before him. (I can see it now, with the little brass ram-rod sticking out of the barrel, and a big black moth perched on the foresight, rubbing its feelers.) Only Brooke was still as offensively chipper as ever, clean-shaven and alert, for all that his eyes looked like streaky bacon; he glanced round at us, and I could guess that he was thinking: this pack can't follow much longer.

"However," says he, grinning slyly, "we ain't as used up as all that, are we? I reckon there's three days' energy left in every man here—and four in me. I tell you what . . ." he squared his elbows on the table ". . . I'm going to give a dinner-party to-morrow night—full dress for everyone, of course—on the eve of what is going to be our last fight against these rascals—"

"Bismillah! I'd like tae believe that," says Paitingi.

"Well, our last on *this* expedition, anyway," cries Brooke. "It's bound to be—either we wipe them up or they finish us—but *that* ain't going to happen, not after the drubbings we've given 'em already. I've got a dozen of champagne down below, and we'll crack 'em to our crowning success, eh?"

"Wouldn't it be better to keep 'em for afterwards?" says Keppel, but at this Stuart raised his head and shook it, smiling wearily.

"Might not all be here by then. This way, everyone's sure of a share beforehand—that's what you said the night before we went in against the Lingas in the old *Royalist*, ain't it, J.B.? Remember—the nineteen of us, four years ago? 'There's no drinking after death.' By Jove, though—there ain't many of the nineteen left . . .''

"Plenty of new chums, though," says Brooke quickly, "and they're going to sing for their supper, just the way we did then, and have done ever since." He shoved Charlie Johnson's nodding head to and fro. "Wake up, Charlie! It's singing night, if you want your dinner tomorrow! Come on, or I'll shove a wet sponge down your back! Sing, laddie, sing! George has given you the lead!"

Johnson blinked and stammered, but Brooke gave tongue with "Here's a health to the King, and a lasting peace", thumping the table, and Charlie came in, croaking, on the lines

So let us drink while we have breath
For there's no drinking after death

and carried on solo to the end, goggling like an owl, while Brooke beat the table and cried, good boy, Charlie, sick 'em, pup. The others looked embarrassed, but Brooke rounded on Keppel, badgering him to sing; Keppel didn't want to, at first, and sat looking annoyed and sheepish, but Brooke worked away at him, full of high spirits, and what else was the chap to do? So he sang "Spanish Ladies"—he sang well, I'm bound to say, in a rolling bass—and by this time even the tiredest round the table were grinning and joining in the chorus, with Brooke encouraging and keeping time, and watching us like a hawk. He sang "The Arethusa" himself, and even coaxed Paitingi, who gave us a psalm, at which Charlie giggled hysterically, but Keppel joined in like thunder, and then Brooke glanced at me, nodding quietly, so I found myself giving 'em "Drink, Puppy, Drink", and they stamped and thumped to make the cabin shiver.

It was a shameful performance—so forced and false it was disgusting, this jolly lunatic putting heart into his men by making 'em sing, and everyone hating it. But they sang, you'll notice, and me along with 'em, and at the finish Brooke jumps up and cries:

"Come, that's none so bad! We'll have a choir yet. Spy-boats will lead tomorrow—5 a.m. sharp, then *Dido*'s pinnace, the two cutters, gig, *Jolly Bachelor*, then the small boats. Dinner at seven, prompt. Good-night, gentlemen!"

And off he went, leaving us gawking at each other; then Keppel shook his head, smiling, and sighed, and we dispersed, feeling pretty foolish, I dare say. I found myself wondering why they tolerated Brooke and his schoolboy antics, which were patently pathetic; why did they humour him?—for that is what it was. It wasn't fear, or love, or even respect; I suspect they felt it would somehow be mean to disappoint him, and so they fell in with every folly, whether it was charging a pirate prau in a jolly-boat or singing shanties when they ought to have been nursing their wounds or crawling away to sink into an exhausted sleep. Yes, they did humour him—G-d only knows why. Mind you, mad and dangerous as he was, I'm bound to say he was difficult to refuse, in anything.

I managed it later that night, though, admittedly not to his face. I was snug under the *Jolly Bachelor*'s ladder when the pirates came sneaking silently out of the mist in sampans and tried to take us by surprise. They were on the deck and murdering our look-outs before we were any the wiser, and if it hadn't been that the deck was littered with tacks to catch their bare feet, that would have been the end of the ship, and everyone aboard, including me. As it was, there was the deuce of a scrap in the dark, with Brooke yelling for everyone to pitch in—I burrowed closer into cover myself, clutching my pistol, until the hurroosh had died down, when I scuttled up quickly and blundered about, glaring and letting on that I'd been there all the time. I did yeoman work helping to heave dead pirates overside, and then we stood to until daylight, but they didn't trouble us again.

Next day it began to rain like fury, and we set off up the Skrang into a perfect sheet of water which cut visibility almost to nothing and pitted the river like small-shot. All day we toiled slowly into the murk, with the river narrowing until it was a bare furlong wide, and d---l an enemy did we see. I sat sodden in Paitingi's spy-boat, reduced to the nadir of misery, baling constantly until my whole body cried out with one great ache; by dark I was dropping with fatigue—and then, when we anchored, d--n my skin if we didn't have to shave and wash and dig out clean duds for Brooke's dinner-party on the *Jolly Bachelor*. Looking back, I can't imagine why I put up with it— I don't attempt to fathom the minds of the others; they all dressed in their best, soaking wet, and I couldn't show unwilling, could I? We assembled in the *Jolly Bachelor*'s cabin, steaming and dripping, and there was the table laid for dinner, silver, glass, and all, with Brooke in his blue swallow-tail and brass buttons, welcoming us like a b----y governor-general, taking wine with Keppel, waving us to our seats, and frowning because the turtle soup was cold.

I don't believe this is happening, thinks I; it's all a terrible nightmare, and Stuart isn't sitting opposite me in his black broadcloth with his string-cravat tied in a fancy bow, and this ain't real champagne I'm drinking by the light of reeking slush-lamps, with everyone crowded round the board in the tiny cabin, and they're not listening breathlessly while I tell 'em about getting Alfred Mynn leg-before at Lord's. There aren't any pirates, really, and we're not miles up some stinking creek in Borneo, drinking the loyal toast with the thunder bellowing outside and the rain gushing down the companion, and Brooke clipping cigars and passing them round while the Malay steward puts the port on the table. I couldn't bring myself to believe that all round us was a fleet of sampans and spy-boats, loaded with Dyaks and blue-jackets and other assorted savages, and that tomorrow we would be reliving the horror of Patusan all over again; it was all too wild and confused and unreal, and although I must have accounted for a bottle of warm champagne, and about a pint of port, I got up from that table as sober as I sat down.

It was real enough in the morning, though—the morning of that last dreadful day on the Skrang river. The weather had cleared like magic just before dawn, and the narrow waterway ahead was gleaming brown and oily in the sunlight between its olive walls of jungle. It was deathly hot, and for once the forest was comparatively silent, but there was an excitement through the fleet that you could almost feel beating in waves through the muggy air; it wasn't only that Brooke had predicted that this would be the last battle—I believe there was a realisation too that if we didn't reach conclusions with the pirates lurking somewhere ahead, our expedition would come to a halt through sheer exhaustion, and there would be nothing for it but to turn down-river again. It bred a kind of wild desperation in the others; Stuart was shivering with impatience as he dropped beside me into Paitingi's spy-boat, drawing his pistol and shoving it back in his belt, then doing the same thing over again; even Paitingi, in the bow, was taut as a fiddle-string, snapping at the Lingas and twitching at his red beard. My own condition I leave you to guess.

Our boy hero, of course, was his usual jaunty self. He was perched in the *Jolly Bachelor*'s bows as our spy-boat shoved off, straw hat on head, issuing his orders and cracking jokes fit to sicken you.

"They're *there*, old 'un," cries he to Paitingi. "All right, I dare say you can't smell 'em, but I can. We'll fetch up with them by afternoon at latest, probably sooner. So keep a sharp look-out, and don't get more than a pistol-shot ahead of the second spy, d'you hear?"

"Aye, aye," says Paitingi. "I don't like it, J.B. It's gey quiet. Suppose they've taken to the side-creeks—scattered and hid?"

"*Sulu Queen* can't hide," calls Brooke. "She's bound to hold to the mainstream, and that's going to shoal on her before long. She's the quarry, mind—take her, and the snake's head is cut clean off. Here, have a mango." He threw the fruit to Paitingi. "Never you mind the side-creeks; the instant you sight that steam-brig, up with a blue light and hold your station. We'll do the rest."

Paitingi muttered something about ambush in the narrow water, and Brooke laughed and told him to stop croaking. "Remember the first chap you ever fought against?" cries he. "Well, what's a parcel of pirates compared to him? Off you go, old lad—and good luck."

He waved as we shot away, the paddles skimming us into midstream and up to the first bend, with the other spies lining out in our wake and the *Dido*'s pinnace and *Jolly Bachelor* leading the heavier craft behind. I asked Stuart what Brooke had meant about the first chap Paitingi had fought, and he laughed.

"That was Napoleon. Didn't you know? Paitingi was in the

Turkish army at the Battle of the Pyramids[31]—weren't you, gaffer?"

"Aye," growls Paitingi. "And got weel beat for my pains. But I tell ye, Stuart, I felt easier that day than I do this." He fidgeted in the bow, leaning on the carronade to stare upriver under his hand. "There's something no' canny; I can feel it. Listen."

We strained our ears above the swish of the paddles, but except for the cries of birds in the forest, and the hum of the insect clouds close inshore, there was nothing. The river was empty, and by the sound of it the surrounding jungle was, too.

"Don't hear anything out o' the way," says Stuart.

"Precisely," says Paitingi. "No war-gongs—yet we've heard them every day for this week past. What ails them?"

"Dunno," says Stuart. "But ain't that a good sign?"

"Ask me this evening," says Paitingi. "I hope I'll be able to tell ye then."

His uneasiness infected me like the plague, for I knew he had as good a nose as any fighting-man I'd ever struck, and when such a one starts to twitch, look out. I had lively recollections of Sergeant Hudson sniffing trouble in the bleak emptiness of the Jallalabad road—by G-d, he'd been right, against all the signs, and here was Paitingi on the same tack, cocking his head, frowning, standing up from time to time to scan the impenetrable green, glancing at the sky, tugging his whiskers—it got on my nerves, and Stuart's, too, yet there wasn't sight nor smell of trouble as we glided up the silent river in the bright sunshine, slow mile after slow mile, through the brilliant bends and reaches, and always the stream brown and empty as far as we could see ahead. The air was empty and still; the sound of a mugger slipping with its heavy splash off a sandbank had us jumping up, reaching for our pistols; then a bird would screech on the other shore, and we would start round again, sweating cold in that steamy loneliness—I don't know any place where you feel as naked and exposed as an empty jungle river, with that vast, hostile age-old forest all about you. Just like Lord's, but no pavilion to run to.

Paitingi stood it for a couple of hours and then lost patience. He had been using his glass to rake the mouths of the little, overhung side-creeks that we passed every now and then, dim, silent tunnels into the wild; now he glowered back at the second spy-boat, a hundred yards in our wake, and snapped an order to the paddlers to increase their stroke. The spy surged ahead, trembling beneath us; Stuart looked back anxiously at the widening gap.

"J.B. said not more than a pistol-shot ahead," says he, and Paitingi rounded on him.

"If J.B. has his way, we'll spring the trap wi' our whole fleet! Then where'll he be? D'ye think he kens more about handling a spy-boat than I do?"

"But we're to hold steady till we come up with the *Sulu Queen*—"

"Shaitan take the *Sulu Queen*! She's lying up in one o' these creeks, whatever J.B. likes tae think. They're not ahead of us, I tell ye—they're either side! Sit doon, d--n ye!" he snaps at me. "Stuart! Pass the word—port paddles be ready to back water at my signal. Keep the stroke going! We'll win him a half-mile of water to manœuvre in, if we're lucky! Steady—and wait for my word!"

I couldn't make anything of this, but it was plainly dreadful news. By what he said, we were inside the jaws of the trap already, and the woods full of hidden fiends waiting to pounce, and he was forging ahead to spring the ambush before the rest of our boats got well inside. I sat gagging with fear, staring at that silent wall of leaves, at the eddies swirling round the approaching bend, at Paitingi's broad back as he crouched over the prow. The river had narrowed sharply in the last mile, to a bare hundred paces or so; the banks were so close I imagined I could see through the nearest trees, into the dark shadows beyond—was there something stirring there, could I hear some awful presence?—the spy-boat was fairly flying round the bend, and behind us the river was empty for a couple of furlongs, we were alone, far ahead—

"Now!" roars Paitingi, dropping to his knees and clutching the gunwales, and as the port paddlers backed water the spy-boat spun crazily on her heel, her bow rearing clear out of the water so that we had to cling like grim death to avoid being hurled out. For an awful instant she hung suspended at a fearful angle, with the water a good six feet beneath my left elbow, then she came smashing down as though she would plunge to the bottom, wallowed with the water washing over her sides—and we were round and driving downriver, with Paitingi yelling to us to bale for our lives.

The water was ankle deep as I scooped at it with my hat, dashing it over the side; the paddlers were gasping like leaky engines, the current helping to scud us along at a frightening pace—and then there was a yell from Paitingi, I raised my head to look, and saw a sight that froze me in my seat.

A hundred yards ahead, downriver, something was moving from the tangle of the bank—a raft, poling slowly out on the bosom of the stream, crowded with men. At the same moment there was a great rending, tearing noise from the jungle on the opposite bank; the forest seemed to be moving slowly outward, and then it detached itself into one huge tree, a mass of tangled green, falling ponderously with a mighty splash to block a third of the stream on our port bow. From the jungle either side came the sudden thunderous boom of war-gongs; behind the first raft another was setting out; there were small canoes sprouting like black fingers from the banks ahead, each loaded with savages— where a moment since the river had been silent and empty it was now vomiting a horde of pirate craft, baying their war-cries, their boats alive with steel and yelling, cruel faces, cutting us off, swarming towards us. There were others on the banks on our beams, archers and blow-pipemen; the whist-whist-whist of shafts came lancing towards us.

"There—ye see?" roars Paitingi. "Whaur's your clever J.B. now, Stuart? *Sulu Queen*, says he! Aye, weel, he's got clear water tae work in—small thanks to himsel'! These sons o' Eblis looked to trap a fleet—they've got one wee spy-boat!" And he stood up, roaring with laughter and defiance. "Drive for the gap, steersman! On, on! Charge!"

There are moments in life which defy description—in my black moods they seem to have occurred about once a week, and I have difficulty distinguishing them. The last minutes at Bala-clava, the moment when the Welsh broke at Little Hand Rock and the Zulus came bounding over our position, the breaching of Piper's Fort gate, the neck-or-nothing race for Reno's Bluff with the Sioux braves running among the shattered rabble of

Custer's Seventh—I've stretched my legs in all of those, knowing I was going to die, and being d----d noisy at the prospect. But in Paitingi's spy-boat running was impossible—so, depressingly, was surrender. I observed those flat, evil faces sweeping down on us behind their glittering lance-heads and *kampilans*, and decided they weren't open to discussion; there was nothing for it but to sit and blaze away in panic—and then a red-hot pain shot through my left ribs, and I looked down bewildered to see a *sumpitan* shaft in my side. Yellow, it was, with a little black tuft of lint on its butt, and I pawed at it, whimpering, until Stuart reached over and wrenched it clear, to my considerable discomfort. I screamed, twisted, and went over the side.

I dare say it was that that saved me, although I'm blessed if I know how. I took a glance at the official account of the action before I wrote this, and evidently the historian had a similar difficulty in believing that anyone survived our little water-party, for he states flatly that every man-jack of Paitingi's crew was slaughtered. He notes that they had got too far ahead, were cut off by a sudden ambush of rafts and praus, and by the time Brooke's fleet had come storming up belatedly to the rescue, Paitingi and his followers had all been killed—there's a graphic account of twenty boats jammed together in a bloody mêlée, of thousands of pirates yelling on the bank, of the stream running crimson, with headless corpses, wreckage, and capsized craft drifting downstream—but never a word about poor old Flashy struggling half-foundered, dyeing the water with his precious gore, spluttering "Wait, you callous b-----s, I'm sinking!" Quite hurtful, being ignored like that, although I was glad enough of it at the time, when I saw how things were shaping.

It was, I've since gathered, touch and go that Brooke's whole fleet wasn't wiped out; indeed, if it hadn't been for Paitingi's racing ahead, sacrificing his spy-boat like the gallant idiot he was, the pirates would have jumped the whole expedition together, but as it was, Brooke had time to dress his boats into line and charge in good order. It was a horrid near-run thing, though; Keppel confessed later that when he saw the fighting horde that was waiting for him, "for a moment I was at a loss what steps to take"—and there was one chap, treading water upstream with a hole in his belly and roaring for succour, who shared his sentiments exactly. I was viewing the action from t'other side, so to speak, but it looked just as confused and interesting to me as it did to Keppel. I was busy, of course, holding my wounded guts with one hand and clutching at a piece of wreckage with the other, trying to avoid being run down by boats full of ill-disposed persons with swords, but as I came up for the tenth time, I saw the last seconds of Paitingi's spy-boat, crashing into the heart of the enemy, its bow-gun exploding to tear a bloody cleft through the crew of a raft.

Then the pirate wave swept over them; I had a glimpse of Stuart, stuck like a pin-cushion with *sumpitan* darts, toppling into the water; of a Linga swordsman clearing a space with his *kampilan* swinging in a shining circle round his head; of another in the water, stabbing fiercely up at the foes above him; of the steersman, on hands and knees on the raft, being hacked literally into bits by a screaming crowd of pirates; of Paitingi, a bristling, red giant, his turban gone, roaring "Allah-il-Allah!" with a pirate swung up in his huge arms—and then there was just the shell of the spy-boat, overturned, in the swirling, bloody water, with the pirate boats surging away from it, turning to meet the distant, unseen enemy downstream.

I didn't have time to see any more. The water was roaring in my ears, I could feel my strength ebbing away through the tortured wound in my side, my fingers slipping from their grip on the wreckage, the sky and treetops were spinning slowly overhead, and across the surface of the water something—a boat? a raft?—was racing down on me with a clamour of voices. Air and water were full of the throbbing of war-gongs, and then I was hit a violent blow on the head, something scraped agonisingly over my body, forcing me down, choking with water, my ears pounding, lungs bursting . . . And then, as old Wild Bill would have said: "Why, boys—I drowned!"[32]

For a moment I thought I was back in Jallalabad, in that blissful awakening after the battle. There was a soft bed under me, sheets at my chin, and a cool breeze; I opened my eyes, and saw that it came from a port-hole opposite me. That wasn't right, though; no port holes in the Khyber country—I struggled with memory, and then a figure blocked the light, a huge figure in green sarong and sleeveless tunic, with a krees in his girdle, and fingering his earring as he stared down at me, his heavy brown face as hard as a curling-stone.

"You should have died," says Don Solomon Haslam.

Just what an awakening invalid needs, of course, but it brought the nightmare flooding back—the reeking waters of the Skrang, the overwhelmed spy-boat, the dart in my side—I was conscious of a dull ache in my ribs, and of bandages. But where the d---l was I? In the *Sulu Queen,* sure enough, but even in that dizzy moment of waking I was aware that her motion was a slow, steady heave, there were no jungle noises, and the air blowing from the port was salt. I tried to speak, and my voice came in a parched croak.

"What . . . what am I doing here?"

"Surviving," says he. "For the moment." And then to my amazement he thrust his face into mine and snarled: "But you couldn't die decently, could you? Oh no, not you! Hundreds perished in that river—but you survive! Every man of Paitingi's —good men—Lingas who fought to the last—Paitingi himself, who was worth a thousand. All lost! But not you, blubbering in the water where my men found you! They should have left you to drown. I should have—bah!" He wheeled away, fuming.

Well, I hadn't expected him to be pleased to see me, but even in my confused state so much passion seemed a mite unreasonable. Was I delirious?—but no, I felt not bad, and when I tried to ease myself up on the pillows I found I could do it without much discomfort; one doesn't care to be raved at lying down, you understand. A hundred questions and fears were jumbled in my mind, but the first one was:

"How long have I been here?"

"Two weeks." He eyed me malevolently. "And if you wonder where, the *Sulu Queen* is approximately ten south seventy east, heading west-sou'-west." Then, bitterly: "What the d---l else was I to do, once those fools had hauled you from the water? Let you die of gangrene—treat you as you deserved? Ha! That was the one thing I could *not* do!"

Being still half-stupid with prolonged unconsciousness, I couldn't make much of this. The last time I'd seen him, we'd been boon-companions, more or less, but since then he'd tried to murder me, kidnapped my wife, and turned out to be the arch-pirate of the Orient, which shed a different light on things. I tried to steady my whirling thoughts, but couldn't. Anyway, he was obviously in a fearful wax because he'd felt obliged, G-d only knew why, not to let me perish of blow-pipe poison. Difficult to know what to say, so I didn't.

"You can guess why you are alive," says he. "It is because of her—whose husband you were."

For a dreadful second I thought he meant she was dead; then my mind leaped to the conclusion that he meant he had taken her from me, and done the dirty deed on her—and at the very thought of my little Elspeth being abused by this vile nigger pirate, this scum of the East, my confusion and discretion vanished together in rage.

"You b----y liar! I *am* her husband! She's my wife! You kidnapped her, you filthy pirate, and—"

"Kidnapped? Saved, you mean!" His eyes were blazing. "Rescued her from a man—no, from a brute—who wasn't fit to kiss her feet! Oh, no—it's not kidnapping to take a pearl from a swine, who fouls her with his very touch, who treats her as a mere concubine, who betrays her—"

"It's a lie! I—"

"Didn't I see you with my own eyes? Coupling with that slut in my own library—"

"Drawing-room—"

"—that harlot Lade? Isn't your name a byword in London

for debauchery and vice, for every kind of lewdness and depravity?"

"Not every kind! I never—"

"A rake, a cheat, a bully and a whoremonger—that's what I rescued that sweet, brave woman from. I took her from the hell of life with you—"

"You're mad!" I croaked. "She never said it was hell! She loves me, curse you—as I love her—"

His hand swept across my face, knocking me back on my pillow, and I had sense enough to stay there, for he was a fearsome sight, shaking with fury, his mouth working.

"What did you ever know of love?" cries he. "Let me hear that word on your lips again, and I'll have them sewn together, with a scorpion in your mouth!"

Well, when he put it like that, I saw there was no point in arguing. I lay there quaking, while he mastered himself and went on, more quietly:

"Love is not for animals like you. Love is what I felt—for the first time—on an afternoon at Lord's, when I saw her. I knew then, as surely as I know there is One God, that there could be no other woman, that I should worship her for life, a life that would be death without her. Yes, I knew then—what love was."

He let out a great breath, and he was trembling. By George, thinks I, we've got a maniac here—he means it. He heaved a minute, and then went on, like a poet on opium.

"She filled my life from that moment; there was nothing else. But it was a pure love—she would have been sacred to me, had she been married to a husband truly worthy of her. But when I saw the truth—that she was shackled to the basest kind of brute"—he shot me a withering look—"I asked why my life, and hers (which was infinitely more precious) should be ruined by a stupid convention which, after all, meant nothing to me. Oh, I was a gentleman, trained in the *English* way, at an *English* school—but I was also a prince of the House of Magandanu, descended from the Prophet himself—and I was a pirate, as you of the West know the word. Why should I respect *your* customs; when I could offer her a destiny as high above life with you as the stars are above the slime, why should I hesitate? I could make her a queen, instead of the chattel of a drunken, licentious bully who had only married her at pistol point!"

"That ain't fair! She was d----d glad to get me, and if that poxy little varmint Morrison says other—don't hit me! I'm wounded!"

"Not by one word, by one gesture, did she complain! Her loyalty, like everything else about her, is perfect—even to a worm like you! But I knew, and I determined to save her for a love worthy of her. So I worked, carefully, patiently, for both our sakes—it was torture to impose on that sweet innocence, but I knew that in time she would bless me for the subterfuge. I was ready to sacrifice anything—millions, what were they to me? I, who was half of the East, half of the West, was prepared to put myself beyond the law, beyond civilisation, for her sake. I would give her a throne, a fortune—and true love. For I still have my kingdom of the East, and she shall share it with me."

Well, you won't want me as British Ambassador, thinks I, but I kept mum, tactfully. He paced about the cabin, looking masterful as he prated on.

"So I took her, and I fought for her—in the face of that vicious madman Brooke! Oh, he'll come too often to Borneo, that one, with his lying piety and promises—he that is the bloodiest pirate of us all! No doubt he made a fine pretext of rescuing her, so that he could come again and harry and burn us, butcher our people—" He was working into a fine froth now, waving his hands. "What's it to him, how we live? What sacred right has he to war on us and our ways? I'd have eaten his fleet alive on the Skrang, but for Paitingi! As it was, I slipped him in the creeks and came downriver, with this one vessel. He thinks he's finished Suleiman Usman, does he? Let him come to Maludu, when I return there!"

He paced some more, chewing over Brooke, and then rounded on me. "But he doesn't matter—not now. You do. You're here, and you're inopportune." He paused, considering me. "Yes . . . you should have died."

I wished to G-d he'd stop harping on that—you could see where it was going to lead. This wasn't Don Solomon of Brook Street any longer, not so you'd notice—this was a beastly aborigine who went plundering about in ships festooned with skulls, and I was an inconvenient husband, 'nuff said. In addition, he clearly had more screws loose than a drunk sapper—all that moonshine about worshipping Elspeth, not being able to live without her, making her a queen—well! It would have been laughable if it hadn't been true; after all, when a man kidnaps a married woman and fights a war over her, it ain't just a passing fancy.

But one thing was plain—his wooing hadn't prospered, or I'd have been overside long ago, with a bag of coal round my ankles. Why the h--l couldn't he have rattled her in London, and got tired of it, and we'd have been spared all this? But here we were, in a pickle whose delicacy made my flesh crawl. I considered, took a deep breath, and tried not to talk shrill.

"Well, now, Don Solomon," says I, "I take note of what you've said, and—ah—I'm glad we've had this little prose together, you know, and you've told me—um—what you think. Yes—you've put it very fair, and while I can't but deplore what you've done, mind—well, I understand your feelings, as any man of sensibility must—and I'm that, I hope—and I see you were deeply affected by . . . well, by my wife—and I know what it's like, of course—I mean, she's a little stunner, we agree—heavens yes," I babbled on, while he gaped in bewilderment, small blame to him.

"But you've got it quite wrong you know; we're a devoted couple, Elspeth—Mrs Flashman—and I, ask anyone—never a cross word—sublimely happy—"

"And that whore Lade?" he snarled. "Is that your devotion?"

"Why, my dear chap! The merest accident—I mean, that I noticed her at all—pure jealousy at seeing my wife flattered by your attentions—a man of your address, I mean, polished manners, charming, stinking rich—no, no, I mean, I found myself quite cut out—and Mrs Lade, well . . . heat of the moment—you know yourself how one can be carried away—"

It was touch and go that he didn't savage me on the bed, considering the drivel I was talking—but it sometimes works, rubbish with a ring of sincerity, when you're stuck with a hopeless case. It didn't here; he strode to the bed, seized me by the shoulder, and drew back his great fist.

"You infernal liar!" cries he. "D'you think you can gammon me with your snivelling?"

"I'm not!" I bawled. "I love Elspeth, and she loves me, and you know it! She don't want you!" I'd done it now, I could see, so I went roaring on: "That's why you wish I'd died—because you know if you harm me now, your last hope of winning her is gone! Don't—I'm an invalid—my wound!"

His fingers bit my shoulder like a vice; suddenly he flung me back and straightened up, with an ugly laugh.

"So that's what you're counting on! Why, you miserable toad, she doesn't even know you're here. I could drop you overboard, and she'd never know. Aye, you go pale at—"

"I don't believe you! If that were true you'd have done me in already—you tried it in Singapore, rot you, with your foul black gangsters!"

He stared at me. "I've no notion what you're talking about," and he sounded sincere, curse him. "I don't expect you to understand it, Flashman, but the reason you're still alive is that I'm a man of honour. When I take her to her throne—and I shall —it will be with a clean hand, not one fouled with a husband's blood—even a husband like you."

That was reassuring enough to banish my immediate terrors; I even recovered sufficiently for a cautious sneer.

"Talk's cheap, Solomon. Honour, says you—but you ain't above wife-stealing, and cheating at cricket—oh, aye, breaking a chap's wicket when you've laid him out foul! If you're such a man of honour," I taunted him, "you'd let Elspeth choose for herself—but you daren't, 'cos you know she'd plump for me, warts and all!"

He stood stock still, just looking at me, without expression, fingering his earring again. Then after a moment, he nodded, slowly.

"Yes," says he quietly. "It must come to that, must it not? Very well."

He threw open the door, and barked an order, glancing oddly at me while we waited. Feet sounded—and I felt my heart begin to thump uncontrollably as I sat up in bed; G-d knows why, but I was suddenly dizzy—and then she was there in the doorway, and for a moment I thought it was someone else—this was some Eastern nymph, in a clinging sarong of red silk, her skin tanned to the gold of honey, whereas Elspeth's was like milk. Her blonde hair was bleached almost white by the sun—and then I saw those magnificent blue eyes, round with bewilderment like her lips, and I heard a sob coming out of me: "Elspeth!"

She gave a little scream, and stumbled in the doorway, putting her hand to her eyes—and then she was running to my arms, crying "Harry! Oh, Harry!" flinging herself at me, her mouth against mine, clutching my head in wild hands, sobbing hysterically, and I forgot Solomon, and the ache of my wound, and fear, and danger, as I pressed that lovely softness against me and kissed and kissed her until she went suddenly limp, and slid from my arms to the floor in a dead faint. It was only then, as I scrambled out, clutching my bandaged side, that I realised the door was closed, and Solomon was gone.

I tried to haul her up to the bed, but I was still weak as a kitten from my wound and confinement, and couldn't manage it. So I had to be content with pawing and fondling until her eyes fluttered open, and then she clung to me, muttering my name, and after we had babbled thankfully for a few minutes and exchanged our news, so to speak, we got down to the reunion in earnest—and in the middle of it, while I was just wondering if my wound was about to come asunder, she suddenly pulled her mouth free of mine and cried:

"Harry—what is Mrs Leo Lade to you?"

"Hey?" I yelped. "What? What d'ye mean? Who's she? I mean—"

"You know her very well! The Duke's . . . companion, who paid you such singular attention. What is between you?"

"Good G-d! At a time like this—Elspeth, my dear, what has Mrs Lade to do with anything?"

"That is what I am asking. No, desist—Don Solomon said . . . hinted . . . of an attachment. Is this true?"

You wouldn't credit it—here she was, on a pirate ship, having been abducted, shanghaied round half the East, through war, ambush, and confounded head-hunters, reunited with her long-lost spouse, and just as he was proving his undying affection at grievous risk to his health, her jealous little pea-brain was off on another tack altogether. Unbelievable—and most unflattering. But I was equal to the occasion.

"Solomon!" cries I. "That viper! Has he been trying to poison your mind against me with his lies? I might have guessed it! Not content with stealing you, the villain traduces me to you—don't you see? He'll stop at nothing to win you away from me."

"Oh." She frowned up at me—G-d, she was lovely, if half-witted. "You mean he—oh, how could he be so base? Oh, Harry"—and she began to cry, trembling all down her body in a way that almost brought me to the boil—"all the rest I could bear—the fear and shame and . . . and all of it, but the thought that you might have been untrue . . . as he suggested—ah, that would have broken my heart! Tell me it wasn't so, my love!"

"Course it wasn't! Good l--d, that raddled pudding Lade! How could you think it? I despise the woman—and as though I could even look at her, or any other, when I have my own perfect, angelic Aphrodite—" I tried a couple of cautious thrusts as I saw the suspicion dying in her eyes, but since attack's the best form of defence I suddenly stopped, frowning thunderously. "That foul kite Solomon! He will stoop to any depth. Oh, dearest, I have been mad these past weeks—the thought of you in his clutches." I gulped in manly torment. "Tell me—in your ordeal—did he . . . I mean—well . . . did he, the scoundrel?"

She was flushed with my attentions anyway, but at this she went crimson, and moaned softly, those innocent eyes brimming with tears.

"Oh, how can you ask? Would I be alive now, if . . . if . . . Oh, Harry, I cannot believe it is you, holding me safe! Oh, my love!"

Well, that was that settled (so far as it ever is with Elspeth; I've never been able to read those child-like eyes and butter-melting lips, so the d---l with it), and Mrs Lade disposed of, at least until we had finished the business in hand and were lying talking in the growing dusk of the cabin. Naturally, Elspeth's story came flooding out in an excited stream, and I was listening with my mind in a great confusion, what with my weakened state, the crazy shock of our reunion, and the anxiety of our predicament—and suddenly, in the middle of describing the rations they'd fed her during her captivity, she suddenly said:

"Harry—you are *sure* you have not been astride Mrs Lade?"

I was so amazed she had to say it twice.

"Eh? Good G-d, girl, what d'you mean?"

"Have you mounted her?"

I can't think how I've kept my sanity, talking to that woman for sixty years. Of course, at this time we'd only been married for five, and I hadn't plumbed the depths of her eccentricity. I could only gargle and exclaim:

"D----t, I've told you I haven't! And where on earth—it is shocking to use expressions of that kind!"

"Why? You use them—I heard you, at Lady Chalmers', when you were talking to Jack Speedicut, and you were both remarking on Lottie Cavendish, and whatever her husband could see in such a foolish creature, and *you* said you expected he found her a good mount. I dare say I was not meant to hear."

"I should think not! And I can have said no such thing—and anyway, ladies ain't meant to understand such . . . such vulgar words."

"The ladies who get mounted must understand them."

"They ain't ladies!"

"Why not? Lottie Cavendish is. So am I, and you have mounted me—lots of times." She sighed, and nestled close, G-d help us.

"Well, I have not . . . done any such thing with Mrs Lade, so there."

"I'm so glad," says she, and promptly fell asleep.

Now, I've told you this, partly because it's all of the conversation that I remember of that reunion, and also to let you understand what a truly impossible scatterhead Elspeth was—and still is. There's something missing there; always has been, and it makes her senselessly unpredictable. (Heaven knows what idiocy she'll come out with on her deathbed, but I'll lay drunkard's odds it's nothing to do with dying. I only hope I ain't still above ground to hear it, though.) She'd been through an ordeal that would have driven most women out of their wits—not that she had many to start with—but now she was back with me, safe as she supposed, she seemed to have no notion of the peril in which we both stood; why, when Solomon's Malays took her away to her own quarters that first night, she was more concerned about the sunburn she'd taken, and if it would spoil her complexion, than about the fate Solomon might have in store for us. What can you do with a woman like that?

Mind you, there was a dead weight off my heart at having seen her, and knowing she'd come to no bodily harm. At least her captivity hadn't changed her—come to think of it, if she'd wept and raved about her sufferings, or sat numb and shocked, or been terrified of her situation, like a normal woman—she wouldn't have been Elspeth, and that would have been worse than anything, somehow.

For the next two days I was confined to my cabin, and didn't see a living soul except the Chink steward who brought my food, and he was deaf to all my demands and questions. I'd no notion what was happening, or where we were going; I knew from what Solomon had said that we were in the South Indian Ocean, and the sun confirmed that we were westering steadily, but that was all. What did Solomon intend?—the one thing that grew on me was that he wasn't likely to do me in, praise God, not now that Elspeth had seen me, for that would have scuppered any hopes he had of winning her. And that was the nub of it.

You see, lunatic though his behaviour had been, the more I thought about it the more I believed him: the blighter was really mad about her, and not just to board and scuttle her, either, but with all the pure, romantic trimmings, like Shelley or one of those chaps. Astonishing—well, I love her myself, always have, but not to put me off my food.

But Solomon had it to the point of obsession, where he'd been willing to kidnap and kill and give up civilisation for her. And he'd believed that, in spite of his behaving like a b----y Barbary corsair, he could eventually woo and win her, given time. But then he'd seen her run to my arms, sobbing, and had realised it was no go; shocking blow it must have been. He'd probably been gnawing his futile passion ever since, realising that he'd bought outlawry and the gallows for nothing. But what was he to do now? Unless he chopped us both (which seemed far-fetched, pirate and Old Etonian though he was) it seemed to me he had no choice but to set us free with apologies, and sail away, grief-stricken, to join the Foreign Legion, or become a monk, or an American citizen. Why, he'd as good as thrown up the sponge in letting Elspeth and me spend hours together alone; he'd never have done that if he hadn't given up all hope of her, surely?

He was in no hurry to repeat his generosity, however. On the third day a little Chink doctor visited me with the steward, but he didn't have a word of English, and busied himself impassively examining the *sumpitan*-wound in my guts—which was fairly healed, and barely ached—while remaining deaf to my demands to see Solomon. In the end I lost patience, and made for the door, roaring for attention, but at this two of the Malay crew appeared, all bulging muscles and evil phizzes, and indicated that if I didn't hold my tongue they'd hold it for me. So I did, until they'd gone, and then I set about the door with my boots, bawling for Elspeth, and calling Solomon every name I could think of—indulging my natural insolence, if you like, since I figured it was safe enough. By George, wasn't I young and innocent, though?

The response to that was nil, and an icy finger of fear traced down my back. For the past two days, with my belly still in a sling, it had seemed natural enough to be in the cabin—but now that the doctor had been, and seemed satisfied, why weren't they letting me out—or why, at least, wasn't Solomon coming to see me? Why weren't they letting me see Elspeth? Why weren't they letting me take exercise? It didn't make sense, to keep me cooped here, if he was going to let us go, and—*if* he was going to let us go. It suddenly rushed in on me that that was pure assumption, probably brought on by my blissful reunion with Elspeth, which had been paradise after the weeks of peril and terror. Suppose I was wrong?

I don't know anyone who despairs faster than I do—mind you, I've had cause—and the hours that followed found me in the depths. I didn't know what to think or believe, my fears mounted steadily, and by next morning I was my normal self, in a state of abject funk. I was even drawing sinister significance from the fact that this cabin I was in was obviously in the forward part of the vessel, with the engines between me and the civilised quarters where Elspeth—and Solomon—would be.

G-d, was he ravishing her, now that he knew he could never seduce her? Was he bargaining with her for my life, threatening to feed me to the sharks unless she buckled to with him? That was it, for certain—it's what I'd have done in his place—and I tore my hair at the thought that like as not she'd defy him; she was forever reading trashy novels in which proud heroines drew themselves upright and pointed to the door, crying: "Do your worst, sinister man; my husband would die rather than be the price of my dishonour!" Would he, by jingo?—surrender, you stupid b---h, if that's all he wants, I found myself muttering; what's another more or less? Charming husband, ain't I? Well, why not? Honour's all very well, but life matters. Besides, I'd do the same to save Elspeth, if any lustful woman threatened *me*. They never do, though.

With such happy thoughts, in a torture of uncertainty, I passed the days that followed—how many I'm not sure, but I guess about a week. In all that time, no one came near me except the steward, with a Malay thug to back him up—I was alone, hour after hour, night after night, in that tiny box, alternating between shivering panic and black despair—not knowing. That was the worst of it; I didn't even know what to be afraid of, and by the end of the week I was ready for anything, if it would only end my misery. It's a dangerous state to be in, as I know, now that I'm old and experienced; I didn't realise, then, that things can always get worse.

Then I saw the American ship, by chance, as I paced past my porthole. She was maybe half a mile off, a sleek black Southern Run clipper with Old Glory at her jackstaff; the morning sun was shining like silver on her topsails as they flapped from the reefs and were sheeted home. Now I'm no shellback, but I'd seen that setting a score of times, when a vessel was standing out from port—G-d, were we near some harbour of civilisation, where the big ships ran? I hallooed for all I was worth, but of course they were too far off to hear, and then I was rummaging feverishly for matches to start a fire—anything to attract attention and bring that Yankee to my rescue. But of course I couldn't find any; I nearly broke my neck trying to squint out of the port in search of land, but there was nothing but blue rollers, and the Yankee dwindling towards the eastern horizon.

All day I sat fretting, wondering, and then in mid-afternoon I saw little native craft from my port, and a low green mainland beyond them. Gradually a beach came into view, and a few huts, and then wooden houses with steep roofs—no flags, and nothing but niggers in loin-cloths—no, there was a uniform, an unmistakable navy coat, black with gold braid, and a cocked hat, among a group on a little jetty. But there was the rumble of the *Sulu Queen*'s cable—we were anchoring a good quarter of a mile out. Never mind, that was close enough for me; I was in a fever of excitement as I tried to figure where it might be—we'd been westering, Southern Indian Ocean, and here was a small port, still important enough for a Yankee clipper to touch. It couldn't be the Cape, with that coastline. Port Natal—surely we weren't that far west? I tried to conjure up the map of that huge sea east of Africa—of course, Mauritius! The navy coat, the niggers, the Arabi-looking small craft—they all fitted. And Mauritius was British soil.

I was trembling as I took stock. What the d---l was Solomon thinking of, putting into Mauritius? Wood and water—he'd probably had no chance of either since bolting from the Skrang. And with me cooped tight, and Elspeth probably likewise, what had he to fear? But it was my chance—there'd never be another like it. I could swim the distance easily . . . and the lock scraped in my door at that moment.

There are split seconds when you can't afford to plan. I watched the steward setting down my tray, and without making a conscious decision I turned slowly towards the door where the Malay thug was hovering, beckoned him, and pointed, frowning, to the corner of the cabin. He advanced a pace, squinting up where I was pointing—and the next instant his courting tackle was half-way up inside his torso, impelled by my right boot, he was flying across the cabin, screaming, and Flashy was out and racing—where? There was a ladder, but I ducked past it instinctively, and tore along a short passage, the Chinese steward squealing in my rear. Round the corner—and there was a piece of open deck, Malays coiling rope, and iron doors flung wide to the sunshine and sea. As I ploughed through the startled Malays, scattering them, I had a glimpse of small craft between me and the shore, a distant jetty and palms, and then I was through those doors like a hot rivet, in an enormous dive, hitting the water with an almighty splash, gliding to the surface, and then striking out, head down, for dear life towards the distant land.

I reckon it took about ten seconds from my cabin to the water, and as many minutes before I was alongside the piles of the wharf. I was half-conscious with the exertion of my swim, and had to cling to the slimy wood while curious niggers in small boats drew up to gape at me, chattering like magpies. I looked back at the *Sulu Queen*, and there she was, riding peacefully, with a few native craft round her. I looked landward—there was the beach, and a fair-sized native town behind it, and a big building with a verandah and a flag-pole—it was a deuced odd-looking flag, striped and blazoned—some shipping line, perhaps. I hauled myself wearily along the piles, found a ladder, dragged myself up it, and lay panting and sodden on the wooden jetty, conscious of a small crowd forming round me. They were all niggers, in loin-cloths or white robes—some pretty Arab-looking, by their noses and head-gear. But there was the navy coat, pushing towards me, and the crowd falling back. I tried to pull myself up, but couldn't, and then the navy trousers stopped beside me, and their owner was bending down towards me. I tried to control my panting.

"I'm . . . a British . . . army officer," I wheezed. "Escaped from . . . that ship . . . pirate . . ." I raised my head, and the words died on my lips.

The fellow bending towards me was in full navy rig, right enough, even to the hat and epaulette—the green sash looked strange, though. But that wasn't the half of it. The face beneath the cocked hat was jet black.

I stared at him, and he stared back. Then he said something, in a language I couldn't understand, so I shook my head and repeated that I was an army officer. Where was the commandant? He shrugged, showed his yellow teeth in a grin, and said something, and the crowd giggled.

"D--n your eyes!" cries I, struggling up. "What the h--l's going on here? Where's the harbour-master? I'm a British army officer, Captain Flashman, and—" I was stabbing him on the chest with my finger, and now, to my utter amazement, he struck my hand angrily aside and snapped something in his heathen lingo, right in my face! I fell back, appalled at the brute's effrontery—and then there was a commotion behind, and I looked to see a small boat ploughing up at the seaward end of the jetty, and Solomon, of all people, springing from her bows and striding towards us along the planking, a massive figure in his tunic and sarong, with a face like thunder. Right, my hearty, thinks I, this is where you receive your ration allowance, once these people realise you're a b----y pirate, and I flung out a hand to denounce him to my epauletted nigger. But before I could get a word out Solomon had seized me by the shoulder and spun me round.

"You infernal fool!" cries he. "What have you done?"

You can be sure I told him, a trifle incoherently, at the top of my voice, drawing the nigger's attention to the fact that here was the notorious pirate and brigand, Suleiman Usman, delivered into his hands, and would he mind arresting him and his ship and restoring me and my wife to liberty.

"And you can swing till the crows peck you, you kidnapping tyke!" I informed Solomon. "You're done for."

"In G-d's name, where d'you think you are?" His voice was shrill.

"Mauritius, ain't it?"

"Mauritius?" He suddenly pulled me aside. "You booby, this is Tamitave—Madagascar!"

Well, that startled me, I admit. It explained the nigger in uniform, I supposed, but I couldn't see it made much difference. I was saying so, when the nigger stepped up and addressed Solomon, pretty sharp, and to my amazement the Don shrugged, apologetically, as though it had been a white official, and replied in French! But it was his abject tone as much as the language that bewildered me.

"Your pardon, excellency—a most unfortunate mistake. This man is one of my crew—a little drunk, you understand. With your permission I shall take him—"

"Balderdash!" I roared. "You'll take me nowhere, you lying dago!" I swung to the nigger. "You speak French, do you? Well, so do I, and I'm no more one of his crew than you are. He's a d----d pirate, who has abducted me and my wife—"

"Be quiet, you clown!" cries Solomon in English, thrusting me aside. "You'll destroy us! Leave him to me," and he began to patter to the black again, in French, but the other silenced him with a flap of his hand.

"Silence," says he, as if he were the b----y Duke. "The commandant approaches."

Sure enough, there was a file of soldiers coming from the landward end of the jetty, strapping blacks in white loin-cloths and bandoliers, with muskets at the shoulder. And behind them, carried by coolies in an open sedan, came an unbelievable figure. It is solemn truth—he was black as your boot, and he wore a turban on his head, a flowered red and yellow shirt, and a 42nd Highlanders kilt. He had sandals on his feet, a sabre at his hip, white gloves, and a rolled brolly in his hand. I've gone mad, thinks I; it's been the strain, or the sun. That thing can't be real.

Solomon was hissing urgently in my ear. "Don't say a word! Your one chance is to prete::d to be one of my crew—"

"Are you mad?" says I. "After what you've done, you—"

"Please!" And unless my ears deceived me he was pleading. "You don't understand—I intend you no harm—you shall both go free—Mauritius, if I can do it safely—I swear—"

"You swear! D'you imagine I'd trust you for an instant?"

And then the black's voice, speaking harsh French, cut across his reply.

"You." He was pointing at me. "You say you were a prisoner on that ship. And you are English. Is it so?"

I looked at the commandant, leaning forward from his sedan in that ludicrous Hallowe'en rig, his great ebony head cocked on one side, bloodshot eyes regarding me. As I nodded in reply to the officer's question, the commandant took a peeled mango from one of his minions and began to cram it into his mouth, juice spurting over his gloved hand and over his ridiculous kilt. He tossed the stone away, wiped his hand on his shirt, and said in careful French, in a croaking rasp:

"And your wife, you say, is also a prisoner of this man?"

"Pardon, excellency." Solomon pushed forward. "This is a great misunderstanding, as I have tried to explain. This man is of my ship's company, and is covered by my safe-conduct and trading licence from her majesty. I beg you to allow—"

"He denies it," croaked the commandant. He cleared his throat and spat comprehensively, hitting one of the soldiers on the leg. "He swam ashore. And he is English." He shrugged. "Shipwrecked."

"Oh, Ch---t," muttered Solomon, licking his lips.

The commandant wagged a finger the size of a black cucumber, peering at Solomon. "He is plainly not covered by your licence or safe-conduct. Nor is his wife. That licence, Monsieur Suleiman, does not exempt you from Malagassy law, as you should know. It is only by special favour that you yourself escape the *fanompoana*—what you call . . . *corvée*?" He gestured at me. "In his case, there is no question."

"What the dooce is he talking about?" says I to Solomon. "Where's the British consul? I've had enough—"

"There's no such thing, you fool!" Solomon was positively wringing his hands; suddenly he was a fat, frightened man. "Excellency, I implore you to make an exception—this man is not a castaway—I can swear he intended no harm in her majesty's dominions—"

"He will do none," says the commandant, and jabbered curtly at the officer. "He is lost"—a phrase whose significance escaped me just then. The coolies lifted the sedan, and away it swayed, the officer barked an order, and a file of his soldiers trotted past us, their leader bawling to one of the boatmen, summoning his craft to the jetty.

"No—wait!" Solomon's face was contorted with anguish. "You idiot!" he shrieked at me, and then he started first this way and that, calling to the commandant, and then running down the jetty after the file of soldiers. The black officer laughed, indicated me, and snapped an order to two of his men. It wasn't till they grabbed my arms and began to run me off the jetty that I came to my senses; I roared and struggled, bawling for Solomon, shouting threats of what would happen to them for laying their filthy hands on an Englishman. I lashed out, and a musket-butt sprawled me half-conscious on the planking. Then they dragged me up, and one of them, his great black face blasting foul breath all over me, snapped shackles on my wrists; they seized the chain and hauled me headlong up the street, with the blacks eyeing me curiously and children running alongside, squealing and laughing.

That was how I became a captive in Madagascar.

* * *

As you know—or rather, you don't, but if you're intelligent you'll have guessed—I'm a truthful man, at least where these memoirs are concerned. I've got nothing to lie for any longer, who lied so consistently—and successfully—all my life. But every now and then, in writing, I feel I have to remind you, and myself, that what I tell you is unvarnished fact. There are things that strain belief, you see, and Madagascar was one of them. So I will only say that if, at any point, you doubt what follows, or think old Flash is telling stretchers, just go to your local libraries, and consult the memoirs of my dear old friend Ida Pfeiffer, of the elastic-sided boots, or Messrs Ellis and Oliver, or the letters of my fellow-captives, Laborde of Bombay and Jake Heppick the American shipmaster, or Hastie the missionary.[33] Then you'll realise that the utterly unbelievable things I tell you of that h--lish island, straight out of "Gulliver", are simple, sober truth. You couldn't make 'em up.

Nor I won't bore you by describing the shock and horror I experienced, either at the beginning, when I realised I had escaped from Solomon's frying-pan into something infinitely worse, or later, as further abominations unfolded. I'll just recount what I saw and experienced, as plain as I can.

My first thoughts, when they threw me chained and battered into a stuffy go-down at Tamitave, were that this must be some bad dream from which I should soon awake. Then my mind turned to Elspeth; from what had passed on the jetty it had seemed that they'd been going to drag her ashore, too—for what fate I could only guess. You see, I was at a complete nonplus, quite out of my depth; once I'd had my usual little rave and blubber to myself, I tried to remember what Solomon had told me about Madagascar on the voyage out, which hadn't been much, and what I recalled was far from comforting. Wild and savage beyond description, he'd said . . . weird customs and superstitions . . . half the population in slavery . . . a she-monster of a queen who aped European fashions and held ritual executions by the thousand . . . a poisonous hatred of all foreigners—well, my present experience confirmed that, all right. But could it truly be as awful as Solomon had painted it? I hadn't believed him above half, but when I thought of that frightful nigger commandant in his bumbee tartan kilt and brolly . . . well.

Fortunately for my immediate peace of mind I didn't know one of the worst things about Madagascar, which was that once you were inside it, you were beyond hope of rescue. Even the most primitive native countries, in my young days, were at least approachable, but not this one; its capital, Antananarivo (Antan', to you), might as well have been on the moon. There was no appeal to outside, or even communication; no question of Pam or the Frogs or Yanks sending a gunboat, or making diplomatic representations, even. You see, no one *knew* about Madagascar, hardly. Barring a few pirates like Kidd and Avery in the old days, and a handful of British and French missionaries—who'd soon been cleared out or massacred—no one had visited it much except heeled-and-ready traders like Solomon, and they walked d----d warily, and did their business from their own decks offshore. We'd had a treaty with an earlier Malagassy king, sending him arms on condition that he stopped slave-trading, but when Queen Ranavalona came to the throne (by murdering all her relatives) in 1828, she'd broken off all traffic with the outside world, forbidden Christianity and tortured all converts to death, revived slavery on a great scale, and set about exterminating all tribes except her own. She was quite mad, of course, and behaved like Messalina and Attila the Hun, either of whom would have taken one look at her and written to *The Times*, protesting.

To give you some notion of the kind of blood-stained bedlam the country was, she'd already slaughtered *one-half* of her subjects, say a million or so, and passed decrees providing for a wall round the whole island to keep out foreigners (it would only have had to be three thousand miles long), four gigantic pairs of scissors to be set up on the approaches to her capital, to snip invaders in two, and the building of massive iron plates from which the cannon-shots of European ships would rebound and sink them. Eccentric, what? Of course, all this was unknown to me when I landed; I began to find out about it, painfully, when they hauled me out of the cooler next morning, still—in my innocence—protesting and demanding to see my lawyer.

My French-speaking officer had disappeared, so all my entreaties earned was blows and kicks. I'd had no food or drink for hours, but now they gave me a stinking mess of fish, beans, and rice, and a leaf-spoon to eat it with. I gagged it down with the help of their vile brown rice-water, and then, despite my objections, I and a gang of other unfortunates, all black of course, were herded up through the town, heading inland.

Tamitave's not much of a settlement. It has a fort, and a few hundred wooden houses, some of them quite large, with the high-pitched Malagassy thatches. At first sight it looks harmless enough, like the people: they're black, but not Negro, I'd say, perhaps a touch of Malay or Polynesian, well-built, not bad-looking, lazy, and stupid. The folk I saw at first were poorer-class peasants, slaves, and provincials, both men and women wearing simple loin-cloths or sarongs, but occasionally we encountered one of the better-off, being toted about in a sedan —no rich or aristocratic Malagassy will walk a hundred yards, and there's a multitude of slaves, bearers, and couriers to carry 'em. The nobs wore *lambas*—robes not unlike Roman togas, although in Antan' itself their clothing was sometimes of the utmost outlandish extravagance, like my commandant. That's the extraordinary thing about Madagascar—it's full of parodies of the European touch gone wrong, and their native culture and customs are bizarre enough to start with, G-d knows.

For example, they have their markets at a distance from their villages and towns—nobody knows why. They hate goats and pigs, and will lay babies out in the street to see if their births are "fortunate" or not;[34] they are unique, I believe, in the whole world in having no kind of organised religion—no priests, no shrines or temples—but they worship a tree or a stone if they feel like it, or personal household gods called *sampy*, or charms, like the famous idol Rakelimalaza, which consists of three dirty little bits of wood wrapped in silk—I've seen it. Yet they're superstitious beyond belief, even to the extent of dispraising those things they value most, to avert jealous evil spirits, and believing that when a man is dying you must stuff his mouth with food at the last minute—mind you, that may be because they're the most amazing gluttons, and drunkards, too. But, as with so many of their practices, you sometimes feel they are just determined to be different from the rest of the world.

I noticed that the soldiers who escorted our chain-gang were of a different stamp from the rest of the people—tall, narrow-headed fellows who marched in step, to a mixture of English and French words of command. They were brutes, who thrashed us along if we lagged, and treated the populace like dirt. I learned later they were from the Queen's tribe, the Hovas, once the pariahs of the island, but now dominant by reason of their cunning and cruelty.

I've endured some horrible journeys in my time—Kabul to the Khyber, Crimea to Middle Asia, for a couple—but I can't call to mind anything worse than that march from Tamitave to Antan'. It was 140 miles, and it took us eight days of blistered feet and chafing chains, trudging along, at first over scrubby desert, then through open fields, with peasants stopping in their work to stare at us indifferently, then through forest country, with the great jungly mountains of the interior coming slowly closer. We passed mud-walled villages and farms, but at night our captors just made us lie and sleep where we stopped; they carried no rations, but took what they wanted from unprotesting villagers, and we prisoners got the scraps. We were sodden by rain, burned agonisingly by the sun, bitten raw by mosquitoes, punished by blows and welts—but the worst of it was ignorance. I didn't know where I was, where I was going, what had happened to Elspeth, or even what was being said around me. There was nothing for it but to be herded on, like an animal, in pain and despair. After the first day or so I was beyond thought; all that mattered was survival.

To make matters worse, there was no road to travel—oh no, the Malagassies won't have 'em, for fear they might be used by an invader. Examine the perverse logic of that, if you like. The only exception is when the Queen travels anywhere, in which case they build a road in front of her, mile by mile, twenty thousand slaves grubbing with picks and rocks, and a great army following, with the court; why, every night they *build* a town, walls and all, and then leave it empty next day.

We were privileged to see this, when we reached the high plain midway on our journey. The first thing I noticed was dead bodies scattered about the place, and then groups of wailing, exhausted natives along our line of march. They were the road-builders; there were no rations provided for 'em, you see, so they just fell out and died like flies. This was the Queen's annual buffalo-hunt, and *ten thousand* slaves perished on it, inside a week. The stench was indescribable, especially along the road itself—which cut perversely across our line of march—where they were lying in rows, men, women, and children. Some of them would haul themselves up as we passed, and crawl towards us, whimpering for food; the Hovas just kicked them aside.

To add to the horrors, we passed occasional gallows, on which victims were hung or crucified, or simply tied to die by inches. One abomination I'll never forget—five staggering skeletons yoked together at the neck by a great iron wheel. They put them in it, and turn them loose, wandering together, until they starve or break each other's necks.

The Queen's procession had passed by long before, up the rough, rock-paved furrow of the road which ran straight as a die through forest and over mountain. She had twelve thousand troops with her, I learned later, and since the Malagassy army has no system of supply or rations they had just picked the country clean, so in addition to the slaves, thousands of peasants starved to death as well.

You may wonder why they endured it. Well, they didn't, always. Over the years thousands had fled, in whole tribes and communities, to escape her tyranny, and the jungles were full of these people, living as brigands. She sent regular expeditions against them, as well as against those distant tribes who weren't Hovas; I've heard it reckoned that the slaughter of fugitives, criminals, and those whom her majesty simply disliked, amounted to between twenty and thirty thousand annually, and I believe it. (Far better, of course, than wicked colonial government by Europeans—or so the Liberals would have us believe. G-d, what I'd have given to get Gladstone and that pimp Asquith on the Tamitave road in the earlies; they'd have learned all they needed to know about "enlightened rule by the indigenous population". Too late now, though; nothing for it but to hire a few roughs to smash windows at the Reform Club—as though I care.)

In the meantime, I'd little sympathy to spare; my own case, as we finally approached Antan' after more than a week of tortured tramping, was deplorable. My shirt and trousers were in rags, my shoes were worn out, I was bearded and foul—but strangely enough, having plumbed the depths, I was beginning to perk up a trifle. I wasn't dead, and they weren't bringing me all this way to kill me—I was even feeling a touch of light-headed recklessness, probably with hunger. I was lifting my head again, and my recollections of the end of the march are clear enough.

We passed a great lake along the road, and the guards made us shout and sing all the way past it; I later heard it was to placate the ghost of a dissolute princess buried nearby—dissolute female royalty being Madagascar's strong suit, evidently. We crossed a great river—the Mangaro—and steaming geysers bubbling out of pools of boiling mud, before we came out on a level grass plain, and beyond it, on a great hill, we beheld Antananarivo.

It took my breath away—of course, I didn't even know what it was, then, but it was like nothing you'd expect in a primitive nigger country. There was this huge city of houses, perhaps two miles across, walled and embattled in wood, and dominated by a hill on the top of which stood an enormous wooden palace, four storeys high, with another building alongside it which seemed to be made of mirrors, for it shimmered bright as a burning-glass in the sunlight. I stared at it until I was almost blinded, but I couldn't make out what it was—and in the meantime there were other wonders closer at hand, for as we approached the city across the plain which was dotted with huts and crowded with village people, I thought I must be dreaming —in the distance I could hear a military band playing, horribly flat, but there could be no doubt that the tune was "The Young May Moon"! And here, sure enough, came a regiment in full fig—red tunics, shakos, arms at the shoulder, bayonets fixed, and every man-jack of them black as Satan. I stood and fairly gaped;

past they went in column, throwing chests, and shaping dooced well—and at their head, G-d help me, half a dozen officers on horseback, dressed as Arabs and Turks. I was beyond startling now—when a couple of sedans, draped in velvet, passed by bearing black women done up in Empire dresses and feathered hats, I didn't even give 'em a second glance. They, and the rest of the crowds, were moving across the front of the city, and that was the way our guards drove us, so that we skirted the city wall until we came presently to a great natural amphitheatre in the ground, dominated by a huge cliff—Ambohipotsy, they call it, and there can be no more accursed place on earth.

There must have been close on a quarter of a million people thronging the slopes of that great hollow below the cliff—certainly more than I've ever seen in one congregation. This great tide of black humanity was gazing down to the foot of the cliff; our guards brought us up short and pointed, grinning, and looking down that vast slope of people I saw that in a clear space long narrow pits had been dug, and in the pits were scores of human beings, tied to stakes. At the end of each pit huge cauldrons were fixed, above roaring fires, and even as we watched a gong boomed out, the enormous chattering crowd fell silent, and a gang of black fiends tilted the first of the cauldrons, slowly, slowly, while the poor devils in the pits shrieked and writhed; boiling water slopped over the cauldron's lip, first in a small stream, then in a scalding cascade, surging down into the pit with a horrible sizzling cloud of steam that blotted out the view. When it cleared I saw to my horror that it only filled the pit waist deep—the victims were boiling alive by inches, while the onlookers bayed and cheered in a tumult of sound that echoed across that ghastly amphitheatre of death. There were six pits; they filled them one by one.

That was the main performance, you understand. After that, figures appeared at the top of the cliff, which was three hundred feet up, and the luckier condemned were thrown off, the crowd giving a great rising whistle as each struggling body took flight, and a mighty howl when it struck the ground below—there was particular applause if one landed in the water-pits, which were still steaming mistily with the contorted figures hanging from their stakes. They didn't just throw the condemned people down the cliff, by the way—they suspended 'em first by ropes, to let the mob have a good look, and then cut them free to drop.

I make no comment myself—because as I watched this beastly spectacle I seemed to hear the voice of my little Newgate friend in my ear—"Interesting, isn't it?"—and see again the yelling, gloating audience outside the Magpie and Stump; they were much the same, I suppose, as their heathen brethren. And if you tell me indignantly that hanging is a very different thing from boiling alive—or burning, flaying, flogging, sawing, impaling, and live burial, all of which I've seen at Ambohipotsy—I shall only remark that if these spectacles were offered in England it would be a case of "standing room only"—for the first few shows, anyway.

However, if the relation of such atrocities nauseates you,[35] I can only say that I swore to tell the truth of what I saw, and any qualms you may suffer were as nothing to poor old Flashy's mental distress as we were herded away from the scene of execution—I'll swear we were only there because our guards didn't want to miss it—and through one of the massive gates into Antan' town proper. Its name, by the way, means "City of a Thousand Towns", and it was as impressive at first hand as it had been from a distance. Wide, clean streets were lined by fine wooden buildings, some of them two and three storeys high (all building must be of wood, by law) and starved and shaken with terror as I was, I could not but marvel at the air of richness there was about the place. Well-stocked booths, shady avenues, neatly-robed folk bustling about their business, expensively-carved and painted sedans swaying through the streets, carrying the better sort, some in half-European clobber, others in splendid sarongs, and *lambas* of coloured silk. There was no making sense of it—on the one hand, the horrors I had just watched, and on the other this pleasant, airy, *civilised*-looking city—with Captain Harry Flashman and friends being kicked and flogged through the middle of it, and no one giving us more than a casual glance. Oh, aye—every building had a European lightning conductor.

They locked us in an airy, reasonably clean warehouse for the night, took off our fetters, and gave us our first decent meal for a week—a spicy mutton stew, bread and cheese, and more of their infernal rice-piddle. We scoffed it like wolves—a dozen woolly niggers snuffling over their bowls and one English gentleman dining with refinement, I don't think. But if it did something for my aching, filthy body, it did nothing for my spirits—this nightmare of existence seemed to have endured forever, and it was mad, incredible, out of all reason. But I must hang on—I had played cricket once, and bowled Felix; I had been to Rugby, and Horse Guards, and Buckingham Palace; I had an address in Mayfair; I had dined at White's—as a guest, granted—and strolled on Pall Mall. I wasn't just a lost soul in a lunatic black world, I was Harry Flashman, ex-11th Hussars, four medals and Thanks of Parliament, however undeserved. I *must* hang on—and surely, in the city I'd seen, there must be some civilised person in authority who spoke French or English, to whom I could state my case and receive the treatment that was my due as a British officer and citizen. After all, they weren't *real* savages, not with streets and buildings like these—a touch colourful in the way they disposed of malefactors, no doubt, and no poor relief worth a d--n, but no society's perfect. I must talk to someone.

The difficulty was—who? When they turned us out next morning, we were taken in charge by a couple of black overseers, who spoke nothing but jabber; they thrust us along a narrow alley, and out into a crowded square in which there was a long platform, railed off to one side, with guards stationed at its corners, to keep the mob back. It looked like a public meeting; there were a couple of black officials on the platform, and two more seated at a small table before it. We were pushed up a flight of steps to the platform, and made to stand in line; I was still blinking from the sunlight, wondering what this might portend, as I looked out over the crowd—blacks in *lambas* and robes for the most part, a few knots of officers in comic-opera uniforms, plenty of sedans with wealthy Malagassies sitting under striped umbrellas. I scanned the faces of the officers eagerly; those would be the French-speakers, and I was just about to raise a halloo to attract their attention when a face near the front of the crowd caught my eye like a magnet, and my heart leaped with excitement.

He was a tall man, wide-shouldered but lean, wearing a

bright embroidered shirt under a blue broadcloth coat, and with a silk scarf tied like a cravat; he and his neighbour, a portly sambo resplendent in sarong and cocked hat, were taking snuff in the local fashion, the lean chap accepting a pinch from the other's box on the palm of his hand and engulfing it with a quick flick of his tongue (it tastes beastly, I can tell you). He grimaced and raised his eyes; they met mine, and stared—they were bright blue eyes, in a face burned brown under a mane of greying hair. But there was no doubt of it—he was a white man.

"You!" I roared. "You, sir! Monsieur! Parlez-vous français? anglais? Hindi? Latin? B----y Greek, even? Listen to me —I must talk to you!"

One of the guards was striding forward to thrust me back, but the lean man was pushing his way through the mob, to my unutterable relief, and at a word from him to the officials he was allowed to approach the platform. He looked up at me, frowning, as I knelt down to be close to him.

"Français?" says he.

"I'm English—a prisoner, from a boat that came in at Tamitave! In G-d's name, how can I get out of this? No one listens to me—they've been dragging me all over the bl----d country for week! I must—"

"Gently, gently," says he, and at the sound of the English words I could have wept. Then: "Smile, monsieur. Smile—what is the word—broadly? Laugh, if you can—but converse quietly. It is for your own good. Now, who are you?"

I didn't understand, but I forced a ghastly grin, and told him who I was, what had happened, and my total ignorance of why I'd been brought here. He listened intently, those vivid eyes playing over my face, motioning me to speak softly whenever my voice rose—which, as you can imagine, it tended to do. All the time he was plainly avoiding glancing at my guards or the officials, but he was listening for them. When I had finished he fingered his cravat, nodding, as though I'd been telling him the latest from "Punch", and smiling pleasantly.

"Eh bien," says he. "Now attend, and not interrupt. If my English she is not perfect, I use French, but better not. No? Whatever I say, betray no amaze', do you see? Smile, if you please. Good. I am Jean Laborde, once of the Emperor's cavalry. I have been here thirteen years, I am a citizen. You do not know Madagascar?"

I shook my head, and he put back his head and laughed softly, plainly for the onlookers' benefit.

"They detest all Europe, and English especially. Since you land without permission, they treat you as *naufragé*—how you call?—shipwreck? Castaway? By their law—please to smile, monsieur, very much—all such persons must be made slaves. This is a slave-market. They make you a slave—forever."

The smiling brown face with its blue eyes swam in front of me; I had to hold on to the edge of the platform. Laborde was speaking again, quickly, and the smile had vanished.

"Say nothing. Wait. Wait. Do not despair. I will make inquiry. I see you again. Only wait, don't despair. Now, my friend— forgive me."

On the heels of the last word he suddenly shouted something in what I took to be Malagassy, gesturing angrily. Heads came round, my guard stooped and wrenched at my shoulder, and Laborde struck me full in the face with his open hand.

"Scélérat!" he cried. "Canaille!" He swung angrily on his heel and pushed his way back into the grinning crowd, while the guard kicked me upright and thrust me back into line. I tried to call to Laborde, but I was choked with horror and my own tears, and then one of the officials mounted a rostrum, shouting an announcement, the chatter of the crowd died away, the first of our coffle was pushed forward, and the bidding began.

No one who has not stood on the block can truly understand the horror of slavery. To be thrust up in public, before a crowd of leering niggers, waiting your turn while your fellow-unfortunates are knocked down, one by one to the highest bidder, and you stand like a beast in a pen, all dignity, manhood, even humanity gone. Aye, it's h--l. It's even worse when nobody buys you.

I couldn't credit it—not even an opening bid! Imagine it— "here's Flashy, gentlemen, young and in prime fettle, no previous owners, guaranteed of sound wind, no heelbug, highly recommended by superiors and ladies of quality, well set-up when he's shaved, talks like a book, and a b----r to ride! Who'll say a hundred? Fifty? Twenty? Come, come, gentlemen, the hair on his head's worth more than that! Do I hear ten? Five, then? Three? For a capital bargain with years of wear in him? Do I hear one? Not for a fellow who dismissed Felix, Pilch, and Mynn in three deliveries? Oh, well, Ikey, put him back on the shelf, and tell the knackers to come and collect him."

It was downright humiliating, especially with the bidding for my black companions as brisk as a morning breeze. Mind you, the thought of being bought by one of those disgusting Malagassies was revolting—still, I couldn't but feel disgruntled when they shoved me back in the warehouse alone, the Selling Plater nobody wanted. It was night before I found out the reason—for night brought Laborde, past bribed officials and guards, with soap, a gourd of water, a razor, and enough bad news to last a lifetime.

"It is simple," says he, when he had slipped a coin to the sentry and we were locked in alone. He spoke French now, which he'd been afraid to do in public for fear of eavesdroppers. "I had no time to tell you. The other slaves were being sold for debt, or crime. You, as a castaway, are in effect crown property; your display on the block was a mere formality, for no one would dare to bid. You belong to the Queen—as I did, when I was shipwrecked years ago."

"But . . . but you ain't a slave! Can't you get away?"

"No one gets away," says he, flatly, and it was now I learned a good deal of what I've told you already—of the monstrous tyranny of Queen Ranavalona, her hatred of foreigners which had caused Madagascar to be quite cut off from the world, of the diabolical practice of "losing"—which is their word for enslaving—all strangers.

"For five years I served that terrible woman," Laborde concluded. "I am an engineer—you will have seen my lightning rods on the houses. I am also skilled in the making of armaments, and I cast cannon for her. My reward was freedom"—he laughed shortly—"but not freedom to leave. I shall never escape —nor will you, unless—" He broke off, and then hurried on. "But refresh yourself, my friend. Wash and shave, at least, while you tell me more of your own misfortune. We have little time." He glanced towards the door. "The guards are safe for the moment, but safety lasts a short while in Madagascar."

So I told him my tale in full, while I washed and shaved by the flickering light of his lantern, and sponged the filth from the shreds in which I was clothed. While I talked I got a good look at him—he was younger than I'd thought, about forty, and almost as big as I, a handsome, decent-looking cove, fast and active, but plainly as nervous as a cat; he was forever starting at sounds outside, and when he talked it was in an urgent whisper.

"I shall inquire about your wife," says he when I'd done. "They will have brought her ashore almost certainly—they lose no chance of enslaving foreigners. This man Solomon I know of—he trades in guns and European goods, in exchange for Malagassy spices, balsam, and gums. He is tolerated, but he will have been powerless to protect your lady. I shall find out where she is, and then—we shall see. It may take time, you understand; it is dangerous. They are so suspicious, these people —I run great risk by coming to see you, even."

"Then why d'you do it?" says I, for I'm inclined to be leery of gifts brought at peril to the giver; I was nothing to him, after all. He muttered something about befriending a fellow-European, and the comradeship of men-at-arms, but I wasn't fooled. Kindness might be one of his motives, but there were others, too, that he wasn't telling about, or I was much mistaken. However, that could wait.

"What'll they do with me?" I asked, and he looked me up and down, and then glanced away, uneasily.

"If the Queen is pleased with you, she may give you a favoured position—as she did with me." He hesitated. "It is for this reason I help you to make yourself presentable—you are very large and . . . personable. Since you are a soldier, and the army is her great passion, it is possible that you will be employed in its instruction—drilling, manœuvring, that kind of thing. You have seen her soldiers, so you are aware that they have been trained by European methods—there was a British bandmaster here, many years ago, under the old treaty, but nowadays such windfalls are rare. Yes . . ." he gave me that odd, wary glance again, "your future could be assured—but I beg of you, as you value your life, be careful. She is mad, you see—if you give the least offence, in any way, or if she suspects you—even the fact that I, a fellow-foreigner, have spoken to you, could be sufficient, which is why I struck you publicly today . . ."

He was looking thoroughly scared, although I felt instinctively he wasn't a man who scared easy. "If you displease her—then it will be the perpetual *corvée*—the forced labour. Perhaps even the pits, which you saw yesterday." He shook his head. "Oh, my friend, you do not even begin to understand. *That* happens daily here. Rome under Nero—it was nothing!"

"But in G-d's name! Can nothing be done? Why don't they . . . make away with her? Haven't you tried to escape, even?"

"You will see," says he. "And please, do not ask such questions—do not even think them. Not yet." He seemed to be on the point of saying more, but decided not to. "I will speak of you to Prince Rakota—he is her son, and as great an angel as his mother is a devil. He will help you if he can—he is young, but he is kind. If only he . . . but there! Now, what can I tell you? The Queen speaks a little French, a few of her courtiers and advisers also, so when you encounter me hereafter, as you will, remember that. If you have anything secret to say, speak

English, but not too much, or they will suspect you. What else? When you approach the Queen, advance and retire right foot first; address her in French as 'God'—'*ma* Dieu', you understand? Or as 'great glory', or 'great lake supplying all water'. You must give her a gift, or rather, two gifts—they must always be presented in pairs. See, I have brought you these." And he handed me two silver coins—Mexican dollars, of all things. "If, in her presence, you happen to notice a carved boar's tusk, with a piece of red ribbon attached to it—it may be on a table, or somewhere—fall down prostrate before it."

I was gaping at him, and he stamped, Frog-like, with impatience. "You *must* do these things—they will please her! That tusk is Rafantanka, her personal fetish, as holy as she is herself. But above all—whatever she commands, do it at once, without an instant's hesitation. Betray no surprise at anything. Do not mention the numbers six or eight, or you are finished. Never, on your life, say of a thing that it is 'as big as the palace'. What else?" He struck his forehead. "Oh, so many things! But believe me, in this lunatic asylum, they matter! They may mean the difference between life and—horrible death."

"My G-d!" says I, sitting down weakly, and he patted me on the shoulder.

"There, my friend. I tell you these things to prepare you, so that you may have a better chance to . . . to survive. Now I must go. Try to remember what I've said. Meanwhile, I shall find out what I can about your wife—but for G-d's sake, do not mention her existence to another living soul! That would be fatal to you both. And . . . do not give up hope." He looked at me, and for a second the apprehension had died out of his face; he was a tough, steady-looking lad when he wanted to be.[36] "If I have frightened you—well, it is because there is much to fear, and I would have you on guard so far as may be." He slapped my arm. "Bien. Dieu vous garde."

Then he was at the door, calling softly for the guard, but even as it opened he was back again, cat-footed, whispering.

"One other thing—when you approach the Queen, remember to lick her feet, as a slave should. It will tell in your favour. But not if they are dusted with pink powder. That is poison." He paused. "On second thoughts, if they *are* so dusted, lick them thoroughly. It will certainly be the quickest way to die. A bientôt!"

If I had my head in my hands, do you wonder? It couldn't be true—where I was, what I'd heard, what lay ahead. But it was, and I knew it, which was why I plumped down on my knees, blubbering, and prayed like a drunk Methodist, just on the offchance that there is a God after all, for if He couldn't help me, no one else could. I felt much worse for it; probably Arnold was right, and insincere prayers are just so much blasphemy. So I had a good curse instead, but that didn't serve, either. Whichever way I tried to ease my mind, I still wasn't looking forward to meeting royalty.

At least they didn't keep me in suspense. At the crack of dawn they had me out, a file of soldiers under an officer to whom I tried to suggest that if I was going to be presented, so to speak, I'd be the better for a change of clothes. My shirt was reduced to a wisp, and my trousers no better than a ragged loin-cloth with one leg. But he just sneered at my sign-language, slashed me painfully with his cane, and marched me off up-hill through the streets to the great palace of Antan', which I now saw properly for the first time.

I wouldn't have thought anything could have distracted my attention at such a time, but that palace did. How can I describe the effect of it, except by saying that it's the biggest wooden building in the world? From its towering steepled roof to the ground is a hundred and twenty feet, and in between is a vast spread of arches and balconies and galleries—for all the world like a Venetian palazzo made of the most intricately-carved and coloured wood, its massive pillars consisting of single trunks more than one hundred feet long. The largest of them, I'm told, took five thousand men to lift, and they brought it from fifty miles away; all told, fifteen thousand died in building the place—but I guess that's small beer to a Malagassy contractor working for royalty.

Even more amazing though, is the smaller palace beside it. It is covered entirely in tiny silver bells, so that when the sun is on it, you can't even look, for the blinding glare. As the breeze changes, so does the volume of that perpetual tingling of a million silver tongues; it's indescribably beautiful to see and hear, like something in a fairy-tale—and yet it housed the cruellest Gorgon on earth, for that's where Ranavalona had her private apartments.

I'd little time to marvel, though, before we were inside the great hall of the main palace itself, with its soaring arched roof like a cathedral nave. It was thronged with courtiers bedecked in such a fantastic variety of clothing that it looked like a fancy-dress ball, with nothing but black guests. There were crinolines and saris, sarongs and state gowns, muslins and taffetas of every period and colour—I recall one spindly female in white silk with a powdered wig on her head à la Marie Antoinette, talking to another who seemed to be entirely hung in coloured glass beads. The contrast and confusion was bewildering: mantillas and loin-cloths, bare feet and high-heeled shoes, long gloves and barbaric feather headdresses—it would have been exotic but for the unfortunate fact that Malagassy women are d----d ugly, for the most part, tending to be squat and squashed, like black Russian peasants, if you can imagine. Mind you, I saw a lissom backside in a sari here and there, and a few pairs of plumptious bouncers hanging out of low corsages, and thought to myself, there's a few here who'd repay care and attention—and they'd probably be glad of it, too, for a more sawn-off and runty collection than their menfolk I never did see. It's curious that the male nobility are far poorer specimens than the common men; Dago blood somewhere, I suspect. They were got up as fantastically as the women, though, in the usual hotch-potch of uniforms, with knee breeches, buckled shoes, and even a stovepipe hat thrown in.

There was a nigger orchestra pumping away abominably somewhere, and the whole throng were chattering like magpies, as Malagassies always do, bowing and scraping and leering and flirting in the most grotesque caricature of polite society—I couldn't help thinking of apes that I'd seen at the circus in childhood, decked out in human clothes. A white man in rags cut no ice at all, and no one spared me more than a glance as I was marched up a side staircase, along a short passage, and into a small ante-room. Here, to my astonishment, I was left alone; they shut the door on me, and that was that.

Steady, Flash, thinks I, what's this? It looked an innocent room enough, overcrowded with artistically-carved native furniture, large pots containing reeds, some fine ornaments in ivory and ebony, and on the walls several prints depicting niggers in uniform which I wouldn't have given house-room to, myself. I stood listening, and through a large muslin-screened inner window heard the murmur and music of the great hall; by standing on a table I could just peep over the sill and through the muslin observe the assembly below. My window was in a corner, and from beneath it a broad gallery ran clean across the top end of the hall, high above the crowd. There were a dozen Hova guardsmen in sarongs and helmets ranged along the balcony rail.

Somewhere deep in the palace a bell rang, and at once the chatter and music died, and the whole crowd below turned to stare up at the balcony. There was the wailing of what sounded like a native trumpet, and a figure stepped out on to the balcony almost directly beneath me—a stalwart black in a gold metal headdress and leopard-skin loin-cloth, with massive muscular arms stretched out before him, carrying a slender silver spear in ceremonial fashion.* The assembled cream of Malagassy society gave him a good hand, and as he stepped aside four young girls in flowered saris appeared, carrying a kind of three-sided tent of coloured silk, but with no roof to it.

Then, to the accompaniment of clashing cymbals and a low, sonorous chanting that made my hair stand on end, there came out a couple of old coves in black robes fringed with silver, swinging little packets on the ends of strings, but not making much of it; they stood to one side, and to a sudden thunderous yell from the crowd of "Manjaka! Manjaka!" four more wenches trooped out, carrying a purple canopy on four slender ivory poles. Beneath it walked a stately figure enveloped in a scarlet silk cloak, but I couldn't see the face at all, for it was hidden by a tall sugar-loaf hat of golden straw, bound under the chin by a scarf. So this is Her Nibs, thinks I, and despite the warmth, I found myself shivering.

She paced slowly to the front of the balcony and the sycophantic mob beneath went wild, clapping and calling and stretching out their hands. Then she stepped back, the girls with the silk

* This spear was known as the "Hater of Lies".

tent contraption carried it round her, shielding her from all curious eyes except the two that were goggling down, unsuspected, from above; I waited, breathless, and two more girls went in beside her, and slipped the cloak from her shoulders. And there she was, stark naked except for her ridiculous hat.

Well, even from above and through a muslin screen there was no doubt that she was female, and no need for stays to make the best of it, either; she stood like an ebony statue as the two wenches began to bathe her from bowls of water. Some vulgar lout grunted lasciviously, and realising who it was I shrank back a trifle in sudden anxiety that I'd been overheard. They splashed her thoroughly, while I watched enviously, and then clapped the robe round her shoulders again. The screen was removed, and she took what looked like an inlaid ebony horn from one of her attendants and stepped forward to sprinkle the crowd. They fairly crowed with delight, and then she withdrew to a great shout of applause, and I scrambled down from my window thinking, by George, we've never seen little Vicky doing that from the balcony at Buck House—but then, she ain't quite equipped the way this one is.

What I'd seen, you may care to know, was the public part of the annual ceremony of the Queen's Bath. The private proceedings are less formal—although, mind you, I can speak with authority only for 1844, or as it is doubtless known in Malagassy court circles, Flashy's year.

The procedure is simple. Her Majesty retires to her reception room in the Silver Palace, which is the most astonishing chamber, containing as it does a gilded couch of state, gold and silver ornaments in profusion, an enormous and luxurious bed, a piano with "Selections from Scarlatti" on the music stand, and off to one side, a sunken bath lined with mother-of-pearl; there are also pictures of Napoleon's victories round the walls, between silk curtains. There she concludes the ceremony by receiving homage from various officials, who grovel out backward, and then, with several of her maids still in attendance, turns her attention to the last item on the agenda, the foreign castaway who has been brought in for her inspection, and who is standing with his bowels dissolving between two stalwart Hova guardsmen.

One of her maids motions the poor fool forward, the guardsmen retire—and I tried not to tremble, took a deep breath, looked at her, and wished I hadn't come.

She was still wearing the sugar-loaf hat, and the scarf framed features that were neither pretty nor plain. She might have been anywhere between forty and fifty, rather round-faced, with a small straight nose, a fine brow, and a short, broad-lipped mouth; her skin was jet black and plump[37]—and then you met the eyes, and in a sudden chill rush of fear realised that all you had heard was true, and the horrors you'd seen needed no further explanation. They were small and bright and evil as a snake's, unblinking, with a depth of cruelty and malice that was terrifying; I felt physical revulsion as I looked at them—and then, thank G-d, I had the wit to take a pace forward, right foot first, and hold out the two Mexican dollars in my clammy palm.

She didn't even glance at them, and after a moment one of her girls scuttled forward and took them. I stepped back, right foot first, and waited. The eyes never wavered in their repellent stare, and so help me, I couldn't meet them any longer. I dropped my gaze, trying feverishly to remember what Laborde had told me—oh, h--l, was she waiting for me to lick her infernal feet? I glanced down; they were hidden under her scarlet cloak; no use grubbing for 'em there. I stood, my heart thumping in the silence, noticing that the silk of her cloak was wet—of course, they hadn't dried her, and she hadn't a stitch on underneath—my stars, but it clung to her limbs in a most fetching way. My view from on high had been obscured, of course, and I hadn't realised how strikingly endowed was the royal personage. I followed the sleek scarlet line of her leg and rounded hip, noted the gentle curve of waist and stomach, the full-blown poonts outlined in silk—my goodness, though, she was wet—catch her death . . .

One of the female attendants gave a sudden giggle, instantly smothered—and to my stricken horror I realised that my indecently torn and ragged trousers were failing to conceal my instinctive admiration of her majesty's matronly charms—oh, J---s, you'd have thought quaking fear and my perilous situation would have banished randy reaction, but love conquers all, you see, and there wasn't a d----d thing I could do about it. I shut my eyes and tried to think of crushed ice and vinegar, but it didn't do the slightest good—I daren't turn my back on royalty —had she noticed? H--l's bells, she wasn't blind—this was lèse-majesté of the most flagrant order—unless she took it as a compliment, which it was, ma'am, I assure you, and no disrespect intended, far from it . . .

I stole another look at her, my face crimson. Those awful eyes were still on mine; then, slowly, inexorably, her glance went down. Her expression didn't change in the least, but she stirred on her couch—which did nothing to quell my ardour— and without looking away, muttered a guttural instruction to her maids. They fluttered out obediently, while I waited quaking. Suddenly she stood up, shrugged off the silk cloak, and stood there naked and glistening; I gulped and wondered if it would be tactful to make some slight advance—grabbing one of 'em, for instance . . . it would take both hands . . . better not, though; let royalty take precedence.

So I stood-stock still for a full minute, while those wicked, clammy eyes surveyed me; then she came forward and brought her face close to mine, sniffing warily like an animal and gently rubbing her nose to and fro across my cheeks and lips. Starter's gun, thinks I; one wrench and my breeches were a rag on the floor, I hooked into her buttocks and kissed her full on the mouth—and she jerked away, spitting and pawing at her tongue, her eyes blazing, and swung a hand at my face. I was too startled to avoid the blow; it cracked on my ear—I had a vision of those boiling pits—and then the fury was dying from her eyes, to be replaced by a puzzled look. (I had no notion, you see, that kissing was unknown on Madagascar; they rub noses, like the South Sea folk). She put her face to mine again, touching my lips cautiously with her own; her mouth tasted of aniseed. She licked me tentatively, so I nuzzled her a moment, and then kissed her in earnest, and this time she entered into the spirit of the thing like a good 'un.

Then she reached down and led me across the room to the bath, undid her scarf and hat and tossed them aside, revealing long straight hair tied tight to her head, and heavy silver earrings that hung to her shoulders. She slipped into the bath, which was deep enough to swim in, and motioned me to follow, which I did, nearly bursting by this time. But she swam and played about in the water in a most provoking way, teasing and rubbing noses and kissing—but never a smile or a word or the least softening of those basilisk eyes—and then suddenly she clapped her long legs round me and we were away, rolling and plunging like d---ation, one moment on the surface, the next three feet under. She must have had lungs like bellows, for she could stay under an agonising time, working away like a lecherous porpoise, and then surfacing for a gasp of air and down again for more ecstatic heaving on the bottom. Well, it was novel, and highly stimulating; the only time I've completed the carnal act while somersaulting with my nose full of water was in Ranavalona's bath. Afterwards I clung to the edge, gasping, while she swam lazily up and down, turning those ugly, glinting eyes on me from time to time, with her face like stone.

Yet the most startling event was still to come. When she had got out of the bath and I had followed obediently, she crossed to the bed and disposed herself on it, contemplating me sullenly while I stood hesitant, wondering what to do next. I mean, usually one gives 'em a slap on the rump by way of congratulation, whistles up refreshments, and has a cosy chat, but I could guess this wasn't her style. She just lay there stark, all black and shiny, staring at me while I tried to shiver nonchalantly, and then she grunted something in Malagassy and pointed to the piano. I explained, humbly, that I didn't play; she stared some more, and three seconds later I was on the piano stool, my wet posterior clinging uncomfortably to the seat, picking out "Drink, Puppy, Drink", with one finger. My audience didn't begin to throw things, so I ventured on the other half of my repertoire, "God Save the Queen", but a warning growl sent me skittering back to "Drink, Puppy, Drink" once more. I played it for about ten minutes, conscious of that implacable stare on the back of my neck, and then by way of variety began to sing the verse. I heard the bed creak, and desisted; another growl, and I was giving tongue lustily again, and the Silver Palace of Antananarivo re-echoed to:

Here's to the fox
With his den among the rocks,
And here's to the trail that we follo-o-ow!
And here's to the hound
With his nose upon the ground,
An' merrily we'll whoop and holl-o-o-o!

And then the chorus, with vim—it's a rousing little ditty, as
you probably know, and I bellowed it until I was hoarse. Just
as I was thinking my voice would crack, blowed if she didn't
glide up at my elbow, glowering without expression from my
face to the keys; what the d---l, thinks I, in for a penny, in for
a pound, so while pounding away with one hand I pulled her
on to the stool with the other, squeezing lustfully and bawling
"He'll grow into a hound, so we'll pass the bottle round", and
after a moment's impassive staring she began to accompany me
in a most disconcerting way. This time, though, we repaired to
the bed for the serious business—and I received a mighty shock,
for as I was waiting for her to assume the supine position she
suddenly picked me up bodily (I'm six feet and upwards of
thirteen stone), flung me down, and began galloping me with
brutal abandon, grunting and snarling and even drumming on
me with her fists. It was like being assailed by a horny gorilla,
but I gather she enjoyed it—not that she smiled, or gave
maidenly sighs, but at the end she stroked her nose against mine
and growled a Malagassy word in my ear several times . . .
"Zanahary . . . zanahary* . . ." which I later discovered was
complimentary.

So that was my first encounter with Queen Ranavalona of
Madagascar, the most horrible woman I've ever met, bar none.
Unfortunately, it was by no means the last, for although she
never ceased to regard me with that Gorgon stare, she took an
unquenchable fancy to me. Possibly it was my piano-playing,[38]
for normally she went through lovers like a rat through cheese,
and I was in constant dread in the weeks that followed that
she'd tire of me—as she had of Laborde and several hundred
others. He had merely been discarded, but as often as not her
used-up beaux were subjected to the dreadful ordeal of the

* Supernatural, divine; (colloq.) wonderful.

tanguin test, and then sent to the pits, or dismembered, or sewn up in buffalo hides with only their heads out and hung up to rot.

No, pleasuring Queenie wasn't a trade you could settle to, and to make it worse she was a brutally demanding lover. I don't mean that she enjoyed inflicting pain on her men, like dear Lola with her hairbrush, or the elfin Mrs Mandeville of Mississippi, who wore spurred riding boots to bed, or Aunt Sara the Mad Bircher of the Steppes—my, I've known some little turtle doves in my time, haven't I just? No, Ranavalona was simply an animal, coarse and insatiable, and you ached for days afterwards. I suffered a cracked rib, a broken finger, and G-d knows how many strains and dislocations in my six months as stallion-en-titre, which gives you some idea.

But enough of romance; suffice to say that my initiation was successful, and I was taken on the strength of her establishment as a foreign slave who might be useful not only as a paramour but also, in view of my army experience, as a staff officer and military adviser. There was no question about this in the minds of the court officials who assigned me to my duties—no thought that I might demur, or wish to be sent home, or count myself anything but fortunate to be so honoured by them. I had come to Madagascar, and here I would stay until I died, that was flat. It was their national philosophy: Madagascar was the world, and perfect, and there could be no greater treachery than to think otherwise.

I got an inkling of this the same afternoon, when I had been dismissed the royal presence, considerably worn and shaken, and was conducted to an interview with the Queen's private secretary. He proved to be a jolly little black butterball in a blue cutaway coat with brass buttons, and plaid trousers, who beamed at me from the depths of an enormous collar and floored me by crying:

"Mr Flashman, what pleasure to see you! I being Mr Fankanonikaka, very personal and special secretary to her majesty, Queen Ranavalona, the Great Cloud Shading the World, ain't I just, though? Not above half, I don't think." He rubbed his little black paws, chortling at my dumbstruck look, and went on: "How I speak English much perfect, so as to astonish you,

I being educated in London, at Highgate School, Highgate, confounded in year of Christ 1565, seven years reigning Good Queen Bess, I say. Please sitting there exactly, and attending then to me. I being an old boy." And he bowed me to a chair.

I was learning to accept anything in this extraordinary country —and why not? In my time I've seen an Oxford don commanding a slave-ship, a professor of Greek skinning mules on the Sacramento stage run, and a Welshman in a top hat leading a Zulu impi—even a Threadneedle Street nigger acting as secretary[39] to the Queen of Madagascar ain't too odd alongside that lot. But hearing English—even his amazing brand of the language—took me so aback that I almost committed the indiscretion of asking how the blazes I was to escape from this madhouse—and that could have been fatal in a country where one wrong word usually means death by torture. Fortunately I remembered Laborde's warning in time, and asked cautiously how he knew my name.

"Ha-ha, we are knowing all manner, no humbuggery or gammon, please," cries he, his fat face shining like boot polish. "You coming ashore from ship of Suleiman Usman, we speaking of him maybe, finding much." He cocked his head, button eyes considering me. "You telling me now of personal life yourself, where coming from, what trade, so to speak, my old covey."

So I did—at least, that I was English, an army officer, and how I'd fallen into Usman's hands. Again, remembering Laborde, I didn't mention Elspeth, although I was consumed with anxiety about her. He nodded pleasantly, and then said:

"You coming Madagascar, you knowing someone here, right enough?"

I assured him he was wrong, and he stuck out a fat finger and says: "M'sieur Laborde."

"Who's he?" says I, playing innocent, and he grinned and cries:

"M'sieur Laborde talking you in slave place, hitting you punch in face, but then coming you cheep-cheep quiet, with dollars for give Queen, razor for shaving, how peculiaring, ain't it?" He giggled and waved a hand. "But not mattering, since you being old boy, Laborde old boy and European chum, my stars, much shake hand hollo old fellow. I understanding, being old boy also,

234

Highgate like. And not mattering, since Queen, may she live thousand year, liking you so much. Good gracious times much! Jig-a-jig-jig and jolly muttons!" cries this jackanapes, making obscene gestures. "Much pleasure, hurrah. Maybe you slave five, six year, pleasing Queen"—his eyes rounded eagerly— "perhaps giving boy child with rogerings, what? Anyway, five year, you not being lost, no more, being free, marrying any fine lady, being great person like me, or someone else. All from Queen liking." He beamed happily; he had my future nicely in hand, it seemed.

"But you slave now—lost!" he added sternly. "Must working hard, not only jig-a-jig. Soldier working, much needed, keeping army best in world, spit and polish, d---e, no mistake. You liking that, staying Madagascar, making fine colonel, maybe sergeant-major, shouting soldiers, left-right-left, pick 'em up, farting about like Horse Guards, quick march, just fine style. I being Highgate, long time, seeing guns Hyde Park, when little boy, at school." The smile faded from his face, and he looked crestfallen. "Little black boy, seeing soldiers, big guns, horses, tantara and galloping." He sniffed and knuckled his eye. "In London. Still raining, not half? Much tuck-shop, footballing, jolly times." He sighed. "I speaking Queen, making you great soldier, knowing latest dodges, keeping army smart like Hector and Lysander, bang-up tip-top, hey? Yes, I speaking Queen."

You may say that was how I joined the Malagassy army, and if Mr Fankanonikaka was a dooced odd recruiting agent he was also an uncommon efficient one. Before night fell I was on the ration strength, with the unique rank of sergeant-general, which I suspect was Fankanonikaka's own invention, and not inappropriate as it turned out. They quartered me in two rooms at the back of the main palace, with an orderly who spoke a little French (and spied on me night and day), and there I sat down and wept, with my head spinning, trying to figure out what to do next.

What, for that matter, could I do, in this nest of intrigue and terror, where my life depended on the whim of a diabolical despot who was undoubtedly mad, fickle, dangerous, and fiendishly cruel? (Not unlike my first governess, in a way, except that their notions of bath-time for little Harry were somewhat different.) I could only wait, helpless, for Laborde, and pray that he might have some news of Elspeth, and bring me hope of escape from this appalling pickle—and I was just reconciling myself to this unhappy prospect, when who should walk in but the man himself. I was amazed, overjoyed, and terrified all in the space of two heartbeats; he was smiling, but looking pale and breathing heavy, like a man who has just had a nasty start and survived it—which he had.

"I have just come from the Queen," says he—and he spoke in French, pretty loud. "My dear friend, I congratulate you. You have pleased her—as I hoped you would. When I was summoned, I confess"—he laughed with elaborate nonchalance —"I thought there had been some misunderstanding about my visit to you last night—that it had been reported, and false conclusions drawn—"

"Frankathingammybob knew all about it," says I. "He told me. For G-d's sake, is there any news—"

He cut me off with a grimace and a jerk of his head towards the door. "I believe it was on the suggestion of her majesty's secretary that I was called to audience," says he clearly. "He was much impressed by your qualifications, and wished me, as a loyal servant of the Queen's, to add my recommendations to his own. I told her what I could—that you were a distinguished officer in the British service—which does not compare, of course, to the glorious army of Madagascar—and that you were full of zeal to serve her in a military capacity." He winked heavily at me, nodding, and I cottoned on.

"But of course!" cries I, ringing tones. "It is my dearest ambition—has been for years. I don't know how many times the Duke of Wellington's said to me: 'Flash, old son, you won't be a soldier till you've done time with the Malagassies. G-d help us if Boney had had a battalion of them at Waterloo.' And I'm beside myself with happiness at the thought of serving a monarch of such graciousness, magnanimity, and peerless beauty." If some eavesdropper was taking notes for the awful black b---h's benefit, I might as well lay it on with a shovel. "I would gladly lay down my life at her feet." There was a fair chance of that, too, if we had many gallops like that afternoon's.

Laborde looked satisfied, and launched into raptures about

my good fortune, and how blessed lucky we were to have such a benevolent ruler. He couldn't say enough for her, and of course I joined in, writhing with impatience to hear what news he might have of Elspeth. He knew what he was doing, though, for while he talked he fiddled with a gourd on the table, and when he took his hand away there was a slip of paper under the vessel. I waited five minutes after he'd gone, in case of prying eyes, palmed it, and read it surreptitiously as I stretched out on the bed.

"She is safe in the house of Prince Rakota, the Queen's son" (it read). "He has bought her. Have no fear. He is only sixteen, and virtuous. You shall see her when it is safe. Meanwhile, say *nothing*, as you value her life, and your own. Destroy this message instantly."

So I ate the d----d thing, speculating feverishly on the thought of Elspeth helpless in the hands of a nigger prince who had probably been covering every woman within reach since he was eight. Virtuous, eh? Just like his dear mama? If he was such a b----y paragon, why had he bought her—to iron his linen? Laborde must be off his head—why, when *I* was sixteen, I know what I'd have done if I'd seen Elspeth in a shop window with a sale ticket on her. It was too horrible to contemplate, so I went to sleep instead. After all, whatever was happening to Elspeth, I'd had a trying day myself.

* * *

[Extract from the diary of Mrs Flashman, October —, 1844]

Madagaskar is the most Singular and Interesting Isle, and I count myself most *fortunate* to have been so kindly received here—which is *due entirely* to the Sagacity and Energy of my darling H., who somehow contrived most *cleverly* to slip ashore from Don S.'s ship and make arrangements for our Enlargement and reception. Oh, happy, *happy* deliverance!! I know not how he accomplished it, for I have not seen my Brave Hero since we landed, but my Love and Admiration for him know no bounds, as I shall make plain to him when once again I know the Rapture of being enfolded in his arms!

I am at present residing in the Palace of Prince Rakoota, in the capital city (whose outlandish name I cannot attempt to reproduce, but it sounds like a dinner bell being rung!), having been brought here yesterday after a journey of many Starts and Adventures. I was brought ashore from Don S.'s ship by some Black Gentlemen—so I must call them, for they are people of consequence, and indeed, everybody's black here. Don S. protested most violently, and became *quite distracted*, so that the black soldiers had to restrain him—but I was not much moved, for his Importunities of late had been most marked, and his conduct quite *wild*, and I was Heartily Sick of him. He has behaved *odiously*, for despite his protestations of Devotion to me, he has put me to the *greatest inconvenience*, very selfishly—and dear H. also, who received a horrid Graze on his person.

I shall say no more of Don S., except that I am sorry so Refined and Agreeable a gentleman should have proved so wanting in behaviour, and been a deep Disappointment to me. But while glad to be shot of him, I was a trifle Uneasy with our Black hosts, the chief of whom I did not like at all, he was so Gross and Offhand, and stared at me in a horrid, *familiar* fashion, and even forgot himself so far as to *handle* my hair, growling to his friends in their Language (although he speaks tolerable French, for I heard him), so I addressed him in that Tongue, and said: "Your behaviour to a Gentlewoman is not becoming, sir, especially in one who wears the tartan of the 42nd, but I'm sure I suspect you have no right to it, for my Uncle Dougal was in the 92nd, and I never heard from him that any persons of your Colour were mustered in the Highland Brigade, not in Glasgow in any event. But if I am wrong I'm sure I apologise. I am very hungry, and *where* is my Husband?"

This being received in discourteous silence, they put me in a sedan or *palankeen*, and brought me into the Country, although I objected *strenuously* and spoke quite *sharply*, but to no avail. I was in such *distress of mind* at having no word of dearest H., or knowing where I was being taken, and the people we passed came to Stare at me, which was disagreeable, although they seemed to be in some awe, and I decided what it was, that *they had never seen a Lady of fair Hair and Complexion before*, they are that Primitive. But I bore this Insolence with Dignity and Reserve, and boxed one of them over the lugs, after which they kept a more respectful distance. To help compose my fears I gave myself into Tranquil Contemplation of the marvels I saw *en route*, the Scenery being beyond description, the flowers of Brilliant Colours, and the Animal life of boundless variety and interest—especially a darling little beastie called the Eye-Eye, which is half-monkey, half-rat with the *drollest* wistful eyes—which I suppose is why they call it Eye-Eye, and they won't kill it. Its antics are diverting.

However, I shall write later at leisure on the Attractions of this singular countryside, when the Descriptive Muse is upon me. Also about the great city of Madagaskar, and my Introduction to His R.H. Prince Rakoota, by a French resident, M. La Board, who is on terms of Intimacy with the Prince. From him I learnt that dear H. has been engaged on Military Business of Importance by no less a Personage than H.M. The Queen of Madagaskar—and I jalouse that my darling very cleverly offered them his Services in exchange for our reception here. They, naturally, would be Eager to avail themselves of so Distinguished an Officer, which doubtless explains the Haste with which he left from the Coast, without even seeing me—which caused me some *pique*, although I am sure he knows best. I don't *quite* understand it, but M. La Board impressed on me the *delicate* nature of the work, and since he and the Prince are insistent that nothing must *prejudice* it, I resign myself with Good Humour and *composure* to wait and see, as a good wife should, and only hope my Hero will soon be spared from his Duties to visit me.

I am v. comfortable in the Prince's delightful Palace, and receive every Consideration and Kindness. The Prince is *just a laddie*, but speaks good French with a pretty hesitation, and is all amiability. He is v. black, well-grown and handsome, smiling readily, and I flatter myself he is more than a little *fetched* by me, but he is so young and *boyish* that an expression of Admiration which might be thought a *little* forward in a person more mature, may be excused in him as a *natural* youthful gallantry. He is a little shy, and has a wistful regard. I could wish that I had my proper wardrobe, for I am in some hope that, when dearest H. returns, he may take me to visit the Queen, who seems from all I have heard to be a Remarkable Person and held in great Esteem. However, if I am so Honoured, I shall make do with what I have, and rely on my *natural breeding* and appearance to uphold my Country's credit among these People, for as our Beloved Bard has it, the rank is but the Guinea Stamp, and I'm sure that an English Lady may move Unashamed in any Society, especially if she has the Grace and Looks to carry it off.

[End of extract—"natural breeding", indeed! And where did you come by that, miss? Paisley, like the rest of us!!—G. de R.]

It's been my experience that however strange or desperate the plight you may find yourself in, if there's nothing else for it, you just get on with the business in hand as though it was the most natural thing in the world. By various quirks of fate I've landed up as an Indian butler, a Crown Prince, a cottonfield slave-driver, a gambling-hell proprietor, and G-d knows what besides—all occupations from which I'd have run a mile if I'd been able. But I couldn't, so I made the best of 'em, and before I knew it I was fretting about silver polish or court precedent or how we were to get the crop in by November or whether the blackjack dealer was holding out, and almost forgetting that the real world to which I rightly belonged was still out there somewheres. Self-defence, I suppose —but it keeps you sane when by rights you ought to be sinking into madness and despair.

So when they gave me the army of Madagascar to drill and train, I simply shut my mind to the horrors of my situation and went at it like Frederick the Great with a wasp in his pants. I believe it saw me through one of the blackest periods of my life—a time so confused, when I look back, that I have difficulty in placing the events of those first few weeks in their proper order, or even making much sense of them. I knew so little then about the place, and that little was so strange and horrid that it left the mind numb. Only gradually did I come to have a clear picture of that savage, mock-civilised country, with its amazing people and customs, and understand my own peculiar station in it, and begin trying to scheme a way out. At first it was just a frightening turmoil, in which I could only do what I had to do, but I'll describe it as best I can, so that you may learn about it as I did, and have the background to the astonishing events that followed.

I had the army, then, to reform and instruct, and if you think that an uncommon responsible job for the newest arrived foreign slave, remember that it was European-modelled, but that they hadn't seen a white instructor in years. There was another good reason, too, for my appointment, but I didn't find out about that until much later. Anyway, there it was, and I'm bound to say the work was as near to being a pleasure as anything could be in that place. For they were absolutely first-class, and as soon as I saw this, when I had the regiments reviewed on the great plain outside the city, I thought to myself, right, my boy, perfection is our ticket. They're good, but there's nothing easier than spending ten hours a day hounding their commanders to make 'em better. And that's what I did.

Fankanonikaka had told me I had a free hand; he came down with me to that first review, when the five regiments stationed at Antan', and the palace guard, marched past under my critical eye.

"Like changing guard, left right, boom-boom, mighty fine!" cries he. "Being best soldiers in world, not half, eh? Right turning, shouldering arms, altogether, ha-ha!" He beamed at the comic opera generals and colonels who were standing with us, puffed up with pride as they watched their battalions. "You liking greatly, Sergeant-General Flashman?"

I just grunted, had them halted, and plunged straight in among the ranks, looking for the first fault I could find. There was a black face badly shaven, so I stamped and swore and raved as though they'd just lost a battle, while the staff stared and shook, and little Fankanonikaka was ready to burst into tears.

"Soldiers?" I bellowed. "Look at that slovenly brute, tripping over his bl----d beard! Has he shaved today? Has he *ever* shaved? Stand still, you mangy b----rds, or I'll flog every second man! Slouch in front of me, will you, with your chins like a monkey's backside? I'll show you, my pretties! Oh, yes, we'll take note of this! *Mr* Fankanonikaka, I thought you spoke to me of an *army*—you weren't referring to this mouldy rabble, I suppose?"

Of course, it put them into fits. There were generals gaping and protesting and falling over their sabres, while I strode about hazing right and left—dull buttons, unpolished leather, whatever I could find. But I wouldn't let 'em touch the offending soldier —ah, no. I degraded his section commander on the spot, ordered his colonel into arrest, and scarified the staff; that's the way to get 'em hopping. And when I'd done roaring, I had the whole outfit, officers and all, marched and wheeled and turned across that square for three solid hours, and then, when they were fit to drop, I made 'em stand for forty minutes stock-still, at the present, while I ranged among them, sniffing and growling, with Fankanonikaka and the staff trotting miserably at my heels. I was careful to snarl a word of praise here and there, and then I singled out the unshaven chap, slapped him, told him not to do it again, pinched his ear à la Napoleon, and said I had high hopes of him. (Talk about discipline; come to old Flash and I'll learn you things they don't teach at Sandhurst.)

After that it was plain sailing. They realised they were in the grip of a mad martinet, and went crazy perfecting their drill and turn-out, with their officers working 'em till they dropped, while Flashy strolled about glaring, or sat in his office yelling for lists and returns of everything under the sun. With my ready ear for languages, I picked up a little Malagassy, but for the most part transmitted my orders in French, which the better-educated officers understood. I built a fearsome reputation through stickling over trivialities, and set the seal on it by publicly flogging a colonel (because one of his men was late for roll-call) at the first of the great fortnightly reviews which the Queen and court attended. This shocked the officers, entertained the troops, and delighted her majesty, if the glitter in her eye was anything to go by. She sat like a brooding black idol most of the time, in her red sari and ceremonial gold crown under the striped brolly of state, but as soon as the lashing started I noticed her hand clenching at every stroke, and when the poor d---l began to squeal, she grunted with satisfaction. It's a great gift, knowing the way to a woman's heart.

I was careful, though, in my disciplinary methods. I soon got a notion of who the important and influential senior officers were, and toadied 'em sickening in my bluff, soldierly way, while oppressing their subordinates most d--nably, and keeping the troops in a state of terrified admiration. Given time I dare say I'd have ruined the morale of that army for good and all.

Since most of the leading aristocrats held high military rank, and took their duties seriously in a pathetically incompetent way (just like our own, really), I gradually became acquainted—not to say friendly—with the governing class, and began to see how the land lay in court, camp, city, and countryside. It was simple enough, for society was governed by a rigid caste system even stricter than that of India, although there was no religious element at all. There were eleven castes, starting at the bottom with the black Malagassy slaves; above them, in tenth place, were the *white* slaves, of whom there weren't many apart from me, and I was special, as I'll explain—but ain't that interesting, that a black society held white superior to black, in the slave line? We were, of course, but it didn't make much odds, since all of us were far below the ninth caste, which consisted of the general public, who had to work for a living, and included everyone from professional people and merchants right down to the free labourers and peasantry.

Then there were six castes of nobles, from the eighth to the third, and what the differences were I never found out, except that they mattered immensely. The Malagassy upper crust are fearful snobs, and put on immense airs with each other—a third-rank count or baron (these are the titles they give themselves) will be far more civil to a slave than to a sixth-rank nobleman, and the caste rules governing them are harsher even than for the lower orders. For example, a male noble can't marry a woman of superior caste; he can marry beneath himself, but he mustn't marry a slave—if he does, he's sold into slavery himself and the woman is executed. Simple, says you, they just won't marry slaves, then—but the silly b-----s do, quite often, because they're crazy, like their infernal country.

The second caste consisted of the monarch's family, poor souls, and at the top came the first caste, an exclusive group of one—the Queen, who was divine, although quite what that meant wasn't clear, since they don't have gods in Madagascar. What was certain, though, was that she was the most absolute of absolute tyrants, governing solely by her own whim and caprice, which, since she was stark mad and abominably cruel, made for interesting times all round.

That much you have probably gathered already, from my description of her and of the horrors I'd seen, but you have to imagine what it was like to be living at the mercy of that creature, day in day out, without hope of release. Fear spread from her like a mist, and if her court was a proper little viper's nest of intrigue and spying and plotting, it wasn't because her nobles and advisers were scheming for power, but for sheer survival. They went in terror of those evil snake eyes and that flat grunting voice so rarely heard—and then usually to order arrest, torture, and horrible death. Those are easy words to write, and you probably think they're an exaggeration; they're not. That beastly slaughter I'd witnessed under the cliff at Ambohipotsy was just a piece of the regular ritual of purge and persecution and butchery which was everyday at Antan' in my time; her appetite for blood and suffering was insatiable, and all the worse because it was unpredictable.

It wouldn't have seemed so horrible, perhaps, if Madagascar had been some primitive nigger tribal state where everyone ran about naked chanting mumbo-jumbo and living in huts. Well, I remember my old chum King Gezo of Dahomey, sitting slobbering like a beast before his death-house (built of skulls, if you please) tucking into his luncheon while his fighting women chopped prisoners into bloody gobbets within a yard of him. But he was an animal, and looked like one; Ranavalona wasn't quite.

She had not bad taste in clothes, for example, and knew enough to hang pictures on the walls, and have her banquets laid with knives and forks just so, and place-cards (Solomon was right: I saw 'em—"Serjeant-General Flatchman, Esq., yours truly" was what mine said on one occasion, in copperplate handwriting). I mean, she had carpets, and silk sheets, and a piano, and her nobles wore trousers and frock coats, and addressed their women-folk as "Mam'selle"—my G-d, haven't I seen a couple of her Comtesses, sitting at a palace dinner, chattering like civilised women, with silver and crystal and linen before them, ignoring the cutlery and gobbling food with their fingers, and then one turning to t'other and twittering: "Permittez-moi, cherie," and proceeding to delouse her neighbour's hair. That was Madagascar—savagery and civilisation combined into a horrid comic-opera, a world turned upside down.

And at the head of the table *she* would sit, in a fine yellow satin gown from Paris, a feather boa stuck through her crown, pearls on her black bosom and in her long earrings, chewing on a chicken leg, holding up her goblet to be refilled, and getting drunker and drunker—for when it came to lowering the booze she could have seen a sergeants' mess under the table. It didn't show in her face; the plump black features never changed expression, only the eyes glittered in their piercing uncanny stare. She wouldn't smile; her talk would be an occasional growl to the terrified sycophants sitting beside her, and when she rose at last, wiping her sullen mouth, everyone would spring up and bow and scrape while two of her generals, perspiring, would escort her down the room and out on to the great balcony, lending her an arm if she staggered, and over the great crowd waiting in the courtyard below would fall a terrible silence—the silence of death.

I've seen her, leaning on that verandah, with her creatures about her, gazing down on the scene below; the ring of Hova guardsmen, the circle of torches flaming over the archways, the huddled groups of unfortunates, male and female, from mere striplings to old decrepit folk, cowering and waiting. They might be recaptured slaves, or fugitives hunted out of the forests and mountains, or criminals, or non-Hova tribesmen, or suspected Christians, or anyone who, under her tyranny, had merited punishment. She would look down for a long time, and then nod at one group and grunt: "Burning," and then at another, "Crucifixion," and at a third, "Boiling." And so on, through the ghastly list—starvation, or flaying alive, or dismembering, or whatever horror occurred to her monstrous taste. Then she would go inside—and next day the sentences would be carried out at Ambohipotsy in front of a cheering mob. Sometimes she attended herself, watching unmoved, and then going home to the palace to spend hours praying to her personal idols under the paintings in her reception room.

While most of her cruelties were practised on common folk and slaves, her court was far from immune. I remember at one of her levées, at which I was in humble attendance with the military, she suddenly accused a young nobleman of being a secret Christian. I've no idea whether he was or not, but there and then he was submitted to ordeal—they have any number of ingenious forms of this, including swimming rivers infested by crocodiles, but in his case they boiled up a cauldron of water, right in front of her seat, and she sat staring fixedly at his face as he tried to snatch coins out of the bubbling pot, plucking and screaming while the rest of us watched, trying not to be sick. He failed, of course—I can still see that pathetic figure writhing on the floor, clutching his scalded arm, before they carried him out and sawed him in half.

Not quite what we're accustomed to at Balmoral, you'll agree, but at least Ranavalona didn't go in for tartan carpets. Her wants were simple: just give her an ample supply of victims to mutilate and gloat over and she was happy—not that you'd have guessed it to look at her, and indeed I've heard some say that she was just plain mad and didn't know what she was doing. That's an old excuse which ordinary folk take refuge in because they don't care to believe there are people who enjoy inflicting pain. "He's mad," they'll say—but they only say it because they see a little of themselves in the tyrant, too, and want to shudder away from it quickly, like well-bred little Christians. Mad? Aye, Ranavalona was mad as a hatter, in many ways—but not where cruelty was concerned. She knew quite what she was doing, and studied to do it better, and was deeply gratified by it, and that's the professional opinion of kindly old Dr Flashy, who's a time-served bully himself.

So you see what a jolly, carefree life it was for her court, of whom I suppose I was one in my capacity of mount of the moment. It was a privileged position, as I soon realised; you recall I told you how I took pains to curry favour with the top military nobles—well, I soon discovered that the compliment was returned, slave though I was officially. They toadied me something pitiful, those black sweating faces and trembling paws in gaudy uniforms—they assumed, you see, that I only had to whisper the word in her ear and they'd be off to the pits and the cross. They needn't have fretted; I never knew one of 'em from t'other, hardly, and anyway I was too alarmed for my own safety to do anything with her d----d black ear but chew it, loving-like.

You may wonder how I stuck it out; or how I could bring myself to make love to that female beast. Well, I'll tell you: if it's a choice between romping and being boiled or roasted, you can bring yourself to it, believe me. She wasn't bad-looking beneath the neck, after all, and she seemed to like me, which always helps—you may find it difficult to believe (I do myself) but there were even moments, on warm, silent afternoons, when we would be drowsing on the bed, or by her bath, and I would steal a glance along the pillow at that placid black face, comely enough with the eyes closed, and feel even a touch of affection for her. You can't hate a woman you sleep with, I suppose. Mind you, once that black eyelid lifted, and that eye was on you, it was another story.

One thing, though, I feel inclined to say in her defence, having said so much ill of her, and rightly. At least some of her excesses, especially in the persecution of Christians (I wasn't one, by the way, during my Madagascar sojourn, as I took pains to point out to anyone who'd listen), were inspired by her idol-keepers. I've said there was no religion in her country, which is true—*their* superstition was not on an organised basis—but there were these fellows who read omens and looked after the stones and sticks and lumps of mud which passed for household gods. (Ranavalona had two, a boar tusk and a bottle, which she used to mutter to.)

Well, the idol-keepers had helped her to the throne when she was a young woman, after her husband the king died, and his nephew, the rightful heir, had been all set to ascend the throne. The idol-keepers, in their role as augurs, had said the omens favoured Ranavalona instead, and since she at the same time was busily organising a coup d'état, slaughtering the unlucky nephew and all her other immediate relatives, you couldn't say the idol-keepers were wrong: they'd picked the winner. They obtained such influence with her that they even persuaded her to kill off the lovers who had helped her coup, and she relied on them for guidance ever after.

I was always very civil to them myself, with a cheery "Good morning" and a dollar or two, mangy brutes though they were, shuffling through the palace with their bits of rag and string and ribbon—which were probably idols of terrific potency, if I'd only known. They helped Ranavalona determine her policy by throwing beans on a kind of chess-board, and working out the combinations,[40] which usually resulted in massacre for someone, just like a Cabinet decision; she would admit them at all times of day—I've seen her sitting on her throne, with her girls helping her try on French slippers, while the lads crouched alongside, mumbling over their beans, and she would nod balefully at their pronouncements, take a squint at her bottle or tusk for reassurance, and pronounce sentence. They once walked in when she and I were having a bath together—deuced embarrassing it was, performing while they cast the bones, but Ranavalona didn't seem to mind a bit.

If there was any other influence in her life, apart from the mumbo-jumbo men and her own mad passions, it was her only son, Prince Rakota—the chap to whom Laborde had managed to steer Elspeth. He was the heir to the throne, although he wasn't the old king's son, but the offspring of one of her lovers —whom she'd later had pulled apart, naturally. However, under Malagassy law, any children a widow may have, legitimate or not, are considered sons of her dead husband, so Rakota was next in line, and my impression was that Madagascar couldn't wait to cry "Long live the King!" You see, despite my misgivings when I'd first heard about him, he was the complete opposite of his atrocious mother—a kindly, cheerful, good-natured youth who did what he could to restrain his bloodthirsty parent. It was common knowledge that if he happened along as they were about to butcher someone on her instructions, and he told them to let the chap go, they would—and mama never said a word about it. He'd have had to spend all his time sprinting round the country shouting "Lay off!" to make much impression on the slaughter rate, but he did what he could, and the populace blessed and loved him, as you'd expect. Why Ranavalona didn't do away with him, I couldn't fathom; some fatal weakness in her character, I suppose.

However, mention of Rakota advances my tale, for about three weeks after I'd taken up my duties, I met him, and was reunited, if only briefly, with the wife of my bosom. I'd seen Laborde once or twice beforehand, when he'd figured it was safe to approach me, and pestered him to take me to Elspeth, but he'd impressed on me that it was highly dangerous, and would have to wait on a favourable opportunity. It was like this, you see: Laborde had told Rakota that Elspeth was my wife, and pleaded with him to look after her, and keep her tucked away out of sight, for if the Queen ever discovered that her new buck and favoured slave had a wife within reach—well, it would have been good-night, Mrs Flashman, and probably young Harry as well. Jealous old b---h. Rakota, being a kindly lad, had agreed, so there was Elspeth snug and well cared for, not treated as a slave at all, but rather as a guest. While I, mark you, was having to pleasure that insatiable female baboon for my very life's sake. They hadn't told Elspeth that, thank G-d, but jollied her along with the tale that I had taken up an important military post, which was true enough.

A strange state of affairs, you'll allow—but nothing out of the way for Madagascar, and no more incredible than some of the things that I've known and heard of in my time. I was so bemused with what had happened over the past few months anyway, that I just accepted the bizarre situation; only two things worried and puzzled me. How had the Queen, who found out everything through her system of spies, which was directed by Mr Fankanonikaka, failed to get word of the golden-haired slave in her son's palace? And why—this was the real conundrum—were Laborde and Prince Rakota in such a sweat to help Elspeth and me? What was I to them, after all? I'm a suspicious brute, you see, and don't put much stock in altruistic virtue; there was something up here. I was right, too.

Laborde presented me to the Prince on an afternoon when Ranavalona was safely out of the way, watching a bull-fight, which was her prime hobby. It was a byword that the fighting bulls were the only living things she had any feelings for; the only times she was known to weep was when one of them died, or was badly gored in the ring. So it was deemed safe for me to take an hour off from parade, and with Fankanonikaka, Laborde, and a leading general named Count Rakohaja, I was borne out to the Prince's garden palace in the suburbs of Antan'.

Rakota received me in his throne room, where I was graciously permitted to prostrate myself before him and his Princess. They were tiny folk—he wasn't more than five feet tall, and dressed like a Spanish matador, in gold tunic and breeches, buckled shoes, and a Mexican sombrero. He was about sixteen, lively and smiling all over his round olive face; he had the beginnings of a moustache.[41] His wife was much the same, a dumpy little bundle in yellow silk; if anything, her moustache was further along than his. They spoke good French, and when I'd clambered upright Rakota said he had brilliant reports of the way I was training the troops, especially the royal guardsmen.

"Sergeant-General Flashman has worked wonders with the men, and the best officers," agreed Count Rakohaja; he was a big, lean Hova aristocrat with a scar on his cheek, dressed in a coat and trousers which would have been perfect St James's, if they hadn't been made of bright green velvet. "Your highness will be enchanted to learn that he has already won the loyalty of all under his command, and has shown himself a most dependable and trustworthy officer."

Which was doing it rather too brown, but the Prince beamed on me.

"Most gratifying," says he. "Winning the confidence of the troops is the first essential in a leader. As commander-in-chief— under the sublime authority of Her Majesty, the Great Cow Who Nourishes All The World With Her Milk, of course—I congratulate you, sergeant-general, and assure you that your zeal and loyalty will be amply rewarded."

It seemed a trifle odd. I wasn't a commander, but a glorified drill instructor, and everyone knew it. However, I responded politely that I didn't doubt the troops would follow me from h--l to Huddersfield and back, which seemed to please his highness, for he ordered up chocolate and we stood about sipping it from silver bowls, two-handed. (The Malagassies have no idea of quantity; there must have been a gallon of the sickly muck in each bowl, and the gurgling of the royal consumption was something to hear.)

It seemed to me the Prince and Princess were slightly nervous; he kept darting glances at Rakohaja and Fankanonikaka, and his little chubby consort, whenever she caught my eye, smiled timidly and bobbed like a charwoman seeking employment. The Prince asked me a few more questions, in an offhand way— about the quality of the lower-rank commanders, the equipment of palace pickets, the standard of marksmanship, and so on, which I answered satisfactorily, noting that he seemed specially interested in the household troops. Then he took one last gulp and belch at his chocolate, wiped his moustache on his sleeve, and says to me, with a little smile and wave:

"You are permitted to withdraw to the other end of the room," and began to talk in Malagassy to the others.

Mystified, I bowed and retreated, a door at the far end opened, and there was Elspeth, smiling radiantly, and dressed in the worst possible taste in a garden-party confection of purple taffeta—purple on a blonde, G-d help us—tripping towards me with her arms out. In a moment Madagascar was forgotten, with its Queen and horrors and dressed-up mountebanks; I had her in my arms, kissing her, and she was murmuring endearments in my ear. Then propriety returned, and I glanced round at the others. They were ignoring us—all except Fankanonikaka, who was having a sly peep—so I enfolded her again, inhaling her perfume while she prattled her delight at seeing me.

". . . for it has been so *long*, and while their highnesses have been kindness itself, I have been yearning for you night and day, my love. Do you like my new dress?—her highness chose it for me herself, and we think it most becoming, and it is so *heavenly* to have proper clothes again, after those dreadful sarongas—but we will not talk of *that*, and the hateful separation, and the *odious* behaviour of that . . . that man Don Solomon—but now we are rid of him, and safely here, and it is such fun—if it were not that your duties keep you from me. Oh, Harry, must they? But I must be a good wife, as I always promised, and not put myself forward where your duty is concerned, and indeed I know the separation is as cruel for you as for me—and, oh, I do miss you . . ."

Here she embraced me again, and drew me down on to a settle—the others were deep in their own conversation, although the dumpy little Princess fluttered her fingers at us shyly, and Elspeth must rise to curtsey—even black royalty was just nuts to her, obviously—before resuming her headlong discourse. I never got a word in edgeways, as usual, but I doubt if I'd have been coherent anyway. For to my amazement, Elspeth seemed to have not a care in the world—well, I've always known she had a slate loose, and was incapable of seeing farther than her pretty nose—which reminded me to kiss it, tenderly—but this was beyond belief. We were prisoners in this heathen h--l-hole, and to hear her you might have imagined it was a holiday at Brighton. Slowly it dawned on me that she had no true notion of the ghastliness of our plight, or even of what Madagascar was like at all, and as she babbled I began to understand why.

". . . of course, I should like to see more of the country, for the people seemed not disagreeable, but the Prince informs me that the position of foreigners here is *delicate*, and it is not advisable for me to be seen abroad. For you, of course, it is different, since you are employed by her majesty—oh, tell me, Harry, what she looks like, and what she says! How does she dress? Shall I be presented? Is she young and well-favoured? I should be *so* jealous—for she cannot fail to be attracted by the handsomest man in England! Oh, Harry, I much admire your uniform—it is quite the style!"

I'd taken advantage of the custom of the country to wear all red, with a black sash, pretty raffish, I admit. Elspeth fairly glowed at me.

"But I have so much to tell you, for the Prince and Princess have been *so* good, and I have the prettiest rooms, and the garden is so beautiful, and there is some very select company in the evenings—all black, of course, and a *leetle outré*—but most agreeable and considerate. I am most happy and interested —but when shall we go home to England, Harry? I hope it is not *too* long—for I sometimes feel anxiety for dear Papa, and while it is very pleasant here, it is not quite the same. But I know you will not detain us here longer than must be, for you are the *kindest* of husbands—but I am sure your work here will be of the greatest service to you, for it is sure to be a valuable experience. I only wish"—her lip suddenly trembled, despite her efforts to smile—"that we could be together again . . . in the same house . . . oh, Harry, darling, I miss you so!"

And the little clothhead began piping her eye, leaning on my shoulder—as though she had anything worth weeping about! It was a d----d letdown, for I'd been looking forward to pouring out my woes and complaints to her, bemoaning my lot, describing the horrors of my plight—the respectable bits, anyway—and generally making her flesh creep with my anxieties. But there seemed no point now in alarming her—she'd just have done something idiotic, and with the others almost in earshot, the less

I said the better. So I just patted her shoulder to cheer her up.

"Now then, old girl," says I, "don't be a fool. What'll their highnesses think of your bleating and bawling? Wipe your nose —you're a lot better off than some, you know."

"I know. I am very foolish," says she, sniffing, and presently, when the Prince and Princess withdrew, she was all smiles again, curtseying like billy-ho, and kissing me a tender farewell. I remarked to Laborde as we returned to the palace that my wife seemed happily ignorant of my predicament, and he turned his steady eyes on me.

"It is as well, is it not? She could be a great danger to you— to both of you. The less she knows, the better."

"But in G-d's name, man! She'll have to find out sooner or later! What then? What when she realises that she and I are slaves in this frightful country—that there's no hope—no escape?" I grabbed his arm—we had left our sedans at the entrance to my quarters at the rear of the palace, Fankanonikaka having parted from us at the main gate. "For the love of heaven, Laborde—there must be a way out of this! I can't go on drilling niggers and piling into that black slut for the rest of my life—"

"Your life will last no time at all if you don't control yourself!" snaps he, pulling loose. He glanced round, anxiously, then took a deep breath. "Look you—I will do whatever I can. In the meantime, you must be discreet. I do not know what can be achieved. But the Prince was pleased with you today. That may mean something. We shall see. Now I must go—and remember, be careful. Do your work, say nothing. Who knows?" He hesitated, and tapped me quickly on the arm. "We may drink *café au lait* on the Champs Elysées yet. À bientôt."

And he was off, leaving me staring, mystified—but with something stirring inside me that I hadn't felt in months: hope.

It didn't stir for long, of course; it never does. You hear news, or a rumour, or an enigmatic remark like Laborde's, and your imagination takes wing with wild optimism —and then nothing happens, and your spirits plunge, only to revive for a spell, and then down again, and up and down, while time slips away almost unnoticed. I'm glad I ain't one of these cool hands who can take a balanced view, for any logical appraisal of my situation in Madagascar would have driven me to suicide. As it was, my alternate hopes and glooms were probably my salvation, as the months went by.

For it was months—six of them, although looking back it's hard to believe it was more than a few weeks. Memory may hold on to horrid incidents, but it's a great obliterator of dull, protracted misery, especially if you help it with heavy drinking. There's a fine potent aniseed liquor on Madagascar, and I sopped it up like a country parson, so between sleep and stupor I don't suppose I was in my wits more than half the time.

And as I've remarked, when needs must, you just carry on with the work in hand, so I drilled and bullied my troops, and attended the Queen when called upon, and warily enlarged my circle of acquaintances among the senior military, and cultivated Mr Fankanonikaka, and found out everything I could that might serve when the time came—if it ever did . . . but it must, it must! For while with every passing week my servitude in Madagascar began to seem more natural and inevitable, there would be moments of sudden violent reaction, as when I'd just seen Elspeth, or been appalled by some new atrocity of the Queen's, or the musky wood and dust smell grew unbearable in my nostrils, and then there was nothing for it but to walk out alone on the parade ground before Antan' and stare at the distant mountains, and tell myself fiercely that Lord's was still over there somewhere with Felix bowling his slow lobs while the crowd clapped and the rooks cawed in the trees; there would be green fields, and English rain, parsons preaching, yokels ploughing, children playing, cads swearing, virgins praying, squires drinking, whores rogering, peelers patrolling—that was home, and there must be a road to it.

So I kept my eye skinned and learned . . . that Tamitave, while it had taken days to cover on the slave-march, was a bare hundred and forty miles away; that foreign ships put in about twice a month—for Fankanonikaka, whose office I visited a good deal, used to receive notice of them . . . the *Samson* of Toulon, the *Culebra* of Havana, the *Alexander Hamilton* of New York, the *Mary Peters* of Madras—I saw the names, and my heart would stop. They might only anchor in the roads, to exchange cargo—but if I could time my bolt from Antan' precisely, and reach Tamitave when a foreign vessel was in . . . I'd swum ashore, I could swim aboard—then let 'em try to get me on their cursed land again! How to reach Tamitave, though, ahead of pursuit? The army had some horses, poor screws, but they'd do—one to ride, three to lead for changes . . . oh, G-d, Elspeth! I must get her away, too—mustn't I? . . . unless I escaped and came back for her in force—by Jove, Brooke would jump at the chance of crusading against Ranavalona—if Brooke was still alive—no, I couldn't face another of his campaigns . . . D--n Elspeth! And so my thoughts raced, only to return to the dusty heat and grind of Antan', and the misery of existence.

There were some slight blessings, though. I became interested in my army work, and enjoyed putting the troops through their manœuvres, teaching them complicated wheels in line, slow marches, and so forth; I became quite friendly with senior men like Rakohaja, who began more and more to treat me as an equal, and even entertained me at their homes, the patronising monkeys. Fankanonikaka noted this and was pleased.

"Doing much fine, what? Dining nibs, much grub, happy boozing like h--l, tip-top society, how-de-do so pleased to meet you, hey? I seeing you Count Rakohaja, Baron Andriama, Chancellor Vavalana, other best swells. Watching Vavalana careful, however, sly dog, peeping or tittle-tattling for Queen. So looking sharp, that's the ticket for soup, rotten rascal Vavalana, him hating old boy Fankanonikaka, hating you too, much jealousing you mounting Queen, happying her much boom-boom, not above half, maybe getting boy child I don't know, Vavalana not liking that, mischief you if possible. Watch out him, I telling you. Meantime you pleasing Queen all while, hearty lovings, she admiring, ain't she just, though, ha-ha?"

And the dirty little rascal would tap his pug nose and chortle. I wasn't so sure myself, for as time went by Ranavalona's demands on me slowly diminished, and while it was a relief in one way—for at first, when I had been summoned to the palace almost every day on her majesty's service, it was so exhausting I daren't wave my hand for fear I floated away—it was worrying, too. Was she tiring of me? It was a dreadful thought, but I was reassured by the fact that she still seemed to like my company, and even began to talk to me.

Not that it was elevating chat—how were the troops? was the ration of *jaka** sufficient? why did I never wear a hat? were my quarters comfortable? why did I never kill soldiers by way of punishment? had I ever seen the English queen? You must imagine her, either sitting on her throne in a European gown, with one of her girls fanning her, or reclining on her bed in her sari, propped up on one elbow, slowly grunting out her questions, fingering her long earring and never taking those black unblinking eyes from mine. Unnerving work it was, for I was in constant dread that I'd say something to offend; it didn't help that I never discovered how informed or educated she was, for she volunteered no information or opinions, only questions, and no answers seemed either to please or displease her. She would just brood silently, and then ask something else, in the same flat, muttered French.

It was impossible to guess what she thought, or even how her mind worked. Well, to give you an example, I was alone with her one day, standing by obediently while she sat on the bed gazing at Manjakatsiroa (her bottle gourd) and mumbling to herself, when she looked up at me slowly and growled:

"Does this dress please you?"

It was a white silk sarong, in fact, and became her not too badly, but of course I went into raptures about it. She listened sullenly, fidgeted a moment, and then got up, stripped the thing off, and says:

* Preserved fried beef, a form of pemmican.

"It is yours."

Well, it wasn't my style at all, but of course I grovelled gratefully and said I couldn't do it justice, but I'd treasure it forever, make it my household idol, in fact, splendid idea . . . she paid not the slightest attention but sauntered over, bare as the back of my hand, to her great mirror and stared at herself. Then she turned to me, slapped her belly thoughtfully two or three times, put her hands on her hips, stared bleakly at me, and says:

"Do you like fat women?"

If the hairs on my neck crawled, d'you wonder? For if you can think of a tactful answer, I couldn't. I stood tongue-tied, the sweat starting out on me as visions of boiling pits and crucifixion flitted across my mind, and I couldn't restrain a moan of despair —which I immediately had the mother-wit to turn into a lustful growl as I advanced on her, grappling amorously and praying that actions would speak louder than words. Since she didn't press the point, I gather my answer was the right one.

Another anxiety, of course, during those long weeks, was that she would get word of Elspeth, or that my dear little wife herself would get restive and commit some folly which would attract attention. She didn't, though, and on the occasional visits I was allowed to make to the Prince's palace, she seemed as cheerful as ever—I still don't understand this, although I'll admit that Elspeth has an unusually serene and stupid disposition which can make the best of anything. She bemoaned the fact that we were kept apart, of course, and never ceased to ask me when we would be going home, but since we were never left alone together there was no opportunity to tell her the fearful truth, and it would have served no good purpose anyway. So I jollied her along, and she seemed content enough.

It was on the last visit I paid her that I saw the first signs of distress, and guessed it had at last penetrated into that beautiful fat head that Madagascar wasn't quite the holiday she imagined. She was pale, and looked as though she'd been crying, but for once we had no opportunity of a private tête-à-tête, for the occasion was a tea-party given by the Princess, and I was held in military small talk by the Prince and Rakohaja throughout. Only when I was leaving did I have a brief word with Elspeth, and she didn't say much, except to grip my hand tight, and repeat her eternal question about going home. I couldn't guess what had upset her, but I could see the tears weren't far away, so I startled her out of her glooms in the only way I know how.

"What's this, old girl?" says I, looking thunderous. "Have you been flirting with that young Prince, then?"

She looked blank, but her dismals vanished at once. "Why, Harry, what can you mean? What a question to ask—"

"Is it, though?" says I grimly. "I don't know—I can see he has more than an eye to you, the presumptuous young pup— yes, and you ain't discouraging him exactly, are you? I'm not well pleased, my lady—just because I can't be here all the time is no reason for you to go setting your cap at other fellows—oh, yes, I saw you fluttering at him when he spoke to you—and a married man, too. Anyway," I whispered, "you're far too pretty for him."

She was pink by this time—not with guilty confusion, mark you, but with pleasure at the thought that she'd stirred the passion in yet another male breast. If there was one thing that could divert the little trollop's attention, it was male admiration; she'd have stood preening herself in the track of a steam road roller if someone had so much as winked at her. I saw by her blushing protests how delighted she was, and that her unhappiness—whatever it was—had been quite forgotten. But now I was being called to the Prince, with Rakohaja at his elbow.

"No doubt we shall see you tonight, sergeant-general, at her majesty's ball," says his highness, and it seemed to me his voice was unduly shrill, and his smile a trifle glassy. "It is to be a very splendid occasion."

I knew about the Queen's dances and parties, of course, although I'd never been to one. Being officially a slave, you see, however much authority I had in the army, I occupied a curious social position. But Rakohaja put my doubt at rest.

"Sergeant-General Flashman will be present, highness." He turned his big scarred face to stare at me. "I shall bring him in my own party."

"Excellent," twitters the Prince, looking everywhere but at me. "Excellent. That will be . . . ah . . . most agreeable." I bowed myself away, wondering what this portended. I didn't have long to wait to find out.

The Queen's galas were famous affairs. They took place every two or three months, on the anniversaries of her birth, accession, marriage—or the jubilee of her first massacre, I shouldn't wonder —and were attended by the flower of Malagassy society, all in their fanciest costumes, crowding into the great courtyard before the palace, where they danced, ate, drank, and revelled all through the night. Proper orgies, from all I'd heard, so I was ready prompt enough, in full fig, when Rakohaja came for me early in the evening.

There was a great crowd of the commonalty waiting at the palace gates as we passed through, peeping to get a look at their betters, who were already whooping it up to some tune. The whole vast courtyard was ablaze with Chinese lanterns slung on chains, potted palms and even whole trees and flower-beds had been brought in for decoration, the arches of the palace front were twined with rammage and cords of tinsel, a fountain had been specially constructed in the centre of the yard, the water playing over glass jars in which were imprisoned clusters of the famous Malagassy fire-flies—brilliant little emerald green jewels which winked and fluttered through the spray with dazzling effect.

Among the trees and arbours which lined the square long tables were set, piled with delicacies, especially the local beef rice which is consumed in honour of the Queen—don't ask me why, because it's mere coarse belly fodder. The military band were on hand, pounding away at "Auprès de ma blonde", and getting most of the notes wrong; I noticed they were all half-tipsy, their black faces grinning sweatily and their uniform collars undone, while their bandmaster, resplendent in tartan dressing-gown and bowler hat, was weaving about cackling and losing his silver-rimmed spectacles. He grovelled on the ground hunting for them and waving his baton crazily, but the band played on undaunted, falling off their seats, and the row was deafening.

Mind you, if they were drunk, you could see where they'd got the idea. There must have been several hundred of the upper crust present already, each one with about a gallon of raw spirit aboard to judge by their antics; I counted four fellows in the fountain when we arrived, and any number staggering about;

the greater number were standing unsteadily in groups of anything from six to sixty, making polite conversation at the tops
of their voices, yelling and back-slapping, seizing glasses from
the loaded trays which the servants passed among them, bawling
toasts, spilling liquor all over each other, apologising elaborately,
tumbling down, and acting quite civilised on the whole.

There was the usual fantastic display of fashion—men in Arab,
Turkish, Spanish, and European costume, or mixtures of all of
them, women in every conceivable colour of sarong, sari, elaborate gown, and party frock. There was abundance of uniform,
too, velvet, brocade, superfine, and broadcloth, with crusts of
silver and gold braid, but I noticed there was more of a Spanish
note than usual—black swallow-tails, cummerbunds, funnel pants,
and sashes among the men, mantillas, high heels, flounced skirts,
lace fans, and flowers among the women. The reason, I discovered, was that it was Rakota's coming of age, and since he
favoured dago fashion the revellers were decked out in his
honour. The heat from that shouting, swaying, celebrating throng
came at you like a wave, with the band crowning the bedlam of
noise with its incessant pounding.

"The dinner has not yet begun," says Rakohaja to me. "Shall
we anticipate the others?" He led the way under the trees, where
the waiters stood, most of 'em pretty flushed, and waved me and
his aides to chairs. There was fine china and glass on the tables,
but Rakohaja simply uncorked a bottle, pulled up his sleeve,
scooped up a huge handful of beef rice, and proceeded to stuff
it into his face, taking occasional pulls of liquor to help it down.
Not wishing to be thought ignorant, I used my fingers on a
whole chicken, and the aides, of course, ploughed in like cannibals.

Half-way through our collation the more sober of the palace
attendants cleared the guests from the main square, and there
was terrific plunging, tripping, swearing, and profuse apologising
as they staggered to seat themselves at the surrounding buffets.
Whole tables were overturned, chaps fell into the undergrowth,
women shrieked tipsily and had to be helped, crockery crashed
and glass shattered, all to the accompaniment of cries of: "Ah,
mam'selle, pardon my absurd clumsiness," "Permit me, sir, to
assist you to your feet," "Holà, garçon, place a chair beneath

madame—beneath her posterior, you clumsy rascal!" "Delight-ful, is it not, Mam'selle Bomfomtabellilaba; such select company, exquisite taste and decoration." "Forgive me, madame, I am about to vomit a while," and so forth. Eventually, to a chorus of cries, smashing, retching, and polite whispers, they were all down, at various levels, and the cabaret began.

This consisted of a hundred dancing girls, in white saris, with green fire-flies bound in their hair, undulating in perfect time across the courtyard to weird nigger music; ugly little squirts for the most part, but drilled like guardsmen, and I've never seen a pantomime chorus to equal them. They swayed and weaved among each other like clockwork in the most complex patterns, and the mob, in the intervals of stuffing and swilling, rose to them in drunken appreciation. Flowers and ribbons and even plates of food were thrown, fellows clambered on the tables to applaud and yell, the ladies scattered change from their purses, and in the middle of it the military band regained consciousness as one man and began to play "Auprès de ma blonde" again. The bandmaster fell into the fountain to prolonged cheering, one of the aides at our table subsided face down in a dish of curry, General Rakohaja lit a cheroot, about twenty chaps ran in among the dancing-girls and began an impromptu waltz, the Prince and Princess made their entrance in sedans draped with cloth-of-gold and borne shoulder-high by Hova guardsmen, the whole assembly raved and staggered in loyal greeting, and at the next table a slant-eyed yellow gal with slim bare shoulders glanced lingeringly in my direction, lowered her eyelids demurely, and stuck out her tongue at me behind her fan.

Before I could respond with a courtly inclination of my head there was a sudden blare of trumpets, drowning out the hubbub; it rose in a piercing fanfare, and as it died away the entire congregation staggered to its feet with a renewed clattering of overturned chairs, breaking of dishes, subdued swearing and apology, and stood more or less silent, leaning on each other and breathing stertorously.

On the centre of the first balcony of the palace, lanterns were blazing, guardsmen were forming, and a brazen-lunged major-domo was shouting commands. Handmaidens appeared bearing the striped umbrella, cymbals clashed, a couple of idol-keepers scurried out with their little bundles, the Silver Spear was borne forward, and here came the founder of the feast, the guest of honour, the captain of the side, imperial in her crimson gown and golden crown, to be greeted by a roar of acclamation which beat everything that had gone before. The wave of adulation beat up and echoed against the towering walls, "Manjaka, manjaka! Ranavalona, Ranavalona!" as she moved slowly forward to the balcony, her stately progress marred only by the obvious fact that she, too, was drunker than David's sow.

She swayed dangerously as she stood looking down, a couple of guardsmen lending a discreet elbow on either side, and then the band, in a triumph of instinct over intoxication, burst into the national anthem, "May the Queen Live a Thousand Years", rendered with heroic enthusiasm by the diners, most of whom seemed to be accompanying themselves by beating spoons on plates.

It ended in a furore of cheering, and her majesty retired about five seconds, I'd say, before collapsing in a heap. We hallooed her out of sight, and now that the loyal toast was drunk, so to speak, the party began in earnest. There was a concerted rush into the square, in which I found myself carried along, willynilly, and with the band surpassing itself, a frenzied polka was danced; I found myself partnering an enormously fat hippo of a woman in crinoline, who used me as a battering-ram to drive a way through the press, screaming like a steam whistle as she did so.

I may say that in keeping with the spirit of the evening, I had taken a fairish cargo of drink aboard myself, and it was making me feel reckless, for I kept craning over the heads of the throng in the hope of a sight of the yellow gal who had been eyeing me. Which was madness, of course, but even the thought of a jealous Ranavalona ain't proof against several pints of aniseed liquor and Malagassy champagne—besides, after months of galloping royalty I was crying out for a change, and that slender charmer would supply it splendidly—there she was, with a froglike black partner clinging to her for support; she caught my glance as the dance swept her past and opened her eyes invitingly at me.

It was the work of a moment to kick my partner's massive legs from under her and thrust her squawking under the feet of the prancing throng; I fought my way to the sidelines, scooping the yellow gal out of her partner's drunken embrace en route, and he blundered on blindly while I bore off the prize with one arm round her lissom waist. She was shrieking with laughter as I swept her into the undergrowth—it was bedlam in there, too, for it seemed that the accepted way of sitting out a dance in Antan' was to crawl into the bushes and fornicate; half the guests appeared to be there before us, black bottoms everywhere, but I found a clear space and was just settling down, choking lustfully in the waves of scent which my lady affected, when some brute kicked me in the ribs, and there was Rakohaja standing over us.

I was about to d--n his eyes heartily, but he just jerked his head and moved behind a tree, and since my yellow gal chose that moment to be sick, I lost no time in joining him, cursing my luck just the same. I was pretty unsteady on my feet, but I realised that he was cold sober; the lean black face was grim and steady, and there was something about the way he glanced either side, at the hullabaloo of the dance and the dim forms grunting and gasping in the shadows about us, that made me check my angry protest. He drew on his cheroot a moment, then, pitching it away, he took my arm and ushered me under the trees, along a narrow path, and so by a dimly-lighted passage into a little open garden space, which I guessed must be to the side of the palace proper.

It was moonlight, and the little space was full of shadows; I was about to demand to know what the dooce this was all about when I realised that there were at least two men half-hidden in the gloom, but Rakohaja paid them no attention. He crossed to a little summer-house, with a chink of light showing beneath its door, and tapped. I stood trying to get my head clear, suddenly scared; faintly in the distance I could hear the sounds of music and drunken revelry, and then the door was opened, and I was being ushered inside, blinking in the lantern-light as I stared round, panic mounting in my throat.

There were four men seated there, looking at me. To my left, in dark shirt, breeches, and boots, his face vulpine in the lantern-ray, was Laborde; next to him, solemn for once, his fat chops framed in his high collar, was Fankanonikaka; to the right, slimly elegant in his full court dress, was one of the young Malagassy nobles whom I knew by sight, although I'd hardly spoken to him, Baron Andriama. And in the centre, his handsome young face tense and strained, was Prince Rakota himself. His glance went past me as the door closed.

"No one saw you?" His voice was a hoarse whisper.

"No one," says Rakohaja behind me. "It is safe to begin."

I doubted that—I really did. Drunk or not, I can smell a conspiracy when it's pushed under my nose, and the presence of royalty and several of Madagascar's most eminent citizens notwithstanding, I knew at once that there was mischief brewing here, but Rakohaja's hand was on my shoulder, firmly guiding me to a seat, and any lingering doubt was dispelled as the Prince nodded to Laborde, who addressed me.

"There is very little time," says he, "so I shall be brief. Do you wish to return to England, in safety, with your wife?"

The honest answer to that was high treason, and the knowledge must have shown in my face, for little Fankanonikaka broke in quickly; it was a sign of his agitation that he spoke, not in fluent French, but in his bastard English.

"Not frightening, no alarms, all's well, Flashman. Friends here, liking you, telling truth, like old boys, ain't we?"

If the Queen's own son, and her secretary and most trusted minister were in it—whatever it was—there could be no point in lying.

"Yes," says I, and the Prince sighed with relief, and broke into a torrent of Malagassy, but Laborde cut him short.

"Pardon, highness, we must not delay." He turned to me again. "The time has come to depose the Queen. All of us whom you see here are agreed on that. We are not alone; there are others, trusted friends, who are in the plot with us. We have a plan—simple, effective, and involving no bloodshed, by which her majesty will be removed from power, and his highness crowned in her place. He will give you his royal word, that in return for your faithful service in this, he will set you and your wife at liberty, and return you to your homeland." He paused; his words had come out in a swift, incisive rush, but now he spoke slowly. "Will you join us?"

Could it be a trap? Some d---lish device of Ranavalona's to

test my loyalty—she was fiend enough to be capable of it. Laborde's face said nothing; Fankanonikaka was nodding at me, as though willing me to agree. I glanced at the Prince, and the almost wistful expression in the fine dark eyes convinced me— nearly. I was sober enough now, and as frightened as any decent coward has any right to be; it might be dangerous to agree, but just the feel of Rakohaja's grim presence at my elbow told me it would be downright fatal to refuse.

"What d'you want me to do?" I said. For the life of me, I couldn't see why they needed me at all, unless they wanted me to strangle the black slut in her bath—the mind shuddered at the thought—no, it couldn't be that—no bloodshed, Laborde had said—

"We need someone," Laborde went on, as though he'd been reading my mind, "who is in the Queen's confidence, entirely above suspicion, yet with the power so to dispose of the armed forces that they will be unable to protect her. Someone who can ensure that when the moment comes, her Hova guard regiment will not be able to intervene. Those guards within the palace can be dealt with easily—provided there is no reinforcement to assist them. That is the key to the whole plan. And you hold the key."

So many thoughts and terrors were jumbling in my mind by now that I couldn't give them coherent utterance for a moment. The prospect of freedom—of escape from that monstrous Poppaea and her ghastly country—I shivered with excitement at the thought . . . but Laborde must be crazy, for what could I do about her infernal soldiers?—I might be G-d Almighty on the drill-ground, telling them where to put their clodhopping feet, but I'd no authority beyond that. Their plot might be A1, and I was all for it, provided I was safe out of harm's way—but the thought of *doing* anything! One hint of suspicion in those terrible eyes—

"How can I do that?" I stuttered. "I mean, I've no power. General Rakohaja here, he could order—"

"Not possible, Queen not liking, all thinking bad of General, chop undoubtedly—" Fankanonikaka waved his hands, and Rakohaja's deep voice sounded behind me.

"If I, or any other noble, attempted to move the Hova Guards more than a mile from the city, the Queen's suspicions would be instantly aroused. And I do not have to tell you what follows on her suspicions. It has been tried, once before, and General Betim-seraba lingered in agony for days, without arms or legs or eyes, hanging in a buffalo skin at Ambohipotsy. He was plotting, as we are, but not so carefully. He forgot that the Queen has spies in every corner—spies that even Fankanonikaka does not know about. Yet all he did was try to detach two companies of the guard to Tamitave. Nothing was proved—but he failed the *tanguin*—and died."

"But . . . but—I can't move the Guards—"

"You **have** done so, twice already." It was Andriama, speaking for the first time. "Did you not give them training marches, one of two days, the other of three? Nothing was said; the Queen was undisturbed. What would excite immediate suspicion, if done by a noble of whom the Queen is jealous—and she is insanely jealous of all of us—may be easily accomplished by the sergeant-general, who is only a slave, and well beloved by the Queen."

Fankanonikaka was nodding eagerly; his lips seemed to be framing the words "jig-a-jig-a-jig". I was going faint at the thought of the risk I'd already run, quite unawares.

"Don't you understand?" says Laborde. "Don't you see— from the moment I saw you in the slave-market, months ago, we have been scheming, Fankanonikaka and I, to bring you to the position where you could do this thing? The Queen trusts you —because she has no reason to suspect you, who are only a lost foreigner. She thinks of you only as the slave who drills her troops—and as a lover. You know how cautiously we have pro-ceeded—so that no hint of suspicion could attach to you; his highness has kept your wife in safety, even beyond the eyes and ears of his mother's spies. We have waited and waited—oh, long before you came to Madagascar. This is not the first time we have plotted in secret—"

"She is mad!" the Prince burst out. "You know she is mad— and terrible—a woman of blood! She is my mother—and . . . and . . ." He was shaking, twisting his hands together. "I do not seek the throne for greed, or for power! I do it to save this country—to save all of us, before she destroys us utterly, or

brings down the vengeance of the world upon us! And she will
—she will! The Powers will not stand by forever!" He stared
from Laborde to Rakohaja and back again. "You know it! We
all know it!"

I couldn't fathom this, until Laborde explained.

"You are not alone, Flashman. Only last month a brig named
the *Marie Laure* was driven ashore near Tamitave; her master,
one Jacob Heppick, an American, was taken and sold into
slavery, like you. I had him bought, through friends of mine—"
He snorted suddenly. "There are five European slaves whom I
have bought secretly this year, to save them from worse; cast-
aways, unfortunates, like you and your wife. They are hidden
with my friends. But there have been inquiries from their govern-
ments—inquiries which the Queen has answered with insults
and threats. She has even been foolish enough to abuse the few
foreign traders who put in here—men have been taken from
their vessels, put to forced labour, virtually enslaved. How long
will France and England and America endure this?

"Even now"—he leaned forward, tapping my knee—"there
is a British warship in Tamitave roads, whose commander has
sent protests to the Queen. She will reject them, as she always
does—and burn another hundred Christians alive to show her
contempt of foreigners! How long before that one British warship is a squadron, landing an army to march on Antan' and
pull her from her throne? Does she think London and Paris will
endure her forever?"

And what the d---l, I nearly burst out, is wrong with that? I
never heard such splendid stuff in all my life—G-d, to think of
British regiments and blue-jackets storming into her beastly
capital, blowing her lousy Hova rascals to blazes, stringing her
up, with any luck—and then it occurred to me that these Malagassy gentlemen might not view the prospect with quite as much
enthusiasm. They wouldn't relish being another British or French
dominion; no, but let good King Rakota mount the throne, and
behave like a civilised being, and the Powers would be happy
enough to leave him and his country alone. So that was why
they were in such a sweat to get rid of mama, before she pro-
voked an invasion. But why should Laborde care—he wasn't a
Malagassy? No, but he was a conniving Frog, and he didn't

want the Union Jack over Antan' any more than the others did. I wasn't in the political service for nothing, you know.

"She will destroy us!" Rakota cries again. "She will bring us to war—and in her madness there is no horror she will not—"

"No, highness," says Rakohaja. "She will not—for we will not let her. This time we shall succeed."

"You understand," says Laborde, eyeing me, "what is to be done? You must send the Guards on a march to the Ankay, a mere thirty miles away. Nothing more than that. A training march, lasting three days, under their subordinate commanders, as usual."

"That will leave the Teklave and Antaware regiments at Antan'," says Rakohaja. "They will do nothing; their generals will be with us as soon as our coup is seen to be successful."

"We shall strike on the second night after the Guards have gone," says Andriama. "I shall be in attendance on the Queen. I shall have thirty men in the palace. At a given signal they will take the Queen prisoner, and dispose of her guards within the palace, if that is necessary. General Rakohaja will summon the commanders of the lesser regiments, and with Mr Fankanoni-kaka will proclaim the new King. It will be done within an hour — and when word of the coup reaches the Hova Guards at Ankay, it will be too late. The enthusiasm of the people will ensure our success—"

"They will rally to me," says Rakota earnestly. "They will see why I do this thing, that I will be a liberator, and—"

"Yes, highness," says Rakohaja, "you may trust us to see to all that."

I couldn't help noticing that they used Rakota pretty offhand, for their future monarch; who would rule Madagascar, I couldn't help wondering? But that was small beer—my mind was racing over this thunderclap that they'd burst on me. They weren't laggard conspirators, these lads, and I'd hardly had time to get my breath. They had it all pat—but, by jingo, it was an appalling risk! Suppose something went wrong—as it had done before, apparently? The mere thought of the vengeance Ranavalona would take set my innards quivering—and I'd be in the middle of the stew, too. I could have wept at the thought that there was a British warship, this very minute, not four days' ride away to the eastward. Was there any way I could—no, that wasn't on the cards. Suppose Laborde could bring it off? Suppose the Queen got wind of it? She had spies—I even found myself looking at Fankanonikaka, and wondering. Who knew—she might have penetrated this conspiracy already—she might be gloating up yonder, biding her time. I thought of those awful pits, and the fellow screaming before her throne, with his arm parboiled . . .

"Then you are with us?" says Laborde, and I realised they were all staring at me—Fankanonikaka, round-eyed, eager but scared; the Prince almost appealing, Andriama and Rakohaja grimly, Laborde with his head back, weighing me. In the silence of the little summer-house I could still hear, faintly, the sounds of the distant music. There was a foolish, useless question in my mind—but funk that I was, I had to ask it, although the answer wouldn't settle my terrors a bit.

"You're sure the Queen doesn't suspect already?" says I. "I've heard of thirty men who'll do the thing—how d'ye know there isn't a spy among 'em? Those two sentries outside—"

"One of the sentries," says Andriama, "is my brother. The other my oldest friend. The thirty whom I shall lead are men from the forests—outlaws, brigands, men under sentence of death already. They can be trusted, for if they betrayed us, they would join us in the pits."

"Neither the Queen nor Chancellor Vavalana suspects," says Rakota quickly. "I am certain of it." He fidgeted and looked at me, smiling hopefully.

"When will my wife and I be free to leave?" says I, looking him in the eye, but it was Laborde who answered.

"Three days from now. For you must send the Guards to Ankay tomorrow, and we will strike on the night of the day following. From that moment, you are free."

If I'm still alive, thinks I. I knew I was red in the face, which is a sure sign that I'm paralysed with fear—but what could I do but accept? Hadn't they cut it fine, though? Not giving old Flash much time to play 'em false, if he'd been so minded, the cunning scoundrels. Even so, they felt it would do no harm to drop a reminder in my ear, for when the Prince had said a few well-chosen words to wind up our little social gathering, and we had dispersed quietly into the dark, and I was making my way tremulously back to the courtyard, where they were still racketing fit to wake the dead, Rakohaja suddenly surged up at my elbow.

"A moment, sergeant-general, if you please." He had a cheroot going again; he glanced around, drawing on it, before continuing. "I was watching you; I do not think you are a calm man."

Heaven alone knew what could have given him that impression. To demonstrate my sang-froid I uttered a falsetto moan of inquiry.

"Calm is necessary," says the big b----rd, laying a hand on my arm. "A nervous man, in your situation, might give way to fear. He might conceive, foolishly, that his interest would be best served by betraying our plot to her majesty." I started to babble, but he cut me short. "That would be fatal. Any gratitude which the Queen might feel—supposing she felt any at all —would be more than outweighed by her jealous rage on discovering that her lover had been unfaithful. Mam'selle Bomfomtabellilaba is an attractive woman, as you are aware. You seemed to be finding her so when I summoned you earlier this evening. The Queen would be most displeased with you if she heard of it."

He took my arm as we approached the courtyard. "I remember one of her earlier . . . favourites, who was indiscreet enough only to smile at one of her majesty's waiting-women. He never smiled again—at least, I do not think he did, but it is difficult to tell after a man's skin has been removed, inch by inch, in one piece. Shall we find something to eat?—I am quite famished."

While I can lie and dissemble with the best as a rule, I'm not much hand at conspiracy; you're too dependent on knavery other than your own. Mind you, they seemed a steady enough gang, and the one blessing was that there was little time left for anything to go wrong; if I'd had to wait days, or weeks, I don't doubt my nerve would have cracked, or I'd have given myself away. When I went on parade next dawn, having had not a wink of sleep, I was twitching like a landed fish; I'd even started guiltily when my orderly brought my shaving-water—what was behind it, eh? wasn't it suspicious that his behaviour was exactly the same as it had been for months? Did he know something? By the time I got to my office, and issued my orders of the day to my small staff of instructors, I was seeing spies everywhere, and behaving like a nervous actor in "Macbeth".

The shocking problem, as I stared at the impassive black faces of my staff and tried to keep my hands still, was to devise a sufficient excuse for sending the Guards off to Ankay. G-d, how had I got into this? I couldn't just order 'em off—that would excite comment for certain. They didn't need the exercise, they'd been behaving well on parade—I couldn't see any way, but I had them mustered in case, trusting the Lord would provide. And He did. The men were steady and well-turned out, as usual, but their junior officers had been at the Queen's party all night, and came on parade half-soused. Seeing my chance, I set 'em to drill their columns, and in five minutes that muster looked like the Battle of Borodino, with Hovas walking into each other, whole companies going astray, and little drunk officers staggering about shrieking and weeping. In happy inspiration I had the band paraded to accompany the drill, and since most of them were still cross-eyed and blowing into the wrong end of their instruments, the shambles was only increased.

At this I flew into a frightful passion, placed the drunker

officers under arrest, harangued the parade at the top of my voice, and told them they could d--n well march in full kit until they were sober and respectable again. Ankay was the place, I said; they could camp out on the plain without tents or blankets, and if one of 'em dared to get fever I'd flog him stupid. It must have sounded convincing, and presently off they went, led by the band playing three different marches at once; I watched them fade into the dusty haze and thought, well, that's my part well done—and if the whole plot goes agley, I can still plead that my actions have been perfectly normal.

But that's small comfort to a conscience like mine. I was a prey to increasing terror all day, fretting about what Laborde and the others might be doing—there was another day and night for word of the plot to leak out, and I started at every voice and footfall. Fortunately, no one seemed to notice; no doubt they attributed my jumps, like their own, to the excesses of the previous night. There was no word from the palace, no hint of anything untoward; evening came, and I prepared to turn in early with a bottle of aniseed to quiet my dark hours.

I lay there, listening to the distant sounds of the palace, sucking at my flask, and telling myself for the thousandth time there was no reason why all shouldn't be well—why, given luck, in two days Elspeth and I would be riding down in style to Tamitave, with Rakota's blessing; then the first English ship, and home and safety, far from this h--lish place. It mightn't be so bad, of course, with Ranavalona out of the way—might be financial advantage to be had—rich country, new market— trading ventures, expert advice to City merchants in return for ten per cent of the profits—not to be sneezed at. Wonder what they'd do with Good Queen Randy—exile to the southern province, likely, with a platoon of Hova bucks to keep her warm ... serve her right ...

The knock on my door sounded thunderously, and I came bolt upright, sweating. I heard my orderly's voice, and here he was, as I scrabbled for my boots, and behind him, the ominous figures of Hova guardsmen, bandoliers and all, their bare chests gleaming black in the lamplight. There was an under-officer, summoning me to the royal apartments; the words pierced my drowsy brain like drops of acid—oh, Ch---t, I was done for. I had to hold on to the edge of my cot as I pulled on my breeches; what could she want, at this hour, and why should she send a guard of soldiers, unless the worst had happened? The gaff was blown, it must be—steady, though, it might be nothing after all —I must keep a straight face, whatever it was. Panic shook me —should I try a bolt? No, that would be fatal, and my legs wouldn't answer; it was all they could do to walk steady as the officer led the way round to the front of the palace, past the broad steps—was it imagination that there seemed to be more sentries than usual?—and across the court to the Silver Palace, gleaming dimly under the rising moon, its million bells tinkling softly in the night air.

Up the stairs, along the broad corridor, with my legs like jelly and the Hova boots pounding stolidly behind me—I wasn't happy about those boots, I remembered; I'd toyed with the idea of trying 'em in sandals, but hadn't been sure how they'd stand up to long marching—ye G-ds, what a thing to think about, with my life in the balance, and now the great doors were opening, the officer was waving me in, and here, in a blaze of light, was the reception room, and I was striding in and bowing automatically, while the picture was emblazoned in my mind.

She was there, black and still, on her throne. It must be midnight, surely, but d---e if she wasn't wearing a taffeta afternoon dress, all blue flounces, and a hat with an ostrich plume. I came up from my bow, feeling the chill stare, but I couldn't bring myself to look at her. A couple of her girl attendants alongside, then the lean, robed figure of Vavalana the Chancellor, his head cocked, looking at me out of his crafty eyes; Fankanonikaka— I struggled for composure, but his bland black face told me nothing. And then my heart leaped sickeningly, and I almost cried out.

To one side, between two guardsmen, stood Baron Andriama. His shirt was torn, his face contorted, and his hands were bound; he seemed barely able to stand. There was a filthy mess on the floor near him—and the word shot into my mind: *tanguin*. She knew, then—it was all up.

Out of the corner of my eye I could see her watching me, her hand at her earring. Then she muttered something, and Vavalana shuffled forward, his staff tapping. His grizzled head and skinny black face looked curiously bird-like; he blinked at me like a cheeky old robin.

"Speak before the Queen," says he, and his voice was a gentle croak. "Why did you send the Guards to Ankay?"

I tried to look slightly puzzled, and to keep my voice steady. "May the Queen live a thousand years. I sent the Guards on a punishment march—because they were drunk and slovenly. So was the band." I frowned at him, and spoke louder. "They were not fit to be seen—I have five of their officers in arrest. Fifty miles in full kit is what they need, to teach 'em to behave like soldiers—and when they come back I'll send them out again, if they haven't learned their lesson!"

It sounded well, I think—the right touch of puzzled indignation and martial severity, although how I managed it G-d alone knows. Vavalana was studying me, and behind him that black face and beady eyes beneath the ostrich plume were as fixed as a stone idol's. I must not falter, or betray fear—

"They were not sent away on the orders of that man?" says Vavalana, and his scrawny hand pointed at Andriama, sagging between his guards.

"Baron Andriama?" says I, bewildered. "He has no authority over the troops. Why—does he say he ordered me? He has never shown any interest in their training—he's not a soldier, even. I don't understand, Chancellor—"

"But you knew"—cries Vavalana, his finger stabbing at me— "you knew he plotted against the life of the Great Lake Supplying Water! Why else should you remove her shield, her trusted soldiers?"

I let my jaw drop in amazement, then I laughed right in his face—and for the first time saw Ranavalona startled. She jumped like a jerked puppet, for I don't suppose anyone had ever laughed aloud in her presence before.

"A plot, you say? Is this a joke, Chancellor? If so, it's in poor taste." I stopped laughing and scowled, seeing the doubt in his eyes—now's your chance, my boy, I thought, rage and indignation, carry it off for all you're worth, bluff loyal old Harry. "Who would dare plot against her majesty, or say that I knew of it?" I almost shouted the words, red in the face, and Vavalana absolutely fell back a step. Then:

"Enough!" Ranavalona took her hand from her earring. "Come here."

I stepped forward, forcing myself to look into those hypnotic eyes, my mouth dry with fear. Had the bluff worked? Did she believe me? The glazed, frozen pupils surveyed me for a full minute, then she reached out and took my hand. My spirits leaped as she held it—and then she grunted one word:

"*Tanguin.*"

My heart lurched, and I almost fell. For it meant she didn't believe me, or at least wasn't sure, which was just as bad; she was holding my hand, sentencing me to trial by ordeal, that horrible, lunatic test of Madagascar, which gave barely a chance of survival. I heard my own teeth chattering, and then I was grovelling and pleading, protesting my loyalty, swearing she was the darlingest, loveliest queen who ever was—only the blind certainty that confession meant sure and unspeakable death stopped me from whimpering out the whole plot; for at least the *tanguin* gave me a slender chance, and I suppose I knew it. The sullen face didn't change. She let go my hand and gestured to the guards.

I could only crouch there while they made their beastly preparations, aware of nothing except the black, muscular hands holding the little *tanguin* stone and scraping it with a knife, so that the grey powdery flakes fell on to the platter on which lay the three dried scraps of chicken-skin. There it was, my poisoned death; one of the guards jerked me roughly to my feet, gripping my arms behind me; the other advanced, lifting the plate up to my face. He seized my jaw—and then paused as the Queen spoke, but it wasn't a reprieve: she was signing to one of her maids, and everything must wait, me with my eyes popping at that venomous offal I was going to have to swallow, while the girl scurried away and came back with a purse, from which the Queen solemnly counted twenty-four dollars into Vavalana's hand. At that final callousness, that obscene adherence to the letter of their heathen ritual, my nerve broke.

"No!" I screamed. "Let me go! I'll tell—I swear I'll tell!" By the grace of God I shouted in English, which no one except Fankanonikaka understood. "Mercy! They made me do it! I'll tell—"

My jaw was wrenched cruelly open; bestial fingers were holding it, and I choked as my mouth filled with the filthy odour of the *tanguin*. I struggled, gagging, but the scraps of chicken were thrust brutally to the back of my mouth; then powerful hands clamped my jaws shut and pinched my nostrils, I struggled and heaved, trying not to swallow, my throat was on fire with that vile dust, I was choking horribly, my lungs bursting, but it was no use. I gulped agonisingly—and then I was staggering free, sobbing and trying to retch, glaring round in panic, knowing I was dying—yet even then aware of the curiosity in the watching eyes of Vavalana and the guards, and the blank indifference of the creature motionless on the throne.

I screamed, again and again, clutching at my burning throat, while the room spun giddily round me—and then the guards had seized me once more, little Fankanonikaka was jabbering at me while they forced a bowl to my lips. "Buvez! Buvez! Drinking—quickly!" and a torrent of rice-water was being poured into me, filling my mouth and nostrils, soaking my whole head; my very lungs seemed to be filling with the stuff. I swallowed and swallowed until I felt I must burst, feeling the relief as that corrosive pain was washed from my mouth—and then an agonising convulsion gripped my stomach, and then another, and another. I was on hands and knees, crawling blindly—oh, G-d, if this was death it was worse than anything I'd imagined. I opened my mouth to scream, and in that moment I spewed as never before, again and again, and collapsed in a shuddering heap, wailing feebly and all but dead to the world, while the spectators gathered round to take stock.

This is the interesting part of the *tanguin* ordeal, you see: will the victim vomit properly? It's true—that's the test. They force that deadly poison into you, douse you with rice-water to help digestion, and await events—but it ain't enough just to be sick, you know, you must bring up the three pieces of chicken-skin as well, and if you do, it's handshakes all round and a tanner from the poor box. If you don't, then you've failed the test, your guilt is established—and her majesty has endless fun disposing of you.

Delightful, ain't it? And just about as logical as the proceedings of our police courts, if rather more upsetting to the accused.

At least you don't have to wait in suspense while they sift the evidence, for you're too racked and exhausted to care; I lay, coughing and whining with my eyes blurred with tears of pain, until someone seized my hair and jerked me upright, and there was Vavalana, solemnly surveying three sodden little objects on his palm, and Fankanonikaka beaming relief at his elbow, nodding at me, and I was still too dazed to take it in as the guards thrust me forward on to my knees, snuffling and blubbering before the throne.[42]

Then followed the most astonishing thing of all. Ranavalona held out her hand, and Vavalana carefully placed eight dollars in her palm. She passed them to her maid, and he then gave her another eight, which she held out to me. I was too used up to recollect that this was the token that I'd survived the ordeal successfully, but then she made it abundantly clear. When I took the money she closed her hand round mine and leaned forward from her throne until our faces were almost touching, and to my utter disbelief I saw that there were tears in those dreadful snake eyes. Very gently she rubbed her nose against mine, and touched my face with her lips. Then she was upright again, turning her glare on the unfortunate Andriama, and hissing something in Malagassy—she may have been reminding him to wear wool next his skin, but I doubt it, for he shrieked with terror and flung himself grovelling in front of her, nuzzling at her feet while the guards fell on him and dragged him writhing towards the doors. My hair stood up shuddering on my scalp as his screams died away; a less comprehensive spew, and that would have been me wailing.

Fankanonikaka was at my elbow, and taking my cue from him I bowed unsteadily, backing out of the presence. As the doors closed on us, Ranavalona was still seated, the ostrich plume nodding as she muttered to her bottle idol; her maids were starting to mop the floor in a disconsolate way.

"Much touching, Queen loving you greatly, so pleased you puking pretty, much happy *tanguin* not dying!" Fankanonikaka was absolutely snivelling with sentiment as he hurried. "She never loving so deep, except royal bulls, which aren't human being. But now hurrying, much danger still, for you, for me, for all, when Andriama telling plots." He thrust me along the passages, and so to his little office, where he shot the bolt and stood gasping.

"What about Andriama? What happened?"

He rolled his eyes. "Who knowing, someone betraying, awful humbug Vavalana maybe spy keyholing, hearing somethings. Queen suspicioning Andriama, giving *tanguin*, he puking no good, not like you. I not there in time, no helping, like for you, with salt, little-little cascara in rice-water, making mighty sickings, jolly happy, all right and tight, I say."

No wonder I'd been sick. I could have kissed the little blighter, but he was fairly twitching with alarm.

"Andriama telling soon. Awful torturings now, worse from Spanish Inquizzing, burnings and cutting away private participles—" He shuddered, his hands over his face. "He crying about plot, me, you, Rakohaja, Laborde—"

"For G-d's sake, talk French!"

"—everything be knowing to Vavalana and Queen. Maybe little time yet, then clink for us, torturings too, then Tyburn jig, I'll wager! Only hope, making plot now—tonight! Guards not here, marching Ankay left-right! Must telling Rakohaja, Laborde, Queen suspicioning, Andriama blowing gaff soon . . ."

He babbled on while I tried desperately to think. He was right, of course: Malagassies are brave and tough as teak, but Andriama would never stand the horrors that Ranavalona's beauties were probably inflicting on him while we stood talking. He'd break, and soon, and we'd be dead men—by George, though, she fancied me, didn't she just, piping her eye when I survived the *tanguin*, the tender-hearted little bundle? Aye, and no doubt she'd weep into her pillow after I'd been flayed alive for treason, too. If we could reach Laborde or Rakohaja, could they bring off the coup at once? Where were Andriama's thirty villains? Did Rakota know what had been happening? Rakota —dear G-d, Elspeth! What would become of her? I pounded my fist in a fury of despair, while Fankanonikaka twittered in Malagassy and pidgin English, and suddenly I saw that there was only one way, and a slender hope at that, but it was that or unspeakable death. The Flashman gambit—when in doubt, run.

"Look, Fankanonikaka," says I, "leave this to me. I'll find Laborde and Rakohaja. But if I'm to move quickly, I must have a horse. Can you give me an order on the royal stables? They won't let me take a beast without authority. Come on, man! I can't run all over b----y Antan' on foot! Wait, though—I may need more than one. Write me an order for a dozen horses, so that I can give 'em to Laborde, or Rakohaja—they'll have to assemble those men of Andriama's somehow."

He goggled at me in consternation. "But what reason? If order say taking all horse, someone suspicioning, crying fire and Bow Street—"

"Say they're for the Guards' officers I sent marching to Ankay! Say the Queen's sorry for 'em, and they can ride back! Any d----d excuse will do! Hurry, man—Andriama's probably crying uncle this instant!"

That decided him; he grabbed a quill and scribbled as I hovered at his shoulder, shuddering with impatience. The minutes were flying, and with every one my chances were growing dimmer. I pocketed the order; there was one more item I must have.

"Have you a pistol? A sword, then—I must have a weapon—in case." I hoped to heaven there'd be no in case about it, but I couldn't go unarmed. He scurried about and found one in a nearby drawing-room—only a ceremonial rapier with a curved ivory hilt and no guard, but it would have to do. As I took it an appalling thought struck me—why not cut upstairs and kill the black b---h where she sat . . . or sick Fankanonikaka on to do it? He fairly squealed with alarm and indignation.

"No, no, no bloodings! Gentle deposings only—great Queen, poor lady—oh, so barmy! If only she peace and quiet, ourselves not needing d--n plottings, not above half! Now all to smash, kicking up rows, arrests and cruellings!" He wrung his hands. "You hurrying Laborde fastly, I waiting sentry, oh my stars, someone maybe nabbing, or Queen suspicioning—"

"Not a bit of it," says I. "Tell you what, though—you're a sharp hand at slipping things into chap's drinks, ain't you? Well, try and find a way of sending poor old Andriama some refreshment—put him out of his misery before he blabs, what? And don't fret, Fankanonikaka! We all old boys, jolly times together. Floreat Highgate and to h--l with the Bluecoat School, hey?"

Then I was off, leaving him twittering, forcing myself to walk slowly as I descended the great staircase, past the incurious palace guardsmen, across the court and out into the street beyond. It was the small hours, but there was plenty of traffic about, for in the royal district of Antan' society folk kept late hours, and there was sure to be much dining-out and discussing of last night's orgy at the palace. They delight in scandal, you know, just like their civilised brethren and sisters. The streets were well-lit, but no one paid me any heed as I made my way past the strolling pedestrians and the sedans jogging under the trees. I had got a long cloak from Fankanonikaka, to wear over my boots and breeches and to cover my sword—for slaves didn't ought to have such things—and apart from my white face and whiskers I was just like any other passer-by.

The stables were only five minutes' walk, and I lounged about in a fever of nonchalance while the under-officer laboriously spelled out Fankanonikaka's note and looked surly. He didn't have much French, but I supplemented the written order as best I could, and since he recognised me as the sergeant-general he did what he was told.

"Two horses for me," says I, "and the other dozen for the Guards' officers out at Ankay. Send 'em out now, with a groom, and tell him to follow the Guards' track, but not to hurry. I don't want the cattle worn out, d'you see?"

"No grooms," says he, sulky-like.

"Then get one," says I, "or I'll mention you to the Queen, may she live a thousand years. Been out to Ambohipotsy lately, have you? You'll find yourself observing it from the top of the cliff, unless you look sharp—and put a water-bottle, filled, with each horse, and plenty of *jaka* in the saddle-bags."

I left him as pale as only a scared nigger can be, and rode at a gentle pace in the direction of Prince Rakota's palace, leading the second horse. I daren't hurry, for a mounted man was rare enough in Antan' at any time, and a hastening rider in the middle of the night would have had them hollering peeler. This is the worst of all, when every second's precious but you have to dawdle—I think of strolling terrified through the pandy lines at Lucknow with Campbell's message, or that nerve-racking wait on the steamboat wharf at Memphis with a disguised slave-girl on my elbow and the catchers at our very heels; you must idle along carelessly with your innards screaming—had Andriama talked yet? Did the Queen know it all by now? Was Fankanoni-kaka, perhaps, already shrieking under the knives? Were the city gates still open? They never closed 'em, as a rule; if I found them shut, that would be a sure sign that the caper was blown—heaven help us then.

Rakota's place in the suburbs stood well apart from the other houses, behind a stockade approached through a belt of small trees and bushes. I left the horses there, out of sight, breathed a silent prayer that Malagassy hacks knew enough not to stray or neigh, and set forward boldly for the front gate. There was a porter dozing under the lantern, but he let me in ready enough —they don't care much, these folk—and presently I was kicking the jigger-dubber* awake on the front steps, boldly announcing myself from the Silver Palace with a message for his royal highness.

This presently produced a butler, who knew my face, but when I demanded instant audience, he cocked his frosty head disdainfully.

"Their highnesses are not returned . . . ah . . . sergeant-general. They are dining with Count Potrafanton. You can wait—on the porch."

That was a blow; I hadn't a moment to spare. I hesitated, and then saw there was nothing for it but the high hand.

"It's no matter, porter," says I, briskly. "My message is that the foreign woman who is here is to be sent to the Silver Palace immediately. The Queen wishes to see her."

If my nerves hadn't been snapping, I dare say I'd have been quite entertained at the expressions which followed each other across his wrinkled black face. I was only tenth-caste foreign rubbish, a mere slave, he was thinking; on the other hand, I was sergeant-general, with impressive if undefined power, and much more to the point, I was the Queen's current favourite and riding-master, as all the world knew. And I brought a command ostensibly from the throne itself. All this went through the woolly head—how much he'd been told by his master about the need to keep Elspeth's presence secret, I couldn't guess, but eventually he saw which way wisdom—and Ambohipotsy—lay.

* Door-keeper.

"I shall inform her," says he, stiffly, "and arrange an escort."

"That won't be necessary," says I, harshly. "I have a sedan waiting beyond the gates."

Butlers are the b----y limit; he was ready to argue, so eventually I just blazed at him, and threatened if he didn't have her down and on parade in a brace of shakes, I'd march straight back to the palace and tell the Queen her son's butler had said "Snooks!" and slammed the door on me. He quivered at that, more in anger than sorrow, and then marched off, all black dignity, to fetch her. You could see he was wondering what things were coming to nowadays.

I waited, chewing my knuckles, pacing the porch, and groaning at the recollection of how long it took the bl----d woman to dress. Ten to one she was peering at herself in the glass, patting her curls and making moues, while Andriama was probably blabbing, and plot, alarm, and arrest were breaking out with a vengeance; Ranavalona's tentacles might be reaching out through the city this moment, in search of me—I stamped and cursed aloud in a fever of impatience, and then strode through the open door at the sound of a female voice. Sure enough, there she was, in cloak and bonnet, prattling her way down the stairs, and the butler carrying what looked like a hat-box, of all things. She gave a little shriek at the sight of me, but before I could frown her into silence another sound had me wheeling round, hackles rising, my hand starting towards my sword-hilt.

Through the open door I could see down the long drive to the main gate. It was dim down yonder, under the flickering lantern, but some kind of commotion was going on. There was a clatter of metal, a voice raised in command, a steady tread advancing—and into my horrified view, their steel and leather glittering in the beams cast by the front door lamps, came a file of Hova guardsmen.

I may not be good for much, but if I have a minor talent it's for finding the back door when coppers, creditors, and outraged husbands are coming in the front. I had the advantage of having my pants up and my boots on this time, and even hampered by the need to drag Elspeth along, I was going like a rat to a drainpipe before the butler even had his mouth open. Elspeth gave one shriek of astonishment as I bundled her along a passage beneath the stairs.

"Harry! Where are you going—we have left my band-box—!"

"D--n your band-box!" I snapped. "Keep quiet and run!"

I whirled round a corner; there was a corridor obviously leading to the back, and I pounded along it, my protesting helpmeet clutching her bonnet and squeaking in alarm. A startled black face popped out of a side-door; I hit it in panic and Elspeth screamed. The corridor turned at right angles; I swore and plunged into an empty room—a glimpse of a long table and dining chairs in the silent dark, and beyond, French windows. I hurtled towards them, hauling her along, and wrenched them open. We were in the garden, dim in the moon-shadows; I cocked an ear and heard—nothing.

"Harry!" She was squealing in my ear. "What are you about? Leave go my arm—I won't be hustled, do you hear?"

"You'll either be hustled or dead!" I hissed. "Silence! We are in deadly danger—do you understand? They are coming to arrest us—to kill us! For your life's sake, do as I tell you—and shut up!"

There was a path, running between high hedges; we sped along it, she demanding in breathless whispers to know what was happening: at the end I got my bearings; we were to the side of the building, in shrubbery, with the front drive round to our left, and from the hidden front door I could hear a harsh voice raised—in Malagassy, unfortunately, but I caught enough words to chill my blood. "Sergeant-general . . .

arrest . . . search." I groaned softly, and Elspeth began babbling again.

"Oh, my dress is torn! Harry, it is too bad! What are you— why are we—ow!" I had clapped a hand over her mouth.

"Be quiet, you silly mort!" I whispered. "We're escaping! There are soldiers hunting us! The Queen is trying to kill me!"

She made muffled noises, and then got her mouth free. "How dare you call me that horrid word! What does it mean? Let me go this instant! You are hurting my wrist, Harry! What is this absurd nonsense about the Quee—" The shrill torrent was cut off as I imprisoned her mouth again.

"For G-d's sake, woman—they'll hear us!" I pulled her in close to the wall. "Keep your voice down, will you?" I took my hand away, unwisely.

"But *why*?" At least she had the wit to whisper. "Why are we—oh, I think you are gammoning me! Well, it is a very poor joke, Harry Flashman, and I—"

"Please, Elspeth!" I implored, shaking my fist in her face. "It's true, I swear! If they hear us—we're dead!"

My grimacing frenzy may have half-convinced her; at least her pretty mouth opened and closed again with a faint "Oh!" And then, as I crouched, straining my ears for any sound of the searchers, came the tiniest whisper: "But Harry, my band-box . . ."

I glared her into silence, and then ventured a peep round the angle of the wall. There was a Hova trooper on the porch, leaning on his spear; I could hear faint sounds of talk from the hall—that d----d butler giving the game away, no doubt. Suddenly from behind us, in the dark towards the back of the house, came the crash of a shutter and a harsh voice shouting. Elspeth squeaked, I jumped, and the Hova on the porch must have heard the shout too, for he called to the hall—and here, to my horror, came an under-officer, bounding down the porch steps sword in hand, and running along the front of the house towards our corner.

There was only one thing for it. I seized Elspeth and thrust her down on her face in the deep shadow at the foot of the wall, sprawling on top of her and hissing frantically to her to keep quiet and lie still. We were only in the nick of time—he rounded the angle of the house and came to a dead stop almost on top of us, his boots spurning the gravel within a yard of Elspeth's head. For a terrible instant I thought he'd seen us—the great black figure towered above us, silhouetted against the night sky, the sword glittering in his hand, but he didn't move, and I realised he was staring towards the back of the house, listening. I could feel Elspeth palpitating beneath me, her turned face a faint white blur just beneath my own—oh, Ch---t, I prayed, don't let him look down! Suddenly he bawled something in Malagassy, and took a half-step forward—my blood froze as his boot descended within inches of Elspeth's face—but right on top of her hand!

She started violently beneath me—and then he must have shifted his weight, for as in a nightmare I heard a tiny crack, and her whole body shuddered. Paralysed, I waited for her scream—he *must* glance down now!—but a voice was shouting from the back of the house, his was bellowing right above us in reply, he plunged forward, his leg brushing my curls, and then he was gone, striding away down the path behind us into the dark, and Elspeth's breath came out in a little, shivering moan. I was afoot in an instant, hauling her upright, half-carrying her into the denser shrubbery on the lawn, knowing we hadn't an instant to lose, bundling her along and hoping to heaven she wouldn't faint. If we could get quickly through the shrubbery unobserved, moving parallel with the drive, and so come to the gate—would they have left a sentry there?

Fortunately the shrubbery screened our blundering progress entirely; we plunged through the undergrowth and fetched up gasping beneath a great clump of ferns not ten yards from the gate. Far back to our left the Hova was still on the house porch beneath the lamp; through the bushes ahead I could make out the faint gleam of the gate-lantern, but no sound, except from far behind us, where there were distant voices at the back of the house—were they coming nearer . . .? I peered cautiously through the fringe of bushes towards the gate—oh, G-d, there was a d----d great Hova, not five yards away, his spear held across his body, looking back towards the house. The light gleamed dully on his massive bare arms and chest, on his gorilla features and gleaming spearhead—my innards quailed at the sight; I couldn't hope to pass *that*, not with Elspeth in tow—and at that moment my loved one decided to give voice again.

"Harry!" She was hissing in my ear. "That man—that man *stood* on my *hand*! I'm sure my finger is broke!" I recall noting that it must have been indignation rather than complaint, for she added a word which frankly I didn't think she knew.

"Ssht!" I had my lips against her ear. "I know! We'll . . . we'll mend it presently. There's a guard on the gate—must get past him!" The voices at the back of the house were growing louder—it was now or never. "Can you walk?"

"Of course I can walk! It is my poor finger—"

"Sssht, for Ch---t's sake! Look, old girl—we must distract his attention, d'you see? The chap on the gate, d---it!" I wouldn't have thought I could yammer and whisper simultaneously—but then I wouldn't have thought I'd be stuck in the bushes in Madagascar plotting escape with a blonde imbecile whose mind, I'll swear, was divided evenly between her wounded finger and her lost band-box. "Yes, he's out there! Now, listen—you must count to five—five, you know—and then stand up and walk out on to the drive! Can you, dearest?—just walk out, there's a good girl! Nod, curse you!"

I saw her lips framing "Why?" but then she nodded—and suddenly kissed me on the cheek. Then I was sliding away to the right, fumbling for my hilt beneath the cloak . . . three . . . four . . . five. There was a rustle as she stood up; she seemed to sway for a moment, and then she had stepped through the bushes and turned to face the gate.

The Hova leaped about four feet, stood with eyes bulging, and let out a yell as he started towards her. Two paces brought him level with me; I clutched the hilt in a frenzy of fear (if it had been any other woman I believe I'd have bolted straight for the gate, but one's wife, you know . . .) and launched myself through the ferns at his flank, drawing as I sprang. There wasn't time to use the point; I continued the draw in a desperate sweep, and as he whirled to meet me the blade took him clean across the face with a sickening jar. I had an instant's glimpse of blood spurting from the gashed mouth and cheek, and then he tripped and fell, screaming.

"Run!" I bawled, and she was past him, her bonnet awry,

her skirts kilted up. I turned with her, plunging for the gate—and out from the shadows of the watchman's hut leaped another of the swine, plumb in our path, whipping up his spear into the on-guard. I stopped dead—but by the grace of God Elspeth didn't, and as he swung to cover her I lunged at his naked chest. He parried, jumping aside, and Elspeth was through the gate, squeaking, but now he was thrusting at me, stumbling in his eagerness. His point went past my shoulder, I cut at him but he turned the blade quick as light, and there we were, face to face across the gateway, his eyes glaring and rolling as he poised, looking for an opening.

"Make for the trees!" I yelled, and saw Elspeth scamper away, holding her bonnet on. There was shouting from the house, footsteps running—and the Hova struck, his spear darting at my face. By sheer instinct I deflected it, straightening my arm in an automatic lunge—God bless you, dear old riding-master of the 11th Hussars!—and he screamed like the d----d as my point took him in the chest, his own rush driving it into his body. His fall wrenched the hilt from my hand, and then I was high-tailing after Elspeth, turning her into the trees, where the horses still stood patiently, cropping at the grass.

I heaved her bodily on to one of them, her skirts riding up any old how, vaulted aboard the other, and with a hand to steady her, forced the beasts out on to the road beyond. There was a tumult of hidden voices by the gate, but I knew we were clear if she didn't fall—she was always a decent horsewoman, and was clinging to the mane with her good hand. We ploughed off knee to knee, in a swaying canter that took us to the end of one road and down the next, and then I eased up. No sounds behind, and if we heard any we could gallop at need. I clasped her to me, swearing with relief, and asked how her hand was.

"Oh, it is *painful*!" cries she. "But Harry, what does it *mean*? Those dreadful people—I thought I should swoon! And my dress torn, and my finger broke, and every bone in my body shaken! Oh!" She shuddered violently. "Those fearful black soldiers! Did you . . . did you kill them?"

"I hope so," says I, looking back fearfully. "Here—take my cloak—muffle your head as well. If they see what you are, we're sunk!"

"But who? Why are we running? What has happened? I insist you tell me directly! Where are we going—"

"There's an English ship on the coast! We're going to reach her, but we've got to get out of this h--lish city first—if the gates are closed I don't—"

"But *why*?" cries she, like a d--n parrot, sucking her finger and trying to order her skirts, which wasn't easy, since she was astride. "Oh, this is so *uncomfortable*! Why are we being pursued—why should they—oh!" Her eyes widened. "What have you *done*, Harry? Why are they chasing you? Have you done some wrong? Oh, Harry, have you offended the Queen?"

"Not half as much as she's offended me!" I snarled. "She's a . . . a . . . monster, and if she lays hands on us we're done for. Come on, confound it!"

"But I cannot believe it! Why, of all the absurd things! When *I* have been so kindly treated—I am sure, whatever it is, if the Prince were to speak to her—"

I didn't quite tear my hair, but it was a near-run thing. I gripped her by the shoulders instead, and speaking as gently as I could with my teeth chattering, impressed on her that we must get out of the city quickly; that we must proceed slowly, by back streets, to the gates, but there we might have to ride for it; I would explain later—

"Very good," says she. "You need not raise your voice. If you say so, Harry—but it is all *extremely* odd."

I'll say that for her, once she understood the urgency of the situation—and even that pea-brain must have apprehended by now that something unusual was taking place—she played up like a good 'un. She didn't take fright, or weep, or even plague me with further questions; I've known cleverer women, and plenty like Lakshmibai and the Silk One who were better at rough riding and desperate work, but none gamer than Elspeth when the stakes were on the blanket. She was a soldier's wife, all right; pity she hadn't married a soldier.

But if she was cool enough, I was in a ferment as we picked our way by back-roads to the city wall, and followed it round towards the great gates. By this time there were hardly any folk about, and although the sight of two riders brought some curious looks, no one molested us. But I was sure the alarm must have

gone out by now—I wasn't to know that Malagassy *bandobast**
being what it was, the last thing they'd have thought to do was
close the gates. They never had, so why bother now? I could
have shouted with relief when we came in view of the gate-
towers, and saw the way open, with only the usual lounging
sentinels and a group of loafers round a bonfire. We just held
steadily forward, letting 'em see it was the sergeant-general;
they stared at the horses, but that was all, and with my heart
thumping we ambled through under the towers, and then trotted
forward among the scattered huts on the Antan' plain.

Ahead of us the sky was lightening in the summer dawn, and
my spirits with it—we were clear, free, and away!—and beyond
those distant purple hills there was a British warship, and
English voices, and Christian vittles, and safety behind British
guns. Four days at most—if the horses I'd sent to Ankay were
waiting ahead of us. In that snail-pace country, where any pursuit was sure to be on foot, no one could hope to overtake us,
no alarm could outstrip us—I was ready to whoop in my saddle
until I thought of that menacing presence still so close, that
awful city crouching just behind us, and I shook Elspeth's bridle
and sent us forward at a hand-gallop.

But our luck was still with us. We sighted the change horses
just before dawn, raising the dust with the groom jogging along
on the leader, and I never saw a jollier sight. They weren't the
pick of the light cavalry, but they had fodder and *jaka* in their
saddle-bags, and I knew they'd see us there, if we spelled 'em
properly. Thirty miles is as far as any beast can carry me, but
that would be as much as Elspeth could manage at a stretch in
any event.

I dismissed the bewildered groom, and on we went at a good
round trot. A small horse-herd ain't difficult to manage, if you've
learned your trade in Afghanistan. My chief anxiety now was
Elspeth. She'd ridden steady—and commendably silent—until
now, but as we forged ahead into the empty downland, I could
see the reaction at work; she was swaying in the saddle, eyes half-
closed, fair hair tumbling over her face, and although I was in a
sweat to push on I felt bound to swing off into a little wood to

* Organisation.

290

rest and eat. I lifted her out of the saddle beside a stream, and blow me if she didn't go straight off to sleep in my arms. For three hours she never stirred, while I kept a weather eye on the plain, but saw no sign of pursuit.

She was all demands and chatter again, though, when she awoke, and while we chewed our *jaka*, and I bathed her finger —which wasn't broke, but badly bruised—I tried to explain what had happened. D'you know, of all the astonishing things that had occurred since we'd left England, I still feel that that conversation was the most incredible of all. I mean, explaining anything to Elspeth is always middling tough—but there was something unreal, as I look back, about sitting opposite her, in a Madagascar wood, while she stared round-eyed in her torn, soiled evening dress with her finger in a splint, listening to me describing why we were fleeing for our lives from an unspeakable black despot whom I'd been plotting to depose. Not that I blame her for being sceptical, mind you; it was the form her scepticism took which had me clutching my head. .

At first she just didn't believe a word of it; it was *quite* contrary, she said, to what *she* had seen of Madagascar, and to prove the point she produced, from the recesses of her underclothing, a small and battered notebook from which she proceeded to read me her "impressions" of the country—so help me, it was all about b----y butterflies and wild flowers and Malagassy curtain materials and what she'd had for dinner. It was at this point that it dawned on me that the conclusion I'd formed on my visits to her at Rakota's palace had been absolutely sound —she'd spent six months in the place without having any notion of what it was really like. Well, I knew she was mutton-headed, but this beat all, and so I told her.

"I cannot see *that*," says she. "The Prince and Princess were all politeness and consideration, and *you* assured me that all was well, so why should I think otherwise?"

I was still explaining, and being harangued, when we took the road again, and for the best part of the day, which took us to the eastern edge of the downs, near Angavo, where we camped in another wood. By that time I had finally got it into her head what a h--l of a place Madagascar was, and what a hideous fate we were escaping; you'd have thought that would have reduced her to terrified silence, but then, you don't know my Elspeth.

She was shocked—not a bit scared, apparently, just plain indignant. It was deplorable, and ought not to be allowed, was how she saw it; why had *we* (by which I took it she meant Her Britannic Majesty) taken no steps to prevent such misgovernment, and what was the Church thinking about? It was *quite* disgusting—I just sat munching *jaka*, but I couldn't help, listening to her, being reminded of that old harridan Lady Sale, tapping her mittened fingers while the jezzail bullets whistled round her on the Kabul retreat, and demanding acidly why something was not *done* about it. Aye, it's comical in its way— and yet, when you've seen the *mem-sahibs* pursing their lips and raising indignant brows in the face of dangers and horrors that set their men-folk shaking, you begin to understand why there's all the pink on the map. It's vicarage morality, nursery discipline, and a thorough sense of propriety and sanitation that have done it—and when they've gone, and the *mem-sahibs* with them, why, the map won't be pink any longer.

The one thing Elspeth couldn't accept, though, was that the outrageous condition of Madagascar was Ranavalona's fault. Queens, in her conception of affairs, did not behave in that way at all; the mother of Prince Rakota ("a most genteel and *obliging* young man") would never have countenanced such things. No, it could only be that she was badly advised, and kept in ignorance, no doubt, by her ministers. She had been civil enough to me, surely?—this was asked in an artless way which I knew of old. I said, well, she was pretty plain and ill-natured from the little I'd seen of her, but of course I'd hardly exchanged a word with her (which, you'll note, was true; I said nothing of bathing and piano-playing). Elspeth sighed contentedly at this, and then after a moment said softly:

"Have you missed me, Harry?"

Looking at her, sitting in the dusk with the green leaves behind her, in her dusty gown, with the tangled gold hair framing that lovely face, so serene in its stupidity, I suddenly realised there was only one sensible way to answer her. What with the shock and haste and fear of our flight it absolutely hadn't occurred to me until that moment. And afterwards, lying in the grass, while she stroked my cheek, it seemed the most natural thing—as if this wasn't Madagascar at all, with dreadful danger behind and unknown hardship before—in that blissful moment I dreamed of the very first time, under the trees by the Clyde, on just such a golden evening, and when I spoke of it she began to cry at last, and clung to me.

"You will bring us there again—home," says she. "You are so brave and strong and good, and keep me safe. Do you know," she wiped her eyes, looking solemn, "I never saw you fight before? Oh, I knew, to be sure, from the newspapers, and what everyone said—that you were a hero, I mean—but I did not know how it was. Women cannot, you know. Now I have seen you, sword in hand—you are rather terrible, you know, Harry—and so quick!" She gave a little shiver. "Not many women are lucky enough to see how brave their husbands are—and I have the bravest, best man in the whole world." She kissed me on the forehead, her cheek against mine.

I thought of her finger, under that crushing boot, of the way she'd stood up in the bushes and walked straight out, of the bruising ride from Antan', of all she'd endured since Singapore —and I didn't feel ashamed, exactly, because you know it ain't my line. But I felt my eyes sting, and I lifted her chin with my hand.

"Old girl," says I, "you're a trump."

"Oh, no!" says she, wide-eyed. "I am very silly, and weak, and . . . and not a trump at all! Feckless, Papa says. But I love to be your 'old girl' "—she snuggled her head down on my chest—"and to think that you like me a little, too . . . better than you like the horrid Queen of Madagascar, or Mrs Leo Lade, or those Chinese ladies we saw in Singapore, or Kitty Stevens, or—my dearest, whatever is the matter?"

"Who the h--l," roars I, "is Kitty Stevens?"

"Oh, do you not remember? That slim, dark girl with the poor complexion and soulful eyes she thinks so becoming— although how she supposes that mere staring will make her attractive I cannot think—you danced with her twice at the Cavalry Ball, and assisted her to negus at the buffet . . ."

We were off again before dawn, crossing the Angavo Pass which leads to the upland Ankay Plain, going warily because I knew the Hova Guard regiment which I'd sent out couldn't be far away. I kept casting north, and we must have outflanked them, for we saw not a soul until the Mangaro ford, where the villagers turned out in force to stare at us as we crossed the river with our little herd. It was level going then until the jungle closed in and the mountains began, but we were making slower time than I'd hoped for; it began to look like a five-day trek instead of four, but I wasn't much concerned. All that mattered was that we should keep ahead of pursuit; the frigate would still be there. I was sure of this because it was bound to wait for an answer to the protest which, according to Laborde, had only reached the Queen a couple of days ago. Her answer, even if she'd sent it at once, would take more than a week to reach Tamitave, so if we kept up our pace we'd be there with time in hand.

I kept telling myself this on the third day, when our rate slowed to a walk with the long, twisting climb up the red rutted track that led into the great mountains. Here we were walled in by forest on either hand, with only that tortuous path for a guide. I knew it because I'd been flogged over it in the slave-coffle, and I had to gulp down my fears as we approached each bend—suppose we met someone, in this place where we couldn't take to our heels, where to stray ten yards from the path would be certain death by wandering starvation? Suppose the path petered out, or had been overgrown? Suppose swift Hova runners overtook us?

I was in a fever of anxiety—not made any easier by the childish pleasure Elspeth seemed to be taking in our journey. She was forever clapping her hands and exclaiming at the saucer-eyed white monkeys who peered at us, or the lace-plumed birds that fluttered among the creepers; even the hideous water-snakes which cruised the streams, with their heads poking out, excited her—she barred the spiders, though, great marbled monsters as big as my hand, scuttling on webs the size of blankets. And once she fled in terror from a sight which had our horses neighing and bucking in the narrow way—a troop of great apes, bounding across the path in leaps of incredible length, both feet together.[45] We watched them crash into the undergrowth, and not for the first time I cursed the luck that I hadn't even a clasp-knife with me for defence, for G-d knew what else might be lurking in that dark, cavernous forest. Elspeth wished she had her sketch-book.

There's forty miles of that forest, but thanks to good Queen Ranavalona we didn't have to cross it all, as you would today. The jungle track runs clear across towards Andevoranto, whence you travel up the coast to Tamitave, but in 1845 there was a short-cut—the Queen's buffalo road, cut straight through the hilly jungle to the coastal plain. This was the track, hacked out by thousands of slaves, which I'd seen on the way up; we reached it on the fourth day, a great avenue through the green, with the mountain mist hanging over it in wraiths. It was eerie and foreboding, but at least it was flat, and with half our beasts already abandoned in exhaustion, I was glad of the easier going.

It's strange, as I look back on that remarkable journey, that it wasn't nearly as punishing as it might have been. Elspeth still swears that she quite enjoyed it; I dare say if I hadn't been so apprehensive—about our beasts foundering, or losing our way if the mist settled down, or being overtaken by pursuers (although I knew there was scant chance of that), or how we were going to make our final dash to the frigate—I might have marvelled that we came through it so easily. But we did; our luck held through hill and jungle, we hardly saw a native the whole way, and on the fourth afternoon we were trotting down through the strange little conical hillocks that line the sandy coastal plain, with nothing ahead of us but a few scattered villages and easy level going until we should come to Tamitave.

Of course, I should have been on my guard. I should have known it had gone too smooth. I should have remembered the horror that lay no great way behind, and the mad hatred and bloodlust of that evil woman. I should have thought of the soldier's first rule, to put yourself in the enemy's shoes and ask what you would do. If I'd been that terrible b---h, and my ingrate lover had tried to ruin me, cut up my guardsmen, and lit out for the coast—what would I have done, given unlimited power and a maniac's vengeance to slake? Send out my fleetest couriers, over plain and jungle and mountain, to carry the alarm, rouse the garrisons, cut off escape—that's what I'd have done.

How far can good runners travel in a day—forty miles over rough going? Say four days, perhaps five, from Antan' to the coast. We were approaching Tamitave on the evening of the fourth day.

Aye, I should have been on my guard—but when you're within the last lap of safety, when all has gone far better than you'd dared hope, when you've seen the Tamitave track and know that the coast is only a few scant miles away over the low hills, when you have the gamest, loveliest girl in the world riding knee to knee with you, that eager idiot smile on her face and her tits bouncing famously, when the dark terrors have receded behind you—above all, when you've hardly slept in four nights and are fit to topple from the saddle with sheer weariness . . . then hope can fuddle your wits a little, and you let the last of your rations slip from your hand, and the dusk begins to swim round you, and your head is on the turf and you slip down the long slide into unconsciousness—until someone miles away is shaking you, and yelping urgently in your ear, and you come awake in bleary alarm, staring wildly about you in the dawn.

"Harry! Oh, Harry—quickly! Look, look!"

She had me by the wrist, tugging me to my feet. Where was I?—yes, this was the little hollow we'd camped in, there were the horses, the first ray of dawn was just peeping over the low downs to the east, but Elspeth was pulling me t'other way, to the lip of the hollow, pointing.

"Look, Harry—yonder! Who are those people?"

I stared back, rubbing the sleep out of my eyes—the distant mountains were in a wall of mist, and on the rolling land between there were long trails of fog hanging on the slopes. Nothing else—no! there was movement on the crest a mile behind us, figures of men coming into plain view, a dozen—twenty perhaps, in an irregular line abreast. I felt an awful clutch at my heart as I stared, disbelieving what I saw, for they were advancing at a slow trot, in an ominously disciplined fashion; I recognised that gait, even as I took in the first twinkle of steel along the line and made out the white streaks of the bandoliers—I'd taught 'em how to advance in skirmishing order myself, hadn't I? But it was impossible . . .

"It can't be!" I heard my voice cracking. "They're Hova guardsmen!"

If any confirmation were needed it came in the faint, wailing yell drifting on the dawn air, as they came jogging down the slope to the plain.

"I thought I had better rouse you, Harry," Elspeth was saying, but by then I was leaping for the horses, yelling to her to get aboard. She was still babbling questions as I bundled her up bareback, and flung myself on to a second mount. I slashed at the three other beasts remaining to us, and as they fled neighing from the hollow I spared another wild glance back; three-quarters of a mile away the skirmishing line was coming steadily towards us, cutting the distance at frightening speed. G-d, how had they done it on foot in the time? Where had they come from, for that matter?

Interesting questions, to which I still don't know the answer, and they didn't occupy me above a split second just then. In the nick of time I stifled my coward's instinct to gallop wildly away from them, and surveyed the ground ahead of us. Two, perhaps three miles due east, across rolling sandy plain, was the crest from which, I was pretty sure, we'd look down on the shore; there was the Tamitave track a mile or so to our right, with a few villagers already on it. I struggled to clear my wits—if we rode straight ahead we ought to come out just above the Tamitave fort, north of the town proper—the frigate would be lying in the roads—Ch---t, how were we going to reach her, for there'd be no time to stop and scheme, with these d---ls on our heels. I looked again; they were well out on the plain by now, and coming on fast . . . I gripped Elspeth's wrist.

"Follow me close! Ride steady, watch your footing, and for G-d's sake don't slip! They can't catch us if we keep up a round canter, but if we tumble we're done!"

She was pale as a sheet, but she nodded and for once didn't ask me who these strange gentlemen were, or what they wanted, or if her hair was disarranged. I wheeled and set off down the slope, with her close behind, and the yell as they saw us turn was clear enough now; a savage hunting cry that had me digging in my heels despite myself. We drummed down the hill, and I forced myself not to look back until we'd crossed the little valley and come to the next crest—we'd gained on them, but they were still coming, and I gulped and gestured furiously to Elspeth to keep up.

I'd have to count up all the battles I've been in to tell you how often I've fled in panic, and I've made a few other strategic withdrawals, too, but this was as horrid as any. There was the time Scud East and I went tearing along the Arrow of Arabat in a sled with the Cossacks behind us, and the jolly little jaunt I had with Colonel Sebastian Moran in the ammunition cart after Isandhlwana, with the Udloko Zulus on our tail—and couldn't *they* cover the ground, just? But in the present case the snag was that very shortly we were going to reach the sea, and unless our embarkation went smoothly—G-d, the frigate *must* be there! . . . I stole another look over my shoulder—we were a clear mile ahead now, surely, but there they were still, just appearing on a crest and streaming over it in fine style.

I took a look at our horses; they weren't labouring, but they weren't fit to enter the St Leger either. Would they last? Suppose one went lame—why the blazes hadn't I thought to drive the spare beasts ahead? But it was too late now.

"Come on," says I, and Elspeth gave me a trembling look and kicked in her heels, clinging to the mane. The last slope was half a mile ahead; as we dropped our pace for the ascent I looked back again, but there was nothing in sight for a good mile.

"We'll do it yet!" I shouted, and we covered the last few yards to the top through slippery sand, the sun blazed in our eyes as we reached the crest, the breeze was suddenly stiff in our faces—and there below us, down a long sandy slope, was the spreading panorama of beach and blue water, with the surf foaming not a mile away. Far off to the right was Tamitave town, the smoke rising in thin trails above the thatched roofs; closer, but still to the right, was the fort, a massive circular stone tower, with its flag, a-flutter, and its outer wooden palisade; there were white-coated troops, about a platoon strong, marching towards it from the town, and looking down from our point of vantage I could see great activity in the central square of the fort itself, and round the gun emplacements on its walls.

The sun was shining straight towards us out of a blue, cloudless sky, the rays coming over a thick bank of mist which mantled the surface of the sea a mile off-shore. A beautiful sight, the coral strand with its palms, the gulls wheeling, the gentle roll of bright blue sea—there was only one thing missing. From golden beach to pearly bank of mist, from pale clear distance in the north to the vague smokiness of the town waterfront to the south, the sea was as bare as a miser's table. There was no British frigate in Tamitave roads. There wasn't even a bl----d bumboat. And behind us, as I turned my frantic gaze in their direction, the Hovas were just coming in sight on the hillside a scant mile away.

I can't recall whether I screamed aloud or not; I may well have done, but if I did it was a poor expression of the sick despair that engulfed me in that moment. I know the thought that was in my mind, as I pounded my knee with my fist in an anguish of rage, fear, and disappointment, was: "But it must be there! It has to wait for her message!" and then. Elspeth was turning solemn blue eyes on me and asking:

"But Harry, where is the ship? You said it would be here—" And then, putting two and two together, I suppose, she added: "Whatever shall we do now?"

It was a question which had occurred to me, as I stared palsied from the empty sea in front to our pursuers behind—they had halted on the far crest, which was an irony, if you like. They could crawl on their bellies towards us now, for all it mattered—we were trapped, helpless, with nothing to do but wait until they came up with us at their leisure, to seize and drag us back to the abominable fate that would be waiting for us in Antan'. I could picture those snake-like eyes, the steaming pits at Ambohipotsy, the bodies turning in the air from the top of the cliff, the blood-curdling shriek of the mob—I realised I was babbling out a flood of oaths, as I stared vainly round for an escape which I knew wasn't there.

Elspeth was clutching my hand, white-faced—and then, because it was the only way to go, I was urging her down the slope to our left, towards a long grove of palms which began about two furlongs from the fort and ran away into the distance along the coastline northwards. That's one thing about a sound cowardly instinct—it turns you directly to cover, however poor and useless it may be. They'd find us there in no time, but if we could reach the trees undetected from the fort, we might at least be able to flee north—to what? There was nothing for us yonder except blind flight until we dropped from exhaustion, or our horses foundered, or those black hounds came up with us, and I knew it, but it was better than stopping where we were to be run down like sheep.

"Oh, Harry!" Elspeth was wailing in my rear as we thundered down the slope, but I didn't check; another minute would have us in the shelter of the grove, if no one in the fort saw us first. Crouched over my beast's neck, I stole a look down towards the stone battlements at the foot of the hill—Elspeth's voice behind me rose in a sudden scream, I whirled in my seat, and to my amazement saw that she was hauling in her mount by the mane. I yelled to her to ride, cursing her for an idiot, but she was pointing seaward, crying out, and I wrestled my brute to a slithering halt, staring where she pointed—and, d'you know, I couldn't blame her.

Out in the roads something was moving in that rolling bank of mist. At first it was just a shadow, towering in the downy radiance of the fog; then a long black spar was jutting out, and behind it masts and rigging were taking shape. In disbelief I heard the faint, unmistakable squeal of sheaves as she came into view, a tall, slim ship under topsails, drifting slowly out of the mist, turning before my eyes, showing her broad, white-striped side—her ports were up, there were guns out, men moving on the decks, and from her mizzen trailed a flag—blue, white, red —dear G-d, she was a Frog warship—and there, to her right, another shadow was breaking clear, another ship, turning as the first had done, another Frenchie, guns, colours and all!

Elspeth was beside me, I was hugging her almost out of her seat as we watched them spellbound, our flight, the fort, pursuit all forgotten—she yelped in my ear as a third shadow loomed up in the wake of the ships, and this time it was the real thing, no error, and I found myself choking tears of joy, for that was the dear old Union Jack at the truck of the frigate which came gliding out on to the blue water.

I was shouting, G-d knows what, and Elspeth was clapping her hands, and then a gun boomed suddenly from the fort, only a few hundred yards away, and a white plume of smoke billowed up from the battlements. The three ships were standing in towards the fort; the leading Frog tacked with a cracking of canvas, and suddenly its whole side exploded in a thunder of flame and smoke, there was a series of tremendous crashes from the fort as the broadsides struck home—and here came her two consorts, each in turn letting fly while sea and sky echoed to the roar of their cannonade, a mighty pall of grey smoke eddying around them as they put about and came running in again.[44]

It was a badly-aimed shot screaming overhead that reminded me we were in the direct line of fire. I yelled to Elspeth, and we careered down to the trees, crashing into the thickets and sliding from our mounts to stare at the extraordinary scene being played out in the bay.

"Harry—why are they shooting? Do you suppose they are come to rescue us?" She was clutching my hand, all agog. "Will they know we are here? Should we not wave, or light a fire, or some such thing? Will you not call to them, my love?"

This, with forty guns blazing away not a quarter of a mile off, for the fort was firing back as well; the leading Frog was almost at point-blank range. Clouds of dust and smoke surged up from the fort wall; the Frog seemed to stagger in the water, and Elspeth shrieked as his foretop sagged and then fell slowly into the smoke, with a wreckage of sail and cordage. In came the second ship, letting off her broadside any old how in lubberly, garlic-eating fashion, and the fort thumped her handsomely in reply, serve her right. My G-d, thinks I, are the Crapauds going to be beat? For the second Frog lost her mizzen top and sheered away blind with the spars littering her poop—and then in came the British frigate, and while I ain't got much use for our navy people, as a rule, I'll allow that she showed up well in front of the foreigners, for she ran in steady and silent, biding her time, while the fort hammered at her and the splinters flew from her bulwarks.

Through the clear air we could see every detail—the leadsman in the chains swinging away, the white-shirted tars on her decks, the blue-coated officers on the quarter-deck, even a little midshipman in the rigging with his telescope trained on the fort.

Silently she bore in until I was sure she must run aground, and then a voice called from the poop, there was a rush of men and a flapping of canvas, she wore round, and every gun crashed out as one in a deafening inferno of sound. The wave of the broadside hit us in a blast of air, the fort battlements seemed to vanish in smoke and dust and flying fragments—but when all cleared, there the fort still stood, and her guns banging irregularly in reply.

The frigate was tacking away neatly, but neither she nor the injured Frogs looked like coming in again—the appalling thought struck me that they might be sheering off, and I couldn't restrain myself at such cowardly behaviour.

"Come back, you sons of b-----s!" I roared, fairly dancing up and down. "D--nation, they're only a parcel of niggers! Lay into them, rot you! It's what you're paid for!" "But, see, Harry!" squeaks Elspeth, pointing. "Look, my love, they are coming! See—the boats!"

Sure enough, there were longboats creeping out from behind the Frogs, and another from the British ship. As the three vessels stood to again, firing at the fort, the smaller boats came heading in for the shore, packed with men—they were going to storm the fort, under the covering guns of the squadron. I found I was dancing and blaspheming with excitement—for this must be our chance! We must run to them when they got ashore—I ploughed back through the fronds, staring at the hill behind, to see how our Hova friends were doing—and there they were, dropping down from the crest behind us, making for the landward side of the fort. They were running any old how, but an under-officer was shouting in the rear, and it seemed to me he was pointing towards our grove. Yes, some of the Hovas were checking—he was sending them in our direction—d--n the black villain, didn't he know where his duty lay, with foreign vessels attacking his b----y island?

"What shall we do, Harry?" Elspeth was at my elbow. "Should we not hasten to the beach? It may be dangerous to linger."

She ain't quite the fool she looks, you know—but fortunately neither am I. The boats were into the surf, only a moment from the shore; the temptation to run towards them was almost more than a respectable poltroon could bear—but if we broke cover too soon, with three hundred yards of naked sand between us and the spot where the nearest Frog boat would touch, we'd be within easy musket-shot from the fort to our right. We must lie up in the grove until the landing-party had got up the beach and rushed the fort—that would keep the black musketeers busy, and it would be safe to race for the boats, waving a white flag—I was tearing away at Elspeth's petticoat, hushing her squeals of protest, peering back through the undergrowth at the approaching Hovas. There were three of 'em, trotting towards the grove, with their officer far behind waving them on; the leading one was almost into the trees, looking stupid, turning to seek instructions from his fellows; then the flat, brutal face turned in our direction, and he began to pick his way into the grove, his spear balanced, his face turning this way and that.

I hissed to Elspeth and drew her towards the seaward side of the grove, under a thicket, listening for everything at once—the steady boom and crash of gunfire, the faint shouts from the fort walls, the slow crunch of the Hova's feet on the floor of the grove. He seemed to be moving away north behind us—and then Elspeth put her lips to my ear and whispered:

"Oh, Harry, do not move, I pray! There is another of those natives quite close!"

I turned my head, and almost gave birth. On the other side of our thicket, visible through the fronds, was a black shape, not ten yards away—and at that moment the first Hova gave a startled yell, there was a frantic neighing—J---s, I'd forgotten our horses, and the brute must have walked into them! The black shape through the thicket began to run—away from us, mercifully, a crackle of musketry sounded from the beach, and I remembered my dear little woman's timely suggestion, and decided we should linger no longer.

"Run!" I hissed, and we broke out of the trees, and went haring for the shore. There was a shout from behind, a whisp! in the air overhead, and a spear went skidding along the soft sand before us. Elspeth shrieked, we raced on; the boats were being beached, and already armed men were charging towards the fort—Frog sailors in striped jerseys, with a little chap ahead waving a sabre and making pronouncements about *la gloire*, no doubt, as the grape from the walls kicked up the sand among him and his party.

"Help!" I roared, stumbling and waving Elspeth's shift. "We're friends! Halloo, mes amis! Nous sommes Anglais, pour l'amour de Dieu! Don't shoot! Vive la France!"

They didn't pay us the slightest heed, being engaged by that time in hacking a way through the fort's outer wooden palisade. We stumbled out of the soft sand to firmer going, making for the boats, all of which were beached just above the surf. I looked back, but the Hovas were nowhere to be seen, clever lads; I pushed Elspeth, and we veered away to be out of shot from the fort; the beach ahead was alive with running figures by now, French and British, storming ahead and cheering. There was the dooce of a dog-fight going on at the outer palisade, white and striped jerseys on one side, black skins on t'other, cutlasses and spears flashing, musketry crackling from the inner fort and being answered from our people farther down the beach. Then there were sounds of British cheering and cries of excited Frogs, and through the smoke I could see they were up to the inner wall, clambering up on each other's shoulders, popping away with pistols, obviously racing to see which should be up first, French or British.

Good luck to you, my lads, thinks I, for I'm tired. At the same moment, Elspeth cries:

"Oh, Harry, Harry, darling Harry!" and clung to me. "Do you think," she whispered faintly, "that we might sit down now?" With that she went into a dead swoon, and we sank to the wet sand in each other's arms, between the boats and the landing party. I was too tuckered and dizzy to do anything except sit there, holding her, while the battle raged at the top of the beach, and I thought, by Jove, we're clear at last, and soon I'll be able to sleep . . .

"You, sir!" cries a voice. "Yes, you—what are you about, sir? Great Scott!—is that a woman you have there?"

A party of British sailors, carrying empty stretchers, were racing across our front to the fort, and with them this red-faced chap with a gold strip on his coat, who'd checked to pop his eyes at us. He was waving a sword and pistol. I yelled to him above

the din of firing that we were escaped prisoners of the Malagassies, but he only went redder than ever.

"What's that you say? You're not with the landing party?
Then get off the beach, sir—get off this minute! You've no business here! This is a naval operation! What's that, bos'un?—I'm
coming, bl--t you! On, you men!"

He scampered off, brandishing his weapons, but I didn't care.
I knew I was too done to carry Elspeth down to the boats a
hundred yards off, but we were out of effective musket shot of
the fort, so I was content to sit and wait until someone should
have time to attend to us. They were all busy enough at the
moment, in all conscience; the ground before the palisade was
littered with dead and crawling wounded, and through the
breaches they'd broken I could see them spiking the guns while
the scaling parties were still trying to get up the thirty-foot wall
behind. They had ladders, crowded with tars and matelots, their
steel flashing in the smoke at the top of the wall, where the
defenders were slashing and firing away.

Above the crashing musketry there was a sudden cheer; the
big black-and-white Malagassy flag on the fort wall was toppling
down on its broken staff, but a Malagassy on the battlements
caught it as it fell; the fighting boiled around him, but at that
moment a returning stretcher party charged across my line of
vision, bearing stricken men back to the boats, so I didn't see
what happened to him.

Still no one paid any mind to Elspeth and me; we were
slightly out of the main traffic up and down the beach, and
although one party of Frog sailors stopped to stare curiously at
us, they were soon chivvied away by a bawling officer. I tried
to raise her, but she was still slumped unconscious against my
breast, and I was labouring away when I saw that the landing
party were beginning to fall back from the fort. The walking
wounded came hobbling first, supported by their mates, and
then the main parties all jumbled up together, British and French,
with the petty officers swearing and bawling orders as the men
tried to find their right divisions. They were squabbling and
jostling in great disorder, the British tars cursing the Frogs, and
the Frogs grimacing and gesticulating back.

I called out for assistance, but it was like talking in a madhouse—and then over all the trampling and babble the distant guns from the ships began to boom again, and shot whistled overhead to crash into the fort, for our rearguard was clear now, skirmishing away in goodish order, exchanging musket fire with the battlements which they'd failed to overcome. All they seemed to have captured was the Malagassy flag; in among the retiring skirmishers, with the enemy shot peppering them, a disorderly mob of French and English seamen were absolutely at blows with each other for possession of the confounded thing, with cries of "Ah, voleurs!" and "Belay, you sod!", the Frogs kicking and the Britons lashing out with their fists, while two of their officers tried to part them.

Finally the English officer, a great lanky fellow with his trouser leg half torn off and a bloody bandage round his knee, succeeded in wrenching the banner away, but the Frog officer, who was about four feet tall, grabbed an end of it, and they came stumbling down in my direction, yelling at each other in their respective lingoes, with their crews joining in.

"You shall not have it!" cries the Frog. "Render it to me. monsieur, this instant!"

"Sheer off, you greasy half-pint!" roars John Bull. "You take your paw away directly, or you'll get what for!"

"Sacred English thief! It fell to my men, I tell you! It is a prize of France!"

"*Will* you leave off, you frog-eating ape? D---e, if you and your cowardly jackanapes had fought as hard as you squeal we'd have had that fort by now! Let go, d'ye hear?"

"Ah, you resist me, do you?" cries the Frog, who came about up to the Englishman's elbow. "It is sufficient, this! Release it, this flag, or I shall pistol you!"

"Give over, rot you!" They were almost on top of us by now, the sturdy Saxon holding the flag above his head and the tiny Frog clinging to it and hacking at his shins. "I'll cast anchor in you, you prancing swab, if— Good G-d, that's a woman!" His jaw dropped as he caught sight of me at his feet, with Elspeth in my arms. He stared, speechless, oblivious of the Frenchman, who was now drumming at his chest with tiny fists, eyes tight shut.

"If you've a moment," says I, "I'd be obliged if you'd assist my wife to your boats. We're British, and we've escaped from captivity in the interior."

I had to repeat it before he took it in, with a variety of oaths, while the Frog, who had stopped drumming, glared suspiciously. "What does he say, then?" cries he. "Does he conspire, the rascal? Ah, but I shall have the flag—death of the devil, what is this? A woman, beneath our feet, then?"

I explained to him, in French, and he goggled and removed his hat.

"A lady? An English lady? Incredible! But a lady so beautiful, by example, and in a condition of swoon! Ah, but the poor little! Médecin-major Narcejac! Médecin-major Narcejac! Come quickly—and do you, sir, be calm!" He was fairly dancing in agitation. "Attend, you others, and guard madame!"

They were all crowding round, gaping, and while a Frog sawbones knelt beside Elspeth, whose eyelids were fluttering, a couple of tars helped me up, and the English officer demanding to know who I was, I told him, and he said, not Flashman of Afghanistan, surely, and I said, the very same, and he said, well, he was d----d, and he was Kennedy, second of the frigate *Conway*, and proud to meet me. During this the little Frog officer was hopping excitedly, informing me that he was Lieutenant Boudancourt, of the *Zelée*, that madame would receive every comfort, and sal volatile, that the entire French marine was at her service, name of a name, and he, Boudancourt who spoke, would personally supervise her tranquil removal without delay—

"Avast there, Crapaud!" roars Kennedy. "What's he saying? Jenkins, Russell! The lady's British, an' she'll come in a British boat, by G-d! Can you walk, marm?"

Elspeth, supported by the Frog doctor, was still so faint, either from fatigue or all this male attention, that she could only gesture limply, and Boudancourt squawked his indignation at Kennedy.

"Do not raise the voice above the half, if you please! Ah, but see, you have returned madame to a decline!"

"Shut your trap!" cries Kennedy, and then, to a seaman who was tugging at his sleeve, "What the h--l is it now?"

"Beggin' your pardon, sir, Mister Heseltine's compliments, an' the blacks is makin' a sally, looks like, sir."

He was pointing up the beach: sure enough, black figures in white loin-cloths were emerging through the broken palisade, braving the shot from the ships and our rearguard's musketry. Some of them were firing towards us; there was the alarming swish of bullets overhead.

"H--l and d--nation!" cries Kennedy. "Frogs, women, an' niggers! It's too bad! Mister Cliff, I'll be obliged if you'll get those men off the beach! Cover 'em, sharpshooters! Russell, run to the boat—tell Mister Partridge to load the two-pounder with grape and let 'em have it if they come within range! Fall back, there! Get off the beach!"

Boudancourt was yelling similar instructions to his own people; among them, the médecin-major and a matelot were helping Elspeth down to the nearest boat.

"Well, go with her, you fool!" cries Kennedy to me. "You know what these b----y Frogs are like, don't you?" He was limping along on his injured leg, the Malagassy flag trailing from his hand, little Boudancourt snapping at his heels.

"Ah, but a moment, monsieur! You forget, I think, that you still carry that which is the rightful property of Madame la République! Be pleased to yield me that flag!"

"I'll be d--ned if I do!"

"Villain, do you defy me still? You shall not leave this shore alive!"

"Shove off, you little squirt!"

I could hear their squabbling above the din as I reached the gunwale of the French boat, with men floundering about her knee-deep in water. Elspeth was being helped to the stern-sheets through a jabbering, groaning, shouting crowd of Frenchmen— some were standing in the bows, firing up the beach, others were preparing to shove off, there were wounded crying or lying silent against the thwarts, a midshipman was yelling shrill orders to the men at the sweeps. There was a deafening explosion as the British cutter nearby fired her bow-gun; the Malagassies were streaming out of the fort in numbers now, skirmishing down the beach, taking pot-shots—they'd be forming up for a charge in a moment—and Kennedy and Boudancourt, the last men off the beach, were splashing through the shallows, tugging at the flag and yelling abuse at each other.

"Let go, G-d rot your boots!"

"English bully, you shall not escape!"

I think of them sometimes, when I hear idiot politicians blathering about "entente cordiale"—Kennedy shaking his fist, Boudancourt blue in the face, with that dirty, useless piece of calico stretched taut between them. And I'm proud to think that in that critical moment, with confusion all around and disaster imminent, my diplomatic skill asserted itself to save the day—for I believe they'd have been there yet if I hadn't snatched a knife from the belt of a matelot beside me and slashed at the flag, cursing hysterically. It didn't do more than tear it slightly, but that was enough—the thing parted with a rending sound, Kennedy swore, Boudancourt shrieked, and we scrambled aboard as the bow-chasers roared for the last time and the boats ground over the shingle and wallowed in the surf.

"Assassin!" cries Boudancourt, brandishing his half.

"Pimp!" roars Kennedy, from the neighbouring boat.

That was how we came away from Madagascar. More than a score of French and British dead it cost, that mismanaged, lunatic operation,[46] but since it saved my life and Elspeth's by sheer chance, you'll forgive me if I don't complain. All that I could think, as I huddled beside her in the stern, my head swimming with fatigue and my body one great throbbing ache, was—by Jove, we're clear. Mad black queens, Solomon, Brooke, Hovas, head-hunters, Chink hatchetmen, poison darts, boiling pits, skull ships, *tanguin* poison—they're all gone, and we're pulling across blue water, my girl and I, to a ship that'll take us home . . .

"Pardon, monsieur." Boudancourt, beside me, was frowning at the piece of sodden flag in his hands. "Can you say," says he, pointing at the black script on it, "what these words signify?"

I couldn't read 'em, of course, but I'd learned enough of Malagassy heraldry to know what they were.

"That says 'Ranavalona'," I told him. "She's the queen of that b----y island, and you can thank your stars you'll never get closer to her than this. I could tell you—" I was going on, but I felt Elspeth stir against me and thought, no, least said soonest mended. I glanced at her; she was awake, all right, but she wasn't listening. Her eyes appeared to be demurely downcast, which I couldn't fathom until I noticed that her dress was so torn that her bare legs were uncovered, and every libidinous Frog face in that boat was leering in her direction. And didn't she know it, though? By George, thinks I, that's how this whole confounded business started, because this simpering slut allowed herself to be ogled by lewd fellows—

"D'ye mind?" says I to Boudancourt, and taking the torn banner from his hand I disposed it decently across her knees, scowling at the disgruntled Frogs. She looked at me, all innocent wonder, and then smiled and snuggled up to my shoulder.

"Why, Harry," sighs she. "You take such good care of me."

*   *   *

[Final extract from the diary of Mrs Flashman, July —, 1845]

. . . to be sure it is very *tiresome* to be parted again so *soon* from my dear, dear H., especially after the Cruel Separation which we have endured, and just at a time when we supposed we could enjoy the repose and comfort of each other's company in Blissful Peace at last, and in the *safety* of Old England. But H.E. the Governor at Mauritius was *quite* determined that H. must go to India, for it seems that there is growing turmoil there among the Seekh people, and that homeward bound regiments have had to be sent back again, and every Officer of *proved experience* is required in case of war.[46] So of course my darling, being on the Active List, *must* be despatched to Bombay, not without Vigorous Protest on his part, and he even went so far as to threaten to send in his Papers, and *quit* the Service altogether, but this they would not permit at all.

So I am left lamenting, like Lord Ullin's daughter, or was it her father, I don't perfectly remember which, while the Husband of my Bosom returns to his Duty, and indeed I hope he takes care with the Seekhs, who appear to be *most disagreeable*. My only Consolation is the knowledge that my dearest would rather far have accompanied me home *himself*, and it was this Dear Concern and Affection for me that caused him to resist so fiercely when they said he must go to India (and indeed he grew *quite violent* on the subject, and called H.E. the Governor many unpleasant things which I shan't set down, they were so shocking). But I could never have him forsake the Path of Honour, which he loves so well, for my sake, and there really was no reason why he should, for I am extremely *comfortable* and well taken care of aboard the good ship *Zelée*, whose commander, Captain Feiseck, has been so obliging as to offer me passage to Toulon, rather than await an Indiaman. He is most Agreeable and Attentive, with the most *polished* manners and full of consideration to me, as are *all* his officers, especially Lieutenants Homard and St Just and Delincourt and Ambrée and dear little Boudancourt and even the Midshipmen . . .

[End of extract—Humbug, vanity and affectation to the last! And a very proper wifely concern, indeed ! ! !—G. de R.]

(On this note of impatience from its original editor, the manuscript of the sixth packet of the Flashman Papers comes to an end.)

Appendixes

Notes

Appendix A: Cricket in the 1840s

Flashman had a highly personal approach to cricket, as to most things, but there can be no doubt that through his usual cynicism there shines a genuine love of the game. This is not surprising, since it is perhaps the subtlest and most refined outdoor sport ever devised, riddled with craft and gamesmanship, and affording endless scope to a character such as his. Also, he played it well, according to his own account and that of Thomas Hughes, who may be relied on, since he was not prone to exaggerate anything to Flashman's credit. Indeed, if he had not been so fully occupied by military and other pursuits, Flashman might well have won a place in cricket history as a truly great fast bowler—the dismissal of such a trio as Felix, Pilch, and Mynn (the early Victorian equivalents of Hobbs, Bradman, and Keith Miller) argues a talent far above the ordinary.

How reliable a guide he is to the cricket of his day may be judged from reference to the works listed at the end of this appendix. His recollection of Lord's in its first golden age is precise, as are his brief portraits of the giants of his day—the huge and formidable Mynn, the elegant Felix, and the great all-rounder Pilch (although most contemporaries show Pilch as being a good deal more genial than Flashman found him). His technical references to the game are sound, although he has a tendency to mix the jargon of his playing days with that of sixty years later, when he was writing—thus he talks not of batsmen, but of "batters", which is correct 1840s usage, as are shiver, trimmer, twister, and shooter (all descriptive of bowling); at the same time he refers indiscriminately to both "hand" and "innings", which mean the same thing, although the former is long obsolete, and he commits one curious lapse of memory by referring to "the ropes" at Lord's in 1842; in fact, boundaries were not introduced until later, and in Flashman's time all scores had to be run for.

Undoubtedly the most interesting of his cricket recollections is his description of his single-wicket match with Solomon; this form of the game was popular in his day, but later suffered a decline, although attempts have been made to revive it recently. The rules are to be found in Charles Box's *The English Game of Cricket* (1877), but these varied according to preference; there might be any number of players, from one to six, on either side, but if there were fewer than five it was customary to prohibit scoring or dismissals behind the line of the wicket. Betting on such games was widespread, and helped to bring them into disrepute. However, it should be remembered that the kind of wagering indulged in by Flashman, Solomon, and Daedalus Tighe was common in their time; heavy, eccentric, and occasionally crooked it undoubtedly was, but it was part and parcel of a rough and colourful sporting era in which even a clergyman might make a handsome income in cricket side-bets, when games could be played by candlelight, and enthusiasts still recalled such occasions as the Greenwich Pensioners' match in which spectators thronged to see a team of one-legged men play a side who were one-armed (The one-legged team won, by 103 runs; five wooden legs were broken during the game.) Indeed, we may echo Flashman: cricket is not what it was. (See Box; W. W. Read's *Annals of Cricket*, 1896; Eric Parker's *The History of Cricket*, Lonsdale Library (with Sir Spencer Ponsonby-Fane's description of Lord's in "Lord's and the M.C.C."); W. Denison's *Sketches of the Players*, 1888; Nicholas ("Felix") Wanostrocht's *Felix on the Bat*, 1845; and the Rev. J. Pycroft's *Oxford Memories*, 1886.)

Appendix B: The White Raja

Nowadays, when it is fashionable to look only on the dark side of imperialism, not much is heard of James Brooke. He was one of those Victorians who gave Empire-building a good name, whose worst faults, perhaps, were that he loved adventure for its own sake, had an unshakeable confidence in the civilising mission of himself and his race, and enjoyed fighting pirates. His philosophy, being typical of his class and time, may not commend itself universally today, but an honest examination of what he actually did will discover more to praise than to blame.

The account of his work which Steward gave to Flashman is substantially true—Brooke went to Sarawak for adventure, and ended as its ruler and saviour. He abolished the tyranny under which it was held, revived trade, drew up a legal code, and although virtually without resources and with only a handful of adventurers and reformed head-hunters to help him, fought his single-handed war against the pirates of the Islands. It took him six years to win, and considering the savagery and overwhelming numbers of his enemies, the organised and traditional nature of the piracy, the distances and unknown coasts involved, and the small force at his disposal, it was a staggering achievement.

That it was a brutal and bloody struggle we know, and it was perhaps inevitable that at the end of it Brooke should find himself described by one newspaper as "pirate, wholesale murderer, and assassin", and that demands were made in Parliament, by Hume, Cobden, and Gladstone (who admired Brooke, but not his methods) for an inquiry into his conduct. Palmerston, equally inevitably, defended Brooke as a man of "unblemished honour", and Catchick Moses and the Singapore merchants rallied to his support. In the event, the inquiry cleared Brooke completely, which was probably a fair decision; his distant critics might think that he had pursued head-hunters and sea-robbers with excessive enthusiasm, but the coast villagers who had suffered generations of plundering and slavery took a different view.

So did the great British public. They were not short of heroes to worship in Victoria's reign, but among the Gordons, Livingstones, Stanleys, and the rest, James Brooke deservedly occupied a unique place. He was, after all, the storybook English adventurer of an old tradition—independent, fearless, upright, priggish and cheerfully immodest, and just a little touched with the buccaneer; it was no wonder that a century of boys' novelists should take him as their model. Which was a great compliment, but no greater than that paid to him by the tribesmen of Borneo; to them, one traveller reported, he was simply superhuman. The pirates of the Islands might well have agreed.*

---

* Suleiman Usman among them. Brooke ran him to earth at Maludu, North Borneo, in August 1845, only a few weeks after the Flashmans were rescued from Madagascar, from which it appears that Usman, having lost Elspeth, returned to his own waters. He was certainly at Maludu when the British force under Admiral Cochrane attacked and destroyed it; one report states that Usman was wounded, believed killed, in the action, and he does not appear to have been heard of again.

Appendix C: Queen Ranavalona I

"One of the proudest and most cruel women on the face of the earth, and her whole history is a record of blood and deeds of horror." Thus Ida Pfeiffer, who knew her personally. Other historians have called her "the modern Messalina", "a terrible woman . . . possessed by the lust of power and cruelty", "female Caligula", and so forth; to M. Ferry, the French Foreign Minister, she was simply "l'horrible Ranavalo".* Altogether there is a unanimity which, with the well-documented atrocities of her reign, justifies the worst that even Flashman has to say of her.

That he has reported his personal acquaintance with her accurately there is no reason to doubt. His account of Madagascar and its strange customs accords with other sources, as do his descriptions of such minutiae as the Queen's eccentric wardrobe, her Napoleonic paintings, furniture, idols, place-cards at dinner, drinking habits, and even musical preferences. His picture of her fantastically dressed court, her midnight party, and the public ceremony of the Queen's Bath can be verified in detail. As to her behaviour with him, it is known that she had lovers —possibly even before her husband's death, although that admittedly is pure speculation based on a study of the events which brought her to the throne, on which Flashman touches only briefly.

King Radama, her husband, had died suddenly at the age of 36 in 1828. Since they had no children, the heir was the king's nephew, Rakotobe; his supporters, foreseeing a power struggle, concealed the news of the king's death for some days to enable Rakotobe to consolidate his claim. In the meantime, however, a young officer named Andriamihaja, who was ostensibly among Rakotobe's supporters, betrayed the news of the king's death to Ranavalona, for reasons which are not disclosed. She promptly

* Speech to the Chamber of Deputies, Paris, 1884.

got the leading military men on her side, put it about that the idols favoured her claim to the throne, and ruthlessly slaughtered all who resisted, including the unfortunate Rakotobe. She rewarded Andriamihaja's treachery by making him commander-in-chief and taking (or confirming) him as her lover—he was presently accused of treachery, put to the *tanguin*, and executed. (See Oliver, vol. i.)

The next 35 years were a reign of terror, religious persecution, and genocide on a scale (considering Madagascar's size and limited population) hardly matched until our own times. That Ranavalona escaped assassination or deposition is testimony to the strength with which she wielded her absolute power, and to her capacity for surviving plots. How many of these there were, we cannot know, but none succeeded—including the Flashman coup of 1845, and a later conspiracy in which Ida Pfeiffer, then aged 60, found herself involved, to her considerable alarm: she describes in her *Travels* how Prince Rakota (still evidently intent on getting rid of mother) showed her the arsenal he intended to use in his revolt, and how she then went to bed and had nightmares about the *tanguin* test.

Since we know that Rakota and Laborde both survived the plot which Flashman describes, it seems likely that it simply died stillborn, or that the Queen, for some reason, forebore to take vengeance on the conspirators. It would be pleasant to think that Mr Fankanonikaka, at least, was spared to continue his devoted service to his queen and country.

Notes

1. Since most of the Flashman Papers were written between 1900 and 1905, it seems likely that Flashman is here referring to the Test Match series of 1901–2, which Australia won by four matches to one, and possibly also to the series of summer 1902, when the Australians retained the Ashes, 2–1. It was in this year that an attempt to amend the ever-controversial leg-before-wicket rule failed. [p. 10]

2. Flashman's behaviour on the football field is memorably described in *Tom Brown's Schooldays*, where Thomas Hughes refers to his late arrival at scrimmages "with shouts and great action". [p. 11]

3. Flashman's memory is playing him false here, but only slightly. The so-called Rebecca Riots did not begin until some months later, in 1843, when a peculiar secret society known as "Rebecca and her Daughters" began a terrorist campaign against high toll charges in South Wales. They went armed, masked, and disguised as women, and would descend by night on toll-houses and toll-gates, which they wrecked. They apparently took their name from an allusion in Genesis xxiv, 60: "And they blessed Rebekah . . . and said . . . let thy seed possess the gate of those which hate them." (See Halevy's *History of the English People*, vol. iv, and *Punch*, vol. v, introduction, 1843.) [p. 18]

4. This is the earliest mention in any sporting or literary record of the "hat trick", signifying the feat by a bowler of taking three wickets with successive balls, which traditionally entitles him to a new hat. The phrase has now, of course, a wider application outside cricket, covering three successive triumphs of any kind – a hat-trick of goals or election victories, for example. It is interesting to speculate, not only that the phrase had its origin in Mynn's impulsive gesture to Flashman, but also that it was first used ironically. [p. 29]

5. Lords Haddington and Stanley were respectively First Lord of the Admiralty and Colonial Secretary; Lord Aberdeen was Foreign Secretary. Flashman is being malicious in coupling Deaf Burke and Lord Brougham as rascals – one was a famous prize-fighter and the other a prominent Whig politician. [p. 38]

6. Alice Lowe, mistress of Lord Frankfort, figured in a notorious court case over gifts he had given her, and which he claimed she had stolen. Nelson's Column in Trafalgar Square, then nearing completion, was something of a laughing-stock – *Punch* noted gleefully that the statue of the great sailor closely resembled Napoleon. The Royal Hunt Cup was first run at Ascot in 1843 and "The Bohemian Girl" opened at Drury Lane in November of that year. [p. 38]

7. Various government reports appeared in the early 1840s on conditions in mines and factories; they were horrifying. The atrocities referred to in Morrison's conversation with Solomon may be traced

in those reports and in others from the preceding decade. As a result, Lord Ashley (later Earl of Shaftesbury) got a Bill through the Commons in 1842 prohibiting the employment of women or children below thirteen in the mines, although the Lords subsequently lowered the age to ten; in 1843 the publication of the report of the Children's Employment Commission ("Horne's report") led to further legislation, including a reduction in factory working hours for children and adolescents. (See Report of the Children's Employment Commission (Mines) 1842; the second report of the C.E.C., 1843; and other papers quoted in *Human Documents of the Industrial Revolution*, by E. Royston Pike.) [p. 41]

8. Lola Montez was Flashman's mistress for a brief period in the autumn of 1842, until they quarrelled; he took revenge by engineering a hostile reception for her when she made her début as a dancer on the London stage in June, 1843. Following this incident, she left England and began that astonishing career as a courtesan which led to her becoming virtual ruler of Bavaria – an episode in which Flashman and Otto von Bismarck were closely involved. (See biographies of Lola Montez, and Flashman's own memoir on the subject, published as *Royal Flash*.) [p. 42]

9. From Flashman's description of the "bluff-looking chap in clerical duds" with the crippled arm, it seems certain that he was Richard Harris Barham (1788–1845), author of *The Ingoldsby Legends*, of which one of the most famous relates how Lord Tomnoddy, accompanied by ". . . M'Fuze, and Lieutenant Tregooze, and . . . Sir Carnaby Jenks of the Blues", attended a Newgate execution, and revelled the previous night at the Magpie and Stump, overlooking the street where the scaffold was erected. However, Barham's inspiration did not come from the execution which Flashman describes; he wrote his famous piece of gallows humour some years earlier, but may well have attended later executions out of interest. Thackeray's presence is interesting, since it suggests that he had got over the revulsion he felt at Courvoisier's hanging three years earlier, when he could not bear to watch the final moment. (See Barham; *The Times*, July 7, 1840, and May 27, 1868, reporting the Courvoisier and Barret executions; Thackeray's "Going to See a Man Hanged", *Fraser's Magazine*, July 1840; Dickens' *Barnaby Rudge* and "A Visit to Newgate", from *Sketches by Boz*; and Arthur Griffiths' *Chronicles of Newgate* 1884 and *Criminal Prisons of London* 1862.) [p. 48]

10. Mr Tighe's bet was that Flashman would "carry his bat" (i.e. would not lose his wicket, and be "not out" at the end of the innings). A curious wager, perhaps, but not extraordinary in an age when sportsmen were prepared to bet on virtually anything. [p. 50]

11. The Regency practice among noblemen of patronising prize-fighters, and using them (usually when they had retired) as bodyguards and musclemen, had not quite died out in Flashman's youth, so his fears of the Duke's vengeance were probably well-founded – especially in view of the names mentioned by Judy. Ben Caunt, popularly known as "Big Ben" (the bell in the Westminster clock tower is said to have been named after him) was a notoriously rough heavyweight champion of the 1840s, and the other fighter

referred to can only have been Tom Cannon, "the Great Gun of Windsor", who held the title in the 1820s. [p. 70]

12. The first sale of Australian horses, imported into Singapore by Boyd and Company, did not in fact take place until August 20, 1844. These were the first of the famous cavalry "walers" (so called after New South Wales) of the Indian Army. [p. 84]

13. Not quite so ancient and shrivelled nowadays, perhaps. Flashman, writing in the *Pax Britannica* of the Edwardian years, could not foresee a time when the tribes of North Borneo would resume the practice of head-hunting which British rule discouraged. The Editor has seen rows of comparatively recent heads in a "head-house" up the Rajang River; the locals admitted that most of them were "orang Japon", taken from the Japanese invaders of the Second World War, but some of them looked new enough to have belonged to the Indonesian tribesmen who at that time (1966) were fighting the British-Malay forces in the Communist rebellion. [p. 92]

14. Frank Marryat, son of the novelist Captain Marryat, served as a naval officer in Far Eastern waters in the 1840s, and confirmed Flashman's opinion of the dullness and prudishness of Singapore society. "Little hospitality, less gaiety . . . everyone waiting to see what his position in society is going to be." His description of the city, its people, customs, and institutions, tallies closely with Flashman's. (See *Borneo and the Indian Archipelago* (1848), by F. S. Marryat, and for a wealth of detail, *An Anecdotal History of Old Times in Singapore*, by C. B. Buckley.) [p. 95]

15. Catchick Moses the Armenian and Whampoa the Chinese were two of the great characters of early Singapore. Catchick was famous not only as a merchant, but as a billiards player, and for his eccentric habit of shaving left-handed without a glass as he walked about his verandah. He was about 32 when Flashman knew him; when he made his will, at the age of 73, seven years before his death, he followed the unusual procedure of submitting it to his children, so that any disputes could be settled amicably during his lifetime.

Whampoa was the richest of the Chinese community, renowned for the lavishness of his parties, and for his luxurious country home with its gold-framed oval doors. His appearance was as Flashman describes it, down to his black silk robe, pigtail, and sherry glass. (See Buckley, Marryat.) [p. 98]

16. As Flashman later admits, the name of James Brooke, White Raja of Sarawak and adventurer extraordinary, meant nothing to him on first hearing, which is not surprising since the fame of this remarkable Victorian had not yet reached its peak. But Flashman was plainly impressed, despite himself, by his rescuer's personality and appearance, and his description tallies exactly with Brooke's famous portrait in the National Portrait Gallery, which catches all his resolution and restless energy, as well as that romantic air which made him the beau ideal of the early Victorian hero. The painting could serve as the frontispiece for any boys' adventure story of the nineteenth century – and sometimes did. All that is missing is the face-wound which Flashman mentions; Brooke had received it in a fight with Sumatran pirates at Murdu on February 12, 1844, so it would still be incompletely healed when they met. [p. 109]

17. If it seems unlikely that even an emotional Victorian can have spoken such purple prose, we can be certain that Brooke at least wrote it, almost word for word. In his journal, about this time, he recorded his emotions on hearing that a European lady was held prisoner by Borneo pirates who were demanding ransom: "A captive damsel! Does it not conjure up images of blue eyes and auburn hair of hyacinthine flow! And after all, a fat old Dutch frau may be the reality! Poor creature, even though she be old, and fat, and unamiable, and ugly, it is shocking to think of such a fate as a life passed among savages!" Obviously, he cannot have had Mrs Flashman in mind. [p. 120]

18. Henry Keppel (1809–1904) was one of the foremost fighting seamen of the Victorian period. An expert in the specialised craft of river warfare, he was known to the Dyaks as "the red-haired devil", and served with Brooke in numerous raids against the pirates of the South China Sea. (See his books, *Expedition to Borneo of H.M.S. Dido*, 1846, and *A Visit to the Indian Archipelago in H.M.S. Maeander*, 1853.) He later became Admiral of the Fleet. [p. 127]

19. Stuart's enthusiastic description of Brooke and his adventures is perfectly accurate; so far as it goes (see *The Raja of Sarawak*, by Gertrude L. Jacob, 1876, *The Life of Sir James Brooke*, by Spenser St John, 1879, Brooke's own letters and journal, and other Borneo sources quoted elsewhere in these foot-notes. Also Appendix B). The only error at this point is a minor one of Flashman's, for "Stuart's" name was in fact George Steward; obviously Flashman has again made a mistake of which he is occasionally guilty in his memoirs, of trusting his ears and not troubling to check the spelling of proper names. [p. 130]

20. Angela Georgina Burdett-Coutts (1814–1906), "the richest heiress in all England, enjoyed a fame . . . second only to Queen Victoria." She spent her life and the vast fortune inherited from her grandfather, Thomas Coutts the banker, on countless charities and good causes, endowing schools, housing schemes, and hospitals, and providing funds for such diverse projects as Irish famine relief, university scholarships, drinking troughs, and colonial exploration; Livingstone, Stanley, and Brooke were among the pioneers she assisted. She was the first woman to be raised to the peerage for public service, and numbered among her friends Wellington, Faraday, Disraeli, Gladstone, Daniel Webster, and Dickens, who dedicated "Martin Chuzzlewit" to her.

The combination of her good looks, charm, and immense wealth attracted innumerable suitors, but she seems to have felt no inclination to matrimony until she met Brooke and "fell madly in love with him". There is a tradition that she proposed to him and was politely rejected (see following note), but they remained close friends, and she is said to have been instrumental in obtaining official recognition for Sarawak. She eventually married, in her sixties, the American-born William Ashmead-Bartlett. She is buried in Westminster Abbey. (See *Raja Brooke and Baroness Burdett-Coutts, Letters*, edited by Owen Rutter, and the *Dictionary of National Biography*.) Flashman's memory has again betrayed him on one small point; he may have known Miss Coutts, but not "at

Stratton Street"; she did not take up residence there until the late 1840s. [p. 136]

21. The truth about Brooke's Burmese wound is far from clear; all that can be said with certainty is that he received it during his service in the Bengal Army in the Assam campaign (1823-5) when he commanded a native cavalry unit and was shot while charging a stockade. Both his principal biographers, Gertrude Jacob and Spenser St John, say that he was hit in the lung; according to Miss Jacob the bullet was not extracted until more than a year later, when it was kept in a glass case by Brooke's mother. On the other hand, Owen Rutter cites John Dill Ross, whose father knew Brooke well, as the authority for the story that the wound was in the genitals. If this is true it is certainly consistent with Brooke's reputed refusal of Miss Burdett-Coutts, and with the fact that he never married.

It is possible, of course, that Jacob and St John were unaware of the true nature of Brooke's injury (although this seems unlikely in the case of St John, who was Brooke's close friend and secretary at Sarawak), or that they were simply being tactful. Remarks occur in their biographies which are capable of varying interpretations: St John, for example, says that in convalescing from the wound Brooke was "absorbed in melancholy thoughts, and often longed to be at rest", but that is not necessarily significant – any young man with a wound that had put paid to his military career might well be gloomy. Again, both Jacob and St John refer to Brooke being in love, and briefly engaged (to the daughter of a Bath clergyman) after he had been wounded, and St John adds that "he from that time seems to have withdrawn from female blandishments". It would be dangerous to draw conclusions from such conflicting evidence, or from what is known of Brooke's character and behaviour; Flashman, naturally, would be ready to believe the worst. [p. 137]

22. Whatever Flashman's opinion of Brooke, he has been an honest reporter of the White Raja's background and conversation. The picture of The Grove – the furnishings and routine, the formal dinners, the reception of petitioners, even his interest in gardening, his pleasure in comfortable armchairs and home newspapers, and his eccentric habit of playing leap-frog – is confirmed by other sources. Much more important, virtually all the opinions which he expressed in Flashman's presence, throughout this narrative, are to be found elsewhere in Brooke's own writings. His views on native peoples, piracy, Borneo's future, missionaries, colonial development, religion and ethics, honours and decorations, personal ambitions and private tastes – all the philosophy of this remarkable man, in fact, is contained at length in his journals and letters, and his conversation as reported by Flashman reflects it accurately, often in identical words. Even the style of his talk seems to have been like his writing, brisk, assertive, eager, and highly opinionated. (See Brooke's papers, as quoted in St John, Jacob, et al.) [p. 139]

23. Brooke had written these very words in his journal only a few days before. [p. 142]

24. Charles Johnson (1829-1917) was Brooke's nephew, and became the second White Raja on his uncle's death in 1868. He took the name Brooke as his surname, reigned for almost 50 years, extended Sara-

wak's boundaries, and earned a high reputation as a fighting man
and just ruler. Despite his background, he was an unusually clear-
sighted colonialist who predicted at the beginning of this century
the end of empire and the ascendancy of new Eastern Powers in the
shape of China and Russia. [p. 151]

25. W. E. Gladstone was one of several liberal politicians who pressed
for charges to be brought against Brooke on the ground that his
actions against the Borneo pirates were cruel, illegal, and excessive.
St John comments bluntly: "James Brooke's sympathies were with
the victims, Gladstone's with the pirates." (See Gladstone's article
on "Piracy in Borneo, and the Operations of 1849".) [p. 152]

26. An excellent description of a sea-going pirate prau. These vessels,
up to 70 feet long, heavily armed with cannon and carrying hundreds of fighting men, were the scourge of the East Indies until
well into the nineteenth century. Cruising sometimes in fleets of
hundreds from the great pirate nests of the Philippines and North
Borneo, they preyed on shipping and coast towns alike in search of
slaves and plunder, and set the small naval forces of Britain and
Holland at defiance.

While piracy was universal in the Islands, the principal fraternities
were the Balagnini, subsidised by the Borneo princes in return for
slaves and treasure; the wandering Maluku from Halmahera in the
Moluccas; the Sea Dyaks of the Seribas and Skrang rivers who
specialised in head-taking; and most feared of all, the Lanun or
Illanun rovers, "the pirates of the lagoon", from Mindanao, whose
praus could cruise for three years at a time and who operated the
great slave market on Sulu Island. Although most of the pirate
leaders were Islanders, some of them, like Flashman's friend, Sahib
Suleiman Usman, were Arab half-breeds – Usman was held to be
especially detestable because he did not scruple to sell fellow-Arabs
into slavery, but he was extremely powerful as head of a strong
confederacy of North Borneo pirates, and also through his marriage
to the Sultan of Sulu's daughter (See Brooke, Marryat, Keppel,
Mundy, and F. J. Morehead, *History of Malaya*, vol ii.) [p. 155]

27. "Jersey" can surely only refer to "New Jersey", where the .40 five-
shot muzzle-loading revolver known as the Colt Paterson was produced between 1836 and 1842. Some of these pistols had barrels a
foot long. [p. 160]

28. Flashman is definitely mistaken. If any pirates were executed at
Linga – and there is no supporting evidence, although the methods
of execution which Flashman describes here were common among
the Dyaks – Makota could not have been among them, since he was
with the pirates at Patusan on the following day. [p. 161]

29. The storming of Patusan, where five pirate forts were burned, took
place on August 7. If Flashman's account does not give prominence
to the part played by Wade and Keppel, or to the outstanding
bravery of the loyal Dyaks and Malays, it is understandable; river-
fighting was more confused than most, and he was obviously fully
occupied by his own share of it. On some details he is exact –
Seaman Ellis was killed in the *Jolly Bachelor* while loading the bow
gun, for example – and other accounts also refer to the plundering
of Sharif Sahib's head-quarters (where his "curious and extensive

wardrobe" was discovered) and to the fact that his harem escaped unscathed from the battle. Plainly the other reporters did not consult Flashman on this last point, or if they did, he was prudently reticent. [p. 179]

30. The fort of Sharif Muller (or Mullah) was taken on August 14, and a great force of pirate praus destroyed. The death of Lt. Wade, and Muller's escape, took place as Flashman describes. [p. 182]

31. The Battle of the Pyramids, fought on July 21, 1798, was one of Napoleon's most complete victories. He beat and captured an Egyptian-Turkish army more than 20,000 strong under the Circassian, Murad Bey. St John tells us that one of Brooke's people had taken part in the battle, on the Turkish side, but refers to him merely as "an old Malay"; Flashman is the only source for the suggestion that this anonymous veteran was Paitingi Ali; it is possible, assuming that Paitingi was in his 60s at the time Flashman knew him. [p. 188]

32. Like Flashman, other participants in the battle on Skrang river thought it the most hectic and bloody of all the encounters fought by Brooke's force in their passage up the Batang Lupar. Six hundred pirates in six praus attacked Paitingi's spy-boat, overwhelming its crew of seventeen; Keppel's account, quoted by Flashman, testifies to the viciousness of the fighting in the waterway choked by a mass of foundering craft and bodies which broke in two as it floated downstream, enabling Brooke and Keppel to drive their gig through the gap, followed by a rocket-firing boat. In addition to Paitingi's crew, the expedition lost 29 other dead, with 56 wounded, in the battle.

Although Flashman was in no position to appreciate it, this action marked the end of the Batang Lupar operation. With the stream too heavy against them, Brooke's fleet returned to Patusan, having effectively destroyed or dispersed the pirates along the river in the fortnight's campaign. Much of the credit for this undoubtedly belonged to Keppel, whose role in the leadership Flashman tends to underrate; otherwise, his account of the expedition is on the whole accurate and fair, although it is as usual a highly individual view, and while he is reliable on dates, names of people, places, and vessels, and the broad conduct of operations, there is no way of verifying his more personal recollections. He seems to have magnified the action at Fort Linga (in which by his own account he played no part), but there is no reason to suppose that the gruesome picture which he paints of Borneo river-fighting, or of conditions along the pirate coast, is in any way exaggerated. (See Keppel, Jacob, St John, Marryat, and Sir George Mundy's *Narrative of Events in Borneo and Celebes*, 1848.) [p. 192]

33. So hostile to foreigners was Madagascar that comparatively few written authorities exist for the first half of the last century, and those named by Flashman are the principal ones in English; they bear out virtually every detail which he gives about that astonishing island and its appalling ruler, Ranavalona I. James Hastie (1786–1826) was a soldier, not a missionary; he was tutor to two Malagassy princes and British agent on the island at a time when Europeans were still tolerated there. His journal is in the Public

Record Office. W. Ellis's *Three Visits to Madagascar*, 1858, *Madagascar Revisited*, 1867, and *The Martyr Church of Madagascar*, 1870, are invaluable sources for Queen Ranavalona's reign, and the island background and people, as is S. P. Oliver's *Madagascar*, 1886. See also H. W. Little's *Madagascar*, 1884, J. Sibree's *The Great African Island*, 1880, and L. McLeod's *Madagascar and its people*, 1865. But none compares with the indomitable and entertaining Ida Pfeiffer, that great tourist whose *Last Travels* contains a wealth of informative detail recorded at first hand. [p. 210]

34. Curiously enough, this barbarous custom was abolished by Queen Ranavalona. It was said to be her only humane act. [p. 212]

35. Flashman's is possibly the only eye-witness account of the fearful cruelties and varied means of execution practised in Madagascar at this time, but the other authorities quote evidence in detail to support him, and there can be no doubt that such atrocities as he describes took place, and were part of the Queen's policy. Ida Pfeiffer, having confirmed Flashman's figures of tens of thousands dying annually from execution, massacre, and forced labour, sums up: "If this woman's rule lasts much longer, Madagascar will be depopulated . . . Blood – and always blood – is the maxim of Queen Ranavalona, and every day seems lost to this wicked woman on which she cannot sign at least half a dozen death-warrants."

[p. 217]

36. Flashman's estimate of Laborde was sound; the Frenchman was a tough and resourceful soldier of fortune who in his time had been a cavalry trooper, steam engineer in Bombay, and (according to some sources) a slave-trader. He was shipwrecked in Madagascar in 1831, enslaved, bought by the Queen and became a favourite. Subsequently he was liberated and married a Malagassy girl, but he was still kept in Madagascar where he served the Queen as engineer and cannon-maker. He became an influential figure at court, and was active in promoting French interest. [p. 224]

37. The few Europeans who met Queen Ranavalona face to face and lived to write impressions of her, confirm what Flashman says of her appearance, although most of them saw her much later in her reign than he did. Ellis, giving a description which is very close to Flashman's, adds that "the whole head and face is small, compact and well proportioned; her expression . . . agreeable, although at times indicating great firmness." Ida Pfeiffer, who apparently did not see her close to, noted that she was "of strong and sturdy build, rather dark". Both she and Mr Ellis seem to have thought the Queen rather older than she probably was; there is no reliable evidence of her birth-date, and although the *Nouvelle Biographie Générale* says "about 1800", which would make her 44 when Flashman met her, it seems more likely that she was in her early fifties.

[p. 229]

38. Flashman's virtuosity on the keyboard was either highly eccentric or less memorable than he imagined, for years later when Ida Pfeiffer was invited to play the palace piano, she understood Ranavalona to say that she "had never seen anyone play with their hands". Mme Pfeiffer found the piano sadly out of tune. [p. 232]

39. Despite her suspicion of Europeans and their ways, the Queen did in fact employ an English-educated secretary. [p. 234]

40. These peculiar divination-boards were known as *sikidy*. According to Sibree, there were three of them, one of four squares by sixteen, a second four by four, and a third four by eight. [p. 248]

41. An unflattering description of Prince Rakota, although not unlike his portrait, which survives. Oliver described him as being like a Greek god, with dark curls and light gold skin, but agrees with Flashman's estimate of his character, and confirms that he was a moderating influence on his mother. [p. 251]

42. Flashman is the only survivor of the *tanguin*, or *tangena*, ordeal to have written of the experience. His account varies from other descriptions only on minor points – it was customary, when time was available, to starve the patient for 24 hours before the scraped stone of the *tanguin* fruit was administered, and some historians say that in order to pass the test the pieces of chicken skin had to be regurgitated in a particular direction. The deposit of 28 dollars (Flashman says 24) was normally put up by the accuser of the person undergoing the test – if the accused failed the test, the accuser got his money back, but if he passed, the accuser recovered only one-third of the deposit, the other thirds going to the accused and the Queen. [p. 278]

43. As a result of its separate evolution, the plant and animal life of Madagascar is ùnique, and it has been estimated that ninety per cent of its living things exist nowhere else on earth. Among its more celebrated fabulous monsters was the giant Roc bird which carried off Sinbad. The "apes" which Flashman saw were probably *sifakas*, a type of lemur capable of prodigious jumps. [p. 294]

44. It was Flashman's good fortune to arrive at Tamitave on the very morning (June 15, 1845) when three European warships, the French *Berceau* and *Zelée* and the British frigate *Conway*, made a concerted attack on the fort and town. The punitive expedition was in retaliation for Ranavalona's ill-treatment of Europeans – she had recently decreed that those trading with the island were liable to Malagassy law (slavery for debt, forced labour, trial by *tanguin*, etc.), there had been fatal incidents between British ships and Malagassy troops, and a British shipmaster of American origin, Jacob Heppick, had been enslaved after his barque, the *Marie Laure*, was shipwrecked. Captain Kelly of the *Conway* was sent to Tamitave to demand redress early in June, and when this was not forthcoming the Anglo-French bombardment followed a few days later. (See Oliver, the "Memorial of Jacob Heppick, mariner, to the Governor of Mauritius", and the *Annual Register*.) [p. 301]

45. The unsuccessful storming of Tamitave fort by landing parties from the Anglo-French squadron took place as Flashman says. The outer palisade was carried under a hail of grapeshot and musketry, the battery overrun and guns spiked, but the attackers failed to carry the main fort and retired after a brisk fight. The British lost four dead and 12 wounded, and the French 17 dead and 43 wounded. Both the *Zelée* and *Berceau* lost topmasts in the gun-battle with the fort.

The incident of the flag is true, although not all the details are clear. It appears that it was shot away from the outer wall, and caught by a Malagassy soldier who put it on a spear. It fell again, and was captured by a British midshipman and two sailors; there was a tussle for it between French and British under Malagassy fire, and the matter was only resolved when someone – the *Annual Register* says Lt Kennedy, but doubtless Flashman knows best – cut it in two. The French received the half bearing the legend "Ranavalona" and the British the piece inscribed "Manjaka". Most of Tamitave town was burned during the attack. [p. 309]

46. After a long period of political unrest and violence in the Punjab, the Sikhs finally invaded British-controlled territory in December, 1845, and the First Sikh War began. [p. 310]